Book 2 of 3

MY SKYLAR

JAKE: Book Two

NEW YORK TIMES BESTSELLING AUTHOR

PENELOPE WARD

First Edition, June 2014

This book is a work of fiction. All names, characters, locations, and incidents are products of the author's imagination. Any resemblance to actual persons, things living or dead, locales, or events is entirely coincidental.

Formatting by Elaine York, Allusion Publishing (http://www.allusion-publishing.com)
Cover by RBA Designs
Stock photo © Shutterstock.com

PROLOGUE

MITCH

Skylar had no idea that I watched her. Once a week, I would sit in my car diagonally across from her house on the quiet suburban street where she lived now—with him. It made me want to vomit just thinking about her with another man, let alone having to witness it.

This spot was one of three where I parked that provided the perfect angle to see into her living room. I would switch positions each week to be less conspicuous, and my car lights were always turned off. A small pair of binoculars came in handy and except for the lack of a partner in crime, it was much like a stakeout you'd see in the movies.

I packed dinner in a brown bag; usually a peanut butter sandwich and a protein shake and made a night of it until the lights shut off downstairs, signaling that she had gone to sleep. Then, I'd drive home to my empty bed and hope that I'd dream about her.

The name of her street was Bayberry Lane. It was the type of neighborhood she deserved: safe, aligned with plush trees and perfectly manicured lawns, about two and a half hours outside of New York City in Jersey. It was the next town over from where we grew up and the type of place I'd always imagined we would end up together, happily ever after.

It had been five, long years since Skylar uttered a single word to me. Most of that time, she had been living out of state. The word on the street was that she left to attend interior design school, but the truth was, she had been running away from me.

Because I broke her heart.

A few years after she left, she met a guy. Our mutual friend, Davey, would give me inside information on her, and as much as I hated the idea of Skylar settling down with another man, if she were truly happy, I knew I had to accept it. It was a whole lot easier when she was far away. I'd assumed she would never come back here. That is, until one night when my world as I knew it turned upside down during a simple run to Target for toothpaste.

I spotted her first. She was looking down at the back label of a bottle of mouthwash when I entered the aisle, and she hadn't noticed me standing a few feet away.

My heart started to pound while my chest constricted. Skylar was always a beautiful girl, but nothing could have prepared me for the sight of her as a full-grown woman. I had always imagined how it might be to see her again, but the intensity of my physical and emotional reaction caught me off guard.

Her long, auburn hair was a bit darker now and tied into a low ponytail cascading down her back. She was wearing a simple black and white plaid wool coat that had a thick belt wrapped around her tiny waist. She seemed a lot taller, but when I looked down, I realized it was because she was wearing high-heeled boots.

She still hadn't turned to notice me, and with my chest tight and my throat closed, I just stared at her, silently urging myself to say something before she walked away. The word was hardly audible when it came out. "Skylar."

When her eyes met mine, it felt as though my heart started beating again for the first time in five years. It made me realize how dead inside I had been.

She took a small step back, and her chest rose up and down in shock. Not only had this been the first time we'd laid eyes on each other since before she left town, but I looked a lot different.

A couple of years ago, at the height of a depression, I started taking my frustrations out on my body and began a rigorous workout regimen that had now become a daily routine. So, I was bigger and probably a little scarier than the college boy she left behind.

She didn't know the half of how hardened I had become, more so on the inside. She, on the other hand, looked delicate and sophisticated compared to my rugged appearance in worn jeans and a soiled, beige construction jacket.

She stood there speechless, looking down at the tattooed letters on my knuckles. She never knew me with tattoos.

Say something, Skylar...anything.

Then, I heard a male voice at the end of the aisle. "Come on, Sky. I don't have all friggin' day."

Sky. No one called her Sky. She hated that nickname. And he was being short with her. I didn't like his choice of words or the look on his face that I spied before turning my head, pretending to look at the toothpaste selection.

I was seething. *Him*. I didn't even know him, and I wanted to destroy him. All I knew was that he had the only thing I'd ever wanted.

She turned around toward this guy who I could only assume was the boyfriend. "I...I'm sorry. I'll be right there." She sounded nervous, discombobulated, nothing like the cool, self-assured Skylar I once knew...and loved. I *still* loved her. She had been my best friend, the most important person in the world to me for so many years...before I fucked us up.

My face was still turned away when I heard her heels clicking away from me and more than that, I *felt* her body leave me as the sudden absence triggered the return of a familiar and unbearable longing that I had only recently learned to keep at bay.

I stayed in the same spot for an undetermined amount of time, staring blankly at the shelves as all of the emotions I tried to bury for years flooded me full force again.

When I finally moved, I saw her standing in line waiting to pay. Her boyfriend must have been waiting in the car because he was nowhere in sight.

Let her go, Mitch.

I almost did...until I saw it.

Skylar lifted her hand to her eyes and began wiping away tears. She looked behind her shoulder to make sure no one was watching and didn't realize I was just on the other side of her a few registers down hiding behind a magazine. My heart felt like it was ready to explode. She was crying, and I knew it was because of me. It should have hurt, but instead, it invigorated me.

She still felt something.

Whether it was sadness or hatred or even a fraction of love, I didn't know. But anything was better than complacency. I had convinced myself that Skylar was gone forever, not only away from town, but that her feelings for me had to have long dissipated. I had never been able to move on from her but assumed that by now, she might have moved past what happened between us.

As she wiped her eyes again, I knew I had to know more. I just needed to know whether she was happy. She sure as hell didn't look it, and that made me angry. I had stayed away all these years, never fought for her, because I thought she was better off. Even if she could never forgive me, I needed to know for my own sanity that Skylar was okay.

So, that's how the stalking came about, although I liked to call it *watching*; that was a little less creepy.

It was freezing, but the heat stayed off because turning the car on would have drawn attention to myself. I shouldn't have been here, but the truth was, being near her felt more like home than anywhere.

Tonight, she was alone, and these were my favorite nights. She'd sit on the couch and read or watch television. Sometimes, when she'd watch TV, she'd laugh out loud to herself. Staring at the lingering smile that followed was the best form of meditation for me. When Skylar smiled, she lit up the room, and there was nothing more calming to look at. It was important for me to see her smile. It meant I hadn't wiped it away altogether.

On the other hand, she seemed tense when *he* was around. Those nights, she spent more time cleaning or cooking, never relaxing. They'd argue a lot and one time, it culminated in his grabbing her and kissing her apologetically. As much as I had tried to prepare myself for what I might have to witness when I decided to do this, that really stung like hell to watch. Thank God it ended there. I wouldn't have stuck around for anything more. That's for damn sure. Show over at that point.

She was reading tonight. With my binoculars, I studied her pensive expression as she concentrated on her book with her legs wrapped in a knit blanket. She had lit a couple of jar candles on the coffee table, and there was one lamp on. She was so friggin' cute in her red-framed reading glasses. I wondered when she started needing glasses and then stopped that thought process because it led me to wonder about all the other things I had missed.

I would have given anything to hold her while she read and to fall asleep with my nose in the crook of her neck. Just the thought of that warmed me inside as I sat in my dark, cold car. I couldn't figure out why some nights he never came home. I would sure as hell be home every night if Skylar were mine.

A howling wind shook my car as I continued to gaze at her through the window. Her eyelids became heavy, and I watched intently as they slowly closed tight. She had fallen asleep on the couch.

I could see my breath as I sighed and leaned my head back against the seat, conceding that it was time to call it quits for the night. My heart hurt every time I had to leave her. But I would keep coming until I had what I needed: assurance that she was happy and safe.

Until next week, my Skylar.

I put the key in the ignition and turned it to start the car when the engine hesitated. Thinking nothing of it, I immediately turned it a second time when the same thing happened.

Please! Not here of all places.

That's what I got for bringing the shit car. I owned a really nice truck, but it was massive and would have attracted too much attention on the quiet street. This car was an older Corvette I purchased for fun, working on it occasionally, but it mainly stayed in my mother's garage.

After a third attempt to start the car, I got a flashlight and kit out of my trunk and opened the hood. The battery wasn't dead, so I tinkered with some wiring in the hopes that I could get it to start. When I cranked it again, it still wouldn't budge. I repeatedly turned the ignition, pumping my foot on the gas, praying that I could get out of here before Skylar woke up and noticed me.

I took a break, slamming my head against the steering wheel in frustration. After about five minutes, I decided to try it one last time before I would abandon my car and walk the several miles home in the freezing cold.

This time, I pumped harder on the gas as I turned the ignition, and to my absolute horror, the car backfired in a loud bang.

Fuck!

I needed to grab my shit and just go. Now. *Go!*

I exited the car, and as I turned to lock it, there was the sound of a door bursting open and footsteps scraping the pavement behind me.

"Is everything okay out here?"

My body froze. My back was toward her. I had a hood on, so she couldn't see my face to identify me. I was almost mad at her for coming out because for all she knew, I could have been a serial killer. But Skylar always had balls too big for her own good.

I had two options: run with my head down or turn around and face her. But how would I explain this?

It felt like my heart was in my mouth when I turned around and removed my hood. "Skylar...it's me."

ONE

MITCH

FIFTEEN YEARS EARLIER

I really hadn't wanted to go to the playground that day. Gram thought it would be a good idea for me to get out of the house because I had done nothing but play video games since I arrived yesterday.

I was staying with my grandmother for the summer because my parents were fighting all of the time, and my mother didn't want me around to witness it anymore. The excuse she gave me was that my grandmother had been lonely and asked for me to live with her, but I knew better.

Things back home were really bad. Some nights, Dad didn't come home, and I was scared that there would be nothing left to go back to.

"Come on, Mitch. Maybe meeting some new kids will brighten your mood."

I begrudgingly slid into the backseat of my grandmother's older, beige Camry. "Gram, I love you. But I just don't want to be here all summer. I want to go home in a couple of weeks."

"Sweetheart, I know. But your folks...they have some things to sort out. Besides, I have been waiting all year to spend quality time with my most handsome grandson." She smiled at me through the rearview mirror.

"I'm your *only* grandson." I offered her a half smile before staring out the window for the rest of the ride.

Gram pulled into the playground parking lot. "You go on and play. I'll be sitting right here in the car knitting if you need me."

I had already made up my mind that I was going to remain miserable. So, while the other kids chased each other around, played ball or climbed the rock wall, I walked across the park and planted myself on the bench farthest away from the action. I had snuck my portable video game player into my shirt before we left the house, so I took it out, trying to drown out the screams and whistles of the other kids.

I felt a whack on my arm. "Tag! You're it!"

My head rose slowly in annoyance. A scrawny girl with two long braids was running away from me, egging me on to chase her. She looked back with a silly smile that soon faded when she realized I still hadn't moved from my spot to play along.

She walked back to where I continued playing the video game. "I said you're it. You're supposed to chase me."

I stared at her for a few seconds. "I'm really not in the mood for this today."

She looked down then sat next to me and whispered, "Then, now would not be a good time to tell you that you have dookey on your shoe." She flashed a shit-eating grin and covered her mouth in laughter.

I lifted my foot. "Shit."

"You shouldn't use that language."

"Excuse me: *crap*," I shouted sarcastically as I rubbed my foot on the grass to remove the dog poop.

She tilted her head. "Why are you such an asshole anyway?"

"Oh, you can say 'asshole,' but I can't say 'shit?'"

She ignored my question. "You should go over there. There's a sprinkler you can turn on to clean your shoe."

I groaned in frustration, walked over to the sprinkler and ran the bottom of my shoe under water, careful not to get the rest of me wet. When I turned around and walked back, the girl had disappeared. So had my video game device.

"Shit!" I mean...*Crap*! Where was she?

"Looking for this?"

I turned around to see the girl waving it in front of me with a teasing expression.

"Give that back to me!"

"See if you can get it from me."

I lunged forward to grab it, and she started running away...fast.

She was giggling. "A-ha! You want to play tag all of a sudden, huh?"

I chased after her and yelled, "Give it to me now!"

She taunted me in a sing-songy voice. "Bet you can't catch me!"

We ran in circles around the park for minutes on end. Her braids were flailing in the air. She was too fast for me, and I couldn't catch up to her. At one point, I sprinted, tackling her to the ground. "Oof!"

She held the device in a death grip as I tugged at it. "Come on. Give it up!"

She just continued to laugh, enjoying this a little too much. I had to think of something, so I started to tickle her. She became hysterical and begged me to stop. Eventually, I started to laugh, too. Before now, I couldn't even remember the last time something had truly made me laugh.

After she couldn't take anymore, she handed me the device out of exasperation. "You win. You win."

We both lay on the ground, huffing and puffing. "That was fun," she said. Her smile lit up her whole face, and it was contagious.

"Yeah...actually, it was."

She smelled like candy, and her tongue was red, probably from a lollipop. "I'm Skylar."

"I'm Mitch."

Then, I heard a woman's voice. "Skylar! Come on, honey. We have to get home. I have soup simmering on the stove."

She hopped up from the ground. "Well...bye, Mitch."

"Hey—" I started to say something, but she ran off before I could. I watched her until she was out of sight.

Skylar. Huh.

She had made me forget about my worries, made me feel alive for just a few moments, and then she was gone. I felt a strange sense of loss. Would I ever see her again? Why did it matter so much?

Why was I still smiling?

I stayed on the ground for a while then noticed that the sun was starting to set. I walked back over to Gram's car where she was looking down at the sweater she was knitting.

"Hey, Gram."

"Did you have fun, honey?"

I thought about it before answering. "Yeah."

"Good. I saw you met Skylar Seymour."

"Huh? Yeah...what...you...you know her?"

"Of course. She lives right across the street from me."

Jackpot.

TWO

SKYLAR

What I loved about Mitch Nichols: He had pointy ears like Dr. Spock from Dad's favorite show, Star Trek. He liked to suck on ketchup packets as a snack. And he called me Skylar, not Sky.

What I hated about Mitch Nichols: At the end of August, he would be gone.

That summer, in two short months, he became the best friend I ever had.

The day after our playground chase, I found a piece of paper that had been slipped under the front door. *You can run, but let's see how you shoot hoops. Meet me out front at three.*

His grandmother, Mrs. Mazza, had a basketball hoop in her driveway that used to belong to her son when he was young. At 2:45, I sat by the window waiting for Mitch to walk outside.

He emerged right on time, bouncing the ball on the pavement, and I ran across the street.

Mitch didn't say anything, just kept dribbling the ball with a smirk on his face as I ran around him. The ball nearly knocked me down as he suddenly passed it to me. I shot, and it missed, much to his amusement. He took the ball, bounced it all the way to the farthest end of the driveway then turned and shot it into the basket.

"Impressive," I said.

"Thank you."

After about twenty minutes of Mitch bouncing the ball while I ran around him, I decided to shake things up a little. "Let's play a game."

He approached me with the ball tucked under his arm. His shaggy brown hair blew in the wind. "I thought that's what we were doing."

"No. This is you showing off. I get it. You can play basketball better than me. Big whoop."

He chuckled. "Okay. What do you want to do, then?"

I thought about it for several seconds and came up with the perfect way to find out more about him, specifically what was eating him yesterday. I was willing to bet it had something to do with why he was here for the summer. There was definitely a story there. Many summers had passed without so much as a visit to his grandmother. I would have noticed him.

"We'll start here close to the hoop and each take turns shooting. If I miss, you can ask me anything you want, and I have to answer truthfully. If you miss, I get to do the same. Then we'll step back further each time to make it harder."

"But I'm gonna get it in every time," he said.

"Well, then you should have no problem with this game, cocky."

I was banking on him missing the shot at least once. I had nothing to hide, and it was a win-win situation for me, so long as he flubbed up a single time so that I could ask that one question.

He shrugged his shoulders. "Alright."

I shot first, and the ball went right into the hoop.

Mitch followed suit.

We kept taking turns, successfully hitting the baskets until I became the first one to miss.

"Aha!" Mitch laughed. "Let's see...what do I want to know?" He scratched his chin and scrunched his lips. "Oh! Yesterday at the park...did you know who I was?"

I nodded. "I knew you were Mrs. Mazza's grandson from the pictures hanging in her house. That's why I left like that. I knew I would see you again anyway."

He nodded in understanding. "Cool."

I passed the ball to him and backed up a step further away from the hoop, gesturing for him to do the same. "Go."

Of course, he made it and passed the ball to me.

I missed again.

"Alright, Skylar...hmm. What was your most embarrassing moment?"

I looked up at the cloudless, blue sky. "I once started laughing at my friend Angie in class and accidentally passed gas out loud in front of everyone."

Mitch's mouth dropped. "I can't believe you just admitted that!"

"We told each other we'd be honest! That was *honestly* the most embarrassing moment of my life."

"That's pretty bad."

"No. What's bad is that everyone thought it was Angie, and I let them believe it."

We laughed at my admission until I passed the ball to Mitch who proceeded to shoot...and *miss*.

I giddily jumped up and down. "Yes!"

"That fart story threw me off track!" Mitch licked his lips and looked down at the ground shaking his head in defeat. "Okay, give it to me."

I looked into his big, blue eyes and asked, "Why are you really here this summer, and why were you so angry yesterday?"

"That's two questions."

"But the answer is the same?"

Mitch didn't say anything right away, just looked at me.

"Things aren't going well back home right now. I'm pretty sure my parents are getting a divorce. They didn't want me around anymore to witness all the fighting. So... yeah."

"My parents are divorced, too."

His eyes widened. "Really?"

"Yeah. For two years now."

Mitch seemed to be thinking hard about something. Then, he turned to me. "Did you ever feel..." He hesitated. "Never mind."

"What? Did I feel what?"

"When you found out about your parents, did you feel like your world was ending...like you couldn't picture the future anymore?"

It seemed Mitch and I had a lot more in common than I originally thought. "Yeah. I did feel like that sometimes. It was hard. I'm an only child, and my parents are my only family, you know?"

"I'm an only child, too. I guess that's why I feel like it's my responsibility to keep them together. Or worse, I think sometimes maybe if I didn't exist, they wouldn't be having these problems."

The game we had been playing was no longer significant. Now, we were just talking as we made our way to Mitch's front steps. The basketball rolled away onto the grass.

"You didn't ask to be born, Mitch. You know this isn't your fault, right? I used to think like you in the beginning with my parents. But after a while, I figured out that it really had nothing to do with me. And honestly, they both seem happier now."

"Why did they get divorced?"

I chuckled. "Well, I overheard my Mom telling my Aunt Diane that my dad couldn't keep it in his pants. But I still haven't figured out what 'it' is. Do you know, Mitch?"

His face turned red. "You're kidding, right?"

I nudged him. "Yeah."

We both started cracking up.

"I can't tell with you." He sighed, picking mindlessly at the shrubs at the side of the stairs before turning back toward me. "Did I really look that miserable yesterday? It was that obvious?"

"Sort of...yeah."

"How old are you anyway?" he asked.

"Ten. How old are you?"

"Eleven. You seem way older than ten."

"My mom says I'm an old soul. I also kind of have this thing. It's like an ESP. With certain people, it's as if I can feel their emotions. It's hard sometimes because I don't always want to. But when I saw you, I just sensed something was wrong, and I felt your sadness, too."

"Wow. What am I feeling right now?"

"Right now, you're not sad."

He stared at me for a while before his mouth spread into a wide smile. "You're right. I'm not anymore."

That night, Mrs. Mazza invited me over for a spaghetti dinner. She let me play in Mitch's room for a while afterward, and he showed me these comic books he made. He did all of the illustrations and captions himself.

We hung out every day that summer.

Each afternoon at exactly three, we would meet at the hoop and play our game. After hundreds of missed shots, we ended up knowing practically everything about each other: our likes, dislikes, embarrassing truths and fears.

It turned out *my* biggest fear came true earlier than expected when one day in mid-August, two weeks before Mitch was scheduled to go back to Long Island, there was a knock at the door.

Mitch looked morose when I opened it, his hair stuffed under a Yankees cap.

"Skylar, my Dad's here. He's taking me home. He made me pack all my stuff just now. My parents didn't agree on how long I should be here, and I guess he got his way, so now I have to leave with him."

It felt like a sucker punch. "Now? We were gonna do that goodbye party thing, and I still haven't made you your gift and—"

"I know. I'm really sorry. I don't want to leave. I didn't want to come here in the beginning. But since I met you, now I wish I could stay...like forever."

"Can you come in?"

"He's waiting out in the car."

The car horn beeped, and Mitch turned around. "Give me a second, Dad. Jeez."

I was frantic. "I don't want you to leave, Mitch."

The tone in his voice broke my heart. "I don't know how I'm gonna handle everything back home. I wish I had you there with me. You always make me feel better about everything."

"Will you keep in touch? Let me know what happens with your parents?"

"I will."

I felt tears forming in my eyes. "What do we do now?"

His voice was low. "I guess we say goodbye."

"I don't want to," I said as the first teardrop fell.

He reached into his jacket and pulled out a large envelope he had tucked under his arm. "Here, I made you something. I was going to give it to you at the end of the summer. Open it later, okay?"

I nodded through tears, "Okay."

The horn beeped again. "Mitch! I don't want to hit rush hour."

Mitch leaned in and pulled me into a hug. Hot tears streamed down my cheek and onto his shoulder.

He sniffled, but I couldn't tell if he was about to cry. "Thank you, Skylar."

"For what?"

"For giving me something happy to think about when I need it."

That was the last thing he said before walking away and getting into the car. His face was barely visible under the cap as he waved goodbye one last time before the car disappeared from sight into the glare of the sun.

My mother's wind chimes blew in the breeze as I stared out into the empty street and across to our desolate basketball court. I was crushed.

I took the envelope straight to my room. Inside was one of the comic books he made. But this one was different. The characters were...us. It was titled *The Adventures of S&M*. (The alternate meaning of which would not occur to me until several years later.) S had two long braids, could fly and had other special powers. M was an ordinary boy in a Yankees cap. M kept getting into trouble and S would rescue him from harm in various situations. He had ended the book with *To Be Continued*.

I never heard from him again after that day.

In the five years that followed, the boy with the Yankees cap and the big, blue eyes became nothing more than a mere fond memory tucked inside my heart.

During that time, Mrs. Mazza moved to Florida, and her house was rented out to new tenants. I assumed that meant I would never see Mitch Nichols again.

But life is full of surprises, and as promised at the end of the comic, our story was far from over.

THREE

SKYLAR

"Angie, can't you go anywhere without that thing?"

Click. Flash.

My best friend Angie wouldn't leave the house without her SLR camera strapped around her neck. Sometimes, people thought we were with the press.

"Are you kidding? This place is a mecca for photo ops," she said.

Angie was odd, but she was a good friend. Because I could pick up on a person's energy, it was hard for me to connect with someone unless they were truly genuine. I could always see through people, and there were very few you could trust with your heart.

Angie didn't have a bad bone in her body and as annoying as the constant clicking of the camera was, she took photos because she truly appreciated everything life had to offer, never wanting to miss an opportunity to capture the unexpected. As embarrassing as it was being the other half of "camera girl" as she became known, I admired the fact that she didn't give a crap what people thought.

Tonight, we were at the high school equivalent of a frat party. Angie and I were freshman at St. Clare's, an all-girls Catholic school. So, we had to depend on parties run by the public school kids for any co-ed mingling.

There were always really cute, older boys at Marcus West's parties, which was why it would have really been helpful if my friend weren't geeking out with her massive camera.

Click. Flash.

"Did you see that? That drunk kid just wiped out on the stairs. I snapped it."

"Annie Liebovitz would be proud, Ang."

Marcus was a junior and a friend of Angie's older brother, so we always got invited to the parties he'd throw when his parents went away. We told our mothers that we were going to the mall, so we'd have to leave by nine.

We never drank. As much as we liked being around the wild stuff, we both had pretty good heads on our shoulders and never put ourselves in situations where we could be taken advantage of.

This party was the same as all the rest. Some cold food from the sub shop that no one touched sat out on an island in the kitchen. In one room, a group of kids would be smoking pot. In another, there would be some dumb drinking game going on. In the main living area, Marcus had his iPod connected to a speaker, and people were either dancing or making out on the couches. And of course, some of those people would head upstairs to do God knows what.

Angie and I mostly just stood in the living room and people-watched. None of the good-looking, older boys ever approached us, but if we hung out in one spot long enough, inevitably some drunk kid with beer breath would come over, put his arm around me and give me some dumb pick-up line.

Tonight it was, "Where have you been all my life?"

"Running from you," I said as I slipped from under his arm.

At one point, Angie left me alone, and I went to find the bathroom. There was one right off the kitchen. When I opened the door, a guy and a girl were making out inside, so I quickly shut it.

Once upstairs to find a different one, I passed another couple kissing in the hallway before rolling my eyes and entering the bathroom.

I splashed some water on my face and decided I was ready to leave. I wasn't feeling it here tonight and wanted to go home to my bed.

On my way out, I approached the same guy and girl who hadn't moved from the spot where he had her pinned against the wall as his mouth hovered over hers.

Right after I passed them, it occurred to me that the guy was wearing a Yankees cap. I thought nothing of it until on my way down the stairs, I heard the girl say, "Mitch, we can't stay here. Let's go to one of the bedrooms."

Mitch? He was wearing a Yankees cap, and his name was Mitch? What were the chances?

I continued down the stairs despite an uneasy feeling. It couldn't have been *my* Mitch because he didn't live around here. But at the same time, I hadn't really gotten a look at his face. It had to be a coincidence, though. *Right?*

The smell of booze and weed saturated the air in the hot, crowded living area.

Angie was now in the corner of the room happily talking to a guy who looked about seven-feet tall. Normally, I would have been thrilled for her, but I wanted to leave.

As I sat alone, I couldn't get the guy named Mitch out of my mind. With each passing minute, my curiosity grew. Butterflies set in as I impulsively made my way back up the stairs.

A door at the end of the hall was cracked open. My heart pounded as I walked over to it, peeked in and saw the guy in the baseball cap lying with the girl on the bed, still fully clothed. I didn't know what to do but felt like I needed to confirm that it wasn't him. There was no way I would sleep tonight if I couldn't.

The room was dark except for a night-light, so it was impossible to see facial features. Who knew how long I would have to wait before they came out? And then, how would I explain my standing outside the room like a creeper?

I went back downstairs where Angie was still in the same corner talking to that really tall guy.

"Angie, I need your help with something."

She gestured to her new friend. "Skylar, this is Cody."

I looked up to meet his face. "Hi, Cody. Can I steal her for a minute?"

"Sure. I'll wait right here," he said. His voice was surprisingly high and undeveloped for a guy who had clearly hit puberty. In fact, if I closed my eyes, it could have been mistaken for a girl's.

I pulled Angie away and led her toward the stairs.

She sighed. "This better be good. I was getting ready to wrap myself around that beanstalk like a vine."

"He *is* really tall." I laughed. "Okay, listen. I'll let you get back to him, but I just need you to do one thing for me."

"Okay...what?"

"I'm a little freaked out right now. Remember my friend Mitch from when I was ten?"

"The one who basically disappeared?"

"Yeah. Well, there's a guy upstairs making out with a girl in one of the rooms. He's wearing a Yankees cap. Mitch used to always wear one. Anyway, I thought nothing of it until I heard her call him Mitch."

"You think it's the same Mitch?"

"I don't know. That's what I want to find out. I couldn't see his face. I need you to just knock on the door and ask, 'Is there a Mitch Nichols in here?'"

Angie had no problem making a fool out of herself, so I knew she'd do it.

"What do I do if he says yes?"

"Chances are, it's not him. So, don't worry about that. I just need to rule it out 100-percent."

She shrugged her shoulders like it was nothing. "Okay."

I let out a deep breath as Angie approached the room. I stayed several feet back closer to the stairs. She looked back at me, and I nodded, giving her the go ahead.

She cleared her throat. "Is there a Mitch Nichols in here?"

I was standing too far away to hear his reply. But when Angie turned to look back at me, the troubled expression on her face made my heart drop.

I lost my breath when he appeared at the doorway.

"I said *I'm* Mitch Nichols. Who wants to know?"

Angie was speechless. "Ugh..."

"What's with the camera?" he asked.

I was too frozen in shock to help my poor friend out. I just stood there unable to believe my eyes. It *was* Mitch. I wanted to run away, but I couldn't move. He hadn't noticed me yet. I turned my head away.

When I peeked over again, the girl came out of the room, her blonde hair mussed and her clothing wrinkled. "What the hell is going on?"

"I have no friggin' idea," Mitch said to her.

A girl's voice yelled from the stairs. "Skylar, where did Angie go?"

I turned around. It wasn't a girl. It was Angie's guy, Cody with the high voice. He came upstairs. "What's going on?"

When I looked back toward the bedroom, I finally let myself look at him. A familiar set of blue eyes stared back at me, and everything else seemed to vanish. He whispered my name in a deep, smooth, unfamiliar voice. "Skylar?"

He was handsome. *So handsome.* And tall. My Mitch...but he wasn't.

A mixture of emotions consumed me, with anger at the forefront. It would have been easier if he just pretended not to recognize me. That would have been better than knowing he'd been here in town and not bothered to contact me. I couldn't handle this. I needed air. So, I turned around and made my way down the stairs.

When I exited the front door, I just kept running down the road away from the house. My mind was in a haze, and my throat felt frozen from swallowing the frigid air as I ran.

Up until this moment, Mitch Nichols represented pleasant childhood memories that I cherished. In seconds, all of that was destroyed. He would no longer be immortalized in my mind as an innocent and vulnerable boy. Now, he'd forever be a cheap manwhore who took girls to back rooms at parties.

It was starting to drizzle, and I found myself running into thick layers of fog. I stopped about three blocks away to catch my breath when I received a text from Angie.

Where are u? He ran after you.

The opaque fog made it impossible to see anything behind me. Then, I heard footsteps running toward me in the distance.

FOUR
MITCH

She wasn't supposed to find out like that, and I damn well never thought she'd be at this stupid party.

After someone shouted, "Skylar," I looked over toward the stairs and nearly lost my ability to breath. I knew it was her, but at the same time, the person standing there wasn't exactly the skinny girl in braids I remembered. She was grown up, really pretty in a classy way, unlike Ava, the girl I came here with. After I called out Skylar's name, I couldn't take my eyes off her, and then she was gone.

"Mitch? What's going on? Who was that girl?" Ava asked.

I just stared speechless at the empty stairs.

The girl with the camera snapped a picture of me before running to chase after Skylar.

What the fuck?

I left Ava and followed the girl downstairs as a seven-foot tall guy I recognized from school trailed me.

"Is Skylar your friend?" I called from behind the girl.

"Yes. I need to find her," she said before asking someone, "Have you seen Skylar?"

Some guy pointed to the door. "She just left a minute ago."

I put my hand on the girl's shoulder to stop her from leaving. "Please. Let me go find her." I ran outside before she could respond.

It was really foggy out, and I had to pick a direction. I chose left because it was toward her house.

After a few minutes of running, I was almost ready to turn around. That was when I noticed her stopped further down the road. When she heard me approaching, she turned around. I slowed down and was out of breath when I finally caught up to her.

"You always could run like hell." When she didn't say anything, I continued, "I didn't expect to see you tonight."

She looked up at the sky and let out a single sarcastic laugh. "Isn't that supposed to be my line?"

She was so pretty.

My heart was pounding. "I guess you're right." I was really taken aback by how different she looked. Long, wavy auburn hair wet from the drizzly rain replaced the two braids I remembered she always wore. She was still petite but definitely wasn't a little girl anymore. I was all too aware of that.

Even though it was dark, the streetlights shined on her face, illuminating her green eyes. She was waiting for me to speak, but I was too busy studying her.

She broke my stare when she said, "This is the part where you open your mouth and say something. Maybe explain why you never called or wrote to me. Maybe explain why you show up five years later screwing some whore at a party on my turf."

"Whoa...wait. I wasn't screwing her," I said defensively. It bothered me how much I needed her to know that.

"It's none of my business anyway. I—"

"I wasn't going to have sex with her," I said with my eyes peering into hers.

"Fine. TMI. Like I said, it's none of my business."

"I don't like the way you're looking at me right now," I said.

"How am I looking at you?"

"Like you're disappointed in me."

Why the fuck did it matter so much what this girl thought of me? It shouldn't have, but it did. It was why I had waited in the first place to tell her I was back here.

She closed her eyes and sighed. Her expression softened. "I'm just a little shocked to see you, okay?"

"I know. I'm sorry." I let out a deep breath before telling her, "I live here now, Skylar."

"What? Since when?"

"Since last week."

"I don't understand..."

"My mother lost her job and has really been strapped for cash over the past year. Since my grandmother moved to Florida and owns her old house outright, she offered it to us so that we could live rent-free. My Dad doesn't give a shit about what we do anymore. So, we moved."

"How did I not see you move in?"

"We didn't have a truck or anything. The house is all furnished. We drove up half our stuff a week ago and go back for the rest next weekend."

"You've been living across the street from me for a week?"

I looked down at the ground unsure of how to explain why I hadn't gone to see her. The truth was, I was scared. That little girl I left behind had meant so much to me. The thought of her and memories of the conversations during our basketball games got me through many difficult nights. I didn't want to find out that she had changed or worse, that she would be disappointed in how I turned out. I knew seeing her again would be inevitable, but each day, I put it off.

"I promise you. I was going to come by soon."

She started to shiver and didn't have a jacket. I took off my hoodie and put it around her arms.

"Thanks," she said.

Several quiet seconds passed. "Let me walk you home."

"I should call Angie."

She walked a few feet away so I couldn't hear the conversation then returned to the spot where I was standing.

"She said Cody is taking her home."

"Is that the tall dude?" I asked.

She nodded. "Yeah."

"That guy sounds like he swallowed his own balls."

When she burst out laughing, my tense body finally relaxed. The sweet sound of her familiar laugh made me smile. For the first time tonight, it had felt like old times.

"What about your girlfriend? You just left her there."

"She's not my girlfriend," I was quick to say. "Ava is a girl I just met at school this week. She asked me to go to the party with her, and I said yes, but I really didn't want to come."

"You left the door cracked open upstairs. From what I saw, it looked like you really wanted to *come* tonight."

Well, shit. There was the wise mouth I remembered. But now that she was older, it was dirty, too. And that intrigued me. But I wished she hadn't seen me making out with Ava because it really didn't mean anything.

"Yeah, well...it was a mistake." I took out my phone. "Hang on." I texted Ava that I wasn't coming back to the party. She'd whine about it and demand an explanation, but I had no interest in continuing what we had started. "I just told her something came up. Now, let me walk you home." I took my jacket off her shoulders and opened it. "Here. Slip your arms through."

She did, and I zipped it up slowly, careful not to catch her hair. My fingers brushed lightly against her breasts on the way up.

Well, those were new.

"Thanks," she said, looking up at me.

My hand was still on the zipper, and I squelched the urge to pull her toward me right before I let go.

Her tiny frame was swimming in my hoodie, and that made me smile. "Let's go."

We walked side-by-side at a slow pace, and I chuckled at the fact that she was a good foot shorter than me.

She was the first to speak when she asked me the question I knew was coming. "So, what have you been up to the past five years, Mitch?" It came out sarcastically casual because we both knew that question was the elephant in the room.

"I'm sorry I never contacted you."

The tone in her voice tugged at something deep inside me when she said, "I just wanted to know you were okay."

"I know. I—"

She interrupted me. "I mean, I would see your grandmother and ask about you. She would always say you were fine, but I wanted to hear it from you, because I knew you didn't share your true feelings with her like you had with me. So, I never knew whether what she would tell me was really the truth."

"Listen...I'm not even going to make an excuse for not calling or writing you. I was a dumb 11-year-old. The situation got really bad after I got home. Things with my parents were way worse than I imagined, and I didn't want to talk to anyone, not even you. I was ashamed of certain things. But you need to know something."

"What?"

"Everything you told me back then stuck with me: that it would get better, that it wasn't my fault. I kept replaying everything we'd talked about and reminded myself that I wasn't alone...that you had been through the same thing and survived. It was the only way I got through it. So, I really need to thank you, Skylar."

The rest of the walk home, she listened as I told her things I hadn't ever told anyone. I explained that shortly after I left my grandmother's, I found out the real reason my parents were getting divorced: my father had a secret girlfriend and had gotten her pregnant. I now had a four-year-old half-sister whom I barely saw because my father eventually took off to live in Pennsylvania with his new family. When I was twelve, my mother had gotten so depressed that she had to be hospitalized, and I had to go to live with my uncle temporarily.

Over the past couple of years, things had finally gotten better. We were getting used to the new normal with my father gone from the picture. When Mom lost her job, the shit hit the fan again, and that's how we ended up here. My mother and I were now back in her childhood home trying to start over.

By the time we got to Skylar's door, I was mentally exhausted from rehashing everything, but it was a relief to have finally let it all out. How ironic that the only two times in my life I had really opened up to someone, it was to her.

What was it about Skylar that made me want to pour my heart out?

"Thanks for being open about everything," she said as she stood on her front steps facing me. "I'm sorry for freaking out and running earlier."

I nudged her with my shoulder. "It was fun chasing you again. And thank you for listening. You know..." I looked down at my feet and shook my head. "Never mind."

"What?"

"This is gonna sound kind of corny, but I always knew I'd see you again, that I'd be back here somehow and that we would still be friends."

She smiled. "To be continued..."

I didn't get it at first but then realized she was referencing the comic I made her when I was eleven. I had forgotten about that. "You still have that book?"

"Of course, I do. It's not everyday you get a starring role in a story about S&M."

I bent my head back in laughter. "Holy shit. When I realized the meaning a few years back, I nearly died. Clueless little kid."

"Well, I better go inside. My mother thought I was at the mall, which closed a half hour ago."

"Oh, yeah...you'd better," I said, backing away. "See you around then?" I pointed across the street. "In case you didn't know, I'm right over there, so..."

She surprised me when she took a step forward and hugged me. "I'm glad you're here."

I closed my eyes, relishing the brief contact of her warm body and the feminine smell of her hair. "Me, too." I never wanted to let go.

She pulled back. "Good night, Mitch."

"Good night."

When I walked into the house, my mother was watching television. "Hey, honey, how was your night?" she asked as she sipped her tea on the couch.

"Unexpectedly good, Mom." I said without further explanation on the way to my room.

Thoughts of her kept me up that night. It felt good to have reconnected, but what was screwing with me were all of the things I wasn't expecting to feel, how attracted I was to her.

She hadn't given me back my hoodie. I thought about her wearing it and how much I loved the thought of her delicate little body in my clothes. I thought about what it would be like to taste her plump, red lips. I imagined burying my nose in her long, silky hair and kissing the nape of her neck.

Sucking on her neck.

It troubled me that I was having these thoughts about Skylar...little Skylar. Not so little anymore.

I was hard. And I was fucked.

She was someone I could see myself really falling for. But there was one thing I knew for sure: I would not let things go any further than friends, fall in love with a girl like Skylar and hurt her.

I remembered how in love my parents seemed when I was small. They were always all over each other, and it grossed me out. My Dad had told my mother how much he loved her all the time, only to leave her years later for a younger woman. My mother almost died from a broken heart. In my experience, love doesn't last forever, and someone always gets hurt.

That wasn't going to be me, and it sure as hell wasn't going to be Skylar. So, when it came to her, I would keep my dick in my pants if it killed me.

Someone should start planning my funeral.

FIVE

SKYLAR

Angie sat on my bed cleaning her camera lens. "I can't believe it doesn't bother you that Mitch dates other girls."

A lump formed in my throat. "He's not my boyfriend, so why should it matter?

Angie took my picture. "Uh-huh."

"What was that for?" I snapped.

"I want you to see what your face looks like when you're lying through your teeth."

I rolled my eyes. "He's like a brother to me, Ang."

"Then, that's just gross because he clearly wants you. I don't understand why you're not together."

"Who says Mitch *wants* me?"

"Have you seen the way he looks at you? I have about a hundred pictures to prove it."

"I don't know what you mean."

I knew exactly what she meant.

Over the past six months since he moved here, Mitch and I had not only picked up where we left off as kids, but we grew closer. We saw each other almost every weekday after school, hung out in our rooms, did homework together and ate dinner at each other's houses. My mother, Tish, and his mother, Janis, also became close and even hung out without us once in a while. Sometimes, the four of us ate together or watched a movie.

To someone looking in from the outside, it would have looked like Mitch and I were brother and sister, part of one big happy family with two lesbian moms. The reality was, the moms were lonely ex-wives of men who abandoned them. And brother and sister secretly wanted to have sex with each other. I would say that's the epitome of dysfunctional.

While Mitch and I were inseparable during the week, on weekends, he would sometimes go out with girls from his school. He was gorgeous with a great body and therefore popular. Despite my pretending not to care, the reality was, his dating hurt like a motherfucker.

He would always tell me where he was going and even who he was going with, but there was a silent understanding that we never talked details, and that was fine with me.

Everyone who knew me would agree that I spoke my mind. If my mother asked me if a dress made her look fat, I'd tell her it did. When Angie said she overheard someone saying her boyfriend, Cody, sounded like a girl, she asked for my opinion. I told her I thought he sounded like Mickey Mouse on helium, but that she shouldn't give a crap what anybody said because she was crazy about that dude.

So, for the most part, I didn't mince words and was an open book—except when it came to my true feelings for Mitch. That was my one sore spot. But I was sick of lying to Angie. I needed to let it out, or I was going to explode.

I plopped down on the bed. "Okay. You're right. It does bother me when he goes out with other girls."

"I knew it! How could it not?"

I took a deep breath because it was the first time I would admit this out loud. "I have feelings for him, okay? But see...I know Mitch better than anyone. We talk a lot. His parents' divorce really screwed him up. He's worried he's going to turn out like his father, and he's seen his mother really hurt by things his father did."

"But what does that have to do with you?"

"We're only fifteen and sixteen. I know he cares about me and wants us to always be in each other's lives. He's afraid to screw it up, and honestly, I kind of am, too. I can sense that he's sexually attracted to me, but I don't think he'll ever cross the line. The problem is...sometimes I wish he would." I exhaled.

"So, you both want each other, care about each other but won't ever find out whether that could lead to more? Meanwhile, he just dates a bunch of bimbos, and where does that leave you?"

I gave the only honest answer. "Screwed."

Mitch worked three days a week at the gourmet coffee shop in the mall food court to help his mother pay the bills. He had to attend this intensive training so that he could learn how to operate the fancy equipment. He was now an expert milk frother and made my vanilla latte exactly the way I liked it: extra hot and foamy.

One Thursday afternoon, Angie, Cody and I decided to pay Mitch a visit at work. While my friends usually took their drinks to go and walked around the mall, I loved to stay and watch him in action in his red apron as he juggled the different orders, flipping cups, pushing buttons, steaming milk.

Strands of his wavy brown hair curled under the red cap he wore. Mitch had the shiniest, thickest, chestnut hair with a hint of copper when the sun hit it. Part of his uniform was a fitted, black polo shirt that hugged his toned chest. I loved the focused expression on his face as he drizzled the caramel just right or carefully poured hot milk into a cup. His tongue always moved slowly across his bottom lip when he was concentrating.

When he placed drinks on the counter, he'd look customers in the eye and flash his gorgeous smile. It was no wonder why the lines were always endless. Girls lined up in droves to visit the brawny, blue-eyed barista. Watching Mitch was a downright turn on.

The thing I loved the most, though, was the moment when he'd first notice me. The genuine smile reserved for me was warmer than the one he'd give the customers, and his eyes always lingered on mine like they were telling me a secret. Then, he'd go back to doing his work, stealing glances at me. He'd smile whenever he caught me watching him.

If he saw me get in line for a drink, he'd gesture for me to sit back down. He'd always make mine before the rest and whistle over to me when it was ready on the counter. The cup would usually have something special written on it in black marker. Sometimes, it was a goofy face or random word like "ass" to make me laugh, and other times, it was a message. Today, he wrote, *Wait for me.* I nodded to indicate that I would hang around until he got off work, and he winked at me.

He would make me as many lattes as I wanted, and

I would do homework or read my kindle amidst the constant steaming sound of the milk frother.

At exactly 7:00, Mitch came from behind the counter with his coat on. “Thanks for sticking around. I like it when you’re here. It makes work go by faster.”

Every time he said something nice to me lately, my heart would pitter-patter.

He grabbed my backpack. “Let’s go. I have a surprise for you.”

Mitch led me down a side corridor of the mall and stopped in front of the pet store with a big grin on his face. “Guess who’s back?”

I gasped and ran to the back of the store. “Seamus!”

Mitch laughed at my reaction. “I heard him on my way into work earlier and couldn’t wait to tell you.”

Seamus was a blue-fronted amazon parrot I had fallen in love with over the past few months. I’d visit him every time we went to the mall. Besides his bright-colored feathers and beautiful, black beak, I loved his attitude. Apparently, the pet store had been trying to get him to mimic common human phrases like some of the other birds. Seamus wasn’t having it. The only thing he said was *“Holy Toledo!”* He must have picked it up from a previous owner.

A few weeks ago, when I had come in to visit him, he was gone. The salesperson told us someone had finally bought him, and it had been heartbreaking to see his cage empty.

“Why is he back?” I asked Mitch.

“They told me the person returned him.”

“Strange.” I turned to the woman at the counter. “Do you know why he was returned?”

“They just didn’t want him anymore. We have a thirty-day policy.”

I pouted my lip. "How could anyone not want you?"

I broke into laughter as he flapped his wings. *"Holy Toledo!"*

Mitch put his hand on my head and playfully messed up my hair. "You're so cute. The simplest things make you happy."

There was the pitter-pattering again.

Mitch didn't touch me a lot, but when he did, even for a second, my body responded.

After fifteen minutes of getting reacquainted with Seamus, we left the store. Mitch waited on a bench for me while I used the mall bathroom.

I was in the stall when I heard two girls talking as they washed their hands.

"Did you see Mitch Nichols out there?"

"Yeah. He's so damn hot. His eyes are insane."

"His body, too. I heard he asked Amber out."

"She's such a bitch. Wait...I thought he was dating Brielle?"

"No, they just hooked up once."

"Oh. Well, I wouldn't mind being next."

"Get in line."

I actually blocked my ears, so I couldn't hear anymore and sat on the toilet frozen until I heard the door slam. My heart was pounding, and I could feel the adrenaline rush as jealousy hit me like a ton of bricks. I breathed in and out slowly until I composed myself enough to get up and wash my hands.

Sure, Mitch cared about me, and I was pretty sure I had at least a piece of his heart, but that wasn't enough for me anymore. I wanted all of him. As I looked in the mirror, I decided it was time to give my friend some of his own medicine.

SIX

MITCH

Davey dropped a bomb on our way home from school. "Did you hear Aidan asked Skylar out for this Friday?"

I fell off my skateboard right as we arrived at my house. "Say what? Aidan Hamilton?"

"Yeah. Apparently, he'd been trying to go out with her for months, but she's always said no. He asked her to go to the fall carnival Friday, and she said yes."

Shit. Aidan went to Crestview High with me. She must have met him through Angie's boyfriend, Cody. Aidan would trip people in the cafeteria for laughs and talk back to teachers. He was a douchelord. He'd been with a lot of girls, too, some of the same ones I dated. I would admit, he was a good-looking guy, but he sure as hell didn't deserve to go out with a girl like Skylar.

"Really…" I was so angry I was practically foaming at the mouth.

"That's all you have to say? Dude, your face is turning colors." Davey followed me into the house and headed straight for the refrigerator.

A dozen thoughts raced through my head. Namely, how I was going to stop this.

Davey knew how protective I was of her. He lived two houses down from us, was our only mutual friend and a go-between. Skylar's friends were mostly girls from her private school. Davey was our common denominator. I didn't like the idea of Skylar having guy friends because they'd all want in her pants eventually—myself included if I were being honest. But Davey was almost as short as Skylar, roly-poly and harmless. Think Pillsbury doughboy with long, black dreadlocks he never washed. That was Davey. Let's just say, Skylar wasn't going to be tempted by our furry little friend, and I liked it that way.

Aidan, on the other hand, was a serious threat, and even though I wanted to spew venom, I tried to play it down while I cleared my head. "Technically, Skylar can go out with whomever she wants," I said coldly.

"Not true," Davey said as he helped himself to a soda.

"What?"

"She wants *you*, you dillweed."

My pulse quickened. "She told you that?"

Davey shook his head. "She doesn't have to say it."

The way she looked at me sometimes with those beautiful almond-shaped eyes made me wonder if she did.

"You know I can't go out with Skylar."

Davey burped. "What I do know is that you mess around with girls you don't even like to get her out of your system."

Maybe, but that was the way it had to be.

"Skylar is like family to me. Going further with her... there is no way that could end well. We're too young, too many years ahead to fuck things up. It would destroy us."

Speaking of destruction, I had to figure out how I was going to keep Skylar from getting mixed up with that dick,

Aidan. If I couldn't have her, he sure as hell wasn't gonna get her. I texted Amber to cancel our movie date Friday night because now I had work to do.

I put my phone in my pocket. "What are you doing Friday night, Dave?"

"Let me check my phone." He lifted it and pretended to check his calendar. "Oh! Waxing my ass."

"Yeah. Postpone that. How do you like cotton candy?"

Whenever I went anywhere with Davey, I felt like we were Arnold Schwarznegger and Danny Devito from that old movie, *Twins,* because I towered over him.

The fall carnival was held in a big field about a mile from where we lived. It was full of people we knew from school and the last place I'd have been were it not for the fact that Skylar would be here on what I was pretty sure was her first official date.

She had told me about her plans, and I played it cool. It wasn't like I could tell her I was going to show up and spy on her. I swore to myself I'd stay away unless I saw Aidan make one wrong move, at which point I would deck him.

It was dark, crowded and chaotic. The bright lights from the rides combined with the dinging sounds from the game booths made it hard to focus on my mission.

I hadn't spotted her yet, and it didn't help that Davey had gotten separated from me in search of funnel cake.

He looked like he had gone swimming in a vat of powdered sugar when I found him. "Davey, can we please focus on finding Skylar? You can eat later."

"Try this," he said, pushing the fried dough into my face.

I waved it away. "I can't think about food right now."

He spoke with his mouth full. "Man, can't you see you have it bad for her? This isn't a normal reaction to your *friend* going out on a date."

"I'm just trying to protect her."

"You're gonna do this every time some guy asks her out?"

"No, just when he's an asshole," I said as I continued to look around.

"Is there really ever going to be a guy good enough for her in your eyes?"

I thought about it. "Maybe not."

Fuck no.

Davey waved the funnel cake as he spoke. "That's messed up. Just admit that you're not here to protect her. You're here cuz you're jealous."

"I'm not jealous."

"Then, it shouldn't bother you that she looks like she is having a really good time right now." He pointed over to the ticket booth.

I turned around and saw Skylar laughing at something Aidan was saying while they were in line. My chest tightened, and it felt like I couldn't breathe. When I could make her laugh like that, it normally made me all gooey inside. Seeing her face light up for another guy made me want to kill someone.

I grabbed Davey. "Come on, I don't want her to see me."

"You should wear green more often. It suits you."

"Shut up."

Davey and I walked back over to the concession stand where he ordered a caramel apple. "I should have gotten the one with the nuts."

The crunch of his teeth sinking into the apple made me cringe. I shook my head at him. "Seriously?"

"Look, I'm here for you, but I'm hungry. Just tell me what I need to do, and I'll do it. In the meantime, I'm eatin.'"

Aidan had taken Skylar over to a game booth. It was the one where you had to shoot water into the clowns' mouths to see which player could fill the biggest balloon. The first to pop won a prize. He sat down to play while Skylar stood next to him.

Her long, straight hair fell loose down her back. She looked sexy as hell, and I might have drooled a little as my eyes traveled from top to bottom. A tight, red shirt hugged her firm breasts, and she wore a short, denim skirt that made me want to pull my hair out. I wanted to scoop her up in my jacket and carry her home.

I knew I was attracted to Skylar. I knew I cared deeply about her and wanted to protect her. But I wasn't prepared for the level of jealousy that hit me tonight.

Aidan kept winning. After each victory, they'd offer him a bigger stuffed animal. If he kept playing, he would eventually get the gargantuan one. After his final win, he stood up from the chair, bent down and lifted Skylar into the air.

His hands were on her ass, and my blood was pumping through my ears. The carnival music began to sound like it was being played backwards along with the drumbeat in my head.

A beastly voice inside me said, *"Get the fuck off my girl."*

After they finally walked away with a pink hippo that was practically bigger than she was, I realized Davey had disappeared on me again.

Several minutes passed, and I had lost track of both Davey and Skylar.

Then, I heard Davey's voice. "Mitch!"

I could have killed him for shouting my name. But it seemed to be coming from the sky. I looked up and saw him waving excitedly from atop the Ferris wheel. He wasn't alone. It took me a few seconds to realize that sitting next to him...was Aidan.

What the...how in the world?

Davey flashed me a maniacal grin and a peace sign. Aidan looked annoyed, and that pleased me to no end.

"What are you doing here?"

Skylar was still holding the massive hippo when I turned around.

I tried to play it cool. "Oh...hey."

"Hey." She wasn't smiling.

"Um...what is...Aidan doing with Davey on the Ferris wheel?" I asked.

"We were standing in line waiting to go on. Aidan got in first, and out of nowhere, Davey pushes past me and steals my seat. Then, it started moving up so the next person could board, and I couldn't do anything."

Remind me to buy Davey another candy apple...with extra nuts.

I bit my lip to stifle a laugh. "No way."

"Any idea why Davey would do that, Mitch?" She asked with a suspicious look.

I held my hands up but couldn't contain my smile. "I swear to God. I had nothing to do with it."

"You didn't tell me you were coming here tonight."

"How were you going to go on the Ferris wheel with that hippo anyway?"

"I was going to leave it on the ground and hope no one took it. You didn't answer my question."

I played dumb. "What was that?"

"Why you didn't tell me you were coming. You knew I'd be here."

"Yeah...that..."

"Are you spying on me?"

"No."

"Your ears are turning red, Mitch. You're lying."

She knew me so well. That really sucked.

"Okay." I rubbed my temples. "I just wanted to check things out. Make sure you were okay."

"Do I do that to you when you go out with a different girl every weekend?"

"No. But it's different. You don't know how guys are, Skylar. We're dirty, dirty fuckers. I don't want him trying to take advantage of you, to touch you. Aidan goes to my school. I know how he is. I—"

"Maybe I want someone to touch me once in a while."

Fuck.

I was stunned silent before I said, "You don't mean that...not him."

"Why wouldn't I? The girls you take out like it when you touch them, right? So...why am I any different from them?"

Shit. I didn't know where this conversation was going anymore, except that I was starting to feel my jeans tighten at the thought of her wanting to be touched. God help me, I'd never wanted to *touch* any girl like I wanted to touch her.

My phone rang. It was Davey. "Davey? What's going on?"

"Have you not realized that this death trap hasn't moved?"

I looked up and saw him waving from the dangling seat. Then, he broke out some kind of hip-hop dance move while Aidan had his head down, hand over his face, looking frustrated. They were stuck at the top. Skylar and I had been so busy talking that we didn't notice.

"They're stuck?" she asked.

I walked over to the conductor who reeked of cigarette smoke. "What's happening?"

He didn't even look up from his newspaper when he said, "Equipment malfunction. We waitin' on support."

"Shit. Davey, are you still there?"

"No."

"I guess they're waiting on help. Hang in there, buddy."

I couldn't help but laugh.

Skylar adjusted her grip on the giant stuffed animal. "I suppose you think this is hilarious."

I shook my head with a grin. "No...*no*."

Her mouth widened into a smile. "Because it is."

We both burst out laughing.

I wiped my eyes and looked up. "Any minute Davey's gonna bust out his Star Wars trivia."

"And if Aidan gets hungry, I'm sure Davey wouldn't mind searching his dreads for some leftover crumbs," Skylar joked.

We waited for about ten minutes until I walked over for another update from the ride operator. "How much longer?"

"They're telling me about thirty minutes now."

I called Davey to let him know.

Poor Davey. But this night could not have ended up better for me. I turned to Skylar. "You hungry?"

She smiled. "I could eat."

I grabbed the hippo from her. We ended up getting a couple of slices of pizza and taking them to a picnic area just outside the carnival gates. It was away from the action, but we could still keep an eye on the Ferris wheel in case it started moving.

When we finished eating, we moved to sit on a grassy hill that overlooked the entire fairgrounds. There was no one else in the vicinity.

We sat in silence until she turned to me. "You were thinking about your sister tonight, weren't you?

Her question floored me because the truth was, I *had* been thinking about her. But how did she know that? "Why do you ask?"

"I saw you looking at the little girl in line when we were getting our pizza. She looked about five, and I know your sister is around that age."

Sometimes, Skylar blew me away with how perceptive she could be.

I had only met my half-sister, Summer, a few times. I always felt guilty about not going to see her more, but things were always tense when I visited my father in Pennsylvania. Summer's mother was one of the main reasons for my parents' divorce and my mother's breakdown, and I couldn't get past it. It wasn't my sister's fault, and I felt guilty a lot for not being there more for her.

"How do you always know everything?"

"I don't know everything. I know *you*."

"Yeah, you do, don't you?" I smiled. "That little girl did remind me of Summer. I was thinking about how I wished I could take her to something fun like this. I worry about her, Skylar."

"Why?"

"I just have this feeling my Dad is going to fuck up again and rip apart her world someday, the way he did mine."

"That could happen, but if it does, she has something you didn't."

"What?"

"She has you, a big brother to turn to and someone who's been through it and can tell her it'll turn out okay. You'll be there for her no matter what, even if he isn't."

She always knew the right thing to say.

I nodded. "She'll have me." I turned to Skylar. "And I had *you*. You were that person for me all those years ago."

"I'm glad."

"I was thinking of taking the train to visit her during school break. Will you come with me if your mother lets you?"

She put her hand on my knee. "Of course."

Skylar's touch felt electric. I looked down and almost put my hand over hers but didn't.

Her hair blew in the breeze, and I wanted to run my hand through it and tell her how much she meant to me.

Instead, I was silent as I looked up at the starry sky. Something beyond my control was building inside of me tonight, and I started to feel inexplicably nervous, as if suddenly this moment were different from the hundreds of other times Skylar and I hung out.

It felt like this was *our* first date instead of hers with the bozo stuck in the Ferris wheel.

She was looking up when I turned to stare at her pretty side profile. She had the smallest, pinned-up nose with a dusting of freckles. When she caught me, I instinctively looked up at the sky again.

A wind blew her flowery scent toward me and I breathed it in, wishing that I could do so much more than smell her. My heart started racing because I felt my inhibitions giving way to something else, something much stronger. It was something I wasn't sure I could fight right now.

"Are you going to let him kiss you later?"

She looked surprised by my question. "I don't know. I hadn't really thought it through. I guess he'd have to be rescued first, or the chances are greater that he'll be kissing Davey." She laughed nervously.

I picked at the grass. "He's gonna try. You know that, right?"

"Yeah."

"Davey told me that Aidan asked you out a lot before, but you always said no. What changed?"

She looked up at the sky again. "I guess I'm growing up." Then, she turned to me. "And maybe realizing certain other things aren't gonna pan out."

Ouch.

My eyes met hers. "Skylar...I—"

"Don't say anything, Mitch. It's okay."

She had no idea how much I wanted to say and wanted to do.

I was pretty sure I knew the answer but asked anyway. "Have you ever kissed anyone?"

She shook her head no but didn't say anything.

"Are you planning to give him your first kiss?"

"Probably."

The jealousy that nearly made me insane earlier returned in full force.

"You can't do that."

"Why?"

My heart pounded in anticipation of what I was about to do. "Because I'm stealing it."

SEVEN

SKYLAR

Mitch placed his warm hands on my cheeks, and my heart skipped a beat when he pulled my face into his. I had imagined this moment so many times but wasn't prepared for how nervous I'd be.

I kept my lips pursed and whimpered as his mouth descended upon me. My body tensed. My eyes shut when his hot lips pressed into mine.

I couldn't believe this was actually happening.

He sensed my nerves, stopping the kiss for a moment, his hands still on my face when he whispered over my mouth, "Open for me, Skylar."

He licked across my lips slowly, and my entire body went limp when his tongue slipped inside my mouth. He tasted like pure sugar and something else that was indescribable. It was *his* taste and suddenly, I couldn't get enough of it.

Mitch groaned when my tongue swirled fast around his. His hands moved from my face, and he gripped the back of my hair, fisting it in his hands.

My nerves were a thing of the past suddenly, and all I wanted was for him to kiss me harder, faster, deeper. Now, my hands were in *his* hair, bringing him closer to me, and he moaned into my mouth. I loved the feel of his silky hair between my fingers. I had always wanted to touch it like this.

His lips opened and closed over mine as he continued to move his tongue around the inside of my mouth. He pulled and sucked on my tongue at one point before slowly letting it go, making my nipples harden instantly.

This was nothing like how I imagined my first kiss. This was what I imagined sex felt like: all-consuming, addictive, and it made me want more. I would have done anything he asked me to, and it didn't even scare me because it was Mitch. This just felt right.

Minutes went by, and we never came up for air. My underwear was completely wet, and that had never happened to me before. He kept his hands on my face or in my hair but never touched me anywhere else.

The only time his lips left mine were to kiss slowly down my neck. I wanted him to go lower, and my breasts tingled in anticipation. But he kissed a line back up to my chin and then returned to my mouth. He growled over my lips. "What are you doing to me? I can't stop kissing you."

Desperate for him to continue, I kissed him harder. "Don't stop."

"I feel like I can't, and it's scaring the shit out of me."

I repeated, "Don't stop, Mitch."

He said in between kisses, "I have to."

He kissed his way up to my forehead and finally pulled away. His eyes were full of lust, but they also looked pained. I leaned in, desperately needing to taste him again, but he backed away.

Then, his phone rang, and he pulled it out of his pocket. I couldn't stop staring at his mouth as he spoke.

"Davey?" He paused. "Good...that's good. Yeah...we just went..." He looked at me. "to get some pizza. We'll meet you by the Ferris wheel in like five minutes."

I rubbed my lips. They were sore in the best way. "Are they off of the ride?"

"Yeah. I guess we missed that development."

I shivered, rubbing my arms. "Apparently."

"Are you cold? Take my jacket."

"I don't know if that's a good idea."

"I don't care what Aidan thinks," he snapped before taking it off and putting it around my shoulders. "Just tell him you were cold, and I gave it to you. He doesn't need to know anything else. You don't owe him an explanation."

I nodded. "Okay. Thanks."

Mitch seemed agitated and looked me up and down. "We should go."

The walk back to the fairground was awkward to say the least. Neither one of us seemed to know what to say about what had happened, so we chose to say nothing at all.

When we approached, Davey was sipping on a giant drink while Aidan was checking his watch.

"Hey, guys," I said.

Aidan looked up, walked over and put his arm around me. "Well, that sucked! Where have you been?"

"I ran into my friend, Mitch, and we went to grab a bite until they got you guys down." I gestured back to Mitch. "You guys know each other from school, right?"

Aidan smirked. "Yeah. Thanks for looking after my date."

Mitch had daggers in his eyes. "The pleasure was all mine."

"Ready to go? I'll drive you home," Aidan said.

Mitch looked over at me, and my heart broke. I knew he was conflicted about our kiss. I was certain he was just as confused as I was right now. Neither of us expected what happened tonight.

Still, I had come here with Aidan and felt I had no choice but to leave with him. I walked away, leaving Mitch and Davey behind. I couldn't look at Mitch as I left.

When Aidan dropped me off at my door and tried to kiss me, I turned my face, giving him the cheek. Between that and my disappearing act at the carnival, I was pretty sure he wouldn't ask me out again.

That night, I lay in bed nestled inside Mitch's hoodie, smelling him on me and replaying our never-ending kiss. My body was still fully aroused. I touched myself and licked my lips, imagining that it was Mitch touching me until I came.

I couldn't fall asleep.

If I was jealous of his seeing other girls before, now that I truly knew all that I was missing, I couldn't fathom how I was going to handle it.

My phone buzzed close to midnight. It was a text from Mitch.

Let me know you got home okay.

Skylar: Home in bed.

A few minutes later, my phone buzzed again.

Mitch: I'm sorry I shut down. I didn't know what to say. And then you left with him. I haven't been able to think about anything else.

Skylar: I know. Me too. Don't overthink it. It is what it is.

Mitch: It was amazing.

I had been trying to play it down. I wasn't expecting him to say that. Since we were being honest...

Skylar: I didn't know a kiss could feel like that.

Mitch: It normally doesn't.

Just when I was getting my hopes up...

Mitch: I don't think we should do that again, okay?

My heart dropped. A sinking feeling developed at the pit of my stomach. I didn't respond.

Mitch: It felt like I was losing control. Like I couldn't stop myself. I don't want to take things too far and lose you.

He kept on.

Mitch: Do you understand what I'm saying?

A teardrop fell down my cheek. I understood where he was coming from, and a part of me worried he was right. But that wasn't going to change how I felt.

Skylar: Loud and clear. Goodnight.

I shut off my phone before he could respond, took off his jacket and cried myself to sleep.

EIGHT

MITCH

It had been a couple of weeks since the kiss at the fairgrounds—the kiss that changed everything. It was proof that I couldn't trust myself with her anymore. All of the reserve I had worked hard to build up was shattered, and it felt like I had to start all over again now.

That meant avoiding being alone with her at all costs, at least for a while. I had Davey come over on the days Skylar and I did homework together. I had to tell him what happened that night, and in typical Davey fashion, he busted my balls about it.

During Spanish homework one afternoon, the dickhead asked Skylar and me if we knew what *beso* meant. When she nonchalantly answered that it was the word for kiss, I wanted to throw my textbook at his head.

She was doing a good job of acting like nothing had changed between us, though, which made it easier but also bothered me a little because for me, it was an internal struggle.

I could try and act like nothing had changed in front of her during the day, but without fail, every night, that kiss replayed in my head. My mouth would water remembering how she tasted or the noises that she made when I kissed her neck. I wanted so badly to experience it again or even worse, to know what noises she'd make with me inside of her.

I had kissed a lot of girls, but it had never felt like that. Then again, I never actually had feelings for any of them. Seeing Skylar with Aidan had triggered a primal reaction and made me realize how deep those feelings actually ran. It was an insoluble problem: keep away from Skylar and keep her away from other guys at the same time.

So, when you can't figure out how to handle something stressful, create a distraction. That was my new motto.

Skylar and her mother would be over for dinner any minute, and I had a surprise for her, one I hoped would help ease the tension between us.

Even though it was a Friday night, I had no other plans. When the doorbell rang, my heart started to beat faster.

Cut the shit. It's just Skylar.

The smell of my mother's eggplant lasagna wafted through the house as I made my way downstairs. The cold, fall air blasted through the door when my mother opened it.

I stood awkwardly with my hands in my pockets, trying to look nonchalant, like I hadn't just been fantasizing about her. "Hey Tish...Skylar," I said.

Skylar took off her black puffer jacket. I was grateful that she had changed out of her sexy school uniform into some sweats.

"Hey," Skylar said before walking over to the living room where she looked through my mother's magazines with her legs crossed on the sofa. I loved how comfortable she was here.

"Mitch, your mother told me about all of the A's you've been getting lately," Tish said.

"Yeah, well, gotta focus my energy on something. Might as well be school."

"Well, keep up the good work."

"Thanks."

That was another thing. I'd been diving head first into my schoolwork in an attempt to transfer my focus onto something other than what happened with Skylar. Apparently, it was paying off.

She was being uncharacteristically quiet tonight and hadn't said anything since they walked in the door. As we sat down to eat, my mother broke the silence.

"So, what are you guys doing for Thanksgiving?"

"Well, Oliver wants Skylar to spend it with him and his beautiful bride down in Florida."

My mother put down her fork. "Beautiful *bride*?"

"You heard me." Tish took a long sip of her wine.

"They got *married*?"

"Apparently, they went to a justice of the peace in the city last week. We just found out when he called about an hour ago. They're doing a little ceremony down in Miami with her family over Thanksgiving, and they want Skylar to fly down."

Shit. That's why she was being quiet.

I looked over at her until she would look at me. The disappointment in her eyes was palpable. I hated seeing her upset. She very rarely let things get to her. *My rock.*

Skylar went to visit her father in Brooklyn about one weekend a month. She wasn't crazy about spending any long amount of time with him, but he was way more involved in her life than my father was in mine. Still, it freaked me out sometimes how similar our family situations were.

While Skylar's Dad didn't leave Tish for another woman specifically, he hadn't exactly been faithful, either. He'd only had one serious girlfriend since the divorce and recently moved in with her. She was apparently now his wife.

My mother turned to Skylar. "Honey, are you okay with all this?"

She wiped her mouth with a napkin then threw it down. "Am I okay with Oliver marrying titanium tits? Sure...whatever. But am I okay with him casually calling to tell us about it *after* the fact, like he was announcing what he had for breakfast? No. I'm not okay with that." She got up from the table abruptly. "Excuse me."

I got up a minute later and found her in the living room where she was standing by the window. It was still early in the evening, but it was already dark out.

"Hey...you okay?"

She turned around to look at me before returning her gaze to the rain that had started to fall outside. "It's not even about me. I'm mad for my Mom. My parents were together for fifteen years. She's acting like this doesn't bother her, but I know it does. I always tell myself they're better off apart, but God, this must sting. She hasn't even dated anyone, and he elopes with the first serious girlfriend he gets and acts like it's nothing. It's the lack of respect that gets me. She just doesn't want it to show, but she's hurting right now."

She was more concerned with her mother's feelings than her own. Typical Skylar.

I wanted to hug her. A few weeks ago, I might have, but now, I really needed to refrain from touching her. "I wish I could say something that would help. But only time usually fixes these things. You know I understand."

She turned to me. "Yeah...out of everyone...I know you do."

"Don't let Oliver's dumb decisions ruin your weekend. Your mom will be okay. She has my mother now, who definitely knows what she's going through, and she's damn lucky to have a daughter who cares about her so much."

She finally cracked a smile. "Why are you home on a Friday night anyway? I figured you'd be out with the girl of the week."

"I decided to stay in for a change and..." I hesitated.

"And?"

"So...I kind of have something that might cheer you up. It's sort of an early birthday gift."

Skylar squinted her eyes suspiciously. "What are you talking about?"

"Come with me."

Come with me? Really? Nice word choice.

She followed me through the kitchen past our mothers who were now polishing off the bottle of wine. My heart was racing in anticipation as we walked up the carpeted stairs to my room.

The look on her face when the door opened was priceless. Where was Angie and her camera when you needed her?

"Seamus?!"

She rushed over to the cage in the corner of the room. The parrot flapped his wings excitedly and tilted his head repeatedly like he recognized her.

"Holy Toledo!"

I laughed because it was the first time he used his signature phrase since we left the pet store earlier. Figures, he would show off for her.

"I've been hiding him in here all day. I got lucky because he was quiet all throughout dinner and didn't ruin the surprise."

"You...you *bought* him?" She looked back at me in disbelief.

"Holy Toledo!"

"Yup. He's ours."

"How...did you afford it? He's expensive!"

"I put him on layaway."

"They have that for birds?"

"The store employees knew how much you loved him, and when I told them I wanted to buy him for you, they worked with me. I've been saving and paying in installments every week since he was returned to the store. They held him until this afternoon when I picked him up."

The only other time I had ever seen Skylar cry was when I left town as a kid. But now, her eyes were filling with happy tears, and I wasn't sure how to react. I just knew that being the one responsible for making her happy made me giddy.

"This is the best gift anyone has ever given me."

I kept my hands in my pockets to squelch the urge to hug her and to discourage her from coming near me. "I was thinking I'd keep him here for you. I know you say you're a light sleeper. I think I can sleep through anything. They said he could get kind of noisy when he gets temperamental. I got him this special breathable blanket to throw over the cage at night, to teach him to sleep on my schedule. He needs it dark to sleep."

"Holy Toledo!"

"Can I take him out?"

"He's yours. Do whatever you want."

She carefully opened the cage and lifted him out onto her finger. "Hey, buddy. Remember me? Guess what?

You're mine now. I can't believe it. I love you. Yes, I do. I love you so much." She kissed his beak and continued whispering sweet nothings.

Lucky-ass bird.

You're mine now. I love you. I closed my eyes for a second, pretending that she was saying those things to me. Damn bird was supposed to distract from my feelings, not enhance them.

Seamus' wings were flapping like crazy now. We actually only guessed on his gender, but something told me he was definitely all male.

"Holy Toledo."

It started to dawn on me why that other customer returned Seamus to the pet store.

My mother walked into my room about two in the morning. "Did you get a dog for her, too? What the hell is going on?"

I had my pillow wrapped around my head. "No! This thing just started barking out of nowhere."

"Apparently, he misses his old stomping grounds," she joked.

I threw the pillow in frustration. "What the hell do I do?"

"Well, you can't exactly return him."

"No. I couldn't do that to Skylar."

My mother sat at the foot of my bed and laughed, "You would do anything for that girl, wouldn't you?"

"Mom..." I said, dismissively.

I hadn't discussed my feelings for Skylar with my mother, and I certainly wasn't going to get into it in the middle of the night with a barking parrot.

"Okay. We'll have to do some internet research on how to get him to stop. In the meantime, I'll put some earplugs in."

I returned the pillow to my ears as my mother left the room.

After another half-hour of barking and some howling now mixed in, I turned on the light and met him face to face.

"Stop BARKING!"

He continued to yelp in my face.

I pointed my index finger. "Look. If you don't cut that out, I don't bring the girl back here to see you. No more girl! You hear me? I'm tired. NO MORE GIRL."

Seamus flapped his wings and tilted his head like he understood. He flew around the cage in a flustered panic, and when I covered him again with the breathable blanket, by some miracle...the barking stopped.

Coincidence? I think not. Seamus and I apparently had something in common.

I had picked up more hours at the coffee shop the following week to help pay for Seamus, and that also meant less time with Skylar, which was probably a good thing.

Thursday was my day off, so she and Davey were supposed to come over and do homework around four.

About an hour earlier, my phone rang. It was Skylar. I picked up. "Hey, you."

"I'm out front. I don't think your doorbell is working. It's pouring rain, and I lost my house key. Can I come in?"

"Uh...yeah. Sure. I'll be right down."

This would be the first time we were totally alone in my house since before the carnival, but what was I supposed to do?

When I opened the door, her hair was sopping wet and so were her clothes. That fucking Catholic school uniform was already a tease, but now, it was stuck to her body. It was the hottest thing I had ever seen.

Inhaling her scent as she brushed past me was like taking a hit of a drug. "Thank goodness you were home."

"Yeah. Thank goodness," I muttered under my breath, watching her go up the stairs to my room. I panicked. "Where are you going?"

"I wanna see Seamus."

Fuck.

"Oh. Yeah."

The bird was flitting around like crazy when she walked into the room. He was practically dead from the neck down and the ass up when it was just the two of us.

"Seamus! Mama's here!" Skylar said.

Some water dripped off of her hair down the back of her white dress shirt. I could see the back of her bra through the wet material, and as she bent to take Seamus out of the cage, my eyes trailed down to the sight of her skirt riding up her legs and those fucking knee socks.

As much as I tried to control it, my mind went there, to that place I tried so hard to stay away from. All I could think about was what it would feel like to be sandwiched between those legs, and I felt myself getting hard. This was not good.

It got worse when she turned around with the bird perched on her finger. Her nipples were completely visible through the thin, wet fabric of her shirt. Water continued to drip down off of her hair onto her chest. My lips tingled as I imagined what it would be like to lick the water right off of her. My body tensed as she approached and sat next to me on the bed.

"You've been a bad boy."

My pulse quickened. "Huh?"

"Seamus. He's been bad. Your mom told me about the barking."

Phew. I thought she had been reading my mind.

"Oh! Yeah. Well, we kind of came to an understanding with that...he and I. It's all good now. He doesn't do it as much."

"That's good." She kissed his beak.

"Holy Toledo!"

He was in his glory, hamming it up for her. I was onto him now.

She was sitting so close to me that I could smell the rain on her body mixed with her perfume. The urge to kiss her was overwhelming, and I wished I could erase the memory of what it actually felt like.

"I'm sorry. I'm getting you all wet, aren't I?"

My breathing was erratic now. "What?"

"I should probably get out of these clothes."

Fuck. What? No.

My dick heard that loud and clear.

"Do you have something I could change into?"

I do. I just can't stand up right now, or you're gonna see how much I want you.

"Yeah. Um...go into my closet and pick whatever you want."

"Thanks."

She returned Seamus to his cage before walking over and taking a long, white t-shirt off a hanger.

Continuing to be paralyzed by my erection, I stayed on the bed and pointed to my chest of drawers. "There are some shorts in there. My pants would be a little too long for you."

She looked back and smiled at me. "You think? Just a little." She grabbed a pair of shorts with a drawstring. "Where can I change?"

Right here. On top of me.

"The bathroom downstairs." That was the safest place because it was the furthest spot from my cock, who was now standing in line for front row tickets to Skylar's wardrobe change. I needed as much time as possible to get rid of his excitement before she came back.

"I'll be right back."

"Take your time."

When I could hear that she was downstairs, I got up and tried to rationalize with my dick.

"Come on. We can do this. Go down."

Nothing was changing. She could not see me like this.

"Fucking boner. Go down!"

I paced the room, continuing my attempt to reason with it.

Seamus was flapping his wings. "What are you looking at? I suppose you think this is funny."

"Holy Toledo!"

"Yeah. Fuck you."

I decided I had no choice but to jump in the upstairs shower. I'd have to make up a story for the sudden need to bathe. *"Skylar, I just shit myself waiting for you to come back upstairs..."*

She was still downstairs when I turned the shower on to the coldest setting and got in. It wasn't working, so I warmed the water and did the only thing I could. I let myself think about undressing her and sucking every ounce of water off her body as I jerked myself off and came all over the tile wall. It was one of the most intense orgasms I had ever given myself.

I dried off and now, I was definitely ready to go back. She'd be out of that wet uniform, dressed in my baggy clothes, and we'd be good to go.

When I returned to the bedroom, she was sitting back on the bed holding Seamus. She had brushed through her wet hair and still looked so fucking beautiful. I loved seeing her in my t-shirt, even though it looked more like a dress.

"You were taking a shower?"

"Yeah...um...sometimes I do that in the afternoon. It's...refreshing."

She laughed with a look of disbelief. "Okay. That's weird."

I changed the subject. "You want to do some homework?"

It was almost four. Where the hell was Davey?

We opened our books, and I moved over to the desk while Skylar lay on her stomach on the bed.

We fell into a nice, comfortable silence as a Coldplay song played from my iPod dock on low volume. Despite my obvious discomfort over my physical attraction to her, these were really the moments I loved best with Skylar, just sitting around, spending quiet time together.

"Fucking boner. Go down!"

Skylar hopped up from the bed and turned toward Seamus. "What was that? What did he just say?"

"Fucking boner. Go down!"

Shit. Shit. Shit.

I tried my best to play dumb. "I don't know what he's saying."

"It sounds like he's saying 'fucking boner...go down?'"

"Yeah, that's what it sounds like, doesn't it?"

I knew I repeated those words several times when Skylar was changing downstairs. It figured Seamus would take this opportunity to suddenly regain his ability to mimic just so he could screw me over.

She covered her mouth in laughter. "That is nuts. He's so unpredictable lately." She walked over to the cage and took Seamus out. He flapped his wings and turned his head slowly toward me, in his own silent way telling me to "fuck off."

I laughed along with her, but really, I wanted to hide in the closet. She was smart and knew damn well where he must have learned his new phrase.

My phone chimed.

"It's Davey. He's downstairs."

I welcomed the opportunity to get out of that room for a minute. Today was definitely not my day.

"Yo," he said, as he entered, carrying a stack of books up the stairs.

Skylar was still playing with the bird when we returned to my room.

"Hey, Davey."

"Fucking boner. Go down!"

"Hey, Skylar. Uh..." He looked at me. "What the hell did that bird just say?"

I shook my head and glared at him in a silent warning not to push it. Davey gave me a knowing but amused look.

Skylar returned Seamus to his perch in the cage and lay back down on my bed. "Are you guys cold?"

"Not really," I said.

"I have the chills for some reason. I think I'm coming down with something. Do you mind if I use your covers?"

"Not at all."

My sheets were going to smell like her tonight.

The three of us opened our books and quietly got to work. From time to time, I would look up at Skylar in my bed. She was still shivering. Davey seemed to catch me staring at her at one point and rolled his eyes. I gave him the finger, and he didn't return it like he usually did. He would get back at me later in his own special way.

"When it comes to Skylar, I can't figure out if you're Himeros or Pothos, Mitch."

"Say what?"

"I'm studying for my Greek mythology test. We have to memorize some of the Gods."

"What does this have to do with me?"

His dreads flew around as he just laughed hysterically and didn't say anything.

Skylar looked up from the bed but didn't seem too affected by the comment. She continued to shiver.

"You okay?" I asked.

"Not really. I'm feeling kind of achy. I think I have a fever. I should probably go home."

"Let me walk you."

She took one of my coats, and we walked across the street. It was already dark, and light snowflakes were starting to fly. We could see our breath.

Skylar continued to shiver as she knocked and rang the doorbell. "She'd better be home."

Tish answered the door. "I got your text. You lost your keys?"

"I think I left them in my locker."

"Hey, Mitch."

I waved to Tish and followed Skylar inside.

"I am not feeling well, Mom."

"What's wrong?"

"I think I might be getting the flu or something."

Tish felt Skylar's forehead. "You should go to sleep early tonight."

She took off my coat and handed it back to me. "You gonna head back?"

"I'll hang out for a few minutes."

For some reason, I just didn't want to leave Skylar. She rarely got sick. In fact, I couldn't recall a single time before this. I followed her into her room, and as she got under her covers, I sat at the edge of her bed by her feet.

"You should get back to Davey."

"You kidding? He's probably having a field day searching my drawers and raiding the fridge. He'll be fine."

Her teeth chattered as she laughed.

"Do you have any NyQuil? That shit will knock you out until tomorrow."

"Oh, good to know. I'll have to be sure to take some with me down to Florida for Oliver's wedding."

"You decided to go?"

She closed her eyes for a moment and sighed. "I think so."

"That's the right decision. It sucks, and it might give you angina, but you'll get through it."

"It might give me what? Vagina?"

"Angina! My grandmother says that all of the time. It's like chest pains or something. You have a dirty mind, girl."

"You love that about me, though."

"You're right. I do. Nothing gets past you, and nothing bothers you. I like not having to walk on eggshells when I talk to you." I playfully squeezed her feet.

"That felt good."

"What?"

"When you squeezed my feet like that."

"You want me to do it again? Give you a foot rub?"

"No, I don't want a foot rub...said no one ever."

"Okay." I laughed and repositioned both of her feet onto my lap, squeezing her toes with both of my hands in firm pulses.

"Speaking of dirty mind...what was up with our bird talking about boners?"

"I have no idea."

"You sure about that?"

My phone chimed. Saved by the bell. Maybe not.

Stop going down on her and get back here and make me a sandwich.

"Fuckin' Davey."

"What? What does it say?"

"I can't tell you. It's—"

"About us?" She put her head down for a bit then looked straight into my eyes. "You told him we kissed, didn't you?"

I stopped rubbing her feet, and my heart was pounding. "Yeah."

"I told Angie. I had to talk about it with someone because *we* weren't talking about it. You know?"

I swallowed, unprepared to discuss this. "Yeah, I know."

She held out her hand. "Show me the text."

I laughed nervously. "No."

"Show it to me."

My tone was serious now. "No, Skylar."

She got up from under the covers and grabbed my phone. She was sick and shouldn't have been exerting herself. I knew she wouldn't back down, so I didn't fight her.

Fuck.

She read it and rolled her eyes.

"I'm sorry he's being a dick," I said.

"You think that bothers me?"

"No...but it's disrespectful."

"I don't care what anybody thinks. I just care about *you*. Did you forget that I can sense what certain people are feeling? With you, it's stronger than most, always has been. You think you're hiding stuff from me, but you're not, not earlier today in your room, not any day. Himeros and Pothos..."

"What?"

"The Greek Gods Davey was studying that he said reminded him of you."

"Yeah...what about them?"

"I studied them, too. Himeros is the God of desire and unrequited love. Pothos is the God of yearning and wanting."

Shit.

I let out a long, shaky breath. "Oh."

"Was he right? Were you just trying to stick it to Aidan with that kiss, or do you really want me? Please be honest."

Her eyes were searing into mine, and I felt like she could see right through me. If that were the case, then she knew I wanted her more than anything in my entire life. There was no point in lying. I may never muster up the courage to make good on my feelings, but I couldn't look her in the eyes anymore and deny what was painfully obvious. I looked down for a moment, and my tense hands formed into fists when I whispered it. "Fuck yes...I want you."

It felt good to finally admit it out loud.

I was sweating, but she was still shivering when I looked up at her. Her lips spread open into a slight, sympathetic smile. It took every ounce of strength in me not to cover her cold body with mine.

"Thank you for being honest."

I nodded, unable to take my eyes off her now. "It's the truth."

She adjusted the blankets over herself and sat up when she said, "I'll talk about almost anything, but it's not easy for me to talk about my feelings for you because getting rejected by you is about the only thing that could destroy my pride. But you mean more to me than my pride, more to me than probably anyone ever has. I don't want to lose moments with you. I don't want you to push me away like you have been because you're afraid. I need you to know that if we screw up and fail, no matter what happens, you won't lose me, okay? I'll always be here."

Hearing her say that meant everything. Now, I had to work on believing it.

"Okay."

"I'm going to go to sleep."

I left her bedroom in a daze.

Her scent was all over my bedding that night as I played her words in my head over and over again.

Over the next several months, that conversation in Skylar's bedroom would haunt me. *I don't want to lose moments with you. I'll always be here.*

I wondered if she sensed something that day, because I could have never predicted that the possibility of losing Skylar would take on a whole new meaning.

NINE

SKYLAR

I perused my closet for just the right outfit. Even though it wasn't technically a date, Mitch had asked me to go to the movies with him, and it would be just the two of us. There was a new Adam Sandler flick he really wanted to see, and he'd be driving us there in Janis' Accord.

It was a Saturday night, but Mitch hadn't been going out on dates with the girls from school lately. We never discussed why. It was obvious that he'd been making excuses over the past few weeks to hang out with me on weekends, too. Normally, we stayed in with Angie and Cody or with Davey. Tonight would be the first in a while where Mitch and I were going out somewhere together alone.

I was nervous, not for the movie but for what would be happening when we got home.

I put on a pair of dark jeans and a flowy, yellow tunic that had gold sequins on the neckline. I blew my hair out pin-straight and sprayed on some of my mother's expensive Jean Paul Gaultier perfume. What the hell, I'd put on some heavy eye make-up and go all out. He needed to remember what I looked like tonight.

It had been about six weeks since the night in my room when Mitch admitted he wanted me while I was holed up in bed with a fever. In the days that followed, I had continued to feel off-kilter physically. Some days, the fever returned and other days, I just felt lethargic.

My mother finally convinced me to go to the doctor a couple of weeks ago. My assumption was that Dr. Stein would send me home with a prescription for antibiotics, and that would be the end of it.

The doorbell rang, startling me out of my thoughts.

"Skylar! Mitch is here," my mother yelled from downstairs.

"Tell him to come upstairs!"

When the door opened, my breath hitched at the sight of him. His hair was wet, perfectly wavy with a loose piece falling over his forehead. He was more dressed-up than I had ever seen him, wearing a navy sweater under a black, wool jacket. He smelled like heaven: a mixture of musk, shower wash and masculinity. The sweater hugged his muscular frame, which was more sculpted lately. He had just turned seventeen, looking less like a boy and more like a man everyday.

He swallowed. "Skylar...you look—"

"I know. I worked hard at it. I damn well better look good."

"Better than good. I was gonna say...beautiful."

My heart fluttered. I took a deep breath, inhaling him. He hadn't ever called me beautiful before. It should have felt good, but instead, it felt like someone had punched me in the gut.

"Thank you."

"You're welcome."

Mitch continued to stand in the doorway. It was quiet except for the noise of my radiator when the heat turned on. When his eyes wandered down the length of my body, it felt like I could feel him on me. My nipples hardened. I didn't know whether this was technically a date, but tonight felt different in more ways than one.

I held up my necklace. "Will you help me put this on?"

He approached me and took it from my hands. I lifted my hair, and he reached his arms over me and connected the lobster clasp. Mitch's hands lingered on my shoulders before he gave them a light squeeze, and his breath warmed the back of my neck.

I closed my eyes and breathed in his scent before turning around to find his blue eyes, steely and striking, staring back at me. He licked his lips and seemed anxious. About what, I couldn't be sure.

It shattered me because he had no idea what was going to be happening tonight.

"Ready to go?" he asked.

"Yeah."

Mitch played Metallica as we drove the few miles to the movie theater, which was packed.

He held the door for me and winked, speaking in a faux British accent. "After you, my lady."

"Why, thank you." I smiled. He didn't know that his attempt at charm in that moment had almost made me cry. He didn't realize how badly I was trying to hold it together.

"You want something to eat?"

"No, I'm not hungry at all."

He examined my face. "You'll regret that decision when you see me eating. I'll get something, and if you change your mind, you can have some of mine."

"Okay." I forced another smile.

The show was nearly sold out, and we struggled to find two seats together. We managed to snag some way in the back.

The lights dimmed, and a feeling of dread came over me.

About fifteen minutes into the movie, I could feel Mitch's eyes on me. My body quivered when he suddenly moved closer and whispered in my ear, "Is everything okay?"

How did I ever think I could make it through this movie?

I nodded, trying to fight the teardrops forming in my eyes. "Yeah."

I could feel his hot breath in my ear again. "You haven't been laughing at anything. Are you not liking it?"

"I'm sorry."

He squeezed my leg. "Don't be sorry. I just want you to have a good time." The smile he gave me after he said it made me feel like my heart was being ripped out. He had no clue I was about to rip his out, too.

When he repositioned himself away from me, I longed for him to say something else just so I could feel his breath on my skin. I needed him. All I wanted was to be with him tonight, but this was the wrong place.

My mind was some place else entirely amidst the muffled sounds of laughter in the theater. My heart started to beat faster, and beads of sweat formed on my forehead.

He noticed me fidgeting. I flinched when his warm hand landed on my own, which was now shaking. When I turned to look at his concerned face—my sweet Mitch—the first teardrop fell from my eye.

I want to see you grow into a man.

I love you, Mitch.

I'm scared.

His expression darkened. His chest was rising and falling when he realized I was crying. The movie seemed to fade into the distance as he looked at me alarmed.

He squeezed my hand and nudged me up out of the seat, pummeling his full popcorn to the ground. We brushed past the legs of the other people in our row as we made our exit. He led me out of the dark theater into the bright lights of the vestibule, which was empty of patrons. I looked down at the red carpet. When I looked up into his terrified eyes in the fluorescent light, my tears came on full force.

I buried my face in his neck, and Mitch pulled me closer into him. His heart was beating a mile a minute onto my chest.

It wasn't supposed to happen here like this. I just wanted a couple of normal hours hanging out with my best friend. Was that too much to ask? I thought of all the moments with him I had taken for granted.

"Skylar, you're scaring me. Please...it's okay. Please tell me what to do. Just tell me what to do. What's wrong?"

My tears had soaked through his sweater.

He knew nothing. I hadn't told him anything at all that could have prepared him for this. I didn't know where to begin. This was going to crush him, and I couldn't bear it.

"Can you just take me home?"

"No. Not until you tell me what's going on."

"I can't...not here."

"Did I do something to upset you?"

I pulled back and touched his cheek. "No, of course not."

He took my hands in his. "You know you can tell me anything, right?"

I nodded through my tears.

He continued, "I think I know what this is all about."

"What?"

Did my mother tell Janis?

He lifted my hands to his mouth and kissed them. "I've been a fucking fool, Skylar...messing with your mind."

"Um—"

He interrupted me. "Let me talk. This isn't easy for me, okay?"

My stomach fell. "What are you doing?"

"I am trying to tell you...that I think...we should try being more than friends. I thought a lot about what you said that night in your room, how you would always be in my life no matter what. You hit the nail on the head. I've just been scared to lose you. But more and more, I want to try it. I want to try...everything...experience everything with you. I can't...stop thinking about it."

This couldn't be happening tonight. I couldn't find the words.

The look in his eyes broke my heart when he said, "I just poured my heart out to you. Say something...please."

The room started to spin, and I grabbed onto him for support. "I have cancer."

TEN

MITCH

There are some moments in life that you just know you will never be able to erase from memory no matter how hard you try.

The moment that the girl that meant more to me than anything uttered those three words was one of them.

At first, it just didn't compute. My nerves were still reeling from building up the courage to tell her I wanted to be more than friends. I had been practicing what I would say for days and was planning to talk to her later tonight.

So, this was an absolute shock.

When I didn't respond, she lowered her voice and repeated, "I have cancer, Mitch."

My hands were on her shoulders and started to shake, my body unsure of how to react. "What do you mean? I mean...how...how did this happen?"

"You know I hadn't been feeling well..."

"Yeah...but that was weeks ago. You went to the doctor. You were feeling better."

She briefly closed her eyes then looked up at me. "I did, but I never told you what happened because I didn't want to scare you until I knew what I was facing. When he examined me, he found a lump in my neck and asked me how long I'd had it. I told him it had been there for a while. I never thought anything of it because it wasn't painful. He checked the rest of my body and found another one in my groin area. He told me not to worry but that he would be ordering some blood tests just to be sure everything was okay." She looked down, and tears returned to her eyes. "I hadn't even taken my mother with me that day."

My stomach began to turn, made worse by the smell of greasy popcorn, and I felt something sour rising in my throat.

You will not do this. You will be strong for her if it's the last thing you do.

I wiped her eyes with my fingertips. "Take your time, but I need you to tell me everything."

She nodded through her tears and sniffled. "The blood test came back abnormal, so I had to go back for an MRI."

I breathed in and out, gearing up for what she would say next and took her hands, wrapping her fingers in mine. They were freezing. "Okay..."

"The images also showed abnormalities. I didn't tell you, but instead of going to my Dad's that one weekend, I had minor surgery to remove parts of the lymph nodes, so they could test them."

The thought of anything cutting into her made me cringe. "And?"

"They found abnormal cells in them."

My heart was beating faster than I could ever remember. My body tensed and felt like it was shutting down and gearing up for war at the same time. "They're sure...that means it's cancer?"

"They told me I have Hodgkins Lymphoma."

As soon as she said it, the door to a nearby theater burst open and loud, laughing people came flooding out. I wanted to kill each and every one of them. She was still talking, but my ears were throbbing, and it felt like she was far away even though her hands were still in mine.

"Stage three..."

"They said I have to have chemo and maybe radiation..."

"I'm going to lose my hair, Mitch. I'm so scared."

My head felt like it was going to explode, and my heart was slamming against my chest. I needed air.

"We need to get out of here." I led her out of the theater into the parking lot. It was freezing out, and I could see my breath. I suddenly stopped walking, turned to her and frantically fastened each button of her coat. "It's cold."

She must have seen that I was losing it. She clasped my hands to stop me from fumbling for more buttons when there weren't any left. "Mitch?"

I looked into her eyes, shook my head in disbelief then pulled her into me, holding onto her for dear life. We stayed there in the middle of the parking lot for minutes on end. My nose was in her hair, smelling every inch of it, thinking about what she had told me, that she was going to lose all of it. This didn't seem real. My eyes started to sting.

You will not cry. She's fine. She's in your arms.

It felt like a dream I couldn't wake up from.

When we returned to the car, we sat and let it idle with the heat on. A Great Big World's *Say Something* came on the radio. That song is depressing under normal circumstances, and I couldn't bear to hear it, so I shut it off.

I stared blankly at a swarm of people who just converged upon the parking lot, their distant laughter piercing me like a knife. Her hand was in mine, and I rubbed over it gently with my thumb. A million thoughts went through my head, but they all led to the same conclusion: I had to be strong for her. I had to take care of her.

Skylar broke my trance. "There's one more thing."

My body tensed. *What else could there possibly be?*

She continued, "My parents discussed it, and they decided that it's best if I get treated in New York. My mother would lose her job if she had to take me to appointments and everything here. She can't afford that, and we would lose the house. Because Oliver works from home and makes his own hours, they think it's better if I live with him and Lizete. He'll take care of me while I'm undergoing chemo. Mom will come out every weekend."

"That's three hours away."

"I know, but it's the only way that makes sense."

My eyeballs moved from side to side trying to think of a solution, anything that could stop her from leaving. "Stay here. I'll take you to your appointments. I'll take care of you."

"How can you do that with school?"

"I'll fucking drop out. Nothing is more important than you."

"I would never let you do that. *Never*. That's not an option. I wouldn't be able to live with that guilt."

I wouldn't be able to live without...you.

"Well, thinking about you going through all that so far away from me where I can't be there for you...is not an option for *me*."

"It'll be okay. This isn't up for negotiation. It has to be this way."

Her body shook from the cold, so I blasted the heat.

The reality of the fact that I wouldn't be able to stop her from leaving set in. "I'm coming to Brooklyn every weekend, then. When does it all start?"

"A week from tomorrow."

No.

The drive home was a blur. I barely remembered walking Skylar from the car to her house or what we said to each other before I ended up standing alone in the middle of our quiet street. It was freezing, and my toes felt numb from the hard snow crunching under my feet.

Lacking even the energy to open my front door, I looked up at the dark sky with an anger I'd never experienced before, wondering how God could have allowed this to happen to her.

I willed the frigid air to take the pain away. *Please.*

When I finally walked into the house, my mother immediately lowered the volume on the evening news, the look of concern on her face revealing that she knew exactly what had happened tonight.

I was too exhausted to speak any louder than a whisper. "You knew?"

She looked at me with tears in her eyes but didn't say anything.

I repeated, "Mom? You *knew* about this?"

"Only for a couple of days. She wanted to tell you herself, Mitch. She had every right to do that."

It felt like my head was burning up. Suddenly, I screamed at the top of my lungs. "How the fuck could you keep this from me?"

"I'm sorry. I promised Tish!"

I'd never spoken like that to my mother before and immediately regretted it. "I need to be alone." I stormed past her, and she pretended not to notice as I opened the liquor cabinet and took a small bottle of vodka to my room.

It was going to be a long road ahead, and alcohol wouldn't solve it, but for one night, I just needed to forget.

The next morning, I forced myself out of bed with a massive hangover and vowed to make every single minute of this week count. I wanted to take her to all her favorite places like the Cheesecake Factory and the butterfly museum. She refused all of it, saying she wanted to just spend time hanging out at home with me.

Two of the days, Davey and Angie joined us for dinner at Skylar's house. Our moms cooked up all of her favorites: homemade pizza, sloppy joes and fettuccini Alfredo. It was like a party every night, but Skylar barely touched any of the food.

We were all putting on a brave face, trying to act as normal as possible: Davey with his crude jokes and Angie taking photos.

On the final night before Skylar had to leave, Angie was being particularly annoying with the camera, telling us to pose, which she normally didn't do. I had pulled her aside and asked as politely as possible if she could lay off the clicking for one night. She told me Skylar had specifically requested she bring the camera tonight and take pictures of all of us, particularly of her and me. That was unlike Skylar to want her picture taken.

For the rest of that evening, I kept obsessing about what Angie told me until I came to a conclusion that I just couldn't accept: Skylar wanted her picture taken because she thought there was a chance she wouldn't be coming back.

My chest tightened in agony, and I filled with a silent rage, having to excuse myself to the bathroom. She couldn't possibly make it through the next few months if that was what she was thinking. I needed to talk to her.

At one point, she said she had to go upstairs to get something. When she didn't come back down right away, I followed her.

She jumped when I startled her as I entered the bedroom. My heart fell when I noticed tears in her eyes. She had come up here to cry alone.

I ran over to the bed and held her in my arms. My eyes were watering, but I fought like hell to keep the tears from falling.

Do your job, Mitch. Be her rock.

"Listen to me, Skylar. You need to keep your head up no matter how hard it gets. There's power in positive thinking. If the two of us do it, that's double the power. You have to believe that everything is going to be okay. I mean, you have to truly *believe* it, and it will happen."

She wiped her red eyes on my shirt. "What if you're wrong? What if I never come home?"

"Questions that begin with 'what if' are based on fear, nothing else. You're scared, but you have to have faith that God won't let that happen."

"How do you know there's a God?"

I knew how I wanted to answer that but stopped to think about the best way to explain it to her. "Because once, when I was a little boy, I felt hopeless, like my world was ending. I prayed hard one night and asked him to send me a sign that he was listening."

"What happened?"

"The very next day, I met you for the first time."

I knew she could see the tears now burning my eyes, but I still wouldn't let them fall. She gave me a chaste kiss on the lips and said, "And he sent *you* to me."

I grabbed her face. "He can't take you away from me because our story's not finished."

She put her forehead on mine. "To be continued."

"To be continued," I said over her lips.

"Can you do me a favor?" she asked.

"Anything."

"Can you tell Davey and Angie I'm very sorry but that I just want to be alone for the rest of the night?"

"Absolutely."

"Then, when they're gone, come back. Spend the night with me."

I looked at her in disbelief. "What?"

"Not like that. I just want you to sleep next to me to-night. I don't want to be alone. Please."

"Of course, I will. My mother would be okay with it, I think, but I don't see Tish allowing it."

"I'll talk to her. After they leave, just go home, get your pajamas and come back."

I ran my hand through her hair, tucking some strands behind her ear. "Okay."

When I returned to Skylar's that night, Tish let me in. She was normally extremely strict and would have never al-lowed me to sleep in her daughter's room under any other circumstances. So, I had to make sure Skylar had cleared it with her. "Are you sure this is okay?"

She took a sip of her wine and nodded. "I trust you."

My chest tightened, unsure I could even trust *myself* 100-percent. "Thank you."

Before I turned to go upstairs, for the first time, Tish cried in front of me. "I've tried everything, Mitch, tried everything to make her smile this week, to keep her hopes up. All she wants is you. She needs to feel safe tonight. I know you need that, too. This has been tough for you, too. That being said, I know you won't do anything stupid." I couldn't tell if it was a statement or a warning.

With that, she watched me walk up to her daughter's room, trusting that I wouldn't take advantage of the rare opportunity gifted to us.

There was one small lamp on, and Skylar had been reading a book. Except for a poster on her closet door of one of those stupid boy bands that was a few years old, her room wasn't girly at all. It was mostly gray and white, no muss, no fuss and classy just like she was.

She placed her book on the nightstand when she noticed me. "Hey."

"Hey." I walked toward the bed unsure whether I was supposed to just plant myself under the covers. I decided to hold my horses and sat at the edge. She was wearing a pink, cotton sleep shirt.

She grinned. "I told you this would be okay."

"I have to admit, I wasn't expecting your mother to go for this."

"You'd be surprised what you can get away with when you have cancer."

She was being funny, but anytime the C word was spoken aloud, I felt sick.

I tried to make a joke. "Wanna go rob a Dairy Queen, then?"

She laughed. "I like your pajamas."

I had worn plaid, flannel bottoms and a t-shirt that Davey gave me for Christmas last year that said, *Tell Your Boobs To Stop Staring at My Eyes.* I suppose it would have been funnier if I weren't *actually* trying to figure out whether or not she was wearing a bra. I scolded myself for even thinking about that at a time like this, but I couldn't help it. She looked so beautiful.

I hadn't moved from my spot. "It feels weird being able to sleep here. I almost don't even know what to do with myself."

"You can start by getting under the covers with me." She pulled her blankets off, and I crawled in next to her, resting my head on her shoulder. She smelled like shampoo and freshly-showered skin. There was no place in the world I'd have rather been.

"This feels nice," I said into the crook of her arm. "What were you reading?"

She giggled. "Just trying to get my mind off of things. You don't really want to know."

"Yes, I do."

"Trust me...you don't."

"Now, I *really* want to know."

"Okay, then." She reached over to her nightstand and handed me a paperback that had a shirtless guy on the cover. There was a blindfolded woman wrapped around his torso.

Well, shit.

"Skylar Seymour...does your mother know you read this stuff?"

She grinned impishly. "I stole it from her room."

"You're a bad girl. It says right here on the back that it's not suitable for people under the age of 18."

She snatched it from me. "I'm almost 16, same difference."

"Not exactly, but I won't tell. Actually, I kind of like it."

"Like you don't have stuff that's worse than this lying around?"

"No comment."

"That's what I thought."

We both laughed then fell into a comfortable silence before she abruptly shut the lamp off and lay down on her left side, facing away from me.

I turned in her direction and wrapped her in my arms, breathing against her back. I was tense, afraid of getting a hard-on, which I knew was inevitable. My heart started to race, filled with so many emotions. Going against my own advice to her, I became filled with worry, scared for tomorrow, albeit immeasurably grateful for tonight. On top of all those emotions, my cock twitched, which really couldn't be helped as long as her body was against mine.

After a few minutes, she turned around, and our faces were just inches apart. "I could feel your heartbeat. What were you thinking about?" she whispered.

"Don't you always *know* what I'm thinking?"

She tapped my head. "There's too much going on in there tonight to figure it out. My signals are crossed." She put my hand over her chest. "Feel mine."

Her heart was beating just as fast. When she slid my hand off, it brushed along her soft breast. I knew now that she definitely didn't wear a bra to sleep, and my dick rose to confirm it.

"Are you okay?" I asked.

"I am, now that you're here."

Hearing her say that made my stomach unsettled because I knew that tomorrow, I wouldn't be. "Tell me what's going on in that pretty little head."

She took a deep breath. "It changes by the minute, but right now, it's that I just wish I knew what to expect with the chemo. The doctor says everyone takes to it differently. I could get really sick, or I could be just fine. There is no way to know."

"You're the strongest person I've ever met. I know you'll be able to handle it even if it's not easy. Anytime you can't, if I'm not there, I want you to pick up the phone, and I'll stay on with you for as long as you need me to. Promise me that you'll call me anytime you need me, day or night."

She was still lost in thought when she said, "Okay."

I was trying to be strong, but deep down, I was scared shitless.

Aside from the occasional sound of a car passing by, the room was completely quiet. We continued to face each other. I wanted to kiss her so badly but didn't know where that would lead. She wasn't wearing a bra or pants under her long shirt. I knew if I started something, I wouldn't be able to stop. Tish had said she trusted me, and I couldn't betray that. Not to mention, now would not be the time to push things with Skylar.

She ran her fingers through my hair. "I'm sorry that I ruined what could have been such a special moment."

I brushed my hand against her cheek. "What are you talking about?"

"The night I told you I had cancer. You were opening up to me. You told me you wanted to take the next step."

"Don't worry about that. I'm not going anywhere. As soon as you make it through this, we can pick up where we left off." When her worried eyes trailed downward, I pulled her face toward me. "Look at me. I'm not going anywhere, Skylar."

"What are we anyway, Mitch? You're not my boyfriend. I call you my friend, but it feels like so much more.

What's the definition? And with what's about to happen to me, what can I possibly be to you now?"

There was only one answer that made the most sense to me. "Everything. You're...everything to me."

Instead of responding, she turned back around facing away and backed into me to spoon her. This time, I allowed myself to fully relax. Unfortunately, with her ass up against me, that meant my dick grew to full attention. I gently brushed my thumb along her side. Being with her like this, was the most intimate thing I had ever done with anyone. Sure, I'd been with girls, but all of it paled in comparison to this moment, just holding Skylar, drowning out the world.

The only thing I knew for sure in life was that I loved this girl, but I couldn't tell her now. She would think it was only because she had cancer when the truth was I'd been in love with her for almost the entire time I'd known her. I couldn't let her believe I was only saying it now out of fear.

My hand ran down the length of her torso. Realization came in waves, and when it hit me this time, it was like a ton of bricks: there was a cancer growing inside of this little, perfect body, a cancer that if left untreated, was a ticking time bomb that would likely kill her.

I grabbed a hold of her tighter and felt tears sting my eyes. *Please stop*. There was nowhere I could run if I started to lose it.

Then, I heard her voice so low it was almost inaudible. "It's okay to cry."

I shut my eyes, willing the tears away, but she knew. She could feel it.

"I'm not crying," I said as the first teardrop fell.

She turned around. "Yeah, and you're not hard, either."

We both burst into laughter with tears pouring from our eyes.

Skylar fell asleep in my arms about fifteen minutes later.

I didn't sleep at all that night. I chose to stay up and listen to the sound of her breathing instead, each breath reassurance that she was still here, that everything was going to be fine.

It had to be.

I watched the sun begin to rise on a day I wished would never come. Then, for the first time since the little girl in braids came into my life, I prayed to a God I hoped was still listening.

ELEVEN

SKYLAR

"Just do it."

Lizete held my father's electric shaver but was refusing to turn it on. My new stepmother was the perfect person for this job. We weren't close enough for it to really affect her like it would my mother, and I couldn't bear to do it myself. So, a few days after my hair started falling out in chunks, I asked her to meet me in the bathroom.

"Are you sure you want to do this?"

"Yes," I said, staring blankly at my father's outdated pink bathroom tile.

"But you still have a lot of hair."

"It's only a matter of days. This way, I can control it."

She nodded. "Okay, m'ija, whatever you want." I hated her nickname for me, the Spanish word for daughter. I wasn't her daughter. I had to give her credit, though. When she married my father, she hadn't signed up to have a sick teenager living with them. As much as I wanted to hate her, I couldn't. She made the best damn arroz con pollo, too.

She clicked a button, triggering the buzzing sound. I saw nothing but her big, fake boobs before closing my eyes as the blade raked over my head. Focusing on the sound, I continued to keep my eyes shut and told myself this was about preserving my dignity and beating chemo to the punch.

It's just hair.

After a few minutes, a draft blew over my head, and I knew it was all gone.

When the buzzing stopped, Lizete gently placed her cold hands on my scalp. I still refused to open my eyes. "Can you give me a minute alone?"

She patted my shoulders. "Sure, m'ija. Come downstairs when you're ready, and I'll make you something to eat."

I heard the door shut.

Ten, nine, eight, seven, six, five, four, three, two... two...two...one.

I opened my eyes. My heart skipped a beat.

It's just hair...until it's gone.

I continued to stare into the mirror, hoping that at any moment, the sight of myself bald would get easier to accept. No matter how much you try to prepare yourself for something, you just don't know how you'll handle it until it happens. Now, I *looked* like I had cancer, and the reality of that was hard to take. Pretending that everything was normal would no longer be an option.

I cried for the first time since arriving in New York over two months ago.

Up until this moment, nothing had been unbearable. I had already completed the first cycle of a type of chemo called ABVD. It sounds like a sexually transmitted disease, but the letters represent each of the four different drugs in the regimen. Even getting those toxins pumped into me hadn't been as bad as losing my hair.

Actually, so far, chemo wasn't as scary as I'd imagined. To avoid frequent needle sticks in my veins, the drugs were administered right through a port that was inserted under my collarbone.

The nurses always did their best to cheer me up and take my mind off it without trying to make it seem like a bed of roses. They gave me what I needed without feeding me a load of bullshit. They'd have sour candies to help rid the bad taste in my mouth caused by one of the drugs, Adriamycin. They'd also turn the television onto the entertainment channel for me. I could block out what was actually happening by involving myself in reality television and would forever associate treatment with watching the Kardashians. *Khemo.*

My father would stay with me for the full three hours. Once they administered all four drugs, they'd flush my port, and I was good to go home where I'd try to pretend I didn't have cancer until the next treatment. Forgetting was easier in the beginning.

I rubbed my fingers along the top of my prickly head now, wondering how I was going to face Mitch looking like this. He was scheduled to visit over Christmas, which was coming up in less than a week. I hadn't even picked out a wig yet. I wasn't expecting to lose my hair so fast since I'd managed to make it through the entire first cycle with no hair loss. To have it come out in chunks all of a sudden was devastating because I was starting to hope that maybe I'd get lucky. Now, Lizete and I had plans to visit a wig shop in Bensonhurst tomorrow.

She had left me an assortment of her hats to choose from on my bed. I picked a gray, knit beret, feeling immediate relief when I looked into the mirror after putting it on.

My phone chimed. I grabbed it from my pocket and noticed a text from Mitch.

Just thinking of you. I can't wait to see you this weekend. How are you doing?

I wanted to tell him that I was miserable and scared about letting him see me without hair, but I didn't see the point in worrying him when he was so far away.

Skylar: Doing okay. How are you?

Mitch: I miss you. So does Seamus. He hates me because he thinks I'm keeping you away.

Skylar: I miss you too.

Typing those words had made me cry again. I lay on the bed staring up at the textured paint on the ceiling, licking my tears as they fell. I missed him. I missed his smell. I missed home. I missed my life before cancer.

I hugged my stuffed Tigger tightly. With pink walls and white furniture, my room at my father's house was girly and filled with my old stuffed animals. When my parents first got divorced, I used to take a lot of my toys with me to feel more at home, and most of them were still here.

I could smell Adobo seasoning. Lizete was cooking something.

She called from downstairs. "Skylar?" I cringed at how the 'r' in my name always rolled off her tongue. "Do you need anything? Lunch is almost ready."

My Dad had a meeting and wouldn't be home until tonight. I wished I were completely alone so that I didn't have to worry about her catching me crying.

I wiped my eyes and yelled, "Everything's fine. I'm gonna stay up here for a while and rest."

It was getting dark out. I shut off the light to take a nap, and it was nearly pitch black in my room.

When my phone rang, I almost didn't pick up. After a few rings, I reached over and saw that it was Mitch.

"Hi, Mitch."

"Hey, you."

A painful longing grew in my chest upon hearing his smooth, deep voice.

I cleared my throat. "What's going on?"

"This is gonna sound strange. I know you said you were doing okay, but I've just had this feeling all day that you weren't, and to be honest, I'm not doing so hot myself. I needed to hear your voice."

How did he know? I closed my eyes and knew that if I opened my mouth, he'd hear that I was starting to cry.

I needed to hear your voice, too.

"Skylar? Are you there?"

My voice was shaky. "Yes. I'm here."

"Are you crying?"

I sniffled. "Yes."

His tone was soothing, almost a whisper. "Talk to me. What's making you sad?"

I hesitated, but he'd find out sooner or later. "I had to shave my head today."

He didn't say anything right away, just breathed into the phone. "I knew something happened. I just knew it." He sighed, and his voice lowered. "I'm so sorry."

"I know it was inevitable. It was just a shock to actually see it all gone."

"I can only imagine." He paused. "Listen, have you checked your email? It's really ironic, but I sent you something this morning. Are you in front of a computer?"

"I can be."

"I'll wait."

I reached for my laptop. When I logged in, I saw that Mitch had sent me a bunch of images of famous people who had shaved their heads for movie roles. The first one was of Natalie Portman, who happened to be his celebrity crush. So, naturally, I hated her. The next was of Demi Moore. Then, there was Megan Fox.

I wasn't exactly sure of his point. "Wow, this is—"

"You see them?"

"Yeah..."

"What do you see when you look at them?"

"Actually, they don't look too bad because they're all beautiful anyway."

"You think they're beautiful?"

"Yeah, I do."

"You're ten times more beautiful, Skylar."

I could never get enough of hearing him call me that. "Mitch..."

"It might take some getting used to, not having your hair, but in the end, you're still gorgeous, and you know what I'm gonna think of when I see your bald head?"

You're never seeing my bald head, buddy.

"What?"

"The fact that the chemo is doing its job, kicking the asses of those cancer cells. I wouldn't have it any other way."

I wasn't sure if he had practiced this spiel to make me feel better or if he truly meant it. Either way, he had succeeded in brightening my mood.

My lips curved upwards into a smile. "What would I do without you?"

"You're never gonna find out."

I heard barking. "Oh no. That's not..."

"Yup. The barking is back. He hates my guts. He thinks I sent you away."

"Let me talk to him."

"Hang on." I heard the cage open, and the barking got louder then Mitch said, "Okay, I'm putting the phone up to his ear."

"Seamus? It's me."

The barking stopped.

I continued talking. "I really miss you. Please be a good boy. Okay? No more barking. Be good for Mitch, and I'll come home soon. I love you."

Dead silence.

Mitch returned to the phone. "Friggin' unbelievable."

I couldn't help but laugh. "Poor baby."

"Poor baby? Poor me, stuck with a lovesick bird. Do you know he shit on me the other day?"

I laughed harder. It felt good.

"You think that's funny, huh?"

"Yes. I do."

"Well, if it's making you laugh, it's worth it. That's gonna be my goal: to make you laugh at least once a day."

Laughter got the best of me at least a dozen more times that night. Mitch stayed on the phone with me for hours until I fell asleep. I didn't even remember saying goodbye.

The following evening, not only would I look like I had cancer, I'd feel like it for the first time, too.

When it rains, it pours. The next few days were brutal. I had to cancel our trip to the wig shop because I couldn't stand up without feeling like I was going to throw up. The chemo nausea I kept hearing about had finally caught up with me. From the beginning, I had been taking Zofran, an anti-nausea med., but it didn't seem to be working for me anymore.

The skin in my mouth also started getting really sore, and I developed mouth ulcers, which went along just great with the vomiting, by the way.

Seeing as though I couldn't even get out of bed, it was hard for me to answer texts and talk on the phone. Even sitting up to watch television felt impossible.

Mitch called the house phone when I didn't answer my cell, and my father had to tell him what was going on.

I heard my father's voice downstairs. "Skylar has terrible nausea, Mitch. She's not able to come to the phone. I'll tell her you called."

He'd be worried, and I hated not being able to explain it myself, but my inability to gather enough energy even to talk to him for a second was a testament to how bad I felt.

After my father hung up the phone, he peeked in on me. "That was Mitch, honey."

I simply nodded and rolled over onto my side.

"You want some ginger ale?" he asked.

"No."

"Mom is coming a day early."

I shook my head in acknowledgement.

My mother normally arrived every Friday night. My Dad and Lizete were cordial to her, and even though Mom was uncomfortable, she tried not to let it show. She'd spend most of her visits in my room, or we used to go out for a little when I was feeling up to it. Then, she'd sleep at her second cousin's house about ten minutes away.

My phone chimed, and I knew it was Mitch. I needed to know what it said and struggled to reach over to the nightstand.

> ***Your Dad told me. Don't worry about texting back. I'm here anytime day or night, though. You're gonna get through this. Counting the days til Saturday.***

My already sick stomach was in knots at the thought of him seeing me like this. I'd have to see how I felt, but if my condition stayed the same, there was no way I could let him visit.

Lizete came into the room with some chicken broth. "M'ija, sit up. You have to eat something. You need your strength."

"I can't. Just the smell is making me want to vomit again."

"Please. Just try."

I knew I needed to have something in my stomach. I sat up and sipped the cloudy broth slowly. It tasted gamey and gross, causing my stomach to rumble, but I forced half of it down.

The nausea kept me up most of that night. Around four in the morning, I started to feel a little better and wished it weren't too early to call Mitch. He had told me to call anytime, but I didn't want to wake him a couple of hours before he had to get up for school.

I decided to check facebook instead, even though I vowed to avoid it lately. It was a constant reminder of everything I was missing back home. Mitch had an account but never used it. I saw that someone had tagged him in a post from last night.

Brielle Decker

Watching the new Batman movie —with Mitch Nichols.

My heart started palpitating. Brielle was a girl he dated at one time. I kept staring at the status. Technically, Mitch and I weren't boyfriend and girlfriend, but if the cancer hadn't happened, we would be together. He did say we'd take up where we left off when I was better, but we never clarified exactly what that meant for us in the meantime. He never explicitly said he wasn't going to date anyone else.

The reality was, girls were constantly after him. I just didn't expect him to run out with one when he was supposedly so concerned about me.

My stomach was still churning when I picked up the phone and texted him.

Hope you had fun on your movie date with Brielle.

He didn't respond.

I rolled over and put the covers over my head just as another bad wave of nausea hit. After several minutes, I started to regret sending the text. It wasn't realistic for me to expect Mitch to stop living for the next six months or more. He would start to resent me. But it was a Catch 22 because the thought of other girls getting to have time with him that would have been mine was impossible to accept. I wasn't able to handle it like before.

Since I hadn't gotten any sleep last night, I ended up nodding off around six am.

My ringtone woke me an hour later. It was Mitch. If I didn't answer, it would bother me all day.

My voice was groggy. "Hello?"

"Thank God you picked up."

"What is it?"

"I just saw your text. I was asleep when you sent it. That's why I didn't answer. We're on our way to school now and running late. Listen—"

"You don't need to explain. You have every right to live your life. You can't wait around while I—"

"Fuck that, Skylar." His tone was angry. "Listen to me, okay? Last night when I called your house and your father told me how sick you were, I felt helpless. I was pacing my room. I had just wanted to hear your voice. Are you there?"

"Yeah."

"Davey shows up at seven, and I had totally forgotten that I promised him we'd go see the new Batman movie. I told him I didn't want to go."

"So, you ended up going with Brielle instead."

I heard some rustling then Davey's voice.

"Skylar?"

"Davey?"

"Romeo is taking too long to get to the fucking point. I showed up last night. He looked like the walking dead. He told me he needed a drink. He was worried sick over you, and I was worried about him. The fucking bird was barking. I dragged him to the movies, reminded him he'd still have his phone if you called. That bitch happened to be there with her friend. They sat next to us, and she tagged him on facebook. He was checking his phone every five seconds to see if you called, not even paying attention to the movie. You know I wouldn't lie to you."

That was the beauty of Davey. He had no stronger allegiance to either one of us and had no reason to lie. Relief washed over me.

"Thanks. Put Mitch back on the phone."

It felt like my blood pressure lowered with the return of his voice. "Hi."

"I'm sorry. This is just so hard."

"No. I'm the one that's sorry. Apparently, I never made things clear to you. I'm not interested in anyone else. I haven't dated anyone since the night we kissed. I thought you already figured that out. I only want you, Skylar."

My bald head shone in the reflection of the mirror over my chest of drawers, and a tear fell. "I'm only half of me right now."

"I'd take a half of you over anything else that's whole in the world."

I heard Davey in the background. "Dude, get me a band-aid cuz my ears are bleeding."

I couldn't help but laugh through my tears. "I miss you. I miss him. I miss home."

"I might be physically here, but every second of every day, my heart is with you. Please promise me you're not going to waste the energy you need to get better worrying about foolish things. Talk to me if something is bothering you."

"Okay. I promise."

"Just think...in two more days, we'll finally be together for Christmas."

It had been over two weeks since that conversation. Cancer didn't get the memo about Christmas and instead of celebrating it with Mitch, I spent it in the hospital.

He was livid because I wouldn't tell him where I was out of fear he would show up. He finally agreed to stay away only because I told him I needed to be isolated due to the risk of infection. That was a white lie since the doctor had only said not to make close contact with people but that it was okay to be around them.

Mitch had a slight cold, and that was the only thing that kept him from pushing the issue. I just couldn't bear to let him see me so weak. My weight had plummeted, and on the days when the fever returned, I couldn't tolerate wearing anything on my head.

It all started the day before Mitch had been scheduled to visit. My fever escalated in the middle of the night, and my oncologist, Dr. Vega, advised my parents to take me to the hospital. Thank God my mother had come early and was with me.

Once admitted, a test showed that my white blood cell count was low. To prevent infection, the doctor on call immediately put me on a drug to help increase cell count along with antibiotics through an IV.

I'd been in and out of the hospital ever since with recurring fevers and had to spend several nights there. They ended up postponing my next chemo treatment, which meant an even longer time before this nightmare would be over.

The worst part was, being stuck in the hospital gave me way too much time to think. The more horrible I felt, the harder it was to see a light at the end of the tunnel. Even though the prognosis with Hodgkins was a promising one, some days I felt like the chemo was going to kill me if the cancer didn't.

I just wanted to live my life. Was that too much to ask? Even though I had no physical energy, my mind was going at warp speed. I felt paralyzed and became obsessed with doing everything I never had a chance to. I wanted to travel, drive a car, try sushi...and I wanted to have sex with Mitch. That was the big one. I didn't want to die without knowing what that felt like. I wasn't ready, but I was scared I'd never have the opportunity.

There was no one I could talk to about it, either. Angie was too young and inexperienced herself, and my mother couldn't handle talking about sex. I wasn't comfortable enough with Lizete and worried she'd tell my father.

The irony was, on top of having all of these grown-up feelings, they stuck me in the pediatric cancer unit. The volunteers there—candy stripers—came by constantly to "cheer me up." Maybe it worked for the ten-year-olds down the hall, but I really could have done without the bullshit. They talked to me like I was five or had a hearing problem. In their defense, my bald head did make me look younger than I was.

After a while, though, I'd had enough. One afternoon, an innocent striper named Fran became the unfortunate recipient of my wrath.

"Hi, Skylar! What a pretty name! How are you doing today? Look what I have here for you. It's a—"

"Wait a minute. Are you on speed? You asked me how I was doing, but you never waited for a response. You just kept talking."

"Oh. Well, I—"

"That's because you don't really want to know how I'm doing, do you?"

"Of course. I—"

"You do? Well, I have sores in my mouth, bruises on my body, and I look like Elmer Fudd. So, I feel like shit, actually. Meanwhile, my pussy is on fire because all I can seem to think about is sex, even though I can't move. Do you have something to fix that?"

"Um..."

"Maybe some weed?"

Fran had to leave suddenly, and two hours later, a psychologist came to "check on me."

Sometimes, you don't realize how badly you need something until it appears out of nowhere. A few days after my outburst, someone new showed up outside of my hospital room. At first, I thought she was just another volunteer. She stood in the doorway and looked lost. I thought maybe she was just hesitant to come in because she had heard about my reputation as a "difficult" patient. I soon realized she was lost and hadn't come to see me at all. For some strange reason, I wished she had.

She looked to be in her early twenties, with long, blonde hair. She was short and skinny but with big boobs and a butt. She looked like a mini Barbie doll with a donkey ass. She was a beautiful piece of the outside world in this stagnant place. I wished she could take me with her wherever she was going when she left.

I felt her energy stronger than most. That usually meant the person was someone I would have a connection with. I didn't know anything about her, but somehow needed to know her. I also sensed that she, too, had a lot on her mind.

When her eyes met mine, there was no pity in them, just curiosity. I was lonely and didn't want her to leave. So, I shut the television off and started a conversation with her. I pretended to assume she was one of the volunteers and asked her to come in. I told her I wanted to talk about sex as a test to see how she handled it.

Her name was Nina. Within seconds, she became everything to me.

She sat down and listened as I told her all about Mitch and my fears: being away from him, ultimately losing him and never knowing what it felt like to truly be with him.

Basically, in one hour, I unloaded everything onto her, and she gave me honest, non-judgmental advice.

I told her how scared I was to let Mitch see me in this condition, and she offered to help get me a proper human hair wig and to make me over so that I felt comfortable enough to see him.

Nina couldn't have truly known how much her showing up that day meant to me. She had given me hope, and just minutes after meeting her, I knew she would continue to be a part of my life forever.

Today was the day I'd been dying for and dreading at the same time. Mitch was coming for his first visit since I got sick and lost my hair. My cell count had finally improved, so I was discharged from the hospital last week and resumed chemo yesterday. The next infusion wouldn't be for another week.

The plan was for Mitch to stay the entire weekend with me at my father's house, so I prayed for no nausea. As of now, I was feeling decent.

There was a knock on my bedroom door.

"Come in!"

Nina was carrying a wig on a Styrofoam head along with some clothing on hangers.

"How are you feeling?"

"Like I look...like ass."

"Well, when we get done, you might still feel like it, but you won't look like it."

She put down all of her stuff and sat on the edge of the bed. "Are you still scared to see him?"

"A little."

"Why?"

"He just doesn't have any clue how different I look now. I know he cares about me, but I want him to want me the way he used to." I closed my eyes and pictured his face. "I love the way he looks at me, Nina."

Her expression was sympathetic. "I hope you don't mind, but I happened to mention what you're going through with Mitch to Jake. I wanted his take on it."

Jake was Nina's boyfriend. From pictures, I knew he was a hot, tattooed God of a man. I hadn't met him yet, but he seemed really down to Earth from how she described him. Seriously, though, he wouldn't have to say a damn thing and that would have been fine with me, too.

"What did he say?"

"First, he told me that if I lost all of my hair, he'd just have to find something else to grab onto while I went down on him. Then, he proceeded to wonder if I would also lose the hair between my legs, and when I told him yes, he did a little fist pump. When he was finally serious about it, he said under no terms would he find me any less beautiful without hair and said to tell you that if Mitch was into you before all of this, you have nothing to worry about."

"He sounds like my kind of guy."

"You have no idea. Why do you think I've kept him away from you for so long?" She winked.

"Well, feel free to bring him over anytime...over...under...wherever he'd like me."

Nina pretended to smother me with a pillow. She knew my sense of humor and wasn't bothered by it. "We should get started. I have to leave at five, and Mitch will be here in a couple of hours, right?"

"Yup. Let's check the inventory. Hair?"

Nina lifted the Styrofoam head. "Check."

"Boobs."

She reached into a large black duffel bag and lifted the silicone chicken cutlets I asked her to buy me, throwing them at me jokingly. "Check!"

I stuffed them into my bra. "It's expensive to look cheap, isn't it? Make up and false lashes?"

Nina took out a floral makeup bag and waved it. "Check!"

"Condoms."

"You didn't say—"

"I'm kidding.

"You'd better be. You're barely sixteen, you little nymphomaniac."

"Ah...don't you mean lymphomaniac?

She shook her head. "Skylar, that was bad even for you."

"In all seriousness...if I wanted to have sex with Mitch, wouldn't you support me?"

She hesitated. "I would, but I'd feel better if you were a little older and if I were sure you were truly ready, not just pushing yourself to grow up too fast out of fear."

I had no real intention of losing my virginity anytime soon, but I wanted to know that she'd be there for me. "Point taken. Now, get over here and work your magic."

"I don't know about magic..."

"You're transforming a hairless cancer patient into a drag queen in less than twenty minutes. Even Copperfield wouldn't touch that."

Nina laughed and helped me get into a simple black sweater dress she let me borrow before starting my make-up. She was by no means an expert beautician, but it was adorable how she pursed her lips and concentrated as she lined my eyes, glued on the lashes and powdered my face.

It started to get dark out, and my nerves kicked in, knowing that Mitch had hopped a late afternoon train and was already on his way.

Nina wouldn't let me look at myself until she was finished. After she placed the wig on my head, she handed me a mirror.

I looked like a different person. "Wow."

"Is that a good 'wow'?"

"Yeah. I mean...I don't look like Caillou anymore. That's for sure."

She grinned. "More like Jessica Rabbit?"

The wig was beautifully made, but once on, it made my scalp hot as hell. The color was also a lot redder than my normal auburn. I did like the smooth, straight style, though. The false lashes brought out the green color of my eyes, but they were too long, and the lipstick was too bright.

I didn't want to make Nina feel bad, but this definitely wasn't me. I had to remind myself that I had specifically asked her to make me up like this to distract from the baldness and weight loss.

She looked worried. "Is it too much?"

"You know what? It just needs to be toned down a little. Hand me that tissue."

I took one out and wiped off most of the lipstick then slowly pulled off the lashes.

I still looked made up, just a little less dramatic. "This is good now. I really do love this wig."

She smiled as she brushed the hair out. "This is about you being comfortable. If you're happy, then I'm happy."

I'd be happy once Mitch saw me and didn't run in the other direction.

On the subway to Brooklyn. See you in about twenty minutes.

I kept staring at the text from Mitch. That was twenty minutes ago, and he would be here any minute. I wanted to save my energy, so I stayed sitting up on the bed and stared out at the bright moon. The reflection in the window of my newly made-up silhouette triggered mixed feelings.

The doorbell startled me, and I let Lizete answer.

I heard her say, "Nice to see you again, Mitch."

The front door shut, and butterflies filled my stomach as the sound of footsteps coming up the stairs got closer.

My hands felt clammy, and I breathed in and out one last time.

I was sitting up on the bed with my arms wrapped around my shins when the door slowly opened.

Mitch dropped his giant backpack on the ground and immediately joined me on the bed. He pulled me into a hug and exhaled as if he'd been holding his breath for a while. I was afraid to look into his eyes, not wanting to see any change in the way they looked back at me. I just stayed with my eyes closed, breathing in the smell of his skin that I had been craving.

He said nothing as he continued to hold me. Then, I felt his hand on my chin as he whispered, "Hey, look at me."

I turned to him and immediately wished I hadn't. How could it be that while I wasted away these past couple of months, he had grown more stunningly handsome? Those butterflies in my stomach were multiplying by the second as I took in his appearance. He had stubble on his chin, which also seemed more angular. His hair was even more grown out and styled into messy perfection. The same navy hoodie he always wore was now snug, conforming to a more muscular frame. He was turning into a man while I was shrinking.

"Look at you. You look nice," he said.

"I wanted to look good for you, so I had Nina help make me up, but it doesn't feel right. None of this feels right."

"None of...this? What are you talking about?"

"You looking like you just stepped out of GQ and me looking like...a crack whore."

His smile faded. "Skylar, come on. You're being a little tough on yourself, don't you think? Look at what you've been through. You look amazing."

"For a cancer patient? That's not saying much."

I stood up off of the bed and must have risen too fast. A feeling of dizziness came over me, and I had to grip the dresser to balance.

He jumped off the bed. "Are you okay?"

"I got up too fast. I feel really nauseous all of a sudden. I think I'm going to throw up. You should go downstairs, Mitch. You don't want to see this."

"I just got here. I'm not leaving you."

I hated this. I couldn't even last five minutes without an outburst and a bout of nausea.

That was the last thought I remembered having before seeing stars and dropping to the floor.

TWELVE

MITCH

I'd never been more petrified of anything in my entire life. When Skylar suddenly collapsed, I practically flew toward her, catching her head in mid-air just before it hit the ground.

"Help!" I yelled, but no one answered. Her stepmother must have left the house.

My heart was pounding through my chest. I tapped her cold cheek. "Skylar! Skylar, please."

Just as I grabbed my phone to call 911, her eyelids fluttered.

"Skylar. Skylar, you're okay. I'm here."

"Mitch? What happened? Where am I?"

"You fainted."

"Oh."

"Has this happened before?"

"The doctor warned me about dehydration with all the vomiting lately. I must have gotten up too fast."

"Do you feel like you can stand up?"

She shook her head. "No. Not yet."

"Okay. We'll stay here. I'm just gonna get up for one second and get a pillow."

"No. Don't leave me."

"Okay. I won't."

I took off my jacket and placed it under her head. After a few minutes, she used my hand to balance herself slowly to a sitting position.

"I think I can stand up now."

I led her over to the bed then grabbed a water bottle from my bag unable to open it fast enough. "Drink some of this."

She sat up slowly against the headboard and drank from the bottle as I held it to her mouth. "Thanks. I never had water today. Dumb move."

"Are you feeling better?"

"A little nauseous."

"Tell me what you need."

"Just stay here next to me." She remained sitting up with a pillow propped against her back and closed her eyes.

She didn't realize her wig had shifted and for the first time, I caught a glimpse of the bald head underneath. She would have freaked if she knew, so I didn't say anything.

Admittedly, it was a shock to see it at first, but everything that had happened from the second I walked in that door had been a rude awakening. Somehow, despite hearing over the phone about everything she'd been going through, I had imagined her physically unchanged, which was easier when I was away and feeling helpless. The reality of how physically weak she had become was hard to accept.

I continued to watch her as she lay with her eyes closed. Black eyeliner was running down her cheek on one side. My heart broke that she felt the need to make herself look unrecognizable, thinking that it would please me. My chest felt heavy, ready to combust in pain, sadness, frustration and love for her all at once.

Even though she looked sick and had lost her hair, not for a second did I love her any less. It killed me that she worried that I'd view her differently because she looked different.

If she only knew how much *more* I loved her right now, how much more I respected her after witnessing firsthand the strength it took to fight the war her body was enduring.

On top of that, the threat of losing her seemed more real now.

In a way, you don't realize the depth of your feelings until something like this happens. Through her frailty, I saw her soul—the essence of why I'd always loved her. It shined brighter, no longer paling in the reflection of her physical beauty. It made me realize that I truly loved her from the inside out, not the other way around.

She suddenly opened her eyes and turned her head in my direction, catching me staring at her. "What are you looking at?"

"Remember on the phone that day, how you said you felt like half of yourself?"

"Now, you can see why, right?"

My tone bordered on angry. She had it all wrong. "No. No...that's not what I was getting at." I grabbed her hand. "I've felt like half of myself, too...until now. I only feel whole when I'm with you. Now that I see with my own eyes what you've been going through, I feel like I've been living a lie all these weeks. I should have been here."

"No. You shouldn't have. I wouldn't want you here all of the time to witness the worst."

Tell her you love her.

The words wouldn't come out. As usual, I convinced myself that she would think I was saying it only because she was sick. So, I decided against it. Another thought popped into my head instead. "Will you come to my prom with me?"

"What? What exactly about this situation screams prom queen?"

"I was just thinking. I know it's a ways away, but it will be after your treatments are done. I could never picture going unless you were with me. It'll be something for us to look forward to."

She smiled for the first time since I had walked in the door. "Okay. I could use that."

"It's settled then."

When I leaned in to hug her, her wig accidentally shifted further off her head. She jumped in a panic, frantically trying to reposition it.

I put my hand on her arm. "Wait. I want to see it."

She let out a single laugh. "No freaking way."

"Skylar, your wig's been slightly off your head this whole time. I didn't say anything, so I've already seen part of it."

"No, you haven't."

"I need you to stop being so afraid. It doesn't matter to me. *You* matter to me. I can't prove that to you if you think it all depends on your wearing that wig."

She shook her head, and a tear fell down her cheek. She mouthed, "I can't."

I fought like hell to stop my own tears from falling and looked deep into her eyes. "Please."

I had honestly not expected her to go for it. When she lowered her arm, she gave me a conflicted look and a slight nod, reluctantly giving me silent permission.

My hand shook a little as I slowly pulled the wig back, letting it fall onto the pillow. I wasn't nervous to see her bald. I was nervous because I knew she was scared. I worried that she'd misinterpret my emotions. The truth was, what she had just handed me amidst her own fear had truly surprised and moved me. It meant that somewhere inside of her beyond the insecurity, she knew how much I cared about her.

Her chest rose, and she wouldn't look at me. I understood. Her self-consciousness didn't keep me from doing the one thing I couldn't help, though.

My rough fingertips rubbed along her smooth, perfectly round scalp. Her head was hot with slight beads of perspiration from the wig, which probably irritated her. And that irritated *me*. The skin on top of her head felt like silk. Her eyes were still closed as I moved my fingers in slow soft circles over it.

All of Skylar's hair transformations during the phases of our friendship ran through my mind like a slideshow: the whimsical braids of the little girl who brought me back to life as a boy, the long, rain-soaked tresses of the vixen in the Catholic school uniform. I loved them all, but none had meant more to me than the vulnerable girl with the soft, smooth head who just put all of her trust in me.

I moved in behind her, and she rested her back against my chest. I lowered my lips and planted a kiss on her head. She was too tired to fight the contact. "You're the most beautiful girl in the world to me." I kissed the same spot again. "Please know that."

Tell her you love her.

My mouth rested against the top of her head as she continued to lean against me.

Coward.

I closed my eyes and felt her breathing start to even out then realized she had fallen asleep in my arms. When I finally opened my eyes, I looked in the doorway to find Skylar's father standing there watching us. I flinched and opened my mouth ready to apologize for being in her bed when he held up his hand.

"Shh. Stay. Don't wake her." His eyes were watery, and his voice was shaky. I wondered how long he had been there and what he had seen.

My back hurt from the couch downstairs. I wasn't able to sleep knowing that Skylar hadn't been feeling well last night. The house was quiet since everyone was still sleeping. I went into the kitchen and started to make coffee. The brown liquid dripped down into the carafe. I counted the drops with disdain, each one signifying another second closer to having to leave her again.

Oliver startled me. "Morning, son."

I turned around. "Hi. I hope you don't mind. I made some coffee."

He nodded. "No, that's good. I'll take one black. How are you holding up?"

"I'm fine, just hoping she's feeling better than yesterday."

"This can't be easy for you seeing her like this," he said.

"I can handle it as long she's feeling okay."

"We've had some rough days lately."

"Is she up?"

"I didn't hear her when I came down." He pulled up a chair and sat down. "Listen, I know before this, I hadn't really been present all that much in her life, but she always has nothing but good things to say about you."

"Thank you, sir."

"Please call me Oliver."

"Okay...Oliver."

"She's stuck with me now, but she would never stay here by choice otherwise. I know she's not happy here. I wish she knew how much I loved her. I tell her all the time now, but I've made a lot of mistakes with her over the years."

I handed him a coffee. "She knows you love her, sir... Oliver."

He took a sip and peeked at me from over the mug. "Does she know *you* do?"

"What?"

"It's okay to say it, you know."

I nodded. He was definitely standing at that door longer than I thought yesterday. "I get it. Thanks."

Throughout the weekend, Skylar continued to be sick as a dog. Despite her showing me her head, she insisted on wearing the wig around me.

I held the strands back for her while she threw up in the toilet Sunday morning.

"Mitch, you should go home."

"No fucking way."

I was scheduled to take the eight pm train out of Manhattan tonight and wasn't going to leave her a second before I had to.

That afternoon, she asked me to run to the store for ginger ale. On the walk home, a thought crossed my mind after passing one of those spinning barbershop poles. I stopped in my tracks.

Should I do it?

Why the hell not? If it would make her feel less alone, it couldn't hurt. I'd do anything for her.

Bells rang as I impulsively opened the door to the shop. "Take it all off."

The owner, Luigi, looked at me like I was crazy. "Do you know how many men would kill for your head of hair, and you want to shave it off?"

When I explained why, not only did he take it off, but he did it for free. Apparently, he had a daughter with breast cancer.

I took one look at myself in the mirror and couldn't help but laugh. My head wasn't exactly as smooth as hers. "I look ridiculous."

He patted me on my back, wishing me the best of luck, and the patrons all clapped.

Back outside, my head felt like it was going to freeze into an ice cube. I put my hood on hoping this would help cheer her up.

When I returned to the house, Oliver and Lizete were watching a movie as I rushed past them up the stairs. Skylar was taking a nap, so I put the ginger ale on her dresser and lay down at the foot of her bed, waiting impatiently for her to wake up.

I ended up nodding off and awoke to the sound of her screaming.

"Mitch! What the hell did you do?"

"Don't freak out," I said groggily.

"Don't freak out? Before I fell asleep, you had hair like David Beckham. I wake up, and you look like Mr. Clean!"

I couldn't help laughing at her reaction. "What...you don't like it?"

"No! I don't. Unlike you...I'm honest about it. Nobody actually looks better bald."

"Well, get used to it. As long as you don't have hair, I won't either."

"Oh, yeah, sure. We'll be the bald brigade, except at least I can wear a wig. You can't. All of the male ones would make you look like a 1970's porn star."

"I don't care. I just want to support you, and this is my way of doing it."

After several minutes, her initial shock seemed to wane, and she rubbed her hand along my head and laughed. "I get why you did it, but you're insane, Mitch Nichols."

"Only when it comes to you."

Tell her you love her.

"Clearly. I can't believe you did this."

"Skylar, I..." *Say it.* "Got your ginger ale."

Coward.

"Thanks."

"I have a few more hours before I have to leave. What do you want to do?"

"Just lie next to me."

"I can handle that."

Over the next several minutes, she became very fidgety and seemed uneasy.

"Are you okay?"

"My nerves are acting up. Some of the meds cause anxiety."

"My mom's therapist told her to create a happy place in her mind whenever she got like that and then meditate on it. Where would you go if you could go anywhere?"

"Hmm. It's not really a specific location, but it would probably be like a beach house right on the water. It would have one of those reading nooks by a large window overlooking the ocean."

"What would you be reading?"

"Probably smut."

I laughed. "Of course. Okay, imagine yourself there reading your smut. Whenever you start to feel nervous, just keep imagining that peaceful place."

"Where's your happy place?"

"Lately? Anywhere you are."

"That's cheesy, baldy."

"That's the truth. As long as you're there, in my mind, the place is interchangeable."

She stared at me for a while and suddenly looked sullen.

I gently shook her arm. "Hey...what's going on? What did I say?"

"Nothing."

"*Something* is bothering you."

She closed her eyes briefly and when she opened them said, "There's something I've always wondered but haven't asked you because I'm afraid of the answer. It's been eating at me lately."

My pulse raced. I had a feeling I knew where this was going. "Okay...ask me anything."

She inhaled. "I know you've dated a lot of girls...but have you ever had sex?"

Honestly, I didn't know how I'd managed to avoid this conversation for so long. I had to be honest with her.

I swallowed. "Yes, I have."

She let out the deep breath she had been holding. She looked devastated. *Fuck.* I hated this. I hated that I just hurt her on top of everything else she'd been going through.

Her eyes were watery, and her neck was breaking out in hives. "I suspected but wasn't sure. God, I feel so stupid. I had this fantasy, that by some miracle, you hadn't and that one day, we'd be each other's firsts."

Hearing her say that crushed me. "I wish so badly that could be true, that I could take it back. I need to explain it to you."

"Explain sex to me?"

"No...God...just let me talk, okay?"

A tear fell down her cheek. "I can't believe I'm crying over this. These damn meds."

I turned to her, and our faces were inches apart when I wiped her eyes. "You're crying because you care about me. If you had just told me you had sex with some guy, I'd probably be on the train right now to go kill him. So, you're handling it better than I would."

She sniffled. "How many?"

"Two."

"Who were they?"

I let out a deep breath. "My first time was with a girl named Leah. She was two years older. It was back in Long Island right before I moved to Jersey. It wasn't special. It was a mistake."

"And your second time?"

"A bigger mistake. It was with Brielle."

She shuddered, closing her eyes. "When?"

"About a month after I moved here. It was one time."

"Did you use protection?"

"Of course."

She looked so sad, and it felt like my heart was in a chokehold. How do I explain to her that it didn't matter without sounding like an asshole? I had always regretted that night with Brielle, but I couldn't take it back.

"I almost wish I hadn't asked you."

I needed to find the words to explain to her that no girl has ever mattered to me like she has.

"The first time happened so fast. I worked with her at the local supermarket. She had been coming onto me for a long time, and I gave in one night. She wasn't a virgin, and I didn't know what I was doing. We never went out again, and then I moved away. With Brielle, it was different. I had made up my mind to do it. It was almost mechanical. I was testing myself during a time I had vowed to stay away from you. I thought if I could move faster with someone else, it would somehow make it easier to be around you and not want you that way."

"So, you were using her..."

"In a way, but I honestly think she was using me, too. She had just broken up with her boyfriend. I don't want to sound like a dick, but it honestly didn't mean anything. Then, she told a bunch of people at school, and that pissed me off. I regret it."

"You make it sound like it's no big deal."

God, I sucked at this. Tell her how you feel.

"It doesn't feel like a big deal if your heart's not in it. All I know is, after the night you and I kissed, I couldn't imagine wanting anyone else. That kiss alone was the most phenomenal thing I had ever experienced in my entire life. I'm sorry I can't give you my first time, but you're the only girl who's ever had my heart. As long as you tell me to wait for you, I will. I can't go back and change the past, but I can guarantee that if you decide to give yourself to me someday, it will damn well mean something."

She didn't have time to respond before we heard footsteps. I jumped up off the bed.

Lizete opened the door. "Oh my God! Wow."

At first, I was confused then realized she was reacting to my shaved head. I was so worried about Skylar that I'd forgotten about my hair being gone.

"Yeah, Mitch came home with a little surprise for me."

Lizete tried to contain her laughter. "Wow...it's...wow. Anyway, dinner's ready. Then, your father's gonna drive Mitch to Manhattan to catch his train."

We followed Lizete downstairs without continuing our conversation. The fried chicken and rice she made tasted great, but I had to force myself to eat it. My stomach was upset because I didn't want to leave Skylar, especially while she wasn't feeling well. She was being really quiet throughout dinner. Oliver made small talk while she and I stole glances at each other. I hoped she wasn't still thinking about my admission upstairs, although I suspected she was.

After dessert, Skylar excused herself to go back to her room. I waited a few minutes before following her and caught her as she was coming out of the bathroom.

The hallway was dark and before she had a chance to open the bedroom door, I pulled her toward me and hugged her tightly.

I buried my face in her neck and whispered, "I'm sorry."

"For what?"

"For everything...for upsetting you, for not being able to make you feel better, for having to leave." I spoke into her skin. "I feel like a failure."

"You didn't do anything wrong. Thank you for telling me the truth earlier."

"I'm sorry it wasn't the answer you hoped for."

"Let's not talk about that anymore, okay?"

"Okay." I kissed her forehead. "I just want this to be over." My voice was shaky, but I refused to cry. "I wish it were me going through this and not you."

"Don't say that. I wouldn't ever wish this on you." She lowered my shaved head to her mouth and kissed the top.

"What if I stayed and went to your treatment with you tomorrow?"

"Mitch, you have school. You can't do that. That would upset me more than you leaving."

"I can't just go home and pretend that everything's normal anymore now that I've seen firsthand what this has been like for you."

"You have to."

She let go of me, opened the door to her room, and I followed her in. She walked over to the mirror. "I'm starting to lose my lashes."

Skylar continued to look at herself while I hugged her from behind, filled with anger. In just two days, I saw this fucking cancer strip away at her bit by bit. That was only what I witnessed, only a fraction of the time she'd been fighting it with several months left to go.

I just wanted to make her forget for a minute. We didn't have much time before her father would come upstairs, so I turned her around, put both of my hands on her face and pulled her lips into mine. I had been dying to kiss her all weekend, but there was never an appropriate time.

Her body was stiff at first, caught off guard by my sudden attack. When my tongue slipped inside her mouth, though, she slowly relaxed into it. It had felt like an eternity since the last time we kissed like this. I was quickly reminded of how sweet she tasted and how out of control it made me feel. Even as sick as she was, I was still so unbelievably attracted her. She sighed as I hungrily opened my mouth wider over hers and began to kiss her more aggressively.

I spoke over her lips. "Have I ever told you how much I love your lips, Skylar?"

She smiled through our kiss and moaned into my mouth. We both pulled back suddenly when someone knocked on the door.

She rubbed her mouth. "Come in!"

Oliver opened the door. "I'm sorry, Mitch. We'd better head out so you don't miss your train."

"Okay. Be right down."

We just stood there staring at each other. My stomach filled with dread as I heard him start his car outside to warm it up.

I grabbed her hand and pulled her toward me. Our foreheads were touching as I said, "I may be walking out of here, but there's not a piece of my heart that's coming with me."

She had to practically push me out the door because I wouldn't let go of her.

The train ride home was like a bad dream. Sounds were louder than normal. The voices of the other passengers were intolerable. I felt like a shell, so disconnected from the rest of the world, a fish out of water. It angered me that all of these people were moving toward something, while with each second, I was moving further away from the one thing that mattered to me. It felt wrong, like I had left not only my heart but my entire self back in Skylar's bedroom. I had no clue how I was going to function tomorrow, knowing that she was getting more of that poison pumped into her.

When the cab dropped me off at home, I looked up into the darkness of Skylar's empty bedroom window across the street and said a silent prayer before entering my house.

My mother was in the kitchen. "Mitch?"

Ignoring her, I walked upstairs in a daze. I had a hood on, so she wouldn't have seen my head.

Seamus was unusually quiet when I opened the door to my bedroom. I was sure he'd start barking again the second he saw me. I opened the cage to make sure he was still alive, and he was just looking at me quietly. He looked how I felt. "Hey, little guy."

He squawked once and tilted his head.

"I know. I miss her, too."

When I leaned in to kiss the top of his head, he nipped my nose. "Ow." I guess I had pressed my luck.

The urge to call Skylar was killing me, but I didn't want to wake her because she had an early appointment tomorrow. I sent her a text instead.

I'm home. Well..."here." Home is wherever you are. I feel lost without you. And I miss your lips.

I felt restless, like I needed to do something for her. I opened my laptop and started a Google search on Hodgkins Lymphoma. The statistics were promising, but of course, that's never the information your mind zones in on. What stuck in my brain were all the potential long-term side effects of chemo, the possibility of a bone marrow transplant if the chemo didn't work the first time around, the risks of radiation, the chance of secondary cancers developing later in life. The list went on and on. I was doing exactly what I urged Skylar not to: focusing on the "what ifs" and letting my fears take over because seeing her suffering had weakened me.

What put me over the edge was an article about a girl around Skylar's age that recently lost her battle. The girl's smiling face in the photo stared back at me, a reminder that nothing was guaranteed. I slammed the laptop closed. The reality that there was a chance Skylar could die from this was unthinkable. The mere thought was so painful that every muscle in my body tightened in an attempt to resist the unwelcome emotions that were rising to the surface.

My mother gasped when she entered the room to find my shoulders shaking as I bawled with my head in my hands. Everything I had been in holding in this past weekend came flooding out.

She ran her hand across my shaved head. "Oh, Mitch."

"I can't lose her, Mom."

"Did something happen?"

I wiped my eyes, angry at my loss of control. "She's just going through hell. It's not fair. Her eyelashes are gone...her fucking *eyelashes*. It's not *about* that, but she can only take so much. This is tearing apart her spirit slowly. I see that happening and can't stand to see her suffering. I love her. I love her so much, and I was too much of a coward to tell her."

"Why? Why couldn't you tell her?"

"I don't know. It's like I associate those three words with bad things happening from when I was a kid. On top of that, I'm so afraid she'll think I'm only saying it because she's sick."

"She needs to hear it. And if you don't want her to think you're saying it only because she's sick, then you need to tell her exactly why you love her, why you've always loved her. It will give her strength. Don't let what happened between me and your father make you afraid. I've watched you fall in love with that girl, and it's real. Your father never loved me like you love her."

She kissed my forehead before I suddenly walked toward the window, staring vacantly across the street at Skylar's house. "I want to be alone, okay?"

"Okay."

"Thanks, Mom."

I stayed awake that night, wired, drawing her a new comic in the *Adventures of S&M* series where S and M were bald bandits banding together to fight the evil C until it was destroyed.

At one in the morning, my phone rang. My heart pounded in terror when I saw her name.

"Skylar? Are you okay?"

"You told me to call you anytime, and I know you didn't really mean one in the morning, but I just had a dream. I don't know if it's the meds or what, but it was so vivid. I almost needed to call you to make sure it didn't really happen."

For the first time all night, I relaxed enough to get into my bed. "A bad dream?"

"No. It was beautiful. We were...having sex, but it was more than that. It was what I imagined it would feel like. It felt so real, and I wished it were. It made me realize how much I—"

"Wait. Don't say it. I love you, Skylar. I love you so much. I should have said it a million times before."

"I was gonna say it made me realize how much I need to get laid, but that's really...wow."

"Seriously?"

"No."

"You little shit." I breathed into the phone. "I love you."

"I love you, too, Mitch, so much it hurts. When I think about worst-case scenarios, out of everything, it's being separated from you that scares me the most."

The tears were burning my eyes. "Skylar, listen to me, okay? I need you to know that I'm not just saying this because I'm afraid or because you're sick. I need you to know that I have loved you since we were kids when you called me out for acting like an asshole and were the first person who cared enough to try and figure out the reason why. I love you because you know what I need or what I'm thinking before I even do. I love you because you make me laugh everyday, especially at myself. I love the way you look at me like I'm the only person in a room full of people. I love the way you smell and the way you whimper when my lips first touch yours. I—"

"Mitch...I already knew you loved me, and I knew how much it scared you to say those words. The way you look at me, the way your heart beats every time you hold me, what you did to your hair for me...actions speak louder than words, and you have been *showing* me how much you love me. That's what matters."

"I feel like I won't be able to breathe until you come home."

That day would be farther away than I could ever have anticipated.

After her first round of chemo ended, cancer gave us a short break.

At the end of that stretch, my prom rolled around and what was supposed to be the most special night of our lives, was anything but.

She had looked so angelic in a white strapless dress. Her friend Nina had come all the way from Boston to help her get ready.

Everything was fine up until we danced to a certain slow song, and then her mood dramatically changed for the rest of the night.

After the prom, on the way to an after party at a hotel, she made a confession in the limo. She hadn't wanted to ruin our night and had been holding back some news. That morning, her doctor had told her that tests showed a recurrence of the Lymphoma.

It had felt like my tie was choking me, and I remember having to undo it because I felt like I was gonna hyperventilate.

Not again.

I ended up taking her home, and it turned out to be one of the worst nights of my life.

The next phase was the lowest point in her cancer journey. A higher level of chemo was followed by a bone marrow transplant, which meant weeks of isolation and a long recovery.

By the grace of God, her tests following that procedure were clear, and it seemed to have been a success.

All in all, from the time she was first diagnosed, it took nearly two years before we would have her back for good.

The months following her return home were the best of my life. Like a spring flower blossoming after a long season of rain, at 18, Skylar emerged from that hell somewhat changed but stronger and more beautiful than ever.

THIRTEEN

SKYLAR

In some ways, recovering from cancer is like coming home from war. You're never fully able to leave it behind because the threat of getting called back always seems to loom. Regardless, you have to move on with your life.

It also changed me. Material things were now insignificant; just being alive was good enough. At the same time, I was learning to live again, to develop a routine that didn't involve treatments or the resulting side effects. You get your life back, but you don't really know what to do with it. In a bizarre way, the cancer had become my normal, and freedom was now foreign to me.

Since my father had arranged for tutoring on the days I felt up to it, I hadn't really fallen too far behind while in Brooklyn. When I returned home, I was able to continue in the middle of my junior year at St. Clare's.

Mitch was a senior now. Despite his support over the course of my illness, any development of a physical relationship had been on hold. We were almost never alone during that time. Either that, or I was too sick to even look at him.

Now, it felt like a giant pause button had been lifted on us. At 19, Mitch was so physically attractive that it was almost painful to be around him without touching. His body was ripped, and his hair had grown back longer, wavy and beautiful again. He still often piled it under that familiar Yankees cap but now sported a constant five o'clock shadow to complete the look. His skin had also tanned from working a new side job cutting lawns.

As for me, my hair was now shoulder-length, and I had gained most of the weight back. Still, even with our newfound freedom, we were taking things slow. Mitch hadn't made any moves even though I knew he wanted to, and that frustrated me. He was handling me with care because of my recovery, but that wasn't what I wanted. It was what he thought I needed. But what I *needed* was him—in the worst way. His eyes always brimmed with desire when he looked at me, and I could feel his resistance running thinner each day. It was just a matter of time.

"When exactly are you planning on telling her?"

My mother and I were supposed to be at Mitch's for dinner at six, but I had arrived early. While in the midst of a private conversation, Mitch and Janis hadn't realized the living room window was open. I leaned in closer to hear.

"I don't know."

"Mitch...this is big. You shouldn't keep this from her."

"I don't want to discuss it right now, Mom. You know how I feel. Stop pressuring me."

The dialog stopped, and I assumed Mitch had gone upstairs.

My chest tightened in anxiety as I rang the doorbell.

Janis opened the door. "Oh...hi, honey. You're early."

"My mother wanted me to put this chicken pot pie in your oven, so it would be nice and hot when we sat down."

"Sure, come in." I smelled a hint of gasoline and knew it was from Mitch who had just returned home from cutting someone's grass. She took the pie from me. "Mitch is upstairs."

I ran up and heard the shower running in the bathroom off the hallway, so I waited in his room.

Pandora radio was streaming from his phone, and Seamus was bopping his head to *Rapper's Delight* by the Sugar Hill Gang. That was his new thing. He was really into music—that and whistling at me lately.

When the door opened, Mitch was wrapped in nothing but a small, white towel. "Whoa. I didn't know you were here. I almost walked in stark naked."

My mouth watered as I marveled at how my childhood friend had transformed into an Adonis. The towel hugged his round ass perfectly. Droplets of water ran down his cut, tan chest. His wet hair was slick back and sexy.

He raised his brow at me, his voice low and intentionally seductive. "Like what you see?"

I cleared my throat. "Actually, I do."

Lay off the truth serum, Skylar.

He smiled mischievously and licked his lips. "Good to know." He grabbed a shirt from the closet and threw it on the chair. "You're about to see a whole lot more if you don't turn around."

My gaze lingered before I reluctantly turned toward the window. I started to obsess over the conversation on the way in until his voice snapped me out of it. "Safe."

He was still shirtless when I turned back around. This was not *safe* at all. His white underwear peeked through the top of his pants, and when I looked down, I noticed a thin trail of hair leading down to the arousal straining against his jeans.

He walked toward me, pulled me up into a standing position and leaned into me, his hot erection pressing into my stomach.

Our lips were almost touching. I was throbbing between my legs when he gripped some of the material of my skirt, and his hot breath tickled my mouth. "I like the way you were looking at me. Actually, it's made me a little crazy. It's like you were eye-fucking me. It makes me want to just—"

The door burst open, and we both jumped.

"Well, well, well, what do we have here?" Davey stood in the doorway, eating out of a bag of Cheetos. "Were you two just about to get it on with that pervy bird bouncing his head, looking on?"

Seamus was still rocking out, this time to *Low Rider* by War.

I was panting, still shocked and turned on by Mitch's sudden aggression and dirty talk.

Mitch looked frustrated and threw a red t-shirt over his head. He said through gritted teeth, "What brings you by Davey?"

Davey made himself comfortable on the bed, wiping his cheese-powdered fingers on his baggy, black pants. "I had an interesting conversation with principal Shipton this afternoon. He asked me if I had heard the amazing news about my friend. Congratulations are in order, man. How could you not have told me?"

Mitch shook his head, silently urging Davey to stop talking.

I turned to Mitch. "What's going on?"

He was giving Davey the evil eye. "Nothing."

"Dude, don't be shy. You should be damn proud."

Mitch stayed silent, so I turned to Davey. "Proud of what?"

"Mitch here...got himself a full ride to Boston University."

My heart beat faster with every passing second as the information set in. "What?"

Davey's eyes widened. "A full four-year scholarship! Some old, rich Crestview alum set it up, and they grant it to the graduate with the highest GPA every year. This year, it was Mitchy!"

My jaw dropped, and I looked over at Mitch. "How long have you known about this?"

His ears were turning red. "Not long."

I feigned happiness even though I was freaking out inside. "This is amazing. I had no idea. I mean, I knew your grades were good but the highest GPA?"

He had a vacant look in his eyes. "I had no clue either to be honest."

I started to feel lightheaded but continued to put on a brave face. "Boston. Wow. I can't believe this. You accepted, right?"

He bit his lip and didn't say anything.

"Mitch?"

Mitch shut off the music that had been playing, and Seamus squawked in protest. "Dave, can you leave Skylar and me alone for a minute?"

Davey huffed, crumpled his Cheetos bag and went down stairs.

When the door shut, the mood suddenly became extremely tense. You could have heard a pin drop. The tormented look in his piercing eyes nearly undid me. "I'm not going to accept it."

"What? Are you crazy?"

"I can't."

"This is what you and your mother were arguing about when I was at the door."

"Boston is five hours away. I'd be gone for four years. Do you understand that? *Four years*. I just fucking got you back. I'm not leaving you."

It felt like all of the air left my body. The fact that he was prepared to throw away this opportunity to be near me was overwhelming.

"You're considering giving up your future...because of me?"

He put his hands on my shoulders. "You *are* my future. It's not like there aren't any colleges here."

"None that will give you a full ride, none that are Boston University! Holy crap, Mitch...you have to take it. Imagine a life with no college debt looming over you, and BU is an awesome school."

He looked down at his bare feet. "You don't understand. This is not up for debate. I've already made up my mind."

"Were you even going to tell me?"

"I don't know. I knew you'd try to convince me to accept it."

"Convince you? Mitch...you ARE accepting it. You're standing here telling me you're turning down the opportunity of a lifetime for me. I would have to live with that for the rest of my life. You've already given up so much over the past two years for me. You will take this...because there will be no you and me if you don't. I am not gonna stand by and watch you ruin your life and use me as the excuse."

His face turned crimson in anger. "Skylar, do you understand what you're asking me to do? I'd be gone. We would only see each other once in a while. We were supposed to finally get to be together now. I want that so badly."

"We'd see each other on breaks and some weekends."

"But it won't be the same."

No, it wouldn't.

"We can make it work. We're stronger than distance."

He began playing with the button on my dress, lost in thought. "I don't feel good about this. Something at the pit of my stomach is telling me going to Boston would be the wrong decision. I fucking miss you already, and you're standing right in front of me."

Hearing him say that had caused me to break down. I had no words, so I reached over to hug him. His beating heart pounded against my own, which felt like it had been turned inside out.

A million thoughts raced through my mind. The thought of him living in a dorm with a bunch of horny girls made me shudder. Maybe I would tell him to stay. No. This was his future. He would never get an opportunity like this again.

He spoke into my neck. "I know accepting this scholarship is the right thing to do on paper, but the only thing that *feels* right is staying with you."

I know. But I still couldn't let him do it.

"I won't let you turn it down. I won't live with that guilt."

"You're saying you won't be here for me if I stay? Don't you love me?"

"I'm doing this *because* I love you."

That night, after further ambush by our mothers at dinner, Mitch reluctantly agreed to accept the scholarship.

The summer before Mitch was set to move to Boston went by way too fast. Despite a bad feeling gnawing at me, I never let him see that I was having doubts about pushing him away. If he knew how sad it was really making me, he'd never leave. Mitch worked hard. He deserved that scholarship. I wasn't going to fuck it up.

That meant controlling myself around him, not allowing things to go any further than kissing. Boy, did we kiss a lot that summer, to the point where I could feel his lips on me at any given moment even when he was nowhere in sight.

He'd grab me the second I'd walk into his room, and we'd just get lost in each other's mouths for minutes on end. He'd be hard as a rock, and I would be wet, but despite our animalistic attraction, we never took it any further. We seriously should have won an award for our resilience. I think deep down, he knew it would complicate things. The kissing was intense, though.

There was only one time that we almost slipped. Mitch had run his palm over my breast, squeezing it hard while he kissed me. I almost came from that sensation alone, but he stopped it before things went too far. He knew just as well as I did that if we ended up having sex, we wouldn't have been able to let each other go. Maybe if we survived the first semester apart, I'd feel more confident about taking that step.

What also helped keep things in check: I'd only go over his house when Janis was home. My body was in a constant state of arousal, and I knew with the first opportunity to be alone, we would give up control.

A certain camping trip at the end of the summer proved that.

It all started with some big news: Davey had a girlfriend for the first time in his life. Her name was Zena, and she was like a female version of him: stalky with dreadlocks except hers were strawberry blonde. They met at a Star Wars convention and realized they lived two miles apart. We were all happy for him because he was no longer the perpetual fifth wheel.

Davey had this idea to take Zena to a campsite in Lake George, New York for her birthday. His grandfather had given him the keys to the family RV, and he invited Mitch, myself, Angie and Cody to tag along.

The RV was older, had a full-size bed all the way in the back and seating with 1980's plaid upholstery on each side in the middle. There was a small kitchen area just before the bedroom.

It was a week before Mitch would be leaving for Boston, and if the ride to Lake George were an indication of how the trip would go, I was in trouble.

Mitch sat next to me for most of the ride, and the heat from his leg that was practically glued to mine radiated throughout my body.

He squeezed my thigh. "Are you excited to go camping?"

"Yeah...you?"

Instead of responding, he took my bottom lip into his mouth, sucking on it hard before slowly releasing it. "I'm excited to go camping with *you*." My body went limp.

Cody was playing his guitar while Angie and Zena sang along with him to *Blowin' in the Wind*. Davey, who was driving, used the opportunity to point out that "blowin" was a prelude to his planned activities with Zena later.

Mitch whispered in my ear, "What the hell is with this music anyway? My grandmother used to listen to this. Peter, Paul and Mary, I think...except Cody sounds like the Mary."

He kept making me laugh as we held hands. When he left our seat to give Davey a break at the wheel, I moved up front. I hadn't even wanted to be away from him for 30 minutes. How was I supposed to handle him going away for four years? My stomach turned at the mere thought.

He'd glance over at me while driving, and I'd melt. The sunlight made his already blue eyes glow into an aquamarine color. He reached for my hand. "I can't wait to spend time with my favorite girl."

Davey overheard and cracked, "There's only one bed. Zena and I have dibs. You two are gonna have to shag in the woods."

"Shut the fuck up, Davey." I had never heard him snap so angrily at Davey before. "I'm sorry," he whispered to me before returning his eyes to the road. Mitch was seriously pissed.

If he only realized how turned on I was at the thought of him taking me in the woods.

Angie snuck up behind us and took a picture of our entwined hands then disappeared.

When we finally arrived in the middle of the afternoon, the guys set up two tents and started to grill hot dogs and hamburgers. I had brought an angel food cake and dressed it with whipped cream and fresh berries.

We threw some blankets on the ground and had a picnic on the dewy grass. There wasn't a cloud in the sky, and a gentle breeze blew around our napkins.

Zena meant well when she asked, "Are you all set for Boston, Mitch?"

Before answering, he looked at me with sadness in his eyes. "Not really."

I gave him a sympathetic smile.

When the others were involved in an argument about sleeping arrangements, he lifted his index finger prompting me to come closer. "You have whipped cream on your mouth." Before I could respond, he pulled my ponytail slowly toward him and slid his hot tongue across my lips. "Mmm," he groaned before kissing me deeply. The sugary sweetness mixed with the taste of him drove me crazy. I wondered how I was going to survive this night.

My focus turned back to the conversation. I heard Angie say, "But Cody can't fit in the tent. His legs would be hanging out. He'd get attacked by a snake in the middle of the night."

"Alright. Let's settle this shit once and for all. Mitch, give me your hat," Davey said. Mitch took off his Yankees cap and handed it over. The flattened hair underneath was sexy as hell.

"We're gonna draw a name. Whichever couple is picked gets the bed inside. The others take the tents."

He ripped parts of a flier and wrote down the names before throwing them into the hat, shaking it and drawing one. "Angie and Cody...shit."

Cody high-fived Angie, and Zena pouted.

Mitch nudged me playfully with his shoulder. "You and me in a tent, huh?"

I swallowed nervously. I wanted him so badly but knew it would only cause problems for him.

Angie stood up. "Let's go swimming in the lake before sundown."

The girls retreated into the RV to change into our bathing suits. I wore a multi-colored string bikini that showed off my assets.

Back outside, Mitch smiled when I approached with my towel in hand. He was still wearing beige cargo shorts but had taken off his shirt.

His gaze slowly descended down the length of my body and gave me chills. "Wow. I like your bathing suit."

I poked his abs with my finger, and they felt like granite. "Who's eye-fucking who now?"

He spoke into my ear. "You can feel that, huh? I'm eye-fucking you so hard right now. You're smokin'."

His words alone made me instantly wet. "Thanks. So are you."

Mitch kissed my nose. "I'm gonna help Davey close up the barbecue. Go ahead, and I'll meet you there?"

"Okay."

On the way to the water, Angie started grilling me. "So...tonight?"

"No. No way."

"Why not? Skylar, that dude's balls are like beyond blue, they're like—"

"Black and blue," Zena chimed in.

Angie laughed. "Right? He wants you bad. You have to know that."

"Of course, I do. The feeling's mutual, but it's not happening right before he's about to leave."

Zena stopped in her tracks. "I hear ya, but do you really want him turned on, unsatisfied and unleashed on a bunch of sex-starved vultures next week? You need to take care of him so he remembers what he has waiting for him at home."

I hadn't thought about it that way.

I became riddled with anxiety. Zena and Angie went in the water while I waited on a blanket for Mitch. Breathing in the earthy smell of the lake, I became lost in thought while watching the dark blue water rippling as the sun reflected upon it.

A male voice emerged from just to the right of me. "Mind if I join you?"

"Um...actually, I'm—"

"I'm Logan." He stuck out his hand and flashed a smile.

Logan was good-looking with short blonde hair and a toned physique.

"Hi." I shook his hand.

"A bunch of my friends and I are here visiting from Western Massachusetts. I saw you sitting here and thought I'd come say hello, find out where you're from."

"Hello."

"Are you here with anyone?"

"Yeah, actually, I'm—"

"She's here with me."

Mitch's voice was gruff, and he was giving Logan a dirty look when I turned around.

"Oh...my bad, man." Logan stood up. "You're a lucky guy. Your girlfriend here is a beauty," he said before jogging back over to his friends.

Mitch was quiet when he joined me on the blanket. His ears were red, and he looked irate.

"I'm sorry about that," I said.

"Why? You shouldn't be. He was right. You are a beauty. But I'm not really a lucky guy, am I? I'm leaving in a few days, and you're not really mine."

"Of course, I am."

"The truth is..." He pointed over to Logan. "That right there was a sneak peak into my biggest nightmare."

"Nightmare?"

"Yeah. You and my mom, pressuring me to take that scholarship...you don't realize it now, but when I'm gone, you'll get lonely. You can't understand that now because I'm still here, but there's going to come a day when you're gonna resent me for leaving. One night, some shithead is gonna move in at just the right time, and I'm gonna lose you."

"That's not true."

"Can you promise me?"

The pleading look in his beautiful eyes was so intense, so vulnerable, it tore down all of my resolve. "I promise. I'm scared, too, okay?"

Instead of responding, he reached out his hand, lifted me up into his arms and ran with me toward the lake, dumping me in. Splashing, kissing and enjoying every second with each other, we played in the water until the sun went down.

After dinner on the barbecue, everyone sat around a bonfire, making S'mores. It had gotten chilly out, and I was still in my bathing suit, so I wrapped myself in a musty blanket from the RV. Some of the other campers joined us, and it was like a party with Cody playing guitar and people taking turns singing.

Mitch was quiet, distancing himself across the fire from me. Through the crackle of the flames and the flying embers, I felt the weight of his stare.

Then, my phone vibrated.

Maybe we should sleep in separate tents tonight.

Skylar: If that's what you think is best.

Mitch: I want to do very bad things to you.

Skylar: Ok, then stay away.

Mitch: Is that what you want?

Skylar: No.

Mitch: Fuck. I have no willpower.

Skylar: 16-year-old Mitch had a ton of willpower.

Mitch: 19-year-old Mitch is a horny bastard who doesn't give a fuck anymore. He just wants you. Are you okay with that?

Skylar: Try me.

Mitch: I do want to try you, a little too much right now.

My heart pounded in anticipation of what I was about to type.

Skylar: Show me.

Mitch: I'm leaving in less than a week. Do you even know what you're asking for?

Skylar: Yes.

Then, he suddenly got up without saying anything and walked into the RV. I wanted to follow him but wasn't sure if that was his intention. He might have just been running away from me. I waited. Then, he texted me.

That was your cue to follow me.

I couldn't help but laugh at my stupidity as I stood up. My pulse was racing. Our friends were all preoccupied with Cody's singing and hadn't noticed me sneaking away. When I entered the RV, it was dark except for a small light in the kitchenette area.

Mitch was sitting in one of the seats and leaning into his elbows. The tone of his husky voice gave me chills. "Lock the door."

I walked back over to the steering wheel and pressed the automatic lock button. The curtains were already closed.

My confidence while texting had disappeared now that we were alone. My heart was hammering against my chest when I turned and saw the raw desire in his eyes. "Don't be nervous. Come here."

I stood in front of him as he stayed seated. Chills rushed down my spine like dominos as he pulled me slowly toward him and softly kissed my torso. He kept his mouth on my skin then reached up and stuck one of his fingers under my bathing suit strap, lightly tugging at it. "Take this off."

My nipples tingled. It was uncharacteristic of him to be so direct, but maybe this was what he was like in the bedroom. It turned me on. I loved horny 19-year-old Mitch.

I undid the tie at the top of my bikini then unhooked the back and let it fall to the ground.

His lips parted, and he let out a slight gasp at the sight of my bare chest. "I just want to look at you for a little bit. Is that okay?"

"Yes."

My nipples were so hard that they actually hurt. Goosebumps covered my chest as he stared at me with a lust-filled expression. It was torture because I wanted to be touched.

Finally, he circled the palm of his hand gently across my right breast and then my left. His breathing was uneven, and his striking blue eyes were glassy, almost like he was in a daze.

"They're more perfect than I could have ever imagined."

I shivered. "Thank you."

He squeezed them together. I closed my eyes and suddenly felt the hot wetness of his mouth as he licked a line up the middle and sucked my left nipple. He took turns licking and sucking and then moved to the right one.

When he began to suck harder, my breathing became erratic. I had dreamt of this, but nothing compared to the reality of his hot mouth feasting on my body.

"You like it when I suck it hard like that?"

I wanted his mouth everywhere. "Uh-huh."

I gripped his beautiful, shiny hair and pulled him harder into my chest. Moisture started to pool between my legs.

"You're sweeter than anything I've ever tasted. I want to taste every inch of you tonight. Will you let me?"

I whispered, "Yes."

"If you want me to stop, just tell me, okay?"

I nodded. My entire body was buzzing in anticipation, every nerve ending hyperaware that something major was about to happen.

His hands slid down my sides and grasped the material of my bikini bottom. "I want to take this off."

"Yes."

He slowly slid it down, and I stepped out of it, completely naked. He groaned through his teeth, "Fucking hell. I'm harder than I've ever been just looking at you."

"Please...touch me," I begged.

"I want to do more than touch you."

I closed my eyes the second his fingers began rubbing against my clit. I had played with myself before, but nothing compared to the feel of his big rough hand on me.

Mitch's eyes were glued to the sight of his fingers rubbing between my legs. When he slowly slipped two of them inside of me, he let out a long, shaky breath. "Holy shit." He just kept looking at his fingers moving slowly in and out of me. "I love how wet you are. Nothing has ever turned me on like this."

I looked down at his cock straining through his board shorts and started to rub over it as he continued to finger me. As soon as my hand touched down on him, his breathing became labored. I loved seeing him lose control.

He suddenly withdrew his fingers from my throbbing sex. "Sit on me," he said gruffly.

I climbed on top and wrapped my legs around him. He was still dressed, and I was completely naked as he pushed me down on him. He took my nipple into his mouth as I gyrated over him. The thin material of his shorts meant it didn't feel like much was separating me from his hot erection. I couldn't get enough and kept bearing down harder and faster.

"Fuuuck...Skylar. Slow down."

I couldn't stop. He leaned back with his eyes closed in ecstasy, guiding my body over him with his hands on my waist. Suddenly, I felt my own orgasm unexpectedly rising to the surface. "Oh my God. I'm gonna come."

He pushed me down on him harder. "Come, baby."

Hearing him say that pushed me over the edge. When my climax pulsated through me, I lost all inhibition and said, "I'm coming all over your dick."

After a few seconds, he yelled, "Shit!" and suddenly pushed me off of him. "Fuck."

I was standing up now. "What's wrong?"

He put his head in his hands. "I'm sorry. When you said that—that you were coming all over my dick—I lost it. I friggin' came. I didn't want it to seep through. That's the only reason I pushed you off like that."

I covered my mouth. "That's okay."

"That's never happened to me before."

"I guess 19-year-old Mitch is also sensitive to dirty talk?"

He shook his head in disbelief. "That right there...was more like 13-year-old Mitch."

We both broke out in laughter. "Let me go change real quick," he said.

He walked to the back of the RV and returned with a new set of shorts, but he had taken his shirt off. I ran my index finger along the thin line of hair that trailed down his washboard stomach, disappearing into his underwear line.

He pulled me into a deep kiss as my heart raced against his rock hard chest. I was still fully naked and could feel that he was already hard again. He playfully bit my bottom lip, squeezing my ass and whispered over my lips. "What have you done to me?"

"What do you mean?"

"I've never come in my pants in my entire life, and not only am I hard again, but it never even went down. I want you so badly. There's a part of me that wants to be gentle with you but a bigger part that just wants to take what I've been dying to have for years."

"Take it. It's yours. It's always been for you."

FOURTEEN

MITCH

Holy shit. *Take it.* Those words unraveled me. Blood rushed through my cock as I lifted her up and wrapped her legs around me, backing her into the counter.

We had been through so much together, not all of it good. Truth be told, ending up in this RV with a naked and ready Skylar urging me to do whatever I pleased made it all worthwhile.

It was dark, so I turned on the overhead kitchen light, needing to see every inch of her gorgeous body.

What I wanted first was something I had never done. With her, I craved it more than anything.

Her ass rested on the counter as I spread her legs open, and she gasped when I lowered my head in between them. I knew she loved how I kissed her mouth, so I mimicked those moves on her soft mound: opening, closing, licking and sucking on her with reckless abandon.

With every sound that escaped from her, my dick throbbed, ready to come the first instance I allowed it.

In between breaths, she said, "Your mouth...it feels... so...good."

"I've never done this before. This is only for you."

When I began flicking my tongue over her clit, she writhed under me. Getting to taste her and knowing it was also driving her mad was the single most arousing experience of my life. I continued pressing down on her swollen bud with my tongue.

I wanted to see her face, so I stopped for a second. She was squeezing her breasts together, her eyes closed. So. Fucking. Hot.

I slipped two of my fingers inside of her tight opening and watched in amazement as she started to fuck my hand. She may have been a virgin, but she knew how to move her body to get exactly what she wanted. I was painfully hard, tempted to replace my fingers with my cock, now oozing with precum.

I pulled my fingers out of her. When my mouth returned to her entrance, she moaned like she had been starving for its return, digging her nails into the back of my head. Suddenly, she started to quake beneath me. She was coming, and I consumed every bit of her pulsating orgasm, devouring her like my life depended on every last drop of her essence. For the first time, my own sounds of pleasure were louder than hers, and I kept going at it long after she came.

Finally, I rested my head on her stomach until she pulled me upwards to kiss her. The fact that she could taste herself on my tongue made me crazy.

She wrapped her arms around me. "That was incredible."

"I'm so screwed. I want to do that to you every day now, and I'm fucking leaving."

She put her hand over my mouth. "Let's just forget about that tonight."

I kissed her forehead. “Okay, baby.”

“Say that again. Call me baby.”

“I love you, baby.”

“I love you, too.” Her mouth spread into a wide grin. “Especially, when you call me baby.”

I tickled her side. “You’ve always been my baby even when I didn’t have the balls to say it.”

“Mitch?”

I kissed down her neck. “Yeah?”

“I want to make you come, too, make you feel the way you just made me.”

Hell. Yes.

“Even just pleasuring you alone made my body feel things it never has before. That being said, I can’t wait to—”

There was a banging knock at the door then Davey’s voice. “I’m really sorry, but I have to take a shit.”

Fuck.

“One second!” I yelled.

We scurried to grab Skylar’s clothes. While she got dressed, I couldn’t keep my eyes off her: the way her breasts bounced when she pulled her shirt over her head, the little blue thong she slid up her thighs. I licked my lips, savoring the taste of her as I watched.

I grabbed a few blankets, a pillow and a lantern then unlocked the door.

Davey practically trampled us. “Thanks for taking your sweet time. I just sharted.”

Back outside, we snuck past everyone still sitting around the bonfire.

“Which one is ours?” she asked.

“That one. Come on.”

We crawled inside the tent, and she immediately straddled me, looking like an angel glowing in the lantern light. The horny beast inside wanted to bury himself inside of her right then and there despite our friends being just feet away.

But she deserved better.

"Skylar, listen to me."

She gently bit at my neck. "Mmmhmm."

"I want you more right now than I've ever wanted anything."

"I can feel that."

"But...I...just can't take your virginity in a cramped tent to the sounds of a bunch of drunk people doing karaoke. You mean too much to me."

"I don't care where we are as long as my first time is with you."

I kissed her hard before pulling back. "I really didn't think you were gonna let me get this far, so I didn't bring any protection, partly to guarantee I'd keep it in my pants. I was wrong in thinking I could control myself."

"What about Davey? Does he have anything?"

"He told me Zena's on the pill."

"So is Angie. Shit."

"Yeah."

She looked truly sad. "In the RV, I had made up my mind that I wanted it to be tonight. Now, I feel like I need you inside of me."

This was killing me.

I pressed my hardness up against her. "I want that too, more than my next breath. You have no idea." I licked a line from the base of her neck to her lips. "But there are other things we can do."

She kissed me. "Like what?"

I whispered over her lips, "Everything but."

Her hand slid down to my crotch. "I want to see you."

I kneeled up onto my knees, unzipped my shorts and slowly pulled them down. Her eyes landed on the erection straining through my boxer briefs.

"Take off your skirt."

She did as I asked and took her shirt off too. My dick twitched at the sight of her in nothing but that baby blue thong.

"Fuck, Skylar. You want to see how much I want you?"

She licked her lips. "Yes."

I lowered my boxers and my engorged cock sprung forward.

She stared down silently with a look of awe then finally said, "Wow. You're...big, bigger than I ever imagined."

"I'm *harder* than I ever imagined. And that's just from looking at you. I can't fathom what it would be like inside you."

"Can I touch you?"

That question alone made moisture bead at my tip.

I sounded tortured. "I'm dying for you to touch me."

She wrapped her delicate hand around my shaft and began to stroke it gently. "Does that feel good?"

I bent my head back. "Hell, yes."

"Tell me how you like it."

"Lick your hand then stroke me harder."

I felt like I was directing the movie version of my wildest fantasy.

She slowly licked across her palm before placing it back on me, twisting and pulling. I closed my eyes, imagining that it was her pussy and nearly came. She circled her thumb over the wetness at my tip, spreading it around as a lubricant.

As if she could read my mind, she said, "I want to see you come."

"Are you sure?"

"Yes."

"Okay, baby. Just keep doing that. Don't stop."

She stroked me harder and within seconds, hot cum spurted out all over her hand. She continued milking me with a look of wonder on her face until there was nothing left.

After we cleaned ourselves off, I put my underwear back on, and she stayed shirtless in her thong. I was still perpetually hard.

We lay down together for a while with no concept of time. Since the sound of crickets replaced the chaos outside, I assumed it was after midnight.

My head rested on her chest. She played with my hair and said, "As much as I was trying to keep it from happening, it feels amazing being with you like this."

"In some ways, the stuff we've done tonight has been hotter and more intimate than sex for me, you know, coming up with unique ways to please each other."

"I'll never forget this night as long as I live."

"Your first time is gonna be even more unforgettable. I'm already planning it in my head. We'll go somewhere overnight, somewhere really nice with candles, roses, the whole nine, and I'm gonna make love to you all night long."

"I wish we didn't have to wait. I want you now, but I know we can't."

The thought had crossed my mind to chance it without protection. That's how badly the urge to take her was. In the end, I just couldn't risk it. Still, the need to feel her somehow wouldn't go away. I had an idea.

"Turn over."

When she turned around, I gently rubbed my hand along her backside. "I'm gonna take off your thong, okay?"

"Yes," she said.

I pulled it down slowly and slipped it off her feet. Then, without my asking, she got on all fours, displaying her perfectly smooth, tight ass. My dick swelled to full capacity in a matter of seconds.

If that wasn't the hottest thing I'd ever seen...

The reflection from the lantern formed a shadow of her lithe silhouette along the side of the tent, an image I'd never forget.

I pulled my underwear down and rubbed my cock along the top of her ass. Her body immediately tensed. I bent down and whispered, "Don't worry...I'm not goin' *there*. Relax, baby."

Her back shook in laughter. She turned around and smiled. "I'd let you do anything you wanted, you know."

Fuck. Me.

"I just want us to feel each other skin to skin. Like this." She moaned as I slid my slick shaft back and forth across the slit of her ass, gripping her cheeks around my length. My legs trembled from the intensity of the sensation. Every single thing we tried tonight topped the last.

She panted. "That feels so good."

It felt like I was in a trance when I muttered under my breath, "I can't wait to fuck you."

When she started to touch herself, it nearly put me over the edge. We stayed like that for minutes, and when she abruptly screamed out in pleasure, I lost it, my hot release erupting all over her back.

After I cleaned her off, I lay down next to her, breathing in her scent mixed with the vague smell of the red spruce tree just outside. "I can't get enough of you. It's almost morning. We haven't slept a wink."

"I can sleep when you're in Boston, Mitch."

I cradled her naked body, feeling possessive and needy at the mention of my impending departure. "Promise me that you'll always belong to me, Skylar. Promise me I'll be your first and your last. I need to go away knowing that."

She turned around, looking suddenly devastated at the realization that I was actually leaving. "I promise."

Those words would haunt me later.

I would have done so many things differently if I knew that the night in the tent would be all I'd have to cling to. Not making love to Skylar when I had the chance would become my biggest regret. Well...my second biggest regret.

FIFTEEN

SKYLAR

"Turn around, you dirty bird." Seamus whistled at me as I changed out of my clothes. He lived with me now that Mitch was away at school.

Things just weren't the same here. Not even my time in Brooklyn had been as difficult as saying goodbye to Mitch. I remembered him always telling me how he'd look across the street at my bedroom window when I was gone. I found myself doing the same thing almost every night now, looking up at the dark second floor of his house, wondering how I was going to make it through the next four years.

Mitch sent me an Amtrak ticket to visit him Columbus Day weekend. As much as he tried to make me feel comfortable in his new surroundings, I was anything but.

He lived in one of the co-ed high-rise dormitory buildings along Commonwealth Avenue, right in front of the

Green Line trolley tracks. It was a far cry from the quaint college campus I imagined. Boston University was more like a bustling city that happened to have a college in the midst of it.

After he picked me up from the train station, we went straight to his dorm. When we exited the elevator, a scantily clad girl who looked like a supermodel traipsed down the hall. "Mitch, tell Rob I stole his blender this morning while he was out," she said in a European accent.

Hearing her reference him by name made my eardrums throb. This was not a good start. "Who was that?"

"That's Heidi. She lives down the hall."

"People just go into each other's rooms and take things?"

He chuckled. "Yeah, pretty much."

Then, another girl appeared. "Hey, Mitch," she said in a long Southern drawl, her blonde hair bouncing as she walked by.

"Hey, Savannah."

I swallowed. "Who's she?"

"That's Savannah. She's the RA."

"What's that stand for, 'really annoying?'" I snorted and suddenly felt really stupid.

Wow. Jealousy does not suit me.

He mussed my hair. "No, my little wiseass. It stands for resident assistant. That means she's in charge of the floor and takes care of things in exchange for free room and board."

She looked like she'd happily take care of you, too.

"I see."

All I knew was, she practically lived with my boyfriend, and therefore, I hated her along with every other tramp in this place.

Once inside his room, I couldn't get over how tiny it was, more like a walk-in closet with two twin beds. A guy with a curly mop of black hair lay on one of them.

"Skylar, this is my roommate, Rob. Rob, this is my girlfriend, Skylar."

Rob took off his headphones, nodded and shook my hand then resumed listening to his music.

I whispered, "He's a talker, that one."

"Yeah. That's about the extent of what you'll get outta him."

A collage of pictures, mostly of Mitch and me, hung on the wall above his desk. He slid the curtain, displaying a view of the flashing Citgo sign, a Boston landmark. As I looked out toward the busy street below, I didn't like the uncertainty shown on the reflection of my face in the glass.

He hugged me from behind and kissed my ear. "I love *you*, Skylar." He turned me around to face his burning stare. "You know what I'm getting at, right?"

Embarrassed that I had been so obvious in my jealousy, I said, "I love you, too. This is just going to be an adjustment."

"Maybe if Rob leaves, I can find a way to remind you whom I belong to."

Rob never left and neither did my paranoia.

The next day, Mitch showed me all around the city. He took me to Newbury Street for gelato, and we sat in the Public Garden. It felt great when it was just the two of us, but once the trolley let us off in front of the dormitory that evening, my discomfort returned.

I hadn't even been able to enjoy the time spent with him because of my preoccupation with examining every last detail of every girl who walked by the open door of his room. This level of jealousy was something I had never experienced and made me feel like I was losing my mind.

We were getting ready to head over to Nina and Jake's for dinner. They lived only a couple of miles from the university, and I couldn't pass up the opportunity to see my best friend while I was here.

When Mitch had gone to shower, I looked around at the Spartan gray walls and calculated that he would spend approximately 800 nights here. Then, I thought about how easy it always was to get him sexually aroused. How could he resist if he was horny or drunk and some hot girl was begging him to take it? There were 800 opportunities for that to happen. I knew he wouldn't hurt me intentionally, but he was human, and now I saw with my own eyes what I was up against.

When he returned from the bathroom, he was shirtless and wiping his wet hair down with a towel. The fact that he had been walking down the hall looking so sexy irked me.

As I watched him get dressed, I couldn't help but ask, "Do you always walk around half-naked?"

"Not always." He winked. "Sometimes, I go full frontal." He examined my timorous expression and was no longer laughing. "That was a joke." He threw the towel on the chair angrily. "Alright. You need to talk to me. Right now."

I looked down at the ground disappointed in myself. "I'm sorry. I don't know what's gotten into me."

"Do you have any idea how excited I've been all week about you visiting? I thought you were gonna have a great time, and I'm fucking pissed that being here has made you nothing but miserable, and now, you're leaving tomorrow."

"It's my own fault. It's just weird seeing this other life you have now. I'm used to having you all to myself."

"You *do* have me. You've been so busy looking for reasons to worry, that you've missed that. Yes...there are a lot of girls who live here. But I don't want a single one of them. I want my girlfriend. I've fantasized about our time in Lake George every single night." He caressed my cheek. "This isn't easy for me, either. All I want to do is make love to you. I'm counting the days til Christmas so that we can go away and be alone."

"Me, too."

"You need to trust me, okay?"

He cradled me in his arms as water dripped down from his hair onto mine. His heart was beating rapidly, and I regretted having upset him. I loved him so much, and suddenly felt like I needed to show him.

I walked over to the door and locked it. "Is your roommate gone for a while?"

"I never know with him," he said, still looking upset by my earlier behavior.

I got down on my knees and began to unzip his jeans.

He gripped my wrist to stop me. "Whoa. What are you doing?"

"What does it look like I'm doing?"

"You don't have to do that."

"I know I don't have to."

"You're doing this because you're feeling insecure. I'm not letting you."

"I promise. It's not because of that. Let me do it."

Despite his insistence that I stop, his rapidly growing erection indicated otherwise.

"Skylar..."

"I just want to taste you. Honest. I've wanted to do this for a while."

His trepidation succumbed to the desire reflected in his darkening eyes that told me he wanted it badly. He didn't say another word as I pulled his sweatpants down. He was fully hard when I wrapped my hand around his thick shaft. His breath hitched as I slowly licked in circles around the wet crown.

"Fuck. That feels so good," he said under his breath while his hands massaged my hair.

I moved my mouth up and down slowly, developing a rhythm as I took him deeply from root to tip. I was surprised how turned on I was, my underwear wetter with each movement. His palms were plastered against the door for balance, and his eyes rolled back. I took him harder, wanting desperately to own him more with each thrust of my tongue.

He moaned from deep in his throat. "In...credible."

His cock was hot and slick in my hand as I pumped it into my mouth. His stomach contracted with each heavy breath, and his eyes were closed. I loved having this total control over him.

After a couple of minutes, his trembling hands gripped the back of my head. "I can't. I...I'm gonna come."

I took him even deeper.

"Shit. Skylar, you need to get off me."

I ignored him, jerking him harder and swallowing every drop of the hot, salty cum that spurted out in a seemingly endless flow.

He panted, still leaning his back against the door. Looking frazzled, he said, "Wow. I think I need another shower. That was...I can't believe you did that."

"I can't believe I didn't do it sooner."

Nina and Jake lived in a brownstone just outside the city in Brookline.

After he buzzed us in, Jake came to the door and immediately started ducking and blocking his face. This was his way of busting my balls over a time back in New York when I showed up at his apartment and decked him with my giant bag as soon as he opened the door. At the time, Nina mistakenly thought he had cheated on her, and I left my father's house at the height of my sickness in a rage with the intent to beat his ass. It was the most impulsive thing I'd ever done, although it ended up being a huge misunderstanding. Still, he never lets me live it down.

"I see you've downsized your purse. I should be good," Jake said as he wrapped his tattooed arms around me. His cologne was intoxicating and as always, touching him gave me the cheapest of thrills. "How's my Skylar?" He slapped hands with Mitch. "Sup, Bitch?" He always called Mitch, *Bitch*. "You takin' care of my girl?"

"Of course, man."

Nina yelled from the kitchen. "Hey, Sissy!" That was our nickname for each other, short for sister since neither of us had one.

The house smelled like Indian spices. Nina must have been practicing some recipe from that international cooking class she told me about.

Their condo was really cozy, decorated in lots of black and red with dark wood furniture. Ornate drawings that Jake created using kohl pencil were framed as artwork on the walls. One of them was a sketch of a pregnant Nina, looking up at the moon. Her hands were covering her breasts.

Jake sipped a beer and joined Mitch on the velvet sofa.

Their two-year-old son A.J. came running into the room. I ran to him and lifted him up. "Look at you!"

His hair was almost black like Jake's and gelled into a Mohawk. I tickled him. "You look just like your Daddy."

"Daddy is bananas," he said in the cutest little voice.

"Nina taught him that. Just for that, I'm gonna try and impregnate her tonight," Jake said.

I laughed. "How's that coming along, by the way?" Nina had told me Jake really wanted another kid, but she wanted to wait.

His lip ring clanked against the beer bottle as he took a sip. "Haven't slipped one past the goalie yet."

Nina overheard and came out from the kitchen wiping her hands on an apron. Her dirty blonde hair was longer than the last time I had seen her. "You'll never believe what he did to me the other day. I opened my birth control pill container, and the pills were missing. Instead, there were a bunch of candies in there with a note that said, *'Even trade: SweeTarts for lady parts.'"*

A giggling A.J. jumped on Mitch's lap, took off his Yankees cap and put it on his own head. Mitch started to tickle him, and A.J. was laughing so hard he got the hiccups.

"You're good with him," Nina said. "Don't be surprised if I call you to babysit."

"I'd do it. Seriously. We'd have fun, right A.J.?" Mitch turned to me and winked. "I wouldn't mind one of these someday."

While I couldn't imagine having a baby anytime soon, the thought of a little blue-eyed Mitch running around made my heart smile.

As if he'd just read my mind, my heart fluttered when he whispered in my ear, "She'd have to have your eyes, though."

Jake turned to Mitch who was now bouncing A.J. on his leg. "So, Bitch, how are you liking BU?"

"It's okay. Statistics is killing me, though."

"Come on. Statistics is easy as balls. Let me know if you need any help."

Nina sat on Jake's lap and wrapped her arm around him. "That's how I got into trouble in the first place, letting this guy tutor me in math."

Jake stuck his tongue out at her, and I could see his tongue ring. "Subtract her clothes, divide her legs and multiply, baby," he joked.

She kissed him. "You're sick."

"You know you love it."

I could have sworn I felt the temperature rise in the room from the explosive chemistry those two had. I envied them because they were at a point in their lives where they could just enjoy each other. I wished that Mitch and I were able to fast forward past the next four years.

Nina hopped off Jake's lap. "Sis, you wanna help me finish up dinner?"

"Sure."

Their kitchen was small but modern. Stainless steel pots and pans hung from above a small island. The cabinets were dark cherry wood with black granite counter tops, and there were at least 20 bananas sitting in a fruit hammock.

I laughed. "Bananas anyone?"

"Jake's like a monkey. He eats them by the bushel." She cleared her throat. "Mitch is really looking hot these days, huh?"

"Why do you say that?" I snapped.

"It was just an observation. You tell me all the time how hot you think Jake is. I'm just saying Mitch has really grown into a man from the last time I saw him."

"Sorry. I'm just—"

"Something is bothering you. Talk to me."

I looked down at the terracotta tile floor. "It's been a bad couple of days. His being here in Boston is tougher than I imagined it would be."

"What about it in particular?"

"He's living with a bunch of girls. It's like a brothel. I'm losing my mind over it."

"So..."

"What do you mean, 'so'?"

Nina poured some orange-looking curry sauce over plates of basmati rice. "He loves you."

"I know, but four years is a long time. So much could go wrong."

"Do you know how many women hit on Jake everywhere we go? If I worried about that crap, it would make me nuts, too. You saw what happened when I jumped to conclusions in the past and stopped trusting him. I was wrong. At the end of the day, trust is all you have."

"I don't think I could handle it if he ever cheated on me. I've always been such a strong person, but when it comes to him, I'm so weak, and I hate it."

"Love makes us crazy. Take one day at a time, Sissy. You've been through a lot the past couple of years, more than most have in a lifetime. Maybe the stress is just catching up with you now."

"Maybe."

Jake walked into the kitchen carrying A.J. "Everything okay in here?" He kissed Nina's neck. "You know they say curry boosts the male sex drive."

"In that case, plain rice for you."

"Nooo, baby. Load me up on the Tikka Masala."

Three weeks after the Boston trip, the feeling of dread that surrounded my relationship with Mitch remained. There was no doubt that I loved him, and he gave me no reason not to trust him. Yet, with him gone, I had too much time to think.

My grades were plummeting, and I started seeing a therapist who reaffirmed Nina's theory that my overreacting to everything was some sort of delayed response to the stress of the cancer ordeal.

Things were just starting to get a little better when a routine visit to my gynecologist sent my life into a tailspin.

My periods had been irregular, and while I remembered discussions with my doctors prior to the cancer treatments about the risks of infertility, I hadn't paid too much attention, mainly because the priority was getting rid of the Lymphoma fast before it spread.

"Skylar?"

A nurse led me into a small room where she took my blood pressure. This was a follow-up appointment, and I was supposed to be getting the results of a blood test I had taken days earlier.

I focused on the butterflies on her scrubs and the pumping sound of the blood pressure monitor.

"The doctor will be right in."

I looked through a pregnancy magazine while I waited, listening to a low instrumental version of a Whitney Houston song coming from a speaker overhead.

Dr. Ottone had a troubling expression on her face as she entered the room and cut right to the chase.

"So, Skylar, I wanted to talk to you about the results of your blood test."

"Okay..."

"It seems that you have poor ovarian reserve."

"What does that mean?"

"Well, everyone is born with a limited number of eggs. Over time, under normal circumstances, they diminish. However, when a woman receives high doses of chemotherapy...that can destroy your eggs. It seems you have a very limited number remaining. It's also possible that they may be of poor quality due to the treatments you received. While we can't be absolutely certain, you'll likely have a hard time conceiving. If you are able to, there's a higher chance of miscarriage."

"Is there anything that can be done?"

"Aside from someone freezing their eggs prior to treatment, there is little we can do at this point. I'm sorry, Skylar. This doesn't necessarily mean total infertility, but chances are, you're going to have difficulty."

The magazine with the smiling pregnant cover model taunted me from my lap and fell to the ground as I got up to leave. My mother had been waiting for me, but I refused to talk and didn't remember much of the ride home.

That night, I kept relaying what Mitch said when playing with A.J. at Nina's house. *"I wouldn't mind one of these someday."*

There was a very good chance I would never be able to give him a child. How could I stay with him in good faith knowing that he wanted one? I loved him too much. But if I told him what I now knew, he would just say it didn't matter to him. Deep down, I knew it would, maybe not right away but someday. The longer I stayed with him, the more it would hurt when he finally arrived at that realization.

I obsessed over it for the better part of a week. Then, one night, came a panic attack that felt like a moving freight train filled with insecurities.

800 nights.

Infertile.

I had myself convinced that his leaving me eventually was inevitable for one reason or another. Whatever the cause, it would destroy me when it happened, and I couldn't let it. It's always easier to be the one doing the leaving than to be the one left behind.

The room swayed when I opened my laptop and started typing:

Mitch, please don't hate me for what I'm about to do.

SIXTEEN

MITCH

Mitch, please don't hate me for what I'm about to do. I don't have the courage to call you because I know if I hear your voice, I will never be able to go through with this. Please know that I love you so much and always will, more than you could ever know. But I think that everything is just happening too fast with us. I don't like the jealous monster I've become lately. You need time to just be away at school without worrying about how it's affecting me.

At the same time, I need time to find myself without the strain of a long-distance relationship. You need to do the same without being tied down at this point in your life. The more I think about it, the more I realize we're too young to settle down. I don't want us to resent each other later.

I hope that someday we can manage to be friends again. I know that will be impossible for a while. I've started applying for internships in New York and plan to move back in with Oliver for the summer to make this easier. I'm so sorry. I know this is going to come as a shock. Remember that I'll always love you.

Reading it never got easier. It had been six months since that email, and I still couldn't wrap my head around it...not one single bit.

My phone lit up in the darkness as I reread it for what felt like the thousandth time. It was the middle of the night, and whenever I couldn't sleep, I'd pull that message up again in an attempt to decipher it. I'd try to find some clue in the wording to understand how Skylar could so easily throw us away. Even though she explained her reasoning, it still made no sense. I knew in my heart, there had to be more to the story.

The weekend after she sent the email, I boarded a train home. We were in her room as she talked in circles, refusing to look me in the eye, only reiterating what she had written without explaining it further. It felt like I was in the middle of a nightmare as she kept her distance, arms crossed against her chest. The fact that she didn't want me to touch her cut like a knife.

When she did offer fleeting glances, the pain in her eyes was almost tangible. She was struggling to hold it together and kept telling me she was "doing this for my own good."

At one point, I lost my cool and screamed at the top of my lungs, "How is it for my own good if I'd rather die than live without you?" Her small lamp came crashing down after I smacked the desk in anger.

That was when Tish came upstairs and asked me to leave. Although a part of me couldn't blame her since I was acting like a lunatic, she had been like a second mother to me and to have her kick me out really hurt. When I turned around one last time before leaving, I noticed that Skylar was crying.

I didn't sleep that entire weekend, just stayed in my room pacing like a zombie with my mouth parched from lack of food or drink. I'd occasionally look across the street to the light in her upstairs bedroom. She was so close, but it felt like I was holding vigil for someone a million miles away. I just couldn't believe I had lost her. It was impossible to accept, and I didn't for a very long time.

The train ride back to Boston at the end of that weekend had felt like the lowest point in my life. Still, after that, I hadn't given up and continued to call, email and text her to no avail.

Then, came Christmas break, which was supposed to have been special for us at one time. I arrived home to New Jersey to find that Skylar had already left for Florida with Oliver to spend it with Lizete's family down in Miami.

The weeks went by, and it felt like my world was ending. The turning point came about a month ago when immense sadness transformed into pure anger.

Davey had sent me a text in the middle of my accounting class.

We're at Chili's and Skylar just walked in with some dude. WTF.

He then texted me a photo that he took without her knowing. She apparently hadn't noticed Davey and Zena a few tables down. My heart felt like it was breaking with every second that passed as I stared at the grainy photo. They were holding hands across the table.

How the fuck could she do this?

I had seen enough. She had finally succeeded in getting her message through to me because at that point, I was done.

Rage enveloped me, and my hands trembled as I grabbed my books and abruptly left the classroom, nearly knocking into someone who was walking by in the hallway outside. As I ran in the rain down Commonwealth Avenue, I couldn't get back to my room fast enough to escape into the bottle of vodka I had been saving in my closet for a special occasion.

I spent the rest of that night drinking myself into oblivion.

I had to force myself to stop looking at Skylar's email.

It wasn't gonna change after six months of staring at it, Mitch.

I shut my phone off, carefully reaching over to the desk and put it down next to an empty condom wrapper. I cringed.

Last night was a mistake.

Heidi lay next to me, and I didn't want to wake her, mainly because I didn't want to have to talk to her. I wished she hadn't stayed over. It wasn't meant to be anything more than a quick fuck. I hated myself for thinking of it that way, but that's what you call sex when it doesn't mean anything.

It was just supposed to be an escape, a distraction because I was now forcing myself to move on. I had finally convinced myself the love of my life wasn't coming back. The pain was something I couldn't deal with alone anymore. When I was by myself, all I thought about was Skylar: Skylar leaving me, Skylar on a date, Skylar having sex with someone else.

That one hurt.

Some other guy would eventually take her virginity. Her first time was supposed to be mine. All of her was supposed to be mine. She was my future. This reminded me of when I was a little boy because the future was now a black hole, just as it had seemed when my parents were divorcing...except this was far worse than that.

I'd never get over her change of heart. With the way she ended things and her showing up at Chili's with some random guy, I should have had no feelings of guilt over what I did last night. Still, it sickened me as I sat here still tasting Heidi's perfume on my tongue. Was this what sex with other women would feel like for the rest of my life? Like it wasn't right somehow because my body belonged to Skylar?

Heidi's long, black hair tickled my arm. I had just wanted her gone but didn't have the heart to kick her out after we'd had sex. So, I let her curl up beside me while I stared at the ceiling, and she fell asleep.

She was from Germany—sexy—but not my type, meaning not Skylar. She wore heavy eye makeup and was extremely tall. She said she used to model. Heidi had always hit on me since the beginning of the year and last night, with Rob staying at a friend's, I gave in when she came to my room under the guise of needing help with her history homework. The rest was, well...history and a night I'd rather forget.

The truth was, Skylar never had a reason to worry about me cheating on her. Plain and simple, it would have never happened because there was no other girl who made me feel the way she did. I just couldn't prove that to her, apparently.

If I couldn't get her back, though, I had to force myself to move on. She was sure as hell doing just that. We were broken up, so last night shouldn't have felt like cheating, but it did.

I closed my eyes, envisioning our night in Lake George. The pain was excruciating. I missed the way her tiny body fit right into the crevice of mine when we lay together. I missed her laugh. I missed her scent. I was pining for her with another girl lying right next to me. It was fucking pathetic. I impulsively reached behind me and picked up my phone, deciding she needed to feel a fraction of my despair.

> ***I know you've moved on. I tried to do the same tonight. I had sex with someone. How does that work for you? It's not working for me. I still fucking love you so much. I always will. I'll never understand. Never. By the way, have you fucked him yet?***

She never texted me back, and I hadn't expected her to.

SEVENTEEN

SKYLAR

I held myself in a fetal position after the text came in: *I had sex with someone*. It was hard digesting those words, but knowing that I had sent him straight into her arms made me want to puke.

This was inevitable, but I didn't think he would be so cruel as to tell me about it. What did I expect? He must have been enraged when I staged that fake date at Chili's. That was the intent. I knew Davey went there every Friday night, so I had asked Jason, a friend of Angie's brother, to have dinner with me and hold my hand so that it would get back to Mitch. I knew the plan had worked when I saw from the corner of my eye that Davey was taking my picture.

The only way Mitch would stay away from me was if he got angry. The one way I knew to do that was to let him see me with another guy. I felt terrible, but what choice did I have? He wasn't backing down in trying to change my mind, because he loved me. That wasn't going to change unless I made him hate me. The anger in the tone of that text showed me I'd finally succeeded.

Congratulations, Skylar.

Images of Mitch's mouth on another woman, his cock inside of her flashed through my brain. I begged my mind to stop, but it only kept getting worse.

What had I done?

Getting out of town before he came home for the summer was more important now than ever. Seeing him would crush me.

The summer after my senior year, I took an interior design internship for a private design firm in Manhattan. I was taking a year off before starting college and wanted to understand the ropes of the design industry before making a decision on whether to choose it as a major.

Oliver and Lizete were happy to have me back for a while. This time, I had Seamus with me. It was ironic because Seamus, like Mitch and I, had also become the product of divorced parents in a way, getting shuffled from house to house.

Although being back in Brooklyn reminded me of my cancer days, there was solace in the fact that I wouldn't have to face Mitch.

I interned three days a week at Harrington Design Studio, which specialized in interior design for high-end clients in Manhattan and the Hamptons. The other two days, I worked at Regal Fabrics, a well-known store in the city that supplied materials to the design studio. My job was to organize their stock by color and texture and also help clients choose a pattern for their needs. My internship manager helped get me the job since she saw what a hard worker I was for no pay.

I had texted Mitch at the beginning of the summer, letting him know what I was up to and where I was working. I figured I at least owed him that much. Even though I was staying away from New Jersey, I didn't want to be totally cruel and not contact him at all. It turned out he decided to stay in Boston for the summer since he had gotten a job at an on-campus restaurant in the student union building. He made sure to stress in his response that he had no reason to come home anymore.

It never got any easier being apart from him. The thought of him sleeping with other girls still made me ill. I hadn't told anyone the real reason I ended it with Mitch. I didn't want to hear my mother or Nina tell me all the reasons I was wrong in thinking that he would leave me someday if I couldn't bear him a child. This was my own private, selfless decision as far as I was concerned, and I didn't expect anyone to understand.

Overall, my routine that summer was pretty predictable. Lizete would make me eat some Cuban-style breakfast in the morning before I'd take the subway into the city. I hadn't made any real friends here, so instead of hanging out in Manhattan after work, I'd just go straight home and read.

All of that changed the day I met Charisma. She looked like the typical wealthy Manhattanite that frequented the fabric store, but she was closer to my age. She had medium-length caramel hair and perfectly manicured nails. She had classic good looks but wouldn't be considered gorgeous. It was obvious she came from money based on how well she was dressed.

"How can I help you?"

"I'm redecorating my bedroom and looking for a bold, black and white damask with a velvet feel for the drapes."

“I think I have just the right thing.” I led her upstairs to where the most expensive materials were housed and showed her what I had in mind.

She gasped as she ran her fingers along the textured fabric. “That’s exactly what I was picturing. How did you do that?”

I smiled. “I’ve just gotten to know the store inside out. Do you have measurements?”

“No. I’ll probably have to come back.” She gave me her hand. “I’m Charisma, by the way.”

“Skylar.”

“Skylar. That’s a pretty name.”

“So is Charisma,” I said as I returned the roll of fabric to the shelf.

She leaned her head to the side. “Are you from around here?”

“I live in Brooklyn with my father. I’m just here for the summer.”

Looking me up and down, she asked, “Do you mind my saying something?”

“Sure.”

“You’re such a pretty girl, like a blank slate. You could be stunning if you wore a little makeup and dressed up a bit. I love to make people over. It’s sort of my hobby. Let me know if you’d be interested.”

“What are you with some kind of ambush makeover show?”

“No. I swear. I just think it would be fun. I guess I have too much time on my hands.”

“Apparently.”

“Where do you go to school?”

“I just graduated high school. I’m taking a year off and thinking of applying at the end of this year, probably majoring in interior design. You?”

"I go to Wellesley. I'll be a junior."

"Wow."

We walked downstairs, and she rummaged through her Coach bag for her phone.

"What do you do for fun, Skylar?"

"I dunno...read? My life is pretty boring."

"You're kidding, right? You're in the city of dreams for the summer, and you're spending your time stuck in a book? We need to change that. You're too young to live like a hermit. What's your number?"

She jotted it down in her phone as I recited it.

"What do you suggest I do for fun?"

"You can start by letting me make you over, and then we'll go out. There are some cool 18 and over clubs downtown. How about this Friday night?"

"Um...not sure if I want to be your pet project."

"I won't take no for an answer."

I shrugged. "Okay. I work here until eight on Fridays."

What did I have to lose?

She clapped giddily. "Yay!"

"What do I wear?"

"Don't worry about that. I have tons of clothes at my apartment. I'll bring the measurements for the drapes and pick you up."

"Okay, see you at eight on Friday."

What the hell just happened?

God, I loved being drunk.

Charisma turned out to be a bad influence in more ways than one. At the time, though, I thought meeting her was the best thing to ever happen to me because it had gotten me out of my funk.

We started hanging out a few times a week. Her family's apartment wasn't too far from the fabric store, so I would walk over after work and sometimes spend the night. The doorman got to know me and would let me go right up. Her parents were vacationing in Fiji that summer, so she had the whole place to herself. The décor was modern, lots of white with sleek geometric furniture.

There was a small bar in the corner of the living room, and Charisma would make me whatever mixed drink I wanted. SoCo and Sours and Cosmos were my favorites.

For the first time in my life, I actually understood the hype. Getting hammered helped to momentarily ease the pain. Nothing else had been able to do that. With each drink, the bad stuff faded away, replaced by a euphoric fogginess. While blissfully intoxicated, I'd also tell Charisma all of my secrets, including the real reason I had broken up with Mitch. She wasn't able to provide much insight, but it was good therapy just to get it all off my chest to someone impartial.

She introduced me to some of the friends she grew up with, and they'd often join us for our cocktail hours. Also in the group was Charisma's cousin, Chad. He was tall, blonde, preppy and had teeth that shined like the top of the Chrysler building. He was home from Harvard for the summer.

Whether it was the way he looked at me or the subtle brushing of his hand on my knee, Chad always made it clear he was interested. Charisma had been trying to get me to give him a chance. He was attractive and nice enough, but I wasn't sure I was ready to date. She told me he never had serious girlfriends, so I knew that meant he just wanted to "hook up."

A part of me knew it was time to lose my virginity. I was the last person I knew who was still a virgin. A bigger part felt a deep sadness at the thought since my first time was always supposed to belong to Mitch. He was truly the only guy I wanted, and if I was going to lose my virginity now, it probably didn't even matter whom it was with; all other guys were interchangeable.

Charisma was pouring Midori into the glass for my drink. "You need a good fuck to get you over that Mitch dude, Skylar."

Tonight, we were scheduled to go to Club Nicole downtown with Chad and a few girls in Charisma's circle.

Chad walked in with his usual fitted sweater smelling like the woodsy cologne he always wore. "Skylar, I wanna see how you dance tonight."

I was already starting to get buzzed. "A few more of these, and you might just get your wish, Harvard punk."

Charisma handed me another drink. "Doesn't Skylar look pretty tonight?"

"She always looks pretty. In fact, pretty isn't a strong enough word for her."

Charisma winked at me. "Should I be leaving the room now?"

I said nothing and continued to sip my drink. She was totally pushing the Chad thing. Maybe I'd give him a chance.

After a long wait in line in front of the club, a large bouncer that looked like the Rock let us in. Chad clasped hands with him, confirming my suspicions that despite his Ivy League status, he was also a well-known party boy. I let out a sigh of relief because it was the first time we'd successfully used the fake i.d.s that Charisma scored downtown.

The humidity outside was replaced by a blast of cold air-conditioning that made my nipples harden. My ears felt like they were going to explode from the loud techno music.

Chad disappeared then returned with a beer for him and a Tom Collins for me. There were girls dancing in cages, and people would dance around them on the sides of these raised platforms. I downed my drink and suddenly felt like I wanted to join them. As if on cue, Charisma pulled me up there, and the two of us, drunk off our asses, started to grind on each other. We caught the attention of a group of men dancing nearby. I normally wouldn't have been caught dead dancing around a cage with some random guy rubbing his balls up against me. At the time, though, and under the influence, it felt totally normal.

Chad whistled at us. When the music switched, he gave me his hand and helped me down.

"That was fun!" Charisma said as she danced away through the artificial smoke toward the bar where the other girls were waiting.

Chad's breath was warm and smelled like beer when he spoke into my ear. "You wanna go upstairs?"

"What's upstairs?"

"It's the VIP area."

I looked up at the balcony, and it seemed dark with a hint of purple lighting. I could only make out shadows of movement up there.

"Sure," I said, suddenly feeling anxious.

"Let's get another round before we go," he said.

Chad returned with our drinks and reached out his hand for me to follow him up the black-carpeted stairs. The music became more distant with each step. A guard stood at the top. "Hello, Mr. Carter."

"Hey, Hollis."

"Why did he call you, Mr. Carter?" I asked as we sat down on one of the purple velour couches.

He smirked. "Because my parents own this club."

"What?"

"My family actually owns three of the nightclubs on this street."

I knew he was loaded but Jeez...

"Wow. That's really cool."

"I think so." He took my drink and placed it on a table. "See that door back there?"

"Yeah."

"That's a private room. The walls and floor are made of glass that overlooks the dance floor downstairs, but nobody can see up into it." He lowered his voice. "We can do whatever we want on top of everyone, and no one will know. Do you see what I'm getting at?"

I thought about it for a good thirty seconds because I knew what he was really asking me. "Sure." Even in my drunken state, I was fully aware of what was about to happen. The hairs on my arms stiffened as he took my hand.

Inside the room, the sound of the music seemed distant, but the beat of the bass was more pronounced.

He shut the door, and I heard the lock click. My heart started to pound as he said, "Stand in front of the wall. Enjoy the view." He came up from behind me and kissed my neck. "I'm enjoying *this* view." He ran his fingertips down my arm. "You have an incredible body. Have you ever been a dancer?"

I stiffened and shook my head. "No."

The contact felt good, but not in a comfortable way. My body responded, but this felt foreign, not like it had been with Mitch. My heart and mind weren't in it. Nerves replaced the intense passion I always experienced before. Still, I needed to grow up and wasn't going to resist anything if he tried. I needed this. Mitch was moving on, and I needed to see if another guy could help me to do the same.

The beat of the music vibrated through my tense body as Chad continued to kiss my neck then began to suck on it.

"I'm gonna make you so feel good, Skylar. I've wanted you for so long."

I closed my eyes, trying to push away my conscience as Chad slowly unzipped my dress and let it fall to the floor. He turned me around and plastered my body against the glass wall.

"Are you sure they can't see?"

"It's one-sided. Don't worry."

I focused on a black chrome chandelier dripping with crystals as he slowly pulled down my underwear.

There's still time to change your mind.

"I bet you've never done it like this before...on top of hundreds of people."

Should I tell him I'm a virgin?

"Definitely not. Not...like this."

He unhooked my bra and began sucking on my breasts. Everything was happening so fast, but in a way, that was how I wanted it. I didn't want to feel it. I just wanted it over with as if my virginity were the last piece of Mitch I needed to let go of in order to move on.

I closed my eyes again and heard the zipper lower on his pants.

He stopped kissing me. When I opened my eyes, he reached into his back pocket. The condom wrapper crinkled as he ripped it open with his teeth. I looked down and watched as he slipped it on then squeezed the tip. I couldn't help but notice how much smaller he was than Mitch.

Chad didn't waste any time. Within seconds, he lifted me up and wrapped my legs around him. I immediately felt the burn as he tried to enter me while Lady Gaga's *Do What You Want* played on the lower level.

How ironic.

"Ow. Slow down," I said.

"I'm hurting you?"

"Yes."

"Okay...sorry, baby."

Don't call me baby.

I inhaled slowly and decided I was going to do whatever it took to withstand the pain. When he pushed inside me again, I whimpered but breathed though it as my back hit the wall.

"You're so tight," he said as his dick thrust harder again into my burning vagina.

I was pretty sure he mistook my heavy breathing for a good thing as he continued to fuck me slowly. When he gradually broke through my hymen, he began to pound into me faster.

As the pain between my legs subsided a little, the realization of what was happening started to sink in. My eyes were closed, and all I could see was Mitch's face. The burning between my legs paled in comparison to the image of his blue eyes burning into my soul in that moment. It should have been him. Tears came pouring out of my eyes as Chad's movements became more pronounced. A few minutes later, he said, "I'm about to come."

I sniffled and lied. "Me, too."

As he moaned, I tightened my eyes to rid them of the tears.

When the movements stopped, he slowly pulled out of me and looked down. "Fuck."

"What?"

"There's blood everywhere."

When I lowered my head, I saw red all over his khaki pants, and it was also running down my leg."

"Shit. Is that your period?"

I covered my mouth unable to fight my tears and shook my head.

He ran his hand through his hair. "You...don't tell me you were a virgin?"

My voice trembled. "Yes."

He seemed angry, like I had tricked him somehow. "Shit. I wouldn't have done this if I knew that. How the fuck am I supposed to go out there covered in blood?"

My own blood was boiling at the insensitive audacity of his question. "I don't know...I—"

He left the room abruptly then came back with a small white towel from the bar, and I used it to wipe my leg down.

He grabbed my hand. "Come on. Let's sneak out the side door." He practically dragged me downstairs and out the side entrance into an abandoned alley. Through the night fog, we walked in silence on gravel to the street where he hailed a cab.

Chad said nothing to me on the ride back to Charisma's apartment. I stared vacantly out the window, still shell-shocked at his Jekyll and Hyde behavior.

When the vehicle stopped, he walked me to the front door and hugged me awkwardly before getting back in the cab, which sped off.

I was speechless, feeling empty. Used.

The doorman let me in, and I took the elevator up in a daze, still feeling like a fire had been put out in my vagina. Once upstairs, I realized Charisma was still at the club. All of my stuff was locked inside her apartment because I was spending the night.

I banged the back of my head against her locked door and slid my body down to rest on the floor of the hallway. I took out my phone and sifted through to the pictures of Mitch and me from Lake George. This was the first time I had allowed myself to look at one single photo of him since I wrote that dreaded email. Seeing his face and the eyes that always reflected a love for me within them made me yearn for him. I clutched the phone to my heart and cried. What happened with Chad did nothing to help me move past my feelings. If anything, it reiterated how indestructible my love for Mitch was. Being with another man had only made me long for him more.

An hour later, the elevator doors slid open, and Charisma came from around the corner. "Hey, girl. What happened? I thought you were with Chad."

I was still on the ground. "Yeah...about that. Your cousin's an asshole."

"What do you mean?"

"I don't want to talk about it."

She opened the apartment door. "You want a drink?"

"No...please. That's how I got into trouble tonight in the first place. I'm done with the drinking. And as for your cousin—if you really want to know—he took off in a cab with my virginity after kicking me to the curb. Apparently, you don't need a soul to get into Harvard."

That summer with Charisma was a learning experience. Between losing my virginity and discovering that alcohol was not my friend, I also realized that it was impossible to move on without your heart. Mitch *was* my heart. My feelings would all come to a head at Jake and Nina's engagement party.

The following November, Jake and Nina had finally set a date for their long-awaited wedding. They had gotten engaged after A.J. was born, but finances were tight, so they waited a couple of years to make wedding plans.

As Nina's maid of honor, I had to travel to Boston to be there for the celebration held at a fancy Italian restaurant in the city's North End. Jake's sister, Allison and her husband, Cedric paid for the party held in a private room with a small dance floor.

The spread included a buffet of things like antipasto, penne with pesto and rack of lamb. For dessert there were cannoli and Italian rum cake brought in from a pastry shop down the street.

The DJ played lots of Big band and mellow songs from artists like Tony Bennett and Michael Buble. The ceilings were adorned with shrimp-colored paper lanterns, and the long table was decorated with white hydrangeas surrounded by tea light candles floating in water.

Jake was wearing a black dress shirt rolled up at the sleeves that showcased his tattoos while Nina donned a simple black and white dress. Jake fed Nina an Italian cookie as A.J. sat in between them.

Even though I was so happy for them, the mood here made my heart feel heavy. It had been over a year now since I'd broken up with Mitch, and every day was harder than the last. I would always wonder what he was doing, whether he was happy or if today were the day he would meet someone he'd fall in love with. Tonight was especially hard because I was in his city, so close yet so far away.

The DJ called Jake and Nina up to dance to Frank Sinatra's *The Way You Look Tonight.* Something about that song always gave me the chills. It was so beautiful. I focused on the way Jake was looking at Nina when they were dancing, how they would whisper things to one another. In that moment, they were essentially all that existed to each other despite the room full of people. The look in Jake's eyes was a familiar one; it was the same look Mitch used to give me.

As the song played, my entire relationship with Mitch flashed before my eyes: our basketball games as kids, the kiss at the carnival, his kissing my bald head, our night in Lake George. An intolerable ache built inside my chest. Just as the music changed to something fast-paced, I ran out of the reception room before anyone noticed me bawling.

I ended up in the crowded restaurant dining room and climbed a set of stairs that led up to an empty rooftop patio. A blast of wind blew my dress Marilyn Monroe-style as I opened the door. Even though it was a chilly night, the starry-sky was breathtaking. It felt like I could feel a hole in my chest as I began to cry harder.

Then, the door burst open. "Skylar? What the hell are you doing up here?"

A plane flew overhead as he walked toward me.

"Jake...." I tried to compose myself. "I just needed some air."

"Bullshit. I saw you leaving in tears."

"You should go back to your party."

"The chicken dance can wait." Jake pulled two chairs off a stack that were lined up on top of each other. "Sit." When I sat down, he said, "Now talk."

"You know I broke up with Mitch..."

"How could I forget? He came by my house after you dumped him, you know."

"He did?"

"Yup...wanted to know if Nina knew anything, wanted my advice. Neither of us knew what to say. I just gave him beer, let him get drunk and drove him home."

"When you and Nina were dancing to that song...it just reminded me of him."

"Hold up. If you're so sad about him, why did you end it? No one seems to know."

"Can I ask you something?"

"Shoot."

"Before A.J. was born, if you found out Nina couldn't have babies, would you have been able to stay with her for the long haul?"

Jake paused, blinking his eyes repeatedly as he put two and two together.

"Without a doubt...yes. *Nina's* my baby. She means more to me than anything in the world. We happened to get lucky practically on the first shot, but if she weren't able to give me a child, yes, it would have been a disappointment but only because I couldn't have a part of her and a part of me. I wouldn't want that with any other woman. Any guy that truly loves you would feel the same." He put his hand on my shoulder. "You never told Nina, did you?"

"No."

"This is all starting to make sense now. You thought you were doing him a favor by letting him go before he had a chance to leave you later."

I wiped my eyes. "Yeah."

"If he truly loves you the way he says he does, you're wrong, Skylar. When I was going through a rough time, a wise girl once told me that life was short and that I would regret it if I let Nina go so easily. This was the same chick who nearly knocked my teeth out. Have you seen this girl?

She was badass. She needs to take her own advice right about now."

I started to laugh a little through my tears, remembering that day. "I'm just scared."

"That's how you really know you love the dude. Love can't exist without fear. If the thought of losing someone doesn't scare the shit out of you, then it's not love."

My heart beat faster as I realized what I was about to do. "Can you tell Nina, I'm so sorry, but I have to leave?"

EIGHTEEN

MITCH

"Good night, princess." I kissed Summer on the forehead as I tucked her into bed. I had been babysitting my sister while my father and his wife were out.

This was the second weekend trip I'd made to Pennsylvania recently. She deserved to have a brother who wasn't completely absent from her life, and for once, I was making an effort to put aside my differences with my father. Something in my life needed to go right when everything else had gone to shit.

We had spent the night playing Monopoly, and I let her show me how to make her favorite Rice Krispy treats. I would have let her stay up way past her bedtime, but she finally got tuckered out and asked to go to sleep.

My father's living room was dark except for the light from the television. The smell of cigarette smoke ingrained in the dated, tweed couch was pungent. I sat, flipping mindlessly through the channels, wishing I could talk to Skylar and tell her all about Summer. I wished a lot of things when it came to Skylar, namely that the past year never happened. I had made a lot of stupid mistakes in my efforts to forget the pain that she inflicted on me. Yet, the longing for her had managed to only intensify.

She hadn't contacted me in months. So, about an hour later, when my phone rang and her name popped up on the screen, I couldn't believe my eyes.

"Skylar?"

"Hi."

My eyelids closed tight, cherishing the sound of her voice. "Are you okay?"

"I'm at the lobby of your dorm. Are you here to let me up?"

"My dorm? You're in Boston?"

"Yes. Nina and Jake had their engagement party, and I left the restaurant to come here."

I threw one of the pillows in frustration. "Shit. I'm in Pennsylvania visiting my sister."

She sniffled. "You are?" Her voice sounded hoarse. "Wow...that's great. I—"

"Skylar, are you crying?"

She hesitated. "Yes. I came here to tell you something."

It was noisy where she was, and I had trouble hearing her. "Listen, can you go somewhere quiet?"

"Where?"

"There's a piano room down the hall of the lobby, the first door on the left before you get to the guard booth. No one's ever in it."

"Okay. I'm walking." The phone shuffled as she moved. "I'm here. It's empty."

"Close the door." I heard it shut, drowning out the earlier noise. "Now, tell me what you came there to say."

"This is hard for me," she said.

"I'll stay on the phone with you as long as you need. You could recite the fucking phone book, and that would okay right about now. It's just so good to hear your voice. Take your time."

"There's stuff I need to tell you. I don't know where to begin. I should really do this in person."

"No. No! I'm not gonna waste another second of my life wondering what you're thinking. I need to know everything, and I need to hear it now."

"I love you, Mitch."

My heartbeat accelerated.

"I love you, too. I never stopped. You know that, right?"

"I have to tell you why I really broke up with you. I thought I was doing the right thing for you."

"You've said that, but I don't understand."

She paused.

"There's a very good chance I can't have babies, Mitch. The treatments...they destroyed my eggs."

I stared at the *Family Guy* episode playing on the television as my mind absorbed what she's said. *What?* I couldn't believe she kept that from me. At the same time, I was devastated for her. It all made sense now.

"Mitch...are you still there?"

"You thought I would leave you if you couldn't have kids?"

"It was more that I was afraid you wouldn't, but that over time, as you got older and wanted a child of your own...you would resent me."

My emotions were all over the place. I needed her to understand, so my voice was louder than I intended. "You got it wrong. I don't want a child if it's not with you. I will never want one with someone else. Do you understand me?

Nothing matters to me but you. I'm just a fucking walking shell without you."

She was quiet and sighed into the phone. "There's something else I have to tell you."

"Okay..."

The long breath that escaped her was loud in my ear. "I spent the summer in New York and met this girl who lived in the city. She introduced me to her cousin. His name was Chad."

My stomach suddenly felt sick. I knew where this was going.

"Okay..."

"I was trying hard to get over you...and I ended up letting him have sex with me."

I let out the breath I had been harboring and could taste the bile forming in my throat. My eyes getting stabbed out would have felt better than hearing that. I tried to act calm, but my labored breathing was a dead giveaway to my true feelings. My hands formed into fists as I resisted punching the wall. "Okay...okay. Is that it? You were protected, right?"

She was talking at warp speed. "Yes, of course. It happened so fast, and it was horrible. I never even saw him again. My first time should have been yours, and I felt so sick about it after. I did it because I thought it would help me move on, and it did just the opposite. I—"

"Okay. Don't tell me anymore, alright? I can't handle it. I just want to move past this."

She directed the conversation toward me. "Have you dated anyone?"

I was silent, unsure of how to explain it to her. Since we were being honest..."I slept with two girls. I was lonely, and the more time that passed, I didn't think you were coming back. The first time was the one-night stand when I stupidly texted you after. Then, at the end of last semester, I started kind of dating someone. Nothing came of it. It continued over the summer, but I was never into her, and she knew it. Shit, I still had your fucking pictures all over my room. She wanted something more serious than I could give her. In the beginning, she acted like she was okay with keeping things casual, but she ended up changing her tune. Anyway, she freaked when I ended it. I told her I was still in love with you. Then, she wouldn't stop calling and started acting kind of psychotic. It was a mess, but it's over."

"What was her name?"

"Her name? Charisma."

I heard a sharp intake of breath, and then it sounded like the phone dropped.

Shit.

"Skylar...are you there?"

Her voice was unsteady when she returned to the phone. "Is she from New York?"

"Yes. Why does it matter?"

"The girl I met in the city—oh my God—it's her."

"What?"

"It's her. She came into my work...pretended to want to buy fabric. How did she know where I worked?" I felt vomit start to rise in my stomach as she continued, "She set me up with her scumbag cousin. I told her all my secrets. Mitch, I...I told her why I really broke up with you!"

Skylar started to cry harder, and my heart couldn't take it.

This couldn't have happened.

I couldn't hold it in anymore as I ran to the bathroom and threw up in the toilet with the phone still in my hand.

I would never forgive myself.

I didn't know then that the worst was yet to come.

NINETEEN

CHARISMA

You know that song, *Whatever Lola Wants*? Yeah. That could've been written about me.

I was used to getting whatever I wanted. My parents never said no to me, so as a young adult, I had a hard time accepting rejection. When I first laid eyes on Mitch, I knew I *needed* to have him. He was the most beautiful male specimen I had ever seen: perfect build, striking eyes and better hair than most girls. There was also something about his unattainable attitude that quickly transformed my normal attraction to him into frenzied lust.

A few of my housemates from Wellesley and I had taken the train over to BU for an off-campus party on Beacon Street. That was where I noticed him sitting in a corner alone, drinking a beer. He was wearing a Yankees cap backwards, his thick hair sticking out from underneath. The gray t-shirt he wore hugged every taut muscle. I watched him wrap his full lips around the bottle, and my panties became wet just imagining it was my breast.

It looked like his mind was somewhere else, though. I needed to turn that attention to me and only me. Since my father was a die-hard Yankees fan, I knew a little something about baseball. So, I started a conversation with him about the Yankees' last win over the Red Sox. After a while, he seemed to loosen up and we spent most of that night talking in the same corner.

I asked if I could see his dorm room and when he took me inside, the first thing I noticed were pictures of some pretty little thing plastered all over the wall above his desk.

"You have a girlfriend?"

"No," he said coldly without offering any other information. I made a mental note to figure out who the hell she was.

He was giving me a vibe that he wasn't that into me. Of course, that only made me want him more. He hadn't tried to make a move on me, and I went home feeling defeated but determined.

In the weeks that followed, I made no secret of my growing feelings for him. I was very touchy feely and finally came right out and told him I wanted him. He made it very clear that he didn't want a relationship but seemed open to something casual. I pretended like that was okay with me but secretly vowed to step up my game.

I'd wear my sexiest outfits and bring him takeout from high-end restaurants on Newbury Street. I even made up a long story about a bad breakup to try and get him to open up to me about *her*. After I shared my "story," he finally started talking.

Skylar.

That bitch broke up with *him*. Unbelievable. I didn't understand how she could drop him like a hot potato after all those years together. The good news was they hadn't had sex. The bad news: the look in his eyes told me he was far from over her. I would have given anything if he had felt that way about me. The more I got to know him, the more I knew I needed to somehow make that happen. He was the whole package: gorgeous, smart and loyal.

A few nights after he opened up to me about Skylar, we slept together for the first time. I sort of pushed it on him, and he didn't back down. Even though he seemed distant and removed from the situation, it was the best sex I'd ever had because I was so physically attracted to him. His cock was enormous, and his body was jacked. I could have come from just rubbing up against him. He was by far the hottest guy I had ever slept with. Being with him did wonderful things for my ego. Like a druggie, I became quickly addicted, vowing to make him mine. I convinced myself he could grow to love me the way he loved her.

It was the middle of the summer. Mitch was allowed to stay at the dorm since he worked on campus. I had an off-campus apartment near Wellesley College and stayed to be near him even though I was supposed to have gone back to Manhattan to house sit for my parents.

When he was asleep one night, I searched his phone to find out if he'd been in contact with her. The last text received from Skylar said she was working in New York City at a fabric store that happened to be close to my parents' apartment. *Lucky me.* That was when I devised my plan. I would meet her, try to figure out what he saw in her and then create a way to keep them apart for good. I told Mitch I had to get home to take care of some things and took the US Airways shuttle the next day.

The first time I went to her work, she wasn't there, but the second time was the charm. I pretended to want to buy fabric, struck up a conversation, and she agreed to go clubbing with me.

Eventually, we ended up getting together a few times a week. She worked Thursday and Friday at the store. We would hang out those evenings and again on Saturday nights. Little did she know, I would fly back to Boston the rest of the week to be with Mitch.

I needed to know whether she still had feelings for him, and the best way to get her to open up was to get her sloshed. She said she didn't drink, so I started making her the fruitiest, girliest concoctions I could think of.

"This doesn't even taste like it has alcohol in it," she'd say.

Yup. That's the point. Drink up.

It started to work. She'd ask me to make her more drinks, and as a good little bartender, I happily obliged. One night, she told me everything I wanted to know. It was a shock to find out what she had been through, especially the cancer and the infertility. I actually felt bad for her but not enough to give her Mitch. I knew then more than ever that I had to be aggressive. She was still in love with him and would eventually realize she couldn't live without him. He'd leave me for her in a heartbeat the second she came calling. I couldn't let that happen.

The first step was to devirginize her. I was pretty convinced part of the reason Mitch held Skylar up on such a pedestal was because she was a virgin. He saw her as this angelic girl saving herself for him. That had to change. So, I enlisted my trusty manwhore of a cousin, Chad, to woo her.

From the beginning, he knew his mission. The problem was, he was supposed to stick around and romance her a little. I was hoping by some miracle, they'd actually like each other. Instead, he bailed after he found out she was still a virgin when he banged her. I knew that would deter him from helping me, so I omitted that little tidbit and let him find out on his own.

My plan backfired because after Chad screwed her over, all she would talk about was Mitch. I put on my best sympathetic front but was panicking inside. My carefully constructed plan was crumbling around me, and desperate times called for desperate measures.

I had to think long and hard. What was the one thing that would keep her away from him? There was only one answer. It also happened to be the one thing that would bind him to me. I needed to get pregnant. It was a little extreme, but keeping him was all that mattered to me. My carrying Mitch's child would traumatize her so badly that she'd have no choice but to leave us alone. He was a good guy who'd stick by me and take responsibility. He'd grow to love me because I'd give him the one thing she couldn't.

The only complication would be when she discovered my identity. What would I do if she ever ratted me out? I tried not to think that far ahead, needing to keep my eye on the prize. I could always make up a story, maybe say I didn't recognize her...call it a coincidence. It would be a long shot, but the good thing was, he didn't know I looked through his phone. If only I hadn't been stupid enough to give her my real name.

There had to be a way to turn it around. For all he knew, she came after me. I could lie and tell him *she* gave me a fake name, twist it so that it seemed like she was a crazy bitch who was stalking her ex and his new girlfriend.

The execution of this plan was going to be the hard part. Mitch was always very careful with protection. He wouldn't go near me until that condom was on. So, I knew I couldn't play the whole "I'm on the pill" thing.

When school started up again, I began suggesting that he come to my apartment instead of my going over to the dorm. I made it very enticing since I had just gotten a 60-

inch flat screen with HD, complete with access to all of the premium sports channels. He loved to watch the baseball games and didn't have cable. Whenever we'd have sex at my place, I'd reach into the nightstand and grab one of the condoms from my stash—the ones I had carefully pinned tiny holes into with a sewing needle. We had sex about six times using them. All I could do was hope.

Things had been going according to plan until one night when Mitch came over and looked like he'd been run over by a train. He told me things were getting too serious between us and that it wasn't fair to me because he was still in love with Skylar. He told me he didn't think he could ever give me anything more than a casual friends with benefits relationship and that since he knew I wanted more, he needed to end it now before it went any further.

I refused to lose him because of that self-righteous bitch. I panicked. That entire week, I called him repeatedly, begging him to reconsider. I even told him I loved him, that I'd do anything for him. I was losing my mind over it. This wasn't how things were supposed to play out. He stopped answering my calls altogether by the end of the week, and when I showed up at his dorm, his roommate said he took off to Pennsylvania for the weekend.

That night, it felt like the walls were caving in on me. There was only one ray of hope left, and I was holding the key to it in my hands. As I opened the wrapper and peed on the stick, I prayed to a God who was probably writing my ticket to hell at that very moment. After an excruciating five-minute wait, I looked at the plus sign and was *positive* that hell was where I'd end up.

PART TWO

FIVE YEARS LATER

TWENTY

SKYLAR

I let out a deep breath. "I saw him."

"You saw Mitch?"

"Yes."

"That explains the emergency appointment. I don't normally see you on a Tuesday." Dr. Rhodes crossed her legs and settled into her upholstered wingback chair. She must have known this session could run long. Since moving back into town, I had only met with her a few times before this.

"Where did you see him?"

"Kevin and I had gone to Target to pick up a few things. I was in the toothpaste aisle, and he was right there. I didn't notice him at first."

"Did you talk to him?"

"No. I froze."

"Did he say anything to you?"

"He said my name, but that was it. He was just as stunned, I think. His eyes..."

"What about his eyes?"

"There was so much emotion in them. He was almost pleading with me without even saying anything. God, he looked so different."

"How so?"

"Not in a bad way, just...new, I guess. He had tattoos on his hands, and I could see one on his neck. He didn't have a single one when we were together. And he's bigger now."

"How did seeing him make you feel?"

I tried to find the right word. There was really only one way to describe it. "Alive."

"Alive...why?"

"Feelings that have been buried for years bombarded me all at once. As long as I didn't have to see him, I could immerse myself into this life I've built with Kevin, but when he was right in front of me, it was just overwhelming. It made me realize that I hadn't really moved forward. I've just been in a holding pattern, making believe it all never happened."

"Name some of those feelings."

"Guilt."

"Why?"

"For leaving when things got rough because I couldn't handle the pain. I knew he was going through hell too because of what that bitch did. He didn't mean for it to happen, but I just couldn't be there for him, couldn't stand by and watch while she..." I shut my eyes.

Dr. Rhodes finished my sentence. "Had his baby."

I nodded as a teardrop fell. Thinking about it never got easier. Saying it out loud was impossible.

My mother and Mitch's mom had grown apart after Janis moved from across the street to live with her boyfriend in the next town over. They were also a bit divided because of what happened. So, my only connection to Mitch over the past five years had been Davey. He had explicit instructions not to tell me anything unless I asked, and he respected that because he understood how hard it was for me. I didn't even have the courage to attend Davey and Zena's wedding a couple of years ago out of fear that Mitch would be there.

All I knew was that Mitch had dropped out of BU, moved back to New Jersey and that Charisma gave birth to a boy who would now be about four-years-old. When Kevin's job transferred him here from Maryland, I had to prepare myself for the fact that I'd have to face the things I had been running from. But I wanted to come home. I missed my mother. It was time.

"You did what you felt you had to do to survive, Skylar. There's no telling that things would have been better off for him if you'd stayed. He would have had to deal with your pain as well as his own. You wouldn't have been able to change the situation if you had stuck around. You knew what you could handle, and you made the decision that was best at the time."

I picked the lint off my skirt. "Maybe."

"Besides guilt, what else did you feel when you saw him?"

This was going to make me sound horrible. "Lust. We always had a strong physical connection. I've never felt anything like it with anyone else. I wanted to touch him, but I couldn't."

"Guilt, lust...what else?"

"Fear. That might have been the most prominent. I'm afraid of what he's been through. I'm afraid that he hates me. I'm afraid he's in love with someone. I'm afraid of the unknown, and I'm not sure I ever want to know everything."

"What does Kevin know about Mitch?"

"He knows what happened before I left New Jersey, but he doesn't know about the Target run-in. When I first moved to Maryland and met Kevin, he saw how broken I was. Mitch is not one of his favorite people to put it lightly, and it's better if I keep this to myself."

"You think he'd be upset?"

"I'm not very good at hiding my feelings. If I tell him about it, he'll know."

"He'll know what?"

"Just that..."

She adjusted her glasses. "That you're still in love with Mitch."

A couple of months after the Target incident, Kevin was preparing for his usual bimonthly business trip to Virginia. He would leave on a Tuesday night and come home on Friday. Kevin worked for a medical device company as a manufacturing manager. The reason for our move home was so that he could manage their new plant in New Jersey. He still had to travel back to his old office from time to time. I didn't mind this because it gave us some space from each other. It wasn't that I didn't want to be around him, but he liked everything just so: the house clean, a warm meal every night, and he wanted to have sex more than I did. It was kind of nice to be able to just lounge around after work, eat cereal for dinner and read my book.

"Have you seen my light blue dress shirt with the white lines?"

"No."

"It's not in the closet. It's got to be in the laundry."

"Then, it's dirty."

"You haven't done any laundry since last week? What have you been doing?"

"I've worked just like you, and then I've been to the hospital a few times to visit the kids. You know that."

"Sky, I have no problem with you volunteering with sick children, but when the house starts going to shit, you really need to budget your time better."

"I can wash it real quick."

"There's no time!"

"Alright. I'm sorry."

"You should be."

Just leave. Please. So, I can breathe.

It wasn't that I hated living with Kevin. I just preferred it sometimes when he was away. He was difficult to live with, but I respected him. He made me feel safe and had saved me during a time when I wasn't sure I was going to survive.

Depression had taken over my life when I first moved to Maryland. It was just one month after Mitch discovered Charisma was pregnant. There were still a lot of unknowns, such as whether she could prove he was the father. I couldn't bear to be anywhere near him, so I took off without a plan, initially moving in with a high school friend who went to college out there.

When I asked Davey about the baby shortly after it was born, he told me that a DNA test confirmed Mitch's paternity. That was all I needed to hear. At that point, I knew I wasn't coming home, so I enrolled in design school and got my own place.

I had just started my freshman year at Maryland School of Design and lived in an off-campus apartment when I met Kevin. He was my downstairs neighbor, five years older and established in his career. Spending time with him gave me something to do besides thinking about what I left behind. It started as a casual friendship. Kevin was a foodie and introduced me to eclectic cuisines, like Ethiopian and Moroccan. Over time, our relationship turned into something more. When I finally opened up to him about Mitch, he vowed to help me forget. Sex with Kevin was good—not as great as what I imagined with Mitch—but certainly better than my first time with Chad. In recent years, though, the spark that existed in the early days had significantly waned. It was sad, but lately, touching myself was preferable to intercourse with Kevin.

He was packing his small suitcase, placing travel-sized toiletries into plastic bags. His flight was at 7:00 in the evening. "I left you a list of stuff I need you to do for me this week on a sticky note. It's hanging on the fridge."

"Okay."

He liked to think I was his secretary. He made more money than I did in my job as an interior designer, so I guess he felt I had to earn my place here. Kevin did provide a good life for me. I didn't want for anything and never had to worry about paying the bills. Even though I resented him sometimes, I felt the good outweighed the bad. No man is perfect, right?

"And Sky, don't forget we have dinner with one of my supervisors, Ray Michaelson and his wife on Friday night. Buy yourself something nice to wear, not like that red dress you wore last time. That was too low cut in the front."

Note to self: buy dress with low back to the ass to compensate.

"Got it."

My anxiety lessened with each second that passed as his suitcase rolled toward the door. "I'll call you when I get in tonight." He gave me a peck on the lips.

"Have a safe flight."

As always, I stood at the window until his car was completely out of sight before I let out a deep breath and plopped on the couch with my kindle.

After an hour or so, I meandered into the kitchen and poured some Lucky Charms into a bowl. Dinner. Done. Leaning against the counter eating my cereal, I noticed the to-do list plastered on the fridge. Pick up dry cleaning. Organize junk drawer. I stuck my middle finger up at the sticky note and took a marker to it.

I remembered that Dancing with the Stars was on and took advantage of the fact that I'd have the television to myself. Kevin wouldn't be caught dead watching one of my shows. When he was home, I'd usually read in the bedroom while he watched the History Channel or BBC America. Halfway into some football player's Paso Doble, I got bored, put on my reading glasses and opted to start my new book.

During a pivotal sex scene, my mind drifted, and suddenly, the image in my head of the main male character transformed into Mitch. He was dressed exactly as I remembered him from Target: paint-stained jeans, unruly hair and big, rough, hands with tattooed letters on his fingers. Mitch had gotten even more painstakingly handsome with age and had clearly been working out. His new rough exterior was definitely working for me. It hurt just as much as it brought me pleasure to have these thoughts. Still, I just couldn't stop. With my eyes closed, I imagined Mitch doing the things to the heroine that the author described—the heroine who happened to be my Doppelganger. I clutched my pink blanket in frustration and continued to read until I fell asleep.

A loud bang woke me up. It sounded like gunfire or an explosion, and I immediately hopped up from the couch. With a palpitating heart, I ran out the front door.

Smoke was billowing from a car across the street. A man in a dark hood stood in front of it with his back facing me as I approached cautiously.

"Is everything okay out here?"

He didn't say anything. My nerves kicked in because it dawned on me that I could have just interrupted an attempted break-in. He wasn't moving, and just as I was about to run back inside and call the police, he turned around.

Crystal blue eyes lit up from under the darkness of the hood. "Skylar...it's me."

The shock nearly knocked the wind out of me, and I shuffled backwards. My breath was visible in the frigid night air as I tried to catch it. "Mitch?"

We silently stared at each other until headlights from an approaching car forced me to move out of the way and closer to him. His familiar smell invaded my senses, triggering an acute onset of unwanted desire. My body was still frozen as I stood there confused. My teeth chattered.

He broke the silence. "I'm sorry. It's cold. Go back inside."

There was that look again, the same pleading look he gave me at Target, like his eyes were screaming a million things at me while he said nothing. Something deep within me was screaming back at him even louder despite my own silence.

"What are you doing here?" I finally managed to ask.

Several seconds later, his voice was hoarse when he said, "I don't know." He looked down at the pavement and repeated in a whisper, "I don't fucking know what I'm doing here."

"You happened to be outside of my house late at night looking like the Grim Reaper setting off fireworks or some shit, and that's all you have to say?"

He looked up at the sky and laughed, shaking his head. "You always manage to make me laugh at myself even in the worst situations. How do you do that?"

My tone softened. "Seriously, what's going on?"

"There's no good answer for that. So, I'd better go. I'll call a tow truck for my car."

He started to walk away.

It felt like I was losing control of my bladder. Even though I was afraid to talk to him for fear of having to face things that would shatter me, I just couldn't let him walk away. "Wait. Don't go."

He stopped in his tracks and turned around, looking surprised as he walked back toward me. "I'm here." He said it with a level of raw emotion that told me he meant it in more ways than one.

I swallowed, and my heart beat faster with every step he took.

What was I doing?

"Do you want to come in?"

TWENTY-ONE

MITCH

Hell yes, I wanna come in.

I nodded and followed her across the street and up the few steps to her door.

"Thank you for inviting me in," I said, wiping my feet on the autumn leaves that were etched on her welcome mat.

Skylar's home was warm and welcoming. Walking in there had felt like a small reprieve from hell for a quick glimpse into heaven. There was simply no place else in the world I'd rather have been.

Still in shock that she even asked me inside, I followed her into the bright white and marble kitchen. She immediately began pouring water into a stainless steel kettle. "I'll make some tea. You look like you could use it."

Spiked with Jack Daniels would be ideal, but I'll take it.

"Thanks," I said as I lowered by hood.

My eyes wandered over to the refrigerator where a list written on a sticky note had the words "Yeah...fuck you" written over it in red Sharpie. *What was that all about?*

She interrupted my thoughts. "How long were you out there anyway?"

"About an hour...or more."

She didn't need to pry any further about what I was doing out there because at this point, it was painfully obvious.

She looked back at me as she reached into her cupboard for cups. "Notice anything interesting?"

"Huh?"

"While you were out there?"

I chuckled. "You still bite your lower lip when you're concentrating on something."

"And?"

"You smile to yourself for a long time after you laugh at the television."

"Anything else?"

"Your roof could use an update."

"Wow...call 1-800-Stalker, get free home improvement advice." When she cracked a small smile, I returned it and started to calm down.

The teapot whistled, and she went to the stove to pour the steaming water into two ceramic cups. She added sugar and milk without asking because she knew how I liked it. She placed the cup on a saucer and as she handed it to me, it shook from her trembling hand. Even though she had been joking around, I was clearly making her nervous. My chest filled with hope because that only confirmed that I still had an effect on her.

My hand intentionally lingered on hers for a few seconds as she handed me the tea. "Thank you." Then, the reflection of something glimmering caught my eyes, which were now glued to the large diamond on her left ring finger. My entire body tensed, and my heart felt like it was going to leap out of my chest.

Fuck. Me. She was engaged.

She noticed me looking down at it, and then our eyes met.

After a long moment of silence, she broke the ice. "So, what have you been up to the past five years, Mitch? Whoa...déjà vu. Haven't I asked you that before?"

"Yes. Except this time *you're* the one that disappeared."

Her smile faded, and it was clear I had touched a nerve. She looked down. "I did, didn't I? I'm sorry. I just couldn't—"

"Please...don't." My tone was harsher than intended. I immediately lowered my voice. "You don't owe me an apology. I understand exactly why you left. I'm just sorry I put you in a position where you felt you had to run away from home. Don't ever blame yourself for my mistakes. *Ever*. What happened was all my fault, Skylar."

She closed her eyes and let out a long, seemingly endless breath.

I just wanted to fucking hold her.

"My being here is upsetting you. Do you want me to leave?"

"No. I knew I'd have to face you sooner or later. I just wasn't prepared for it to be tonight."

"I know. It wasn't supposed to be like this. I didn't mean to—"

"Get caught?"

I couldn't help but smile. "Yeah."

"You're not a very good stalker. You should keep your day job."

"Well, what kind of victim are you, inviting me in for Sleepytime tea?"

Every time our eyes met, you could practically feel the static in the air. It pleased me to no end that despite all that had happened, our connection was still as strong as ever.

The heat in her house was blasting, and I was burning up. "Do you mind if I take off my jacket?"

"Sure."

Her eyes wandered down to my chest as soon as I removed it. At least my workout addiction was paying off. I did it to burn off steam, but if Skylar liked what she saw, then that was a huge bonus.

She swallowed. "You look good."

"So do you...amazing, actually." Did she ever. She had filled out in all the right places. She was still petite, just a little curvier than I remembered. She wasn't wearing a bra under her white cotton shirt, probably because she wasn't expecting guests. So, I had to force my eyes upward. Now was not the time to get caught staring at her tits. She already outed me as a "stalker," a not so distant cousin to "perv." My jaw tightened when it hit me that her beautiful body belonged to another man now. *Him*. That was impossible to accept. Adrenaline pumped through me. I needed to get her back. I didn't care if it took me forever.

The first step was getting the hard part out of the way.

I put my tea on the counter and looked deeply into her eyes. "I know you don't want to hear it, but please let me tell you everything."

She looked away and then quickly nodded her head. "Okay." She wrapped her arms around herself. Whatever light mood existed minutes ago was gone. "It's like I've been in a coma for five years, and I'm just waking up, Mitch. It still feels like it was just yesterday."

It took everything in me not to reach for her. I was dying to take her in my arms, to tell her how sorry I was for all of the pain my actions had caused, but I knew I needed to keep my distance.

"I'll only tell you what you want to know. Davey told me about your little agreement, that you didn't want him to tell you anything unless you asked. So, I want you to direct this conversation. Ask me anything, okay? Don't be afraid."

"Let's go in the living room."

I followed her into the room that had been the backdrop of my window into her world these past couple of months. It felt strange to be sitting on the same cream-colored sofa I used to stare at from my car. It was like walking into my favorite television show.

She sat on the farthest end of the couch from me. A picture of Skylar and *him* standing in front of the Washington monument taunted me from the end table.

"You have a little boy..."

"Yes. His name is Henry."

A teardrop fell from her eye almost instantly after I said his name. I guess that made it real for her. I wished she could have known him. She would have felt differently. He was my world now.

She sniffled. "He's four?"

"Yes."

Her mouth quivered. "Is she around? Are you with her?"

"With Charisma?" I couldn't believe she would even think that. My tone was shrill. "Of course, not...after what she did to you...to us? You think I would get involved with that crazy bitch?" That question had angered me, and I suddenly realized why she was so scared to find out information about me. She actually thought there was a chance Charisma was a part of my life. That broke my heart. I needed to clarify this real fast. "The only good thing that woman ever did was give birth to my son. Other than that, she's garbage as far as I'm concerned. Actually...she did one other good thing. She took off."

"What?"

"I have full custody."

"I don't understand. How could she do that?"

"I need to tell you the whole story. Can I?"

Clutching the pink blanket, she nodded and settled into her seat.

I took a deep breath and geared myself up. "After you left, my grades were in the toilet, and I lost my scholarship because it was contingent on keeping up a certain GPA every semester. One strike, you're out. So, I moved home. Charisma stayed back at Wellesley the whole time she was pregnant. I still didn't know at that point if the baby was even mine. I was in a really rough place. The following summer, he was born in Manhattan. She put my name on the certificate as the father. A DNA test later confirmed it. I still don't understand how it happened since I was never with her without protection. Anyway, she tried one last time to convince me to give her a chance. She tried to lie to me about what happened between you and her and tried to make it seem like she didn't have this whole thing planned out. But I knew better. You have to know, I never once considered being with her, Skylar...not even for a split second."

She let out a sigh of relief but said nothing.

I continued, "That summer, I got a job working in construction and would travel to New York on weekends to see Henry. She told me she was planning on going back to Wellesley to finish her last year that fall. When I asked who would be taking care of the baby, she told me her parents were going to hire someone. It didn't feel right. I told her I wanted to take my son to live with me while she was in school. My mother offered to stay home and watch him while I worked. Charisma actually agreed to it. She saw him maybe three times that school year. I didn't care because I didn't want her bad energy around him. After she graduated, she took a job in New York and told me she was gonna fight for full custody. She took me to court, and the judge ruled that she could have him during the week, and I'd get him on weekends. I'm pretty sure hired strangers were taking care of him during those weeks."

"I don't get it. How did she end up agreeing to your getting full custody?"

"When Henry turned two, things changed. We started to notice that he didn't have the same kind of eye contact as other kids, and he wasn't using any words. He wasn't pointing to things. He stopped sleeping through the night and was having a lot of tantrums where he'd be inconsolable. Even with the little time she spent with him, she couldn't handle him anymore. She was too self-centered to deal with it. Her new boyfriend was from Europe and wanted her to travel. Let's just say, Henry wouldn't do well on a Transatlantic flight. She started letting me have him more often. Eventually, I asked for full custody, and she just...gave it to me. Skylar, she didn't even put up a fight."

"I just...wow. I can't believe that."

"A year ago, she moved to London with the boyfriend. She's seen her son one time since then. So, anyway...fuck her. Around the time she moved, I got him in to see a neurologist. They diagnosed him with something called pervasive developmental disorder, but it's since been upgraded to autism."

"Henry still can't talk?"

I offered a slight smile, unable to contain my relief that she used my son's name. I didn't want her to view him in a negative light because of how he came into the world. He didn't deserve that. "No. He tries to sound out some words, but he's non-verbal. It's not easy. My mother has been a huge help. We finally got him on this waiting list for state-funded therapy, but it hasn't started up yet. Thank God my job has good benefits to cover all these doctor appointments."

"You're still working in construction?"

"Yeah, but I manage the company now, too. I'm also a part owner. So, it's a mix of site work and office stuff. It's a good gig. Where are you working?"

"I'm actually trying to start my own interior design business. I only have a couple of private clients right now. So, business is slow, but self-promotion is the full-time job. I'm designing a website myself at the moment."

"That's really cool. That was always what you said you wanted to do...interior design."

She changed the subject back to Henry. "Do you have a picture of him?"

"As a matter of fact, I do." I took out my phone and scrolled through, pulling up a photo of Henry in the bathtub smiling with suds all over his head. "He loves the water."

She covered her mouth with her hand, and her eyes became watery again as she took the phone from me. I didn't ask what she was thinking because it felt like a private moment. I had to remind myself she was seeing him for the first time. As she continued to gaze at the image, I took the opportunity to gaze at her. With every passing second, I wondered how the hell I was going to walk out of here tonight. I couldn't even seem to move from this couch.

I didn't want to ask, but I had to know what I was up against. "Tell me about this guy you're with. Where is he tonight?"

"Kevin."

Kevin.

"You're really going to marry him?"

"He asked me. I said yes."

"But is there a date set?"

"No."

Thank fuck. I think I just got hard.

"You never said where he was."

"He goes away for a few days to Virginia twice a month."

That explained why sometimes he wasn't home.

"Are you happy?"

She didn't respond.

"This house is a fucking mess, Sky."

"What the hell was that?" I asked.

"You don't know who that is?"

"Seamus? He's still alive?"

She got up from the couch, went upstairs and returned with the bird propped on her finger. She handed him to me.

"Hey, little guy. Remember me?"

He flapped his wings in excitement. *"This house is a fucking mess, Sky."*

"Why is he saying that?"

"He overheard Kevin and me arguing one night. That was the phrase that stuck. You know how unpredictable he can be."

Kevin sounds like a real winner.

I looked Seamus in the eye. Over the past five years, this bird has seen everything I wasn't able to. He was being really friendly to me, which was uncharacteristic. I liked to think he was sending me a message. At least that was what I thought until he sprayed me with lime green shit droplets. "Aw, man! You haven't changed one bit!"

Skylar couldn't contain her laughter. "You look like you got slimed at the Kids Choice Awards."

"What have you been giving him to eat? Goddamn."

She took Seamus. "I'll bring him back to his cage and get you a clean shirt."

She ran upstairs and returned with a plain white t-shirt, throwing it to me. "Here. He won't miss this."

"Are you sure?"

She was still laughing. "It's fine."

As I lifted off my soiled shirt, I watched closely to gauge her reaction.

"Whoa. When did you get all those?"

Her eyes zoned in on the three tattoos on my chest, specifically the one of her name scrawled across the top.

"Does that make you uncomfortable?"

"No."

I pointed to the name tattoo. "This one was done right after you left. I got most of them during the time I'd moved back home before Henry was born. It became like an addiction. I was trying to find a way to express how lost I was without you—still am in many ways. The only difference is now I have my son to take my mind off it."

She slowly walked toward me and ran her fingertips from left to right across the letters that spelled out *SKYLAR*. She placed her hand over my heart that was beating out of control. She kept her hand there as she looked down at the words spread across my abdomen.

To be continued...because true love never ends.

Then, she placed her hand on my inner forearm where it said, *Time can't heal wounds that cut through your heart.*

She looked up at me. "They're beautiful."

"So are you."

Fighting the urge to grab her and kiss her senseless, I slipped the clean garment over my head. As she continued to look up at me, I felt it. Her heart still belonged to me. I didn't want to live without her anymore, but it would be a long road to getting her back. It would be worth it. I just had to be patient and not rush things. I needed to start by being her friend again. I would rebuild what we had from the ground up.

In that moment, I vowed that no matter what it took, the shirt wouldn't be the only thing I'd be stealing from him.

TWENTY-TWO

SKYLAR

Kevin pulled out my chair. “You really look stunning tonight.”

“Thanks.”

I decided not to intentionally embarrass him for once and kept my wardrobe choice modest. Even though ruffling his feathers was more fun, I figured it was the least I could do considering the better part of the past week was spent fantasizing over my ex-boyfriend’s chest, which had apparently become a shrine in honor of me.

Tonight, we were at dinner with one of Kevin’s co-workers, Ray Michaelson and his wife, Linda.

Linda placed a cloth napkin on her lap. “So, Sky, Kevin tells me you’re an interior designer?”

“Yes. I’m starting my own company, actually. It’s still in the early stages. What do you do?”

“I don’t work, but I chair my community Agriburbia board.”

“Agri what?”

“Agriburbia.”

"That sounds like a digestive issue..."

Kevin put his fork down. "Sky..."

I whispered, "I was just making a joke. Sorry."

Linda continued, "Actually, it's a concept for integrating agricultural production with housing developments."

"Ah...very nice." I took a sip of water.

Kevin rolled his eyes.

"Have you two set a date?" Ray asked.

I hated this question. "Well—"

Kevin chimed in. "I was thinking summer. What about you, Sky?"

"We haven't really discussed it, Kev."

"I know, but summer would be ideal, and we're not having anything big anyway, so we should have enough time to plan."

"Okay, well, we should talk about this in private another time."

Linda clasped her hands together. "Summer weddings are fabulous. You could book something down the shore or...Ray, what about your uncle who lives in the Hamptons? Do you think he'd be willing to rent out his house for the event? Wouldn't that be the perfect venue for a wedding?"

Great. Now, agriburbibitch was planning my wedding?

"I think we'll be good, but thank you."

Kevin turned to her. "Actually, Linda, would you mind looking into that? A Hamptons wedding might be nice."

I cleared my throat. "Excuse me. Don't I have a say in this?"

"Sky...come on. I just asked her to look into it."

"Well, I don't want to get married in the Hamptons."

Ray and Linda quietly munched on their salads as the mood became tense.

After dinner that night, Kevin paused before starting the car.

"Do you mind telling me what's going on with you? They were trying to be helpful, and you shit all over it."

"I just don't like people prying into my life when I didn't ask them to."

"It's more than that."

"What do you mean?"

"You've been distant. It's been that way for a couple of months."

I hadn't realized how transparent it was. Mitch was all I could focus on lately. My feelings for him weren't going to disappear, but it wasn't feasible to think that he and I could actually have a future, that we could just pick up where we left off. There was a child involved now, and I wasn't sure I could ever move past what happened in order to accept Henry the way he deserved and the way I would need to in order to be with Mitch. But I just couldn't stop thinking about him: the passionate way he looked at me, the love he had for Henry, his smell, how his heart beat against his smooth, hard chest that now bore my name. Thoughts of Mitch were consuming my life.

At the same time, I truly cared about Kevin. He didn't deserve to be strung along while I dealt with these other feelings. We had our moments, but deep down, he was a good man. Kevin had been my safety net for so long, and losing him could mean ending up alone altogether.

I needed to say whatever it took to keep the peace while my head got sorted out. "I'm sorry. It's just the stress of starting the business. I'll try not to let it show in front of other people like that."

"I'm sorry, too. I've been so busy with work and hadn't realized it was getting to you like that. I know I'm tough to live with sometimes. I'll try to be more understanding of the stress you're under." He leaned in and kissed me. "Speaking of stress, let's go home, get into bed and relieve some of it. I know just the way to make you feel better. You'll see."

Unfortunately, that night, as Kevin made love to me, the only thing I *saw* was Mitch.

It had been a couple of weeks since the night Mitch came over. We had exchanged cell phone numbers, and he told me to call him if I ever needed anything. The temptation to contact him was ever present, but I couldn't come up with an excuse.

It was a Wednesday night and Kevin was in Virginia when a text came in.

Did you know stalkers deliver food now? Are you hungry?

Butterflies fluttered in my stomach at the thought of seeing him.

Skylar: How did you know I was alone?

Mitch: I remembered you saying he goes away on business every other week. I have it marked on my calendar.

Skylar: That's very stalkerish of you.

Mitch: I'm perfecting my craft.

Skylar: Apparently.

Mitch: Would you prefer to go out to eat?

My hands were on the keypad, but I wasn't sure what to type. He must have sensed my apprehension when he didn't wait for my response.

Mitch: I'm not asking you on a date. I know you're engaged. Don't worry. I respect that. I just want to spend time with you.

Why did it disappoint me that he wasn't asking me on a date? I was sick in the head and suddenly felt guilty. *Kevin.*

For all I knew, Mitch might have been involved with someone, too. We never actually discussed that.

Despite all of the logical reasons why this was a bad idea, the need to see him again was overwhelming.

Skylar: Pick me up at 8. What should I wear?

Mitch: Casual. I'll be wearing all black as usual.

Skylar: Don't forget your binoculars, creeper.

Mitch: ;-)

When the bell rang, my legs shook in anticipation as I walked to the door and opened it.

He lifted his hand up. "Hi."

His smile nearly melted me, and I had the urge to run my tongue along his perfect teeth. This wasn't a good start.

"Hi," I whispered. Any promise I had made myself to view him platonically tonight had gone down the tubes the second our eyes met. "I'll get my coat."

Calm down, Skylar.

Mitch was wearing dark jeans and a gray ribbed sweater that clung to his muscles. His wet hair was messy in the best way, and he smelled like the same musky cologne I remembered sniffing all over my body after our one night together in Lake George. I hated being reminded of that right now. The muscles in between my legs clenched, and I wasn't even touching him.

He'd brought the same Corvette that was broken down last time.

I joked, "I see you fixed the stalker mobile."

"Yeah...that plan *backfired*, right?" He laughed and the familiar sound momentarily took me back to a place in time I never wanted to leave.

"Good one," I said.

"Seriously, I'm grateful it broke down. I'd be sitting out here in the cold tonight watching you instead of taking you out to dinner."

"Do you mind if I drive it?"

"Sure." He threw me the keys.

"How do you drive Henry around with no backseat?"

"I have a Ford F150. This car is just a hobby. It's older. I got a good deal on it and fixed it up."

When I turned the engine on, *Every Breath You Take* by The Police was playing. "Ah, the stalker's anthem, I see."

"I dug up my old c.d. just for you."

I shook my head and pulled out onto the street.

"Where are we going anyway?" I asked.

"I thought maybe you'd want to hit Bev's."

Bev's was my absolute favorite diner. It was closer to the neighborhood where my mother lived. We'd gone there quite a bit before he left for college, so we had a lot of good memories at that restaurant. The menu was massive, and it was a 24-hour place, so you could order breakfast for dinner or vice versa.

Once on the freeway, I decided to have a little fun. Before I knew it, I was going 90 with the windows down.

Mitch yelled through the vibrating wind. "Whoa, take it easy. We're in no rush."

My hair was blowing around as I shouted the first thing that came to mind, "This from the guy who came in his pants."

My leg stiffened when he smacked it playfully. "You little shit. Thanks for remembering that...of all things." The quick contact of his hand on my thigh had given me goosebumps. I hated that I wanted him to do it again.

We laughed a lot during that ride. By the time we got to Bev's, I was sure my hair looked like a bird's nest. "How do I look?"

"Like you've been driving around in a car with the window down going 90."

"Hideous?"

"You are *so* hideous," he said with an expression on his face that told me he was thinking the opposite as his eyes lingered on mine.

"I'm starving," I said as I opened the car door, slamming it unintentionally hard.

"Easy now."

"Sorry, I guess I'm a little nervous all of a sudden."

"Nervous...why?"

"It's weird being back here with you."

"Do you want to leave?"

"No."

"Good."

Bells jingled as we entered the diner. The nostalgic smell of freshly baked pie and coffee was the first thing that hit me. Nancy, a longtime waitress, brought us to a booth in the corner. "I haven't seen you kids in ages."

"Yeah, it's been a long time," Mitch said.

She looked down at my ring finger as she handed me a menu. "Congratulations, you two. What a rock! I always knew you would end up getting married."

She walked away faster than we could respond. The smile on Mitch's face had disappeared, and he was now staring at my ring, looking more upset than I had seen him since we reconnected.

I moved my hand to my lap out of sight. "I'm sorry about that."

"Don't be," he said abruptly.

I needed to change the subject stat. "Do you know what you want?"

Without looking down at the menu, he said, "Yes." His eyes never left mine. I looked at the ceiling, feeling suddenly shy because it seemed like he wasn't talking about the food.

I coughed. "I think I'm gonna get the pastrami on rye."

"You always get that."

"Yeah...but I haven't had one as good as this one in five years."

"I know how that feels," he said under his breath, looking down. When he looked at me again, he said, "It doesn't seem like that long, does it?"

"No."

Nancy came back. "What would you like?"

Mitch gestured for me to start.

"I'll have the pastrami on rye and a Diet Coke."

He continued to look at me while he said, "Bacon cheeseburger with extra ketchup and a Sprite."

"You got it," Nancy said as she took our menus.

An awkward silence ensued after she left. Having no menu to hide behind left me feeling suddenly naked under the weight of his stare. He looked so handsome, and I worried he could see the want all over my face. As he licked his lips, I imagined running my fingers through his hair and pulling him toward me into a kiss. Someone needed to notify my body that this wasn't a date and that it was inappropriate to be having these thoughts while engaged to another man.

I looked down at his tattooed knuckles to distract myself from the glare of his hypnotic eyes. I was afraid to ask what the letters stood for. Then, my eyes traveled up to the neck tattoo peeking out from the top of his sweater. It was some sort of tribal or Celtic marking. I felt guilty for wanting to lick it in a line up to his mouth. I hated myself for all of these feelings and started fidgeting, causing our legs to collide under the table.

"Sorry," I said.

He ignored me and crossed his arms. "Why do you let him call you Sky?"

"He doesn't know I hate it."

"Why don't you tell him?"

"He started calling me Sky from the very beginning.

When I first met him, I wasn't exactly thinking straight. I wasn't sure if I even wanted to be Skylar anymore back then."

He momentarily shut his eyes. "Tell me about that... about your time in Maryland."

"What do you want to know?"

"Everything."

Over the next several minutes, I explained as best as I could, how bad my mental state was when I left and how I met Kevin soon after but that it took a while for us to actually get together. He nodded in silence as I recalled the past five years. He clung to each and every word as if he didn't want to miss any part of it.

When our food arrived, I wanted to lighten the mood. I couldn't eat unless something changed. "What kinds of foods does Henry like?"

"Unfortunately, he's very picky. He'll only eat chicken nuggets, McDonald's fries and mac and cheese easily. It has to be certain nuggets, too, like the dinosaur ones and only Kraft macaroni. Everything else is a struggle. I make him protein shakes for nutrients, mixing peanut butter and some fruit with almond milk. He'll drink those, but I can't get him to pick up a fruit or a vegetable on his own."

"That's typical of kids with autism, right? Food texture issues?"

"Yeah. How did you know that?"

"I was looking up autism online after you told me about Henry."

He stopped chewing and wiped his mouth with a napkin. "Wow...that's...thank you...for doing that."

"I don't like being ignorant. I hadn't thought about autism all that much before and never knew anyone affected by it. But now, I do. So...I want to understand."

"Thank you." He smiled at me. "You said something last time about volunteering at the hospital?"

"Yeah. I visit kids who are sick with cancer and try to cheer them up. I'm basically a—"

"Candy striper!" He laughed and pointed at me. "Oh my God. You—Skylar Seymour—have become one of those broads you used to tell me annoyed the crap out of you when you were sick."

"Yes...yes, except I'm a progressive striper. I'm the cool one. I don't blow smoke up their asses and try to make them feel like they should be happy when they're not. I give them what they need and let them know it's okay to be angry. I spruce up their rooms and bring them stuff they want, like candy cigarettes..."

"You're giving a kid with cancer cigarettes?"

"*Candy* cigarettes! One little boy wanted those. So, I got them for him. My job is to do whatever it takes to make them happy. That's what I'm there for."

"They're lucky."

"Lucky? Not quite..."

"No, I mean...they're lucky because they have you. Anyone who's been lucky enough to have you in their lives has been blessed."

"I don't know what to say."

"I just hope Kevin knows how lucky *he* is." He took a sip of his Sprite. He looked hesitant to say something and began playing with his straw before looking up at me. "Are you happy?"

I was silent because I honestly didn't know how to answer that. Happy wasn't the right word. *Safe*, maybe. In some ways, that might have been more important to me after everything I'd been through. With Kevin, I felt secure, albeit not 100-percent fulfilled. With Mitch, I had been truly happy in every way at one time, only to have it all implode.

He continued through my silence. "Look, Skylar, I meant it when I said I respect your situation. I want us to be friends again and won't try to interfere in your relationship. If you're genuinely happy, I would never impose on that."

He looked out the window and seemed to be lost in thought. Silverware clinked all around us while I stared at his reflection and wondered what he was really thinking. Why did it suddenly disappoint me that he wasn't begging me to break up with Kevin or that he wasn't trying to fight for me?

Instead of answering his earlier question, I simply said, "I appreciate that."

Mitch opened one of the ketchup packets and began to squeeze it into his mouth. It was a habit he had since childhood.

"You still do that?"

"Yup," he said, opening another one.

The image of his mouth sucking hard on the plastic triggered an unintentional flashback of those same lips doing the very same thing when he went down on me. The muscles between my legs contracted as I imagined him doing it to me right then and there, remembering all too clearly how amazing it had felt. Kevin never did it, and I hadn't missed it...until now.

"Actually, that's kind of gross," I said. "Can you stop?"

Mitch took the driver's seat on the way home from Bev's.

"Did your mom tell you I built an addition on my mother's house? Well, technically, it's my house now that she lives with Fred."

"No. She didn't."

My mother, like everyone else, was under strict instructions not to talk about Mitch. So, it was no surprise she hadn't mentioned it.

"I don't really see Tish anymore, but I know she must have noticed me working out there from across the street. It was under construction for months. I wasn't sure if she mentioned it to you."

"What kind of addition?"

"Well, you know our house doesn't have much space. So, I wanted a room where Henry could play and run around in the winter. I built one off the side of the living area."

"That's so cool that you were able to do that yourself."

He glanced at me and smiled. "I've learned a few things working in construction over the past several years. Would you want to drive by real quick and see it? We're not far. We won't go inside. I'll just show you the exterior."

"Sure."

Jitters developed as we drove down my old street and pulled into his driveway. My mother had been to visit Kevin and me since we moved home, but I hadn't been back here, mainly out of fear of running into Mitch. The lights were off in my mother's house across the street, and I remembered she had her book club tonight. Mitch came around and opened the passenger door, helping me out of the Corvette.

"We'll just walk around the side real quick. Then, I'll take you home."

I was surprised at how big the new structure looked from the outside. "This must have been a lot of work. That's no small room."

"Yeah, well, we've got a trampoline in there and a lot of stuff for his therapy when it starts, so we kind of need all of the space."

"Wow, good job."

"Thanks. It's cold. We can get going. I just wanted you to see it."

Just as we were about to enter the car, a light came on, and the front door opened. Janis came running out. "Mitch, I'm glad you're home. He's upstairs. I can't get him to sleep. He's—" She stopped talking when she noticed me in the passenger seat and squinted. "Skylar? Is that you?"

She looked like she had seen a ghost.

I waved awkwardly like a teenager sneaking around who just got caught. "Hi, Janis."

She approached the car. "Hi. I, uh, wasn't expecting to see you, honey. I...I'm sorry. I thought Mitch was alone. I'll let you two —"

"Mom, it's okay. Skylar's back in town, and we were just meeting up for some dinner to catch up. I wanted to show her the addition from the outside before I drove her home. What's wrong with Henry?"

"He's been up. He just won't stop crying. Something is frustrating him, and he started biting his hand."

Mitch put his head on the steering wheel. "Shit." He turned to me. "I better go in real quick, see if I can get him down. Do you mind?"

"Of course, not. I'll wait here."

"It's cold. This could take a little bit. Will you come in?"

"I—"

"Skylar and I will have some tea while you get Henry to sleep," Janis said, nodding to me in a silent plea to come inside.

"Okay. Sure."

My heart was beating rapidly, unsure of what to expect. The door creaked as we entered the house. It was dark except for a lamp on in the living room, and the evening news was on low volume. I could immediately hear Henry crying upstairs, and it made my heart beat faster. It sounded like he was jumping on the bed.

Mitch turned around at the bottom of the stairs before heading up. "I'll be back, okay?"

Janis put her hand on my arm. "Come sit with me."

As we entered the familiar kitchen with the same wooden chairs and the same flowered seat cushions, I thought how about ironic it was that everything was the same, yet so different.

She turned on the stove and put a pot of water on to heat then sat across from me. "He didn't tell me he was going to see you. He said he had to meet a friend."

"Technically, that was the truth."

"You're no friend, Skylar. You mean so much more to him, more than you could ever comprehend. You don't know what things were like here after you left."

I felt ill-prepared to have this conversation but wanted to know more. I noticed that the crying upstairs had stopped.

"Tell me."

She leaned in and whispered, "He would kill me if he knew I was saying any of this to you." She got up to grab the kettle and poured hot water into two mugs. "I was so worried for him after you left. He was drinking all of the time. Then, there was the arrest."

"Arrest? For what?"

"He was cleared, but I think you should let him tell you that story."

An image of Mitch behind metal bars appeared in my head. I was silent as she continued.

"He wouldn't talk to me, wouldn't talk to anyone. I was really scared I was going to lose him." She steeped the tea bag into my mug and handed it to me. "By the time Henry was born, Mitch was still hurting, but he stepped up to the plate and stayed strong for his son. When he finally opened up to me months later, I realized he was more tormented about the fact that he thought he'd hurt you beyond repair than anything else."

"I was devastated. That was why I left, but I never fully blamed him. It still hurts, but I'm okay. I don't think it's anyone's fault but hers."

"I'm sorry about everything that happened, Skylar. I'm sorry you left, that you were hurt, and I'm most sorry that Tish and I grew apart because of it. I really miss her."

I reached for her hand across the table. "That makes me more sad than you know."

She looked down at my ring. "You're engaged?"

"Yes."

"Promise me something?"

"Okay..."

"Promise me you won't lead Mitch on. If you say you're his friend...be one. Don't cross the line then leave. He couldn't handle losing you again. I know my son, and I know how much he still loves you. He never stopped. He may be telling you he's okay with this friendship thing, but you're still very much under his skin. I can't bear to see him hurt again."

It was a lot to take in. "I won't hurt him, Janis."

She took my tea from my hands and placed it on the table. "Go meet my grandson."

"What?"

"Don't be scared. He's a little Mitch. He's got the same big blue eyes. He can't speak, but I know he can understand us."

"She's really not around at all?"

"No, honey. Were you worried about that? She was never a part of our lives. She calls to check on Henry once in a blue moon, mostly when she knows my son is at work. She doesn't want to deal with Mitch, and the feeling is mutual. She claims she might be coming in the summer, but who knows? We're better off without the aggravation. It would only screw up Henry's routine if she came around."

"I have recurring dreams about beating the shit out of her."

"Don't pay them any mind. She's not worth any of our time. Go upstairs. See Henry. He might even be sleeping by now."

I stood up and put the mug on the counter. Tensely gripping the handrail, I slowly walked up the stairs.

The door to Mitch's bedroom was slightly open, and he was lying on the bed with Henry. There was one night light on. He didn't see me peeking through the crack of the door and was unaware that I could hear him talking to his son.

"She was everything to me once, like you are now. I want you to meet her. Her name is Skylar. I can't believe she's actually here."

Henry was awake, staring vacantly, humming but non-responsive. That didn't stop Mitch from talking to him in the same manner he would were he expecting the boy to say something back.

Mitch kissed him on the head. "You feel better now that I'm here, don't you? I love you, buddy."

A feeling so intense it was unidentifiable built inside my heart upon seeing Mitch as a father like this. Yet, his situation was different than most. You had to be an extraordinary person to parent a child who needed round the clock care and still demonstrate the patience and love he clearly had for Henry.

I coughed so that he knew I was there.

Mitch sat up. "How long were you standing there?"

"Not long."

"Come in." He turned to Henry who was calm but staring into space. "Henry, this is who I was telling you about...Daddy's special friend. This is Skylar."

I sat at the edge of the bed. "Hi, Henry. It's so nice to meet you."

He said nothing and didn't look at me. He blinked a few times as he stared at the wall.

"Is he feeling better?"

"Yeah. He's used to me putting him to bed. So, I think he was just acting up for my mother. As soon as I got up here, he stopped crying. I brought him here to my room in the hopes that if I lay down with him, he'd fall asleep. I'll transfer him back to his own bed once he's out, but he's a little wired from all the jumping."

I was still looking up at Mitch when I felt Henry reach for my hand. I looked down at his tiny dimpled fingers, which were now gripping my own. My palm was facing up as he began folding my fingers down one by one as if he were counting as he went along. Then, I would open my hand up again and he would repeat it. Even though he wouldn't look at me, he was looking at my hand.

"Does he do this a lot?" I smiled.

"No. He doesn't usually touch people like that. He seems to be playing with *you*, though."

After a few more rounds of the same pattern of opening and closing in sequence, he stopped and just continued to hold my hand without making eye contact. I could feel Mitch staring at me as I looked down at Henry's hand in mine. When I got a closer look at the boy's face, I realized he really was the spitting image of Mitch. There was no physical sign of *her*. I continued to stare in awe at the beautiful human being I once perceived as the main source of my angst. In reality, he was an angel.

Mitch startled me when he placed his hand over Henry's and mine. My entire body warmed upon his touch.

"Thank you for coming upstairs to meet him. I didn't want to pressure you, but I'm really glad you did."

"He's beautiful, Mitch."

"Thank you."

"And you're an amazing father."

He looked down at our hands then up at me. "You have no idea how much that means to hear you say that. I like to think that everything happens for a reason, even the bad stuff. I just know I was meant to be his father, you know? I don't regret having him. Hurting you is my only regret."

"You need your strength for this little boy. I really see that now. Don't waste your energy worrying about the past. I'm strong. I'm fine. He needs you now."

"He does need me." His eyes seemed to be glowing in the darkness as he stared into mine. "But I need *you*."

I didn't know what to say. Despite my declaration of strength, I felt like I wanted to cry...not exactly out of sadness. Out of what, I couldn't be sure. Henry was now fast asleep. I slipped my hand from beneath Mitch and Henry's and stood up. "You should take him to his room. I'll meet you downstairs."

"I'm sorry. It just came out. I don't mean to make you uncomfortable. I just said what I felt in that moment."

I turned around in the doorway. "It's okay. See you down there."

I went down the stairs as fast as I could to avoid his seeing that I was about to cry.

Janis got up from the table. "Well?"

She could see that my eyes were watering and hugged me.

"He's so beautiful, Janis. He held my hand and was playing a game with me."

As my head leaned against her shoulder, the seriousness of this situation really hit me. She was right. I had to make sure I didn't cross any lines if I wasn't planning to leave Kevin. This wasn't a game. Mitch still had strong feelings for me and couldn't afford to have his heart broken. *I* couldn't afford to fall in love with that little boy and hurt both of them if I chose to stay with Kevin.

I wiped my eyes just as I heard footsteps behind me and then Mitch's deep, smooth voice.

"Apparently, Skylar's presence did the trick. Henry's out like a light now. Ready to head back?"

"Yes." I hugged Janis one last time. "It was so nice to see you again."

"You, too, honey. Don't be a stranger."

Mitch was deep in thought the entire car ride home while I kept thinking about Henry.

By the time he pulled into my driveway, the silence had become impossible to take any longer. "Are you okay?"

He rubbed his temples, looking frustrated. "I'm fine."

"You don't look fine."

He suddenly turned to me. "It's just...not easy."

"What?"

"You really want to know? I was supposed to be..." He wiggled his fingers into air quotations. "Respecting your situation. It might be better if I just let you go inside because if I start talking right now—"

"What's not easy?"

I flinched when he reached his hand over to my cheek and rubbed his thumb along my chin. "Pretending that you're just a friend."

My heart felt like it was trapped inside my chest along with all the words that wanted to escape held captive by an overwhelming fear of my own emotions.

I'm scared. I want you so badly that it hurts. I've never loved you more than I have tonight after seeing you with your son.

He let go of me. "Just go inside, Skylar, before I say or do something I'll regret tomorrow."

"I don't want to leave you like this."

"Why can't you answer my question?" he asked, turning his whole body toward me.

"What question?"

"I've asked you twice whether you're happy, and you haven't given me an answer. It's what I need to know in order to move on. It's why I fucking started stalking you."

"I guess I'm just not sure how to answer that."

"That's a no, then."

My tone was defensive. "I feel safe with Kevin, okay? He's never hurt me, and I'm pretty sure he never will."

He moved away from me. "Unlike me."

"I didn't mean that against you. I just—"

"That's okay. I get it now."

"No. You don't."

"You don't realize that the words coming out of your mouth don't match the look in your eyes, Skylar. Your eyes are betraying you and confusing the fuck out of me. You still look at me the way you always have, like I'm the most important thing in the world to you. As long as you keep doing that—until you tell me to walk away—I'm not sure that I can move on."

"You're right. I shouldn't be leading you on. This is all just really confusing."

"Look...I'm a different person now. I've been through a lot. I'm not that boy anymore that was scared to tell you how he felt. I'm a damaged man that feels like he's been to hell and back with nothing to lose. I want you more in this moment than I've ever wanted you. You're *all* I want, and I can't even show you how much. You have no idea the things I'd do to you right now if I could. I can't even think straight around you. There's just no one else, Skylar. There hasn't *been* anyone else. I haven't—"

"You haven't what?"

"This is so fucked up." He slammed his head against the steering wheel. "Fuck! I didn't want to have this conversation tonight."

"What are you talking about?"

He looked over at me and whispered, "I haven't been with anyone."

"What? What do you mean?"

"I mean...I haven't *been*...with a woman in over five years."

"You haven't had a girlfriend...but certainly you've..."

He shook his head. "No. No one. I haven't *touched* a woman in five years, Skylar."

I covered my mouth. "Oh my God."

"I haven't *wanted* any other woman, not even for sex. I'd throw myself into work or my son and just try not to think about you. Now that I'm around you again, it's like my body's come alive all of a sudden. I have these urges. I feel out of control, and I don't know what to do with all of it. The fact that I know you're off limits makes it even worse. I'm sorry. You said you wanted honesty. Sometimes, the truth is ugly."

My phone was in the center console when it rang. Mitch looked down at it then handed it to me. "It's Kevin. You'd better take it."

He opened the car door and slammed it shut, leaning his back against the window. My heart was breaking because I knew how hard it must have been to admit what he just did. I was still in shock.

I let the phone go to voicemail and then texted Kevin.

I'll call you back in a few.

I felt guilty, but I couldn't take the call right now. I exited the car and stood beside him.

Mitch wasn't looking at me. "What did he have to say?"

"I didn't take it. I sent him a text that I'd call him back."

He let out a single laugh that seemed bitter and looked up at the sky. It was a clear night as we stood against his car gazing at the stars.

We said nothing for several minutes until he faced me. "You weren't the only one who was devastated." Then, he turned around, got into the car and rolled down the window.

I leaned in. "Where does this leave us?"

He reached out and tucked a piece of my hair behind my ear. "That's for you to decide. I guess you need to figure out whether or not you're happy first, since you don't seem to know. Here's a hint: if you happen to see my face the next time he takes you to bed, chances are good, you're not happy. If I were the one fucking you, I can guarantee you wouldn't have to think twice."

He started the engine and put the car in drive. "Good night, Skylar."

I stood there dazed and confused. *Aroused.* "Bye."

That night, I got under my covers and replayed those words over and over again.

"If I were the one fucking you..."

My fingers circled my clit as I gave myself an intense orgasm while I imagined him doing just that.

TWENTY-THREE

MITCH

"I messed up, Dave."

Davey handed me the capicola sandwich he brought from the local deli. He had come down to the work site to have lunch with me. My company was leading the construction of a new shopping center in town. It was one of our biggest projects to date.

"You'd better figure out the problem before that thing comes crumbling down."

"No, not with the building. With...Skylar."

"Skylar? You've been in touch with her?"

"She hasn't said anything to you?"

"No. We haven't even gotten together since she's been back. How the hell did this happen?"

"It's kind of a long story. I never told you, but I started stalking her a few months back."

"What the fuck, Mitch..."

"It's not as bad as it sounds. Long story short...she caught me one night. Instead of calling the police or freaking out, she invited me in, and we've hung out a couple of times. She's met Henry."

"You're playing with fire. You know that, right?"

"You knew she was engaged?"

Davey hesitated. "She told me a while ago. I didn't tell you."

"Why not?"

"Oh—I don't know—because when it comes to her, you're a little unstable? I thought maybe you'd do something rash...like *stalk* her or something."

"Alright...point taken. Anyway, we went to Bev's last week. I was trying to play it cool, act like we were friends again."

Davey took a sip of his soda and pointed it at me. "I'm sure you did a great job," he said sarcastically.

"Everything went according to plan until we stopped by my house after, and she met Henry."

"I'm surprised she went for that."

"Me, too. She was really sweet with him, and he was actually interacting with her. All of a sudden, I just started to see the three of us together."

"Meaning you, her and *Kevin*, right? Because you do realize she's about to marry him?"

"Just let me finish."

"Okay."

"After I drove her home, I lost it."

"Nooo...really?"

"I told her how I felt and how there hasn't been anyone else."

"Please don't tell me you told her you're a virgin."

"I'm not a fucking virgin."

"Five years with no sex has got to qualify you for some kind of reestablishment of that title. What's the opposite of vaginal rejuvenation?"

"Can you be serious for one friggin' second?" I rolled my eyes. "I did tell her that I hadn't been with anyone."

"That was dumb, but I have a feeling there's even more to this."

"I also told her I didn't think she was happy with him, especially if at any point she saw my face while fucking him."

"Wow. That was graceful."

"Well, yeah...so that's my problem. I have a feeling I scared her away."

"Dude, that was premature ejaculation at its best."

"What?"

"No pun intended, but you blew your load way too fast."

"My load?"

"Yes. It's not that you shouldn't have told her how you felt. You just need to stick to a timeline and do it incrementally. Take a hint from your son. I bet Henry charmed the pants off of her, right?"

"Yeah...actually, he did. He didn't have to say anything at all and just connected with her."

"Sometimes, less is more. You need to control your words and your emotions at this early stage in the game."

"I couldn't help it, Davey. She's not happy with this guy, and I still love her."

"I know you do, man. If there's one thing I know, it's that. I just don't want to see you get your hopes up and then be crushed if she ends up going through with the marriage."

"You don't think I stand a chance, do you?" I bit angrily down at my sandwich even though I had lost my appetite.

Davey shouted through the sound of drilling behind us, "You just have to understand that her meeting Henry and bonding with him for a few minutes doesn't necessarily mean she's gonna be able to put the past five years aside and be his mother all of a sudden. That girl wouldn't even let me mention your name a year ago. This guy she's with...he's solid. Zena and I met up with them while we were down in D.C. once. I'm not saying she doesn't love you, but there are other people involved in this situation. There are a lot of obstacles, but —"

"Whose fucking side are you on?" I said with my mouth full.

"Let me finish. There are a lot of obstacles...but I'll brainstorm, alright? I'll do whatever it takes to help you get her back. As much as I've always busted your balls when it came to her over the years...you two were meant to be together."

"You'll help me come up with a plan?"

"Yeah. At some point, we need to get her away from him for a little while in the right venue. I don't know exactly how to do that."

"What are you talking about? Kidnapping her?"

"Not exactly. Don't get excited."

"He goes away every other week on business for a couple nights."

"Okay...that's a start. I'll come up with something."

I adjusted my hard hat. "I think I love you, Dave."

"Save it. I'm not popping your cherry."

That night, after putting Henry to bed, I opened a beer and pulled up my DVR list to watch one of the several *Pawn Stars* episodes that had been piling up. I had just pressed play when a text from Davey came in.

Davey: I've got it.

Mitch: Got milk? Got herpes? Got what?

Davey: I'm just warning you. You're gonna wanna blow me after this.

Mitch: This better be good after that visual.

Davey: You've got that flip your company is doing for the family down in Virginia Beach coming up in a few weeks, right?

Each year, my company donated its resources to help a family in need by rebuilding a house damaged in a storm or fire. This year, we were surprising a family down in Virginia Beach. The plan was to flip their house while they were staying with relatives on the other side of the state. A tropical storm wrecked their home, and they hadn't been able to live in it for months. They also had two special needs kids, one in a wheelchair, so we'd be putting in a ramp. I had plans to meet my guys down there for five out of the last seven days. It would be the first time I'd be away from Henry, but my mother insisted I go when she found out what we were doing.

Mitch: What about it?

Davey: Hang on. I'm gonna call you.

The phone immediately rang.

"Yo."

"You're flipping the house, and then it has to be set up for them and shit, right?

"Yeah. We pay for all new furniture and decorate it."

"You need an interior designer."

"Actually, I'm not sure—"

"You *need* an interior designer."

"Wait...you're saying I should hire Skylar to do it?"

"You're really smarter than I give you credit for. Of course, that's what I'm saying! That's her specialty, isn't it?"

I scratched my chin and paced the floor. "This is fucking genius."

"Thank you."

"I don't even know if we have it in the budget for a designer. I think we were just going to wing that, but I'll pay for it myself if I have to just to make this happen. The real issue is, how am I going to get her to agree to go away with me? Don't you think she'll see right through this?"

"It's all in how you present it. That's your job. I can't do everything for you. By the way, where are you staying?"

"I'm getting a hotel for myself and for the other guys, too."

"Well, now you're getting a house on the beach."

"A house on the beach?"

"Yes."

"She's not gonna agree to stay in a beach rental with me. Are you fucking kidding?"

"*You're* not staying in it. You'll say the company booked it for her as part of the deal."

"I'm not following you."

"Trust me. Just don't plan to sleep there. It's too presumptuous. You get a hotel, and she sleeps at the beach house. She'll invite you over at some point, and that will be your opportunity. It'll be a nice, romantic setting away from all of the complications here. And she'll actually get some work out of this trip to add to her resume. It's a win-win."

"I have to give you credit, Davey. This is a brilliant idea. I'm just not sure I can get her to do it."

A week later, it was a Wednesday evening, and I had left work early to be home for Henry because my mother had a party to attend with my stepfather, Fred.

The Virginia trip would be coming up in a few weeks. If I was going to propose this job to Skylar, I needed to get in touch with her. I'd been anxiously waiting for tonight because according to my calendar, this was a week he would be away on business.

Henry was running back and forth on his toes across the carpeted playroom. Then, he grabbed his iPad and an automated voice said, *"I want to go to McDonald's."*

The teacher in his special ed preschool class had put an application on there where he could point to a picture, and it would sound out what he wanted in a full sentence. You could program any sentence to match the picture. He would point to a cookie, and it would say, *"I want a cookie."* If he touched the picture of my mother's house, it would say, *"I want to go to Grammy's house."* Tonight, he kept pressing the golden arches. *"I want to go to McDonald's."*

"Not tonight, Bud. Daddy's got to make an important phone call, and Grammy made you some mac and cheese. It's on the stove."

He jumped up and down with his iPad, pressing the icon. *"I want to go to McDonald's."*

"Maybe tomorrow."

He kept it up, pressing on the picture repeatedly. *"I want to go to McDonalds. I want to go to McDonalds. I want to go to McDonald's."*

I laughed at his persistence. "I get it! You want to go to McDonald's." I was such a sucker sometimes. "Okay, let me change your diaper, and we'll go." Even though Henry was four, he wasn't able to be potty trained yet.

After I changed him and got him dressed, as I was zipping up his jacket, an idea crossed my mind. I took my phone out of my pocket and scrolled down to Skylar's name.

She answered. "Hello?"

I closed my eyes at the sound of her sweet voice. "Hey."

"Long time no speak," she said.

"Yeah. I wasn't sure if you wanted to hear from me after the way I left last time."

She didn't acknowledge my statement. "What's going on?"

"I'm actually calling on business."

"Business?"

"Yeah, believe it or not. My company tasked me with finding an interior designer for a project we have coming up. I wanted to see if you had some time right now to meet up for dinner and discuss it."

"Tonight?"

"Yeah...if you're free."

"I am."

"Great. Would you want to meet me at the McDonald's on Franklin, close to your house?"

"A business meeting at McDonald's?"

"My mother's not here, so I'll have Henry. That's where he likes to go. Theirs are the only fries he'll eat."

"Oh...of course you have Henry. I feel stupid now. That makes total sense."

"Don't feel stupid. You didn't know."

"Sure. I can meet you there."

"Great. Wanna say a half hour?"

"Okay. See you then."

Henry and I arrived about ten minutes early and got a booth in the farthest corner away from the action. In case he had a tantrum, I wanted to handle it with the least amount of rolling eyes and whispers. I squeezed him into one of the plastic, gray high chairs, clasping the belt to secure him. Even though he was too big for it, it was the easiest way to get him to sit still and eat, otherwise he'd be climbing all over the greasy booth or trying to crawl on the floor.

It was after the dinnertime rush, so there were only a few tables occupied.

I handed him his iPad while we waited for Skylar. He immediately began playing a Sesame Street matching game.

Five minutes later, the front door opened, and the sight of her nearly took my breath away. She was so cute as she looked around unaware that we were all the way in the back. I chuckled and raised my hand, waving it. The smile she flashed when she noticed us squeezed at my heart, which was beating faster with every step she took. Yeah, I was screwed.

She was wearing a little white dress with spaghetti straps, and her long, wavy hair was swaying as she moved. When she got to our table, her clean, delicate scent immediately hit me. It was like catnip. I wanted to rub my nose through her hair and sniff her all over.

Down, boy.

She sat down. "Sorry I'm a few minutes late. There was a ton of traffic." She turned to Henry. "Hey, little guy."

He continued to stare at his iPad and ignored her.

She turned to me. "How are you?"

I had been staring at her lips, and suddenly looked up. "I'm good."

"So, I'm curious about this business proposition you mentioned."

"Yeah. You know what? Let's get food first. Do you mind sitting here with Henry while I order?"

"Of course, not."

"What would you like?"

"I'll have a fish sandwich, a small fry and a Diet Coke."

I winked. "Okay. Be right back."

While waiting in line, I looked over and noticed that Skylar had placed her hand out for Henry. He took it and started folding her fingers down, playing that same game he created the first time he met her. Focusing on her beautiful smile while she engaged with my son, I realized that everything that mattered to me in the world was in that booth.

When I returned with our food, Henry was back to looking at his iPad.

"We can start eating first," I said. "His fries have to cool off. He won't eat them if they're even a tad hot."

I placed a fruit smoothie in front of Henry. "Drink." He took a small sip. After I bit into my burger, I said, "So, let's get the job stuff out of the way while he's occupied with that game."

"Okay," she said, dipping her fry into some ketchup and taking a bite.

Over the next several minutes, I explained what HM Construction would be doing down in Virginia Beach and why I needed her help.

"So, I would have complete control over the décor?"

"Yes. The family doesn't even know we're doing this. The idea is to have them walk into the place and be blown away. Some local newspapers and media will actually be there to capture it. We'd give you a budget to purchase the items you need down there. As each room is completed, you'll have access to it to do your magic. We'd have you pick paint colors, too."

"Why me?"

"Why not?"

"What's the catch? Virginia Beach in the middle of summer? This sounds too good to be true."

"There is no catch. I just wanted to throw this business your way if you're interested."

"Where would I stay?"

"The company would provide housing for you."

"Are you going to be down there?"

"Yes. I'll be overseeing it and helping my guys."

"How will we get there?"

"I'll get you a flight."

"I have to be honest. This is really tempting. I haven't had much luck getting new clients here in New Jersey."

"HM Construction would be an excellent addition to your resume. This is a good thing. Trust me."

Trust me.

"I really can't see any reason not to say yes."

I tried not to leap out of my seat. "So, you're in?"

"Can I just have a few days to think about it? I'd have to talk it over with Kevin."

Buzz kill.

"Of course."

She took of a sip of her soda. "Thank you."

I took a bite of one of Henry's fries to make sure they had cooled. I handed him the container, and he immediately began to play with them.

"What is he doing?"

"He has some OCD tendencies. One of them is arranging things in a row. He does this to his fries all the time. He lines them up one by one, counts them and then eats them from left to right. Don't worry. I wiped down the table earlier."

"What would happen if I took one? How would he react?"

I grinned. "That's a good question. Try it out."

Skylar took a fry out of the line up. Henry immediately started yelling and reaching for it. It amazed me how aware of things he was when he wanted to be.

"Mine," she said as she held the fry away from him toward her chest.

He looked down at his organized fries and back up at Skylar with a look of urgency.

He was looking at her.

"Say mine," she said.

Henry reached his hand out.

She repeated in a sing-songy voice, "Mine...mine... mine."

Henry opened his mouth. "Mm...mi..."

Holy shit. He was trying to say it.

She happily stomped her feet. "Good boy. Mine. Mine! Here you go." She handed him back the French fry. "Wow. Mitch...it's really all in there. He just needs the motivation."

Proud could not begin to describe how I was feeling. "Well, up until this moment, the only thing he's ever tried to say was, 'hi.' You have a way about you that brings out the best in people."

"I think he would have done that for anyone that messed with his order, but it was cool to see him interact a little. I guess we're all capable of anything if we really want something."

Mine.

I could certainly relate to desperately needing something you can't have and wanting to beg for it.

As Henry started eating his fries from left to right, Skylar looked at me and appeared hesitant to say something.

I moved our tray out of the way. "You have something on your mind."

"I was just thinking about something your mother said."

"Okay..."

"She mentioned that you were arrested around the time I moved away. What happened?"

Shit. My mother had a big mouth. I really hadn't wanted Skylar to find out about that.

I breathed in and out slowly. "I beat the shit out of someone."

"What?"

"Yeah. He had it coming."

"Who?"

I hesitated, reluctant to start the conversation this would inevitably lead to. "It was Chad."

"Charisma's cousin...Chad?"

"Yes. He took advantage of you. Then, he had the gall to come to the hospital when Henry was born. The second he introduced himself, I knew exactly who he was. So, I asked him to help me carry some stuff out to the car. When we got outside, I punched his lights out and knocked out one of his teeth."

"Oh my God..."

"You have to understand how angry I was at that time. I hated him probably more than anyone but not more than myself for indirectly bringing him into your life through Charisma. I was in so much pain and couldn't see past it. I wanted to kill him and was sorry I hadn't put him in the hospital. Do you think less of me for saying that?"

"No. I understand that kind of anger. I have recurring dreams about doing the same kind of thing...to her. But a dream is one thing. You were actually put in jail?"

"Briefly. Then, she somehow convinced him to drop the charges."

"Wow."

"Yeah."

"I'm sorry you felt like you had to do that because of me."

"I'd do anything for you."

I'd die for you.

I needed to change the subject before diarrhea of the mouth developed. I couldn't risk saying something that would make her decide not to come to Virginia Beach. "Stay right here with him, okay?"

I went up to the counter and returned with two M&M McFlurries. She always used to make me stop here when we were teenagers because that was her favorite kind of ice cream.

She smiled. "You remembered."

"I haven't forgotten a thing."

It would be easier if I could.

She took a spoonful and moaned. "Mmm. There's nothing like this."

I watched as she closed her eyes. *No, there isn't.*

"It *is* really good," I said, clearing my throat.

"There's still no other ice cream I like better. Will Henry eat some?"

"He usually won't touch ice cream."

Skylar moved her plastic spoon toward Henry's mouth, and he immediately turned his head away as if she were offering him poison. Then, he snatched the utensil from her.

She pretended to be upset. "Hey! That's my spoon."

He reached it into her cup. We both watched in anticipation, thinking maybe he was planning to eat some. Instead, he whipped the spoon toward Skylar, smacking her in the face with a huge dollop of ice cream.

She squealed in surprise.

"Shit! I'm sorry." I jumped up and ran to get some napkins.

When I returned, she had fallen into a fit of hysterical laughter. To my amazement, Henry was giggling and kicking his legs.

"Again, I'm so sorry for that."

"If it got him to laugh, it was worth it."

I turned to him. "You think that was funny? You get away with murder."

She was wiping the ice cream off her face. It had dripped down onto her chest.

I was not thinking about sopping it up with my tongue.

I handed her more napkins. "Do you need water?"

"No...I'm fine. I needed a good laugh." She wiped the happy tears from her eyes. *Beautiful almond eyes.* "Gosh, that felt good."

I lifted my brow. "Really?"

"Really."

The customers seated diagonally across were smiling over at us. They must have thought we were a crazy family. How I wished that were real, that Skylar were my wife and Henry's mother. We'd go home, put Henry to bed, and then I'd take her to our room and make love to her all night. Instead, she'd be sleeping in another man's bed, and I'd be alone dreaming of her, replaying every moment of tonight.

When her amusement died down, our eyes locked.

I used the opportunity to bring up the last time we were together. "I'm sorry if I was out of line that night in my car."

"You were just being honest with your feelings. I'll never fault you for that."

I paused, looking down at my melted ice cream, swirling it around the styrofoam cup. "Does he know about me?"

"He knows what happened after I left home. He knows everything, but he doesn't know we've been back in touch."

"How do you think he'd feel about that?"

"Honestly?

"Yeah."

"He'd go ballistic."

I nodded, pretending to get it while anger built inside me.

Fuck him. He could never love her as much as I do.

We didn't go into it further. She changed the subject and started asking me about Henry's school. I talked to her about the type of therapy we were waiting for him to receive. We sat for another half hour or so. Despite our five years apart, being with her always felt like home.

I got us two coffees, and Henry kept busy snapping pictures of the table, floor and ceiling via the camera on his iPad. He must have had about 700 images in the library because he just kept taking photo after photo.

I looked down at my watch. "Holy crap. It's almost 10 o'clock."

"What time does Henry go to sleep?"

"8:30."

"Whoops."

"He's being so good tonight. Normally, he would have had a tantrum by now, and then I would have known it was time to leave. I think he likes your company."

She gave him an affectionate look. "Well, then, that makes me happy."

"I like your company, too," I said.

Leave it at that. Don't tell her how much you miss her, how much you love her. It's too much. Remember what Davey said.

She blushed as if she were reading my mind anyway. "You should get him home."

"Yeah. I could stay here all night with you, but he does need to sleep. At this point, he'll be so wired, he'll probably be up all night."

Henry's iPad battery had died, which meant it could be a rocky ride home. I held his hand as we walked out the door with Skylar. The warm summer wind blew her dress up, and the quick peek at her underwear was pure torture.

We stopped in front of my truck, and I got Henry into his booster seat. She leaned into the backseat. "It was nice hanging with you, Henry. Next time, I'm wearing an old t-shirt, though."

My pulse raced. *Next time.*

Henry reached his hand out and squeezed her nose hard. "Ow," she said laughing.

"I should have warned you. He likes to pinch people's noses if you get too close to his face. He's got some strong hands."

She stood in front of me, her hair blowing in the soft breeze. I looked down at the ice cream stain on her dress. Red and blue dye from the M&Ms had bled onto the white fabric. "I want to pay to have that cleaned."

"Are you kidding me?"

"No. I insist."

She looked up at the moon then into my eyes. "Do you really think I care about this dress? This stain is life, Mitch. When I was sick as a teenager, I promised God if He let me live, I'd never sweat the small things again. I'm proud to wear this. I used to worry that I'd never get to experience things like seeing you as a grown man. That was a big fear for me. Not only have I lived long enough for that, but I just got to hang out with your son, too. That's pretty damn cool."

My heart felt like it was going to explode. The visceral need to kiss her weighed on my lips. "That's beautiful."

"I didn't think I'd ever be able to handle meeting him, Mitch. But the reality is, he's so special that it makes me forget about the rest."

Fuck it. I pulled her into a warm embrace, relishing every second and trying to burn the feeling into memory: the smell of her, the softness of her breasts, her heart pounding against mine. My mouth was so close to her neck, and I bit my lip to hamper the need to devour her skin. I whispered in her ear, "I'm so grateful you're here, too."

After a minute of holding each other, she pulled back. She must have known I wouldn't be the first to let go.

"When do I need to let you know about the job?"

"By the end of the weekend would be good."

"Okay. Will do. Thank you for dinner."

"My pleasure."

"Good night."

"Good night, Skylar."

As I watched her walk to her car, I muttered three words over and over.

Please say yes.

TWENTY-FOUR

SKYLAR

Nina put me on speakerphone while she did the dishes. She spoke in an echo through the sound of running water. “So, you think there’s an ulterior motive to this job offer?”

“I mean, I think the job is legitimate,” I said as I kicked back on my bed.

The water stopped, and I could hear Jake in the background. He coughed out the word, “Bullshit.”

Nina laughed. “Sorry, he’s been listening the whole time.”

He spoke into the phone. “You want my two cents? Nina, what’s your favorite drink?”

“Sex on the Beach,” she said.

“Exactly.” He snickered.

“What are you getting at, Jake?” I asked.

“Bitch might be offering you a job, but that is not the reason he wants you to go with him to Virginia Beach. He could have hired anyone. Instead, he chooses his ex-girlfriend he’s still in love with?”

"So, if that's true, I'd be betraying Kevin in accepting it."

"If you do this, are you going to tell Kevin that Mitch is the person behind it?" Nina asked.

"Are you crazy? He doesn't even know we've been in touch."

"Well, then you need to decide whether it's worth lying to Kevin and whether you want to deal with the fact that Mitch might have more he wants to offer you down there besides money."

"Like his stiff cock," Jake said loudly into the phone.

Nina laughed. "You're terrible."

"Trust me. I'm a guy. If we want a woman badly enough, we'll come up with all kinds of clever shit. I'm not saying all he wants is sex. I know he cares about her. He's trying to be slick with this job offer, though, and I'm calling him out. He's a typical guy who's crazy over a girl."

"It takes one to know one," Nina said.

"Damn straight."

I heard their lips smacking together.

"Can you two stop making out for one second?"

"Sorry, Sissy." She whispered to him away from the phone. "Go run the shower. I'll meet you in there."

I heard him growl and rolled my eyes.

She spoke into the receiver again. "The bottom line is, we can't tell you what to do. You have to look inside your heart and do what you think is right for you—not for Kevin or Mitch—for you. What do *you* want?"

I sighed. "Okay. Thanks for listening."

I hung up, more confused than ever and decided to feel Kevin out about the offer when he returned tomorrow.

It was Friday night, and Kevin had taken me to Spinelli's, a local Italian eatery. Earlier, he had returned from his trip in a jovial mood, announcing that we were going out to celebrate. He said he wanted to save the news until we got to the restaurant. I mentioned that I had something to discuss with him as well.

Kevin poured two glasses of Chianti as he picked at the antipasto appetizer. "So...you go first because I don't want to overshadow your news immediately."

I took a sip and placed my glass down. I inhaled to grab my composure, ingesting the smell of olive oil and garlic. "Well, I was offered a new design gig."

"Really? Honey, that's great. Who's the client?"

I placed a hot pepper into my mouth. "It's actually a construction company that's remodeling a home down in Virginia Beach. They want to fly me down there for five days."

"When would this be?"

"In a couple of weeks." I nervously rolled a toothpick in between my fingers waiting for his reaction.

"How's the money?"

"We actually didn't discuss it."

"You didn't discuss compensation?"

"No. They're definitely paying me, but this is sort of a charity thing for them. They're rebuilding a home that was damaged in a storm. The family was displaced and has no idea this is happening. It's supposed to be a surprise. It's going to be this big media event when they walk in and see the transformation. That'll be good exposure for my work."

"Sounds like a good deal, then." Staring at me through the glass, he took a long sip of his wine then said, "The change of scenery might be good to get you out of your malaise lately, too."

He was referring to my lack of interest in the bedroom. I had managed to avoid sex with Kevin since the night Mitch and I first went out. I had been struggling with guilt over my carnal thoughts of Mitch and felt awkward whenever Kevin touched me. That needed to be worked out soon, or he was going to suspect something.

I nervously bit into a breadstick. "So, you think I should take it?"

"Why not?"

I had to remind myself that without knowing about Mitch, Kevin had no real reason to want me to turn it down. My lie of omission was only making *me* feel hesitant.

I shrugged my shoulders as if to laugh off my trepidation. "Right."

He reached across the table for my hand. "So, from good news to great news. It's funny you mentioned travel because...well, how do you like California?"

"California? I've only been there once when I joined you on that business trip, but it's nice enough. Why?"

"We're moving there."

I instinctively moved my hand away. "What? What do you mean?"

"You're looking at the new vice president of operations for Leland, Corp."

"Vice president?"

"Yup. Honey, all my hard work's paid off. This is a bigger promotion than I could have ever hoped for. Everyone knew Stenner was retiring, but I hadn't thought for a second that I was being considered for his job. They flat out offered it to me. I'll be overseeing three plants, and my salary will almost double."

News that should have made me ecstatic instead made my heart instantly ache. I wondered if my sad attempt at a smile reflected the terror I felt. "Kev, that's amazing, but we'd have to move? You can't do that position from here?"

He shook his head as he sipped his wine. "That's where the corporate headquarters are. All of the bigwigs work out of Fresno. That's non-negotiable."

It felt like I was about to regurgitate the breadstick. My head was throbbing. All I could see was Mitch's face when I'd have to tell him I was leaving again. My eyes swelled, and the sudden pain in my chest was unbearable.

"Are you crying, Sky?"

"I'm sorry. I just wasn't expecting this. When does the position start?"

"We have to be moved out there in six weeks time. I'll be transitioning into the role in the meantime."

I downed my water then slammed the glass on the table. "But we just got here. This is my home."

"Sky...I understand, but I can't turn down a vice president job because you want to be close to Mommy. We haven't even been to visit your mother since we moved back. This job will set us up for life. You won't have to worry about working. If you get clients, fine. If not, I'll be making enough so that we can live very comfortably on my salary alone. We can have the wedding of our dreams. We could even afford to do it in Hawaii like we used to fantasize about."

"This is just...a shock."

"I understand it's sudden. I guess I thought you'd be more excited. You haven't been back here long enough to really get attached. I don't understand the big deal."

No, you wouldn't.

A group of restaurant employees entered the dining area singing the happy birthday song to a man at the table next to us. I wanted to scream, and my thoughts were drowning in the noise.

It hit me that if I were really going to move away with Kevin, I couldn't let myself get any closer to Mitch. The Virginia Beach trip would be a bad idea. So, why did I want it more than anything now? Our dinner with Henry the other night was truly the best time I'd had since we were teenagers. Something about being in a place that reminded me of my childhood with Mitch and *his* child had truly touched me. Getting Henry to connect had been exhilarating. I wasn't seeing Charisma when I looked at him. I just saw *him*...a boy without an ego, who knew nothing of how he came to be. He just enjoyed the simple things in life. I would miss him, too.

Maybe I wouldn't leave.

What was I saying?

I couldn't just abandon Kevin, who truly cared about me, supported me and protected me for over five years. He hadn't done anything to deserve that. He was supposed to be my future.

"Sky? Have I lost you? You look like you're about to pass out."

Since I wasn't able to admit the real reason I didn't want to move, I was at a loss for words as he stared at me from across the table.

He continued, "You'll get used to the idea, okay? Let's try to celebrate this. I love you. I want to make a good life for us."

It would be a perfect life. So, why did I feel like running from it?

I took another sip of my water. The waiter arrived with my Chicken Marsala, and I pretended to enjoy it, all the while thinking about what my next move would be.

Sunday was the deadline to let Mitch know about the job, and I had no idea whether that trip was the only decision I'd have to make in the coming days.

It was a lazy, sunny Saturday in the late afternoon. Kevin and I drove with the windows down as we headed to my mother's house for dinner. It was her birthday, and a few of her closest friends would be joining us to celebrate.

"We need to stop and get wine," he said. "What kind does your mother like again?"

"Merlot."

When we arrived at my old neighborhood, Kevin pulled up to a small gourmet market that apparently also sold liquor. I had never noticed it before, so it must have been built sometime after I left for Maryland.

When we walked in, I sampled some Brie and peppercorn crackers that were being given out, while Kevin went in search of the wine. This was an eclectic little place and reminded me of Trader Joe's, although it seemed to be independently owned. At another station, someone was pouring samples of flavored coffee, so I took one and proceeded to wander, browsing the shelves. I passed the aisle where Kevin was still deciding on a wine.

Three aisles down, I had been looking at organic cacao chocolate bars when I heard a familiar voice.

"What, buddy? What do you see?"

One of the bars slipped out of my hands. I turned around to find Mitch standing there with Henry who was seated in the front of a shopping cart.

His face lit up when he saw me. "Hi."

"Hi," I said softly.

"You dropped something." He bent down and handed me the chocolate.

The wrapper crinkled as I took it from him. "Thanks."

Mitch was wearing a Yankees cap backwards. I hadn't seen him in one since we were teenagers. He looked more like the Mitch I used to know in that moment with his hair sticking out from under the cap. It made my heart flutter and ache at the same time.

My Mitch.

His eyes seared into mine. "Are you alone?"

He smelled so good. Like the push of a button, my body immediately awakened with desire as it always did around him.

"No."

His eyes darkened. "He's here with you?"

"Yes."

He let out a deep breath, and his nostrils flared. "We'll go. I don't want to get you in trouble," he said abruptly.

I looked behind my shoulders.

When he started to walk away, I put my hand on the cart to stop it. "Wait." I turned to the boy. "Hi, Henry."

Henry wasn't looking at me, but I saw he had pulled up a photo of me on his iPad. He must have taken it when he was snapping all those pictures at McDonald's. My head was cut off, but you could see my chin and the ice cream dripping down my dress.

Mitch leaned into the photo, and I could feel the vibration of his voice. "He noticed you before I did. He kept pointing to the picture, and there you were."

His proximity had caused the hairs on the nape of my neck to stiffen. I cleared my throat. "Do you shop here a lot?"

"Sometimes. They have these flaxseeds I put in Henry's smoothies. What are you doing in this part of town, anyway?"

"It's Mom's birthday. We're having dinner at her house."

I smiled at Henry who was still staring at the picture of my decapitated body.

A few seconds later, I heard Kevin's voice behind me. "Sky. There you are."

Before I could answer him, Mitch had already disappeared with Henry down the aisle. Unsure of whether Kevin had seen me talking to them, I waited for to him to say something.

"I lost you. Ready to go?"

I let out a sigh of relief. He had no idea what Mitch looked like, so chances were good even if he had seen us making small talk, he would have thought nothing of it.

My throat felt thick, and my heart was palpitating. "Yeah. I was just looking at these chocolate bars."

"You want one? Get one."

"No, I need to watch my diet."

"No, you don't. You're perfect. Here, take two." He threw the bars into his shopping basket and kissed me on the cheek before wrapping his arm around me.

I immediately felt guilty. We may have had our spats, but Kevin didn't deserve a lying fiancée obsessed with her ex-boyfriend.

We walked to the register where there was a long line. Kevin scratched my back, and my body tensed as I wondered whether Mitch could see us.

The line hadn't moved when I heard loud screaming coming from one of the aisles. It was Henry. He was having a tantrum.

Beads of sweat formed on my forehead as I listened to the wailing. I felt helpless.

I heard one of the employees. "Sir, do you need some assistance?"

"No. Thanks. He has autism. This happens out of the blue from time to time. We're fine. I'm gonna need to abandon my stuff in the cart and leave, though."

"No problem, sir."

Everyone in the market stared as Mitch carried a kicking and screaming Henry past the line of people. The boy's arms and legs were flailing as he struggled to wiggle from his father's grasp while his screams grew louder and louder. Mitch's eyes briefly darted toward mine. His face was red. Then, he disappeared out the door.

Kevin whispered in my ear. "That—right there—is precisely why I don't want kids."

I wished I could explain to him that Henry couldn't help it, that his autism trapped him inside his body and that he had tantrums because he couldn't express his feelings. Instead, I said nothing. A gnawing feeling continued to eat away at me as we waited in line.

My mother was president of the Kevin Blanchard fan club. Why wouldn't she be? She knew how messed up I was when I left town, and she'd always been grateful to him for saving her little girl from the depths of despair. She also admired his success, and the fact that—unlike Oliver—he was loyal.

She put her arm around me at the dinner table. We had just finished up her birthday cake. "As much as I hate to see you move away from me again, this job Kevin has accepted is one hell of an opportunity for both of you."

Kevin held up his wine glass in a salute. "Thank you for your support, Tish. I know Skylar doesn't want to leave you, but I appreciate your understanding."

I downed my wine as my mother and he discussed the future being laid out for me. They had no clue that my mind was somewhere else completely.

I hadn't been able to get the encounter with Mitch today out of my head. It felt like my two lives collided in that grocery store. It was a physical manifestation of my mental tug of war: on one side, Kevin who was my brain and my perfect, safe haven...on the other, Mitch who was my heart and my flawed, deepest desire.

"Tish, would you consider relocating out West in a few years?"

"I might, if that's definitely where you'll settle." She put her hand on my knee. "And if my daughter wants me around, of course."

It felt like my clothes were getting tighter by the second. Needing a breather from this conversation, I got up.

"Excuse me. I need to use the bathroom."

I ran upstairs to my old bedroom, which was now my mother's sewing room. Feeling like I might hyperventilate, I closed the door and clutched my stomach. When my breathing calmed, I noticed that Mitch's bedroom light was on across the street. It was a comfortable summer night, and his window was open. I stared out into his room, which looked empty. A thin curtain blew in the breeze and slightly obstructed my view. My body flinched when his shirtless, statuesque frame suddenly appeared at the window. He stood facing me. Then, he waved.

He saw me.

I waved back. I couldn't help but giggle.

Mitch put something in his mouth, and I saw the light of a small flame at the tip. He was smoking something, but I couldn't tell what it was.

My phone was in my pocket and buzzed. I answered.

Mitch's voice sounded raspy and sexy as hell. "Are you stalking *me*, now?"

"No, not really. What is that you keep putting in your mouth? You're smoking something?"

"Why are you so interested in what I'm doing with my mouth?"

I closed my eyes. "Ugh..."

"Sorry. Joke. I shouldn't have said that."

"So, what is it?"

"I'm smoking a cigar, actually."

"I didn't know you smoked cigars."

"I only do it once in a while. It calms me down when I've had a long day."

My mouth tingled at the thought of tasting cigar on his tongue. I shook my head to stop that train of thought.

I cleared my throat. "I'm sorry about what happened earlier with Henry."

"Don't be. He was fine by the time we got home. He's fast asleep now."

"Good. I was worried about him."

"Where's your guy?"

"He's downstairs."

"Why are you upstairs talking to me, then?"

"I don't know."

"You sound like me when I got caught stalking you." He made fun of his own excuse. "Gee, I don't know what I'm doing here, Skylar."

"Except I'm not wearing a creepy hood and carrying explosives."

The sound of his deep laughter in my ear soothed me. "True. Very true. Seriously, why are you alone upstairs looking out the window?"

"I haven't been able to stop thinking about things, about what happened today, about your job proposal. I needed a breather, so I could think straight."

He was silent for a while, and then I saw him take a puff of the cigar again. His voice was low...sexy. "I wish you could come over right now."

"Mitch..."

"I know. I'm overstepping my boundaries again."

"That's not what I was going to say." I couldn't believe what I was about to admit. "I wish I could come over, too."

He didn't say anything, but I could hear his breathing quicken, and he seemed frustrated as he ran his fingers through his hair.

"I haven't been able to stop thinking about you, Mitch, and I'm really confused." I exhaled. It was the first time I admitted my feelings to him.

"Skylar..."

"Yeah?"

"Take the job. Come to Virginia Beach with me."

I was silent.

"Please," he urged.

He had just made what I already suspected abundantly clear: this wasn't just a business trip. I knew it was so wrong, but my entire body was buzzing...because I had made my decision.

"I'll go."

TWENTY-FIVE

MITCH

It felt too good to be true. As I threw my clothes into the suitcase, I still couldn't believe that Skylar agreed to go away with me. It would only be five days, but I would make the most of every last second.

The logistical planning went into effect from the moment she said yes. That night, I literally put my cigar out and immediately went searching for beach rentals on the Internet. I had a hard-on the entire time just thinking about being alone with her away from here. I was going to need to control myself, or I'd blow it.

With such late notice, properties were either unavailable or expensive. I eventually contacted a realtor the following week, and she found me the perfect place on Sandbridge Beach that cost an arm and a leg. The second I saw the photos of the inside, though, I knew it was the one. It didn't matter how much it cost at that point.

I got to Virginia Beach a day before she did. I had booked her a plane ticket but decided to drive down myself.

Skylar was set to arrive at the work site any minute. A text came in from her when the plane landed. She had rented a car at the airport and went straight to a home improvement store to pick out paint. I'd already given her a copy of the floor plan, so we weren't wasting time.

The keys to the beach house were burning a hole in my pocket. I'd take her there tonight after our work ended for the day. I couldn't wait to see her reaction.

The weather was perfect, so we kept the front door to the property open while we worked to let the balmy, dry breeze in. The house smelled like sawdust and primer, so it was good to air it out. My guys had made great progress before I arrived, and everything was on target to be completed by the end of the week.

A Steely Dan song played on an old boom box that was splattered with white paint. There were empty beer bottles everywhere. Technically, we weren't supposed to be drinking on the job, but I let it slide this time. This job couldn't have been more different from all previous ones. Case in point: every head in the place turned toward the doorway when Skylar walked in. She waved awkwardly when she realized the guys were all checking her out.

She wore a short, gray skirt and a sleeveless blouse that had a bow in the front that begged to be untied. She looked very business-like, which was a huge turn-on. That get-up was like a grown-up version of the Catholic school uniform.

I introduced her to all the guys and tried to ignore the once-overs they gave her as she shook their hands. What

I did make sure to catch was the once-over she gave *me*. I was wearing beige cargo pants and no shirt. I couldn't really tell what Skylar was thinking lately when it came to everything else. The one thing I did know: she was as physically attracted to me as I was to her.

She flinched when I put my hand on the small of her back and led her into the first completed room. "You made it in good time." I reluctantly slid my hand slowly off of her.

"Yeah. I was actually able to find some neutral paint colors in the bargain mistake section, so that will free up some money for other things."

I hadn't realized how obvious my staring was until she interrupted it.

"Did you hear what I said?"

"Yeah. Paint, right?"

"Yes. We should be all set. I put the gallons out front whenever you're ready for them. I marked each can with a label indicating which room it's for."

"You're so organized. You want a full time job when we get back?" I joked.

"And what would that be?"

I wiggled my eyebrows. "You can be my personal assistant."

She looked down at my hands that were covered in primer. "And what exactly would that entail?"

"It requires full-time residency, actually."

"Oh...in your house?"

"Yeah."

"I see. What else?"

"There's sort of a dress code."

"Let me guess...a lack of dress?" She laughed.

I fucking loved flirting with her.

I hadn't intended for this conversation to veer in the direction it had, but this was a good sign. It surprised me that she was playing along...until she cut it short.

"I should head to the fabric store."

"Hey. You know I'm playing around with you. I promise to be good this trip."

She smiled. "I hear you."

I leaned against the doorway and as she walked away, I said, "Unless you tell me you want me to be bad. I'd be up for that, too."

She turned around briefly, her face flushed. "Goodbye, Mitch."

Getting through the next fifteen minutes without killing someone seemed like an impossible task because all of the guys wouldn't shut up about how hot she was. They didn't know anything about our past, although they should have put two and two together based on the massive tattoo of her name on my chest. Getting arrested for assaulting an employee was not on my list of things to do while here, so I gritted my teeth and controlled my fists as best as I could.

It really did impress me how fast Skylar operated that first day. She decided she'd make all the curtains herself to stay within budget, borrowing a sewing machine from the wife of one of the local volunteers. She came back that afternoon with a massive amount of material and planned to spend the entire day tomorrow sewing at the beach house. She also visited a local consignment shop and scored some artwork for next to nothing.

That night, we worked later than I had hoped in order to stay on deadline, but it would be the only late work night. By the time 10:00 rolled around, I was exhausted but exhilarated, knowing she'd be following me to the beach house. I threw my navy hoodie over my bare chest.

She was hanging a couple of pictures on the wall of a room that had been fully painted. Her hair, which was perfectly coiffed earlier in the day, now fell loose and messy. *Sexy*. It was how I'd imagined it would look after sex. *Fuck*. I needed to get that thought out of my head before I got hard.

"Ready to go?" I asked.

Too late. Hard.

She stepped down from the stool. "Sure."

Skylar followed me in her car. When I pulled up to the rental, my palms got sweaty because the place was a shitload nicer than expected. She would have a tough time believing that this was the house HM Construction paid for. Every red cent had come out of my own money.

We parked next to each other on the gravel driveway and got out.

She slammed the car door. The ocean air blew her hair around in wispy strands. She spit one out of her mouth. "What is this?"

"What do you think?"

"What's going on?"

I must have looked guilty as shit. "What?"

"This house is—"

"Let's go in."

I reached into my pocket for the key and opened the front door.

Her jaw dropped. "Okay…this is like that show *Cribs* on MTV minus the ten cars out front. Exactly how much money did your company spend on this place?"

"I shut the door. We got a good deal. Don't worry about it."

She dropped her bag lazily and walked around in awe. "This kitchen is way better than mine at home." She ran her fingertips along the granite of the countertop. "I'm gonna make a nice meal for us tomorrow night."

Fuck. Yes.

"That sounds great."

She covered her mouth and walked in silence over to the one thing I had been waiting for her to notice. She sat down on it. I walked over and joined her on the plush cushion. She turned to me. "I can't believe you did this."

"Did what?"

"You picked this place out and paid for it, didn't you?"

I sighed. "I did."

"Why?"

Our faces were just inches apart. "I don't know what's gonna happen one day from the next with you, and I hate not being able to control that. I just wanted to have some time with you in the best possible place I could imagine. When you were sick, I never forgot where you told me your happy place would be: a reading nook overlooking the ocean. When I saw online that this house had one, I didn't give a shit what it cost. I knew I had to get this one for you."

She lay back into the wall, kicked her feet up onto my lap and closed her eyes. She opened them and looked out at the waves crashing in the distance. "I don't know what to say. I feel like I don't deserve this."

"This is for me, too." I looked out the window. "Do you remember where my happy place was?"

She nodded. "Anywhere I am."

I lightly squeezed her shin. "I just want to be with you even if it's just for a few days. No other expectations, okay? Please don't worry about that. I want you to have a good time."

"Was any part of this trip really about the job?"

I couldn't lie to her. "What do you want me to say?"

"Where are you staying?"

"The Holiday Inn down the street."

She looked conflicted. "I know there's plenty of room, but I can't offer you to stay."

"I understand, believe me. I would never expect that."

"This is wrong, Mitch. This whole thing: my lying to Kevin, my taking this offer when I knew deep down it was more than work."

"Don't you dare feel guilty, Skylar. After everything we've been through, we deserve this break even if it's nothing more than that."

"I just wanted to spend time with you, too. I don't know what it all means."

It pained me to have to lift her leg off of me and stand up. "Tell you what, it's been a long day. I'm going to head back to the hotel and let you get some rest. Tomorrow, we'll call it quits with work early, do dinner and enjoy the beach. Don't overthink this. We only live once. If we want to spend time together, that's not a sin. Nobody's getting hurt by that."

She stood up. Her blouse was wrinkled and halfway untucked. She was a beautiful mess.

I licked my lips, wanting to kiss her so badly. "Make sure you lock up tonight."

"I appreciate all of the effort you put into this. I hope I didn't come across as ungrateful." She walked a few steps toward me. "I never thought I'd actually get to visit my happy place. Thank you for giving that to me."

If I didn't walk away now, I'd never leave. I headed straight for the door. Then, I turned to look at her one last time. "Thank you for giving me mine."

The next day seemed to drag at work even though we'd gotten a lot done. All of the rooms were now drywalled and painted. Skylar had spent the entire day shopping for décor or at the beach house sewing drapes. I missed her. I kept checking my watch to see how close it was to 3:00.

I got to my hotel at 3:15 and took a quick shower. As the hot water beat down on me, my thoughts turned anxious. I only had four more nights with her. This trip was my chance to get her to see that we belonged together. But I promised her there were no expectations, and I didn't plan to pressure her. I just wanted us to get closer organically, but there just wasn't enough time.

Skylar was expecting me at 4:00. She was making dinner, and we were going to take a walk on the beach at some point. I was giddy with excitement and a need to see her, to smell her, to touch her even if it were just a brush of her hand.

I put on a black button down shirt and some dark jeans. I sprayed on cologne and slicked my hair back with gel.

When I arrived at the rental, she opened the door, and my heart immediately started beating out of control. She looked good enough to eat in a tiny peach-colored dress. I wanted to wrap her in her my arms but instead tightened my fists and said, "You look nice."

"Thanks. So do you."

I walked toward the kitchen. "What is that I smell?"

"It's Chicken Cacciatore. I remembered you used to like it when your mother made it. I hope this is just as good."

"If you made it, I'm sure I'll love it."

"Are you hungry now?"

My eyes drifted down to her mouth and then her neck. "I'm starving." I wondered if she could tell I wasn't referring to the food.

Her heels clicked against the tile floor as she walked over to a bottle of red wine on the counter, opened it and poured it into two stemless glasses. "Cabernet okay?"

"Love it. Thanks," I said, taking the glass from her and making sure to skim the skin of her hand. I took a sip. "Mmm."

"You want to take these up to the deck?"

"Yeah, I'm dying to get up there to see that view."

She smiled and nudged her head to follow her. "Come on."

Two white Adirondack chairs sat on the gray wooden deck that overlooked Sandbridge Beach. It was like they were made for the two of us to sit in. We sat down and quietly sipped our wine. We gazed out at the rolling waves and listened to the sound of the seagulls. I stole glances at her beautiful side profile.

She was the first to speak. "So, I say we sit out here for about ten minutes, have dinner downstairs, then take that beach walk when the sun is setting."

"Perfect."

Nothing could be more perfect than this.

And it was, until reality rang when we got downstairs. She picked up her cell phone. I knew by the tone of her voice that it was him. I walked over to the window, so she wouldn't be uncomfortable. I listened to every word and stared out into the ocean. The reminder that she was engaged to someone else took my appetite away and slapped me out of the fantasy I'd been living out just a moment ago.

"Yeah. Everything's going great. It's beautiful here. Saturday. My flight gets in at four-thirty."

My jaw tightened just thinking about leaving Saturday. I polished off my wine.

"Did you remember to buy Seamus' food? Good. Okay. Me, too. Bye."

Me, too.

I wondered if he had told her he loved her. Did she not say it back to avoid hurting my feelings or because she didn't really love him?

She walked over to me. A new tension replaced the relaxed atmosphere of five minutes ago. "That was Kevin."

"You should have given him my regards."

"Mitch..."

"Oh, that's right. 'He'd go ballistic.'" I walked over the counter, refilling my empty glass. "Is that because he'd know he has a reason to worry?"

She didn't say anything, and I regretted putting her in that position.

I put my glass on the counter and rubbed my eyes in frustration. "I'm sorry."

"It's okay. I understand. Let's just try to have a nice dinner, okay?"

"I would love that."

We fell into an easy conversation while devouring the meal she made: Chicken Cacciatore with a side of lemon garlic Brussels sprouts.

"This is by far the best Cacciatore I've ever had."

"Really? You're just saying that."

"I don't have any reason to lie."

"You don't, huh?"

My lips slowly spread into a smile. "Maybe I do, but I didn't have to. It was damn good."

"Well, thank you."

She wiped her mouth. "There's dessert, too, but I think we should take a walk on the beach before it gets dark."

"Agreed. The sun just started to set."

We took our shoes off and walked down to the shore. The urge to grab her hand was overpowering, but I restrained myself. I was pretty sure she'd let me, but I'd only want more, so it was best if I didn't touch her for any great length of time.

I looked down at Skylar's tiny feet, her red painted toes kicking the sand. I wanted to nibble on them along with every other part of her body. She looked so content as she walked quietly alongside me. It made me think of the last time I was on a beach with her. "Being here reminds me of the summer before I went to college."

"Yeah, we went to the beach a lot that summer. Remember when Davey shaved his chest hair into the shape of a bikini top?"

I burst into laughter. "How could I forget? Then, there was that time right before he met Zena. He was checking out that girl sunbathing on her stomach only to find it was a guy with long hair and a beard when the person finally flipped around."

She shook her head. "Davey always got himself into the funniest situations. I wish I could remember them all."

We walked and reminisced until we made our way back inside the beach house. We sat down on opposite sides of the white couch in the living room.

My mind was still moonlighting in the past. "You know what I remember most about that summer?"

"What?"

"Being so happy that you were home from Brooklyn and in remission. That and kissing the shit out of you every chance I got. Those were seriously the two best months of my life. I feel like everything changed so fast after that."

"We had a lot of good times, Mitch."

"Good times? No. You were the best thing that ever happened to me."

Whoa. Way to be subtle, Nichols.

She looked like she didn't know how to respond to that and promptly changed the subject. "Did you know that Angie just had a baby?"

"Really? No."

Angie and Cody had gotten married and moved to Seattle a few years ago. I wasn't sure if Skylar had still been in touch with them.

"Yeah. They had a little girl. Her name is Ainsley."

"That's a cool name. I'm sure she'll grow up to sound just like her father."

Skylar threw a pillow at me playfully. "You're bad."

"It's the truth though, isn't it?" I threw it back.

"Yes. Of course, it is!" She wiped tears of laughter from her eyes. "Anyway...she quit her job. She's home with the baby now, probably taking a zillion pictures all day."

"Baby's first 9,257 hours..."

"Exactly."

Skylar stared off, and I knew why. It was something I tried to block out whenever it would cross my mind because it hurt like hell to think about. There was no one in the world that would make a better mother, and my heart ached for her. She looked at me, and I realized she knew what I was thinking.

She floored me when she said, "Kevin doesn't want kids."

"Does he know?"

"Yes. I was always up front with him about it."

"You do, though...want kids."

"You know I always have, but what does that matter if I can't conceive?"

"There's always adoption."

"He doesn't want kids period. If he doesn't want one of his own, he's certainly not going to want to adopt."

I wasn't talking about him. I was talking about us.

"Is that why you stay with him because you think you don't have to worry about him leaving you if you can't give him a child?"

She started to shut down. "No. That's not why I'm with him. I don't want to talk about this anymore."

I thought it was a fair question, considering it was the very reason for our demise. If she hadn't left me over that fear, we wouldn't be in this position right now. I felt I had a right to ask.

"Okay." I needed to change the subject. "Hey...I wanted to ask you. I don't usually have a big birthday party for Henry. His birthday's in the summer, but there's this place that opens up in the fall. It's an indoor kids gym, and you can rent it out. I was thinking of having a belated party for him at the end of September. He doesn't really have any friends, so there won't be too many kids there. He'll just be able to jump around and go crazy and enjoy it without the chaos of a crowd. They have one of those moonbounces and a ball pit. They let you bring in pizza and cake. Do you think you'd be able to make it?"

Her face turned pale.

"Did I say something wrong? You don't have to come. It was just an innocent invitation."

"You said...the end of September?"

"What's wrong?"

"I would love to go, but—"

"But what? What aren't you saying?"

"There's something I haven't mentioned. I didn't want to ruin this trip. I don't really know how to tell you."

I felt a sudden rush of panic. I started to sweat. "Say it."

"Kevin was offered a vice president position in California. He's taking it, and we're supposed to be moving in a month."

My heart felt like it had been ripped out of my chest. All efforts to remain calm and composed during this trip were destroyed in that moment. "You're moving away?"

"I don't want to."

She moved closer. I backed away.

"In a month? How long have you known about this?"

"Two weeks, maybe three."

"Were you ever gonna tell me? Or were you going to just fucking disappear again?"

"I was going to tell you. I just—"

"WHEN?"

I got up from the couch and paced the floor.

"Please don't get upset. You have no idea how badly this is hurting me. I don't want to leave, but—"

"But you were going to anyway...maybe not even tell me until the last minute or never?" I rubbed my temples to soothe my pounding head as old wounds from her past abandonment burst open. "You knew...before you agreed to come here." I looked deeply into her eyes, desperate for the truth. "This trip...it's not a chance for us to get closer. It's goodbye, isn't it?"

Her voice trembled. "I don't know what it is. I'm scared and so confused."

"Well, I'll make it easier for you." I needed to get out of there before I totally lost it. I walked to the door and turned around one last time. "Thanks for dinner."

A tear fell down her cheek. "Please don't go away mad..."

"I'll see you tomorrow at work."

I slammed the door behind me.

When I got into the car, I couldn't move. My hands shook as I gripped the steering wheel. I needed to calm down, so I could drive home. If she saw that I was still sitting out here, she would come outside. I needed to be away from her to think clearly.

I pulled out of the gravel and onto the dark road leading back to my hotel. A car driving toward me nearly blinded me with its high beams.

I replayed the night in my head as I drove. She loved me. I knew it in my heart. But love may not have been enough because she didn't feel safe with me.

The text alert on my phone sounded, and I quickly looked down while trying to keep an eye on the road.

I didn't say anything to you because I'm not sure I'm going with him.

My heart filled with hope and fear at the same time. While her words were encouraging, it was still a mixed message. Either way, it became abundantly clear that with this new threat looming, I had to fight harder and faster. I no longer had months to get her to see that she belonged with me. Maybe I would never be the safe choice, but I was the right choice. I would love her harder than I ever hurt her.

With only three nights left, I needed to capitalize on what strengths I had, including her physical attraction to me. I needed to show her how much she needed me, how happy and fulfilled I could make her in ways he couldn't. Fuck my original plan to get her back gracefully.

Now, it was time to play dirty.

TWENTY-SIX

SKYLAR

When my alarm sounded at six, my eyes were groggy, and my headache was splitting. I hadn't been able to sleep most of the night. I stretched and walked over to the window. When I opened it, the salty smell of the ocean immediately greeted me along with the morning call of the seagulls.

I missed him.

After I'd made him angry, I felt guilty staying in this beautiful house that he paid for. My stomach was upset because I just didn't know what to expect when I got to work this morning. He never responded to my text last night. Today was supposed to be one of my busiest days, as I'd be putting up all of the window treatments. I didn't want to be spending all of that time inside the house if he'd just be giving me the cold shoulder.

I decided to stop by Starbucks on the way to get a latte for me and a coffee and muffin for Mitch. Maybe that small gesture would help get the day off on the right foot.

When I arrived, all of the guys were out front. I had forgotten that today was the day they would be putting in the wheelchair ramp.

When Mitch spotted me, he put down the tool he was using and walked over to where I was getting out of my car.

Butterflies swarmed in my belly as he approached. It was early, but his shirt was already off. A tool belt was wrapped around his waist where his jeans hung low. I don't think I'd ever seen anything hotter in my life. I was expecting him to be mad, but instead when he stopped in front of me, he gave me a wicked grin.

He took the coffee and muffin from my hands. "Thank you. You shouldn't have."

"Well, I figured it was the least I could do after upsetting you with that news last night."

I stepped back in surprise when he leaned in. I thought he was going to kiss me on the mouth, but instead he plastered a warm, firm kiss on my cheek.

His voice was low and deep as he spoke close to my ear. "Don't worry about last night."

Okay.

Then, he turned around without saying another word. I watched as he walked away. I tilted my head, admiring the way his jeans hugged his tight ass. My body was still tingling from the shock of feeling his mouth on my skin for the first time in so many years. My cheek was still wet from his saliva as I stood motionless, hating myself for wishing the kiss had been on my lips with his tongue down my throat.

When I walked inside the house, the fresh paint fumes were overwhelming. I got to work immediately, putting up the hardware for the curtains in the bedrooms.

After an hour or so, I jumped in surprise when Mitch appeared in the threshold, his chest glistening.

"Oh, hey," I said.

"Hey."

I stepped down from the stool. "What's up?"

"I need a favor."

"Shoot."

He lifted a tube of sunscreen. "The sun is blazing. I'm starting to burn. Can you put some of this on my back?"

Oh God.

"Uh, yeah. Sure."

He handed it to me and turned with his back facing me. "Thanks."

His skin was flawless, smooth and golden from the sun. This was my first close-up of the large cross tattoo in the middle of his back. There was an awkward squirting sound as I squeezed the lotion into my palm and closed the cap, holding the tube between my knees.

I started at the top, rubbing in slow circles at the base of his neck before moving down over his shoulders and the rippling muscles of his upper back. They tightened and flexed at my touch. My massage was more sensual than appropriate. I couldn't help it. It had been years since I could touch him like this. He was breathing fast, and I knew he felt the same electricity. My hands moved over the cross then to his lower back. I fantasized about slipping my hands into the waistband of his jeans, grateful that he couldn't see the look of awe on my face, which would have been a dead giveaway to my weakness.

He turned around suddenly, and slowly reached down between my knees to grab the bottle. I felt weak, and my hands tremored with a need to touch him again.

I wished I could do the front.

As he looked at me, his blue eyes reflected the sunlight pouring into the room. They were filled with more raw desire than I had seen in a long time. "Thank you."

I gulped the saliva that built up from my drooling. "You're welcome."

Then, he just turned around and disappeared.

He spent the rest of the afternoon outside, leaving me rattled as I struggled to focus on my work and not the memory of how his skin felt.

Around three in the afternoon, he came into one of the bedrooms where I was arranging furniture. Sweat was dripping down his chest, and he wiped his head with his forearm. "I'm heading out of here. You should do the same."

"I just have a couple more things to finish up."

"I'm picking you up at five."

"Where are we going?"

"Don't worry about it. Wear the nicest thing you have."

Before I could respond, he was gone. My body filled with excitement. I fiddled with my engagement ring in the hopes that it would magically knock some sense into me. Unfortunately, it did nothing to curb the throbbing between my legs.

I put on a tiny, red dress that left little to the imagination and slipped my feet into a pair of my highest stilettos. I styled my hair in long, loose curls and finished up getting ready just as the doorbell rang.

A whiff of his delicious scent greeted me when the door opened. Wearing a fitted, white linen shirt, Mitch was more dressed up than I'd probably ever seen him. His sleeves were rolled up and a few buttons at the top were opened just enough to see the beginning of my name tattoo. He wore dark, khaki pants that fit snugly. After all these years, a sense of pride filled me upon seeing him so grown-up and dapper.

"Well, don't you look like a member of the yacht club."

His eyes moved from top to bottom. "And you—much to my delight—in those heels, could be a member of the gentleman's club."

"Good one."

My nipples practically turned to steel when he rubbed my arm. "You know I'm kidding."

"You want to come in first? Or do we have a reservation?"

"We should get going now. We'll come back here after dinner."

The thought of us being alone later made me jittery.

He opened the car door for me. "You still like seafood?"

"Yeah. You know it's my favorite."

I could feel Mitch glancing over at me constantly as he drove.

"What?" I asked.

"You look really pretty."

I rubbed both hands over my arms to tame the goosebumps. "You look nice, too."

"You seem nervous. You okay?" he asked.

"You're acting differently today."

"You're right. Today is a new day. This trip will be over in the blink of an eye. I want you to know if I'm thinking something over the next few days, I'm gonna say it. Until last night, I thought I had more time to remind you of who

I am and to tell you things you need to know. I'm not going to waste the rest of this time talking about the possibility of your moving with him. This is about me and you and no one else."

I gave him a slight smile to show him that I understood.

His eyes returned to the road, and he didn't look at me the rest of the quiet ride.

We pulled into the parking lot of a high-end restaurant, Rowlings on the Water. He held the door open for me. The smell of fresh seafood immediately hit me. There was a room off to the left with lobsters swimming around in a large tank. To the right, was the dining area that was pretty crowded for so early in the evening. There was indoor seating and an outdoor area that overlooked the water.

A hostess greeted us. "Would you prefer inside or out?"

Mitch looked at me.

"It's so nice out. Let's eat outside," I said.

She grabbed two menus. "Outside it is. Right this way."

Once seated, our waitress, a pretty redhead named Ginny, came over. "What can I get you started with?"

"I'll have a glass of Pinot Grigio," I said.

"I'll have a Sam Adams."

When I handed her my drink menu, her eyes landed on my diamond, which was shining brightly in the sun. "Whoa, stunning ring," she said before looking at Mitch. "You have nice taste."

"Oh, I didn't pick it out. She's not my fiancée. We're just friends," he said curtly.

"Really? I would have never guessed that." She took his menu. "Does that mean you're single?"

"I am," he said while looking right at me.

"I'll be right back with your drinks."

An awkward silence ensued as Mitch and I browsed the food menu.

When she returned, the focus of her attention shifted solely to Mitch. She totally made eyes at him when she handed him his beer.

"Are you ready to order?"

Mitch pointed to me. "Skylar?"

"I'll have the one pound lobster with a side of baked potato and a salad."

"And I'll have the sea scallops with rice and a salad. Can we also have the oysters on the half shell appetizer?"

"Absolutely. You know what they say about oysters, right?"

Mitch was still looking at me while answering her. "What do they say about oysters, Ginny?"

She blinked her eyelashes. "They're an aphrodisiac."

His eyes were still burning into mine. "Good to know."

She winked at him, oblivious to his clear disinterest. "I'll be right back."

He unfolded his napkin with a guilty laugh. He knew she wanted him. "Did you know that about oysters, Skylar?"

I rolled my eyes. "She's a little bit too obvious, don't you think?"

"About what?"

"She wants to fuck you, and she's letting you know it."

He took a long sip of his beer. "Does that bother you?"

"No. I'm just...pointing it out."

"Okay. So, you wouldn't mind if I asked her to meet up later, then?"

The thought made my stomach sick. His behavior had been so unpredictable today, though, that I couldn't be

100-percent sure he was kidding. For all I knew, he might do it to prove a point and then end up really liking her.

"If that's what you want. Is it?"

He leaned in. "Oh, it wouldn't be what I want. What I want is for all these people to magically disappear and to take you on this table until you scream my name. So, what I want is irrelevant, isn't it? I was just wondering if you'd care."

All of the color must have drained from my face.

"What's wrong?" he asked, knowing exactly the effect his words had on me.

I was so turned on. I could hardly breathe.

I took a long sip of my wine in an attempt to cool myself down. "You weren't kidding when you said you weren't holding back."

"I'm done wasting time with bullshit. Think hard before you ask me something. From now on, I'll damn well give you the honest answer. When we were kids, you used to always do the same. I used to love that about you."

Ginny arrived with our oysters, placing the entire plate in front of Mitch as if I were invisible. "Just let me know if there's anything else I can get you. Anything at all."

Bitch.

Mitch ignored her and pushed the plate into the middle of the table. "Have one."

I stuck my hand out. "I didn't realize they were raw."

"You didn't? I thought you knew what these were. You like sushi, don't you?"

"Yeah, but these are kind of slimy-looking."

I watched closely as he lifted one to his mouth and licked the oyster out of the shell, sucking out the juices. He licked his lips, and it made me instantly wet. Talk about food porn. He took another and reached across the table.

"Open your mouth."

I did as he asked and sucked it into my mouth, swallowing the sludgy oyster as fast as possible.

I made a face. "Okay, I've tried it."

"No more?"

"No."

"Thank you for trying it."

"I'll try anything once." It came out more suggestive than I intended.

I was completely egging him on, and I couldn't stop myself.

When our meals arrived, things cooled down. It never ceased to amaze me how the mood with Mitch could easily turn from sexually tense to comfortable in minutes. That had always been our modus operandi.

We talked about everything from my health to our families. It was sweet to see the look of genuine relief on his face when I explained that my doctors were more optimistic each visit. All routine scans and blood work in the years since my transplant had checked out clear. Then, we moved to the topic of his sister whom he'd remained close with in recent years. He lamented over the fact that Summer was now in her preteens and that he might have to physically harm any boys who break her heart.

Ginny returned to our table. "Did you want dessert?" she asked, looking only at Mitch.

I just wanted to get home and intercepted. "We still have a ton of tiramisu left over from the other night back at the house," I said.

He looked at her. "I guess that's a no. We'll just take the check."

She returned with our bill and two mints.

He looked down at it and made a funny face.

I reached out my hand "What's the damage?"

"It's nothing."

"Mitch, you've paid for this whole trip. The least I can do is cover dinner. Please let me."

"No way."

I suddenly snatched the bill out of his hand and saw that Ginny had left more than those two candies. His earlier smirk made total sense now.

I think you're adorable, and I'd love to go out sometime. Call me. 757-969-2352.

My body stiffened as a feeling of primal protectiveness surged through me. It was unfair to feel this way given my circumstances, but the thought of Mitch with another woman made me crazy.

"You okay?" he asked.

"Yeah."

He gave me a knowing look. I guess I wore my jealousy on my sleeve.

"I'm not gonna call her, Skylar."

"You don't owe me an explanation. You'd have every right to be interested in someone else."

He looked around to see if anyone was listening then looked into my eyes. "I *wish* I could fucking want someone else." His stare was penetrating. "It doesn't feel good, though, does it? Times that by 1000, and that's what I've been going through."

For the first time tonight, I saw genuine sadness in his eyes.

"No, it doesn't...feel good."

He ripped the bill from my grasp and cracked a smile. "For the record, you're adorable when you're jealous."

I didn't put up a fight about paying. I just wanted to get out of there as fast as possible, angry at my sudden and selfish desire to be alone with him.

Mitch took two small plates out of the cupboard. "Let's take dessert out to the beach while there's still a little light, unless you'd want to go swimming?"

"No, the water's too cold. It's high tide, and the waves are rough. Dessert on the beach sounds good. I'll grab a blanket from upstairs."

We took our shoes off and walked out onto the sand where we spread the blanket down.

It was windy, and our hair was blowing all over the place. A flock of a dozen seagulls decided to join us once they saw we were eating.

Mitch threw one a remnant of his dessert. "They must know we're bird people."

I let out a giggle. "Aw, I miss Seamus. He's probably miserable without me."

"That old bird and I always did have that in common."

He startled me when he moved closer and rubbed his thumb against my chin. "You had a ton of whipped cream right there." When he licked his thumb, a shiver ran down the length of my body.

He didn't realize he had some whipped cream, too, on the corner of his mouth, and it was taunting me. I imagined licking it off.

"You have some, too," I said.

"Where?"

"Right here." I brushed my index finger along the corner of his mouth. The tip of his tongue peeked out from in between his teeth and grazed my finger as I moved it along his lower lip."

He shut his eyes as if to fend off the feelings produced by the contact. I didn't know why I was torturing myself. Touching his mouth wasn't going to help if I couldn't kiss it deeply the way I was dying to.

Now, he was staring at *my* mouth, a silent invitation to continue what I started. I tried to change the subject. "I have a confession. I didn't make this tiramisu. I bought it at the bakery down the road."

"Ah...you sneak," he said, taking another bite.

"Isn't it the most delicious thing you've ever tasted?"

He slowly pulled the spoon from his mouth and shook his head. "No, actually. It's not."

It took me a few seconds to understand why he was looking at me like he wanted to eat me. Then, I figured out that he was referring to going down on me. I squeezed the muscles between my legs in response to the immediate reaction triggered by the memory of his hot mouth devouring me. He was the only man who had ever done that to me.

In another attempt to change the subject, I looked toward the seagulls that were now yards away. "The night is still young. What do you want to do?"

"I want go inside and light up that electric fireplace. Have you tried it?"

"No. I haven't yet," I said.

"That's what I want to do. I want to sit by the fire with you and just chill."

"Okay."

"But first I want to make you wet."

Excuse me?

"What?"

Before my mind could fall further into the gutter, he lifted me up over his shoulder and sprinted toward the choppy ocean.

I whacked him repeatedly as my body bounced against him while he ran. "Mitch! No. No. No. Put me down! Put me down!"

My back slapped against the cold water when he dumped me in. I swallowed some of the salt water and started coughing incessantly. My dress was drenched, and so were his clothes.

"You jerk!" I started to splash him as fast and furiously as I could.

He didn't even try to block me. He just stood there and let me do it with a devilish smile on his face, periodically pushing his hair back with his hands and spitting out water. At one point, I got taken out by a wave and lost my balance. I started to laugh fervently after it knocked me down.

As he held his stomach in laughter, I trudged through the water and knocked him in the chest. "You think that's funny, huh?"

"No," he said, grabbing me again and lifting me over his head. "I think *this* is funny." He threw me down hard into the water again.

We frolicked in the ocean for at least an hour until every drop of sun disappeared. The light from the house was like a lamp in the darkness.

"It's getting chilly. Let's go inside," he said.

We squeezed the water out of our clothes and raced to the door. It felt like we were teenagers again. We were laughing and panting as we wiped our feet free of sand in the doorway.

"I'll go get some towels," I said before running up the stairs.

I quickly got out of my dress, putting on a cami and shorts before returning downstairs.

He had turned on the electric fireplace that was built into the wall in the living room. I threw one of the towels at him.

He rubbed it through his hair. His skin was transparent through the wet white shirt. "This wasn't a very smart idea. I have no change of clothes."

"I could see if there are any in the drawers or closet upstairs. The owner might have left some stuff behind."

"Worth a shot," he said as he unbuttoned his wet shirt.

I watched until every last button came undone and ran back upstairs, still thinking about it.

The drawers were mostly empty. In the back of the first closet, there were a few ladies winter coats, and then I hit the jackpot: one set of obnoxious tropical shorts. The motif was a combination of bright colors and palm trees. There were no shirts in sight.

I ran excitedly down the stairs. "I have good news and bad news. I found some great shorts for you but no shirt."

"I can live with that."

So could I.

I threw the shorts at him. "You can change in the bathroom off the kitchen."

"These are...wow. Hideous," he said, holding them up. They might be a little small for me."

When he came back out, I was amazed at how good he looked even in those ridiculous shorts. With muscles and a six-pack like that, what he wore didn't really matter. His damp hair was messy, sticking up in all directions, which I found amazingly sexy. The shorts fit him like a glove. They didn't look nearly as bad on him as they had on the hanger.

"I feel like my package is an advertisement for Hawaiian tourism."

I giggled. "They don't look half-bad." I couldn't help checking out his body. "When did you start working out so hard?"

"A few years after you left town."

"Really?"

"It was my outlet, still is. You have to blow off steam somehow, right? Plus, I want to be around for a long time for my son." He walked over to the fire. "Come sit here by me."

There was a couch right under the fireplace on the wall. He sat on one end facing me, and I sat on the other end and put my feet up.

"I saw you were checking your phone when I was coming out of the bathroom. I'm guessing he called?"

"Yeah."

"How come you didn't call him back?"

"I texted him that I was turning in early and that I'd talk to him tomorrow."

"You didn't have to lie for me. You could've called him."

"This whole trip is a lie, isn't it? What's the difference?"

"The difference is, you're not doing anything wrong. He could never begin to understand our history and the need for closure."

"So, that's what this is about...closure?"

"There's no one else here, Skylar—just you and me. Tell me what you're really feeling. Please. I need to know what I'm facing when we get home."

The fire cast a glow around his face. His translucent eyes reflected the flames. Mitch's strong hand gripped the back of the couch as if that were the one thing keeping him from touching me. He waited for me to say something.

When he pointed out that no one would ever know what was said in this room tonight, it resonated with me. Suddenly, as I looked at this beautiful, vulnerable man with my name etched onto his chest, I wanted to pour my soul out to him.

"I'm feeling...like I wish we could stay here forever. I wish everyday could be a happy one, like how we were in that water tonight."

"We *can* have that kind of happiness. Everyday."

"It's not that simple. Someone would have to get hurt for that to happen. And then, there's Henry..."

"Henry is fine. He has me and always will. He doesn't need a mother, Skylar, if that's where you're going with this. We've done just fine without one. Your coming into our lives wouldn't have to mean becoming Henry's mother. I know you may never be able to fully accept him because of—"

"No! I don't let her impact the way I look at him. He doesn't deserve that. He's been through enough. I'm just afraid of hurting him."

He rested his forearms on his legs and rubbed his eyes in frustration then abruptly turned to me. "Because you think I'll do something to hurt *you* again, and then you'll have to leave, right? You don't feel safe with me. I get it. But are you content? Every time I ask you if you're happy with him, you skirt around the question. Fuck, Skylar. Are...you... *happy* with him?"

"You want the answer?"

"Yes."

"A question for a question, then. I'll answer, and then I get to ask you one."

"Like our old game...without the basketball."

"Yeah."

"I'm down for that," he said.

"You asked if I was happy…" I stared into the fire, feeling incredibly guilty for what I was about to admit for the first time, both to him and out loud to myself. "I'm not. I feel safe, but I'm not happy. You used to make me happy. You were the only person who ever made me truly happy. When that was ripped away, it became more important to feel safe than happy." I exhaled. "My turn."

"Okay."

"How is it possible that you haven't been with anyone in five years?"

He leaned his head back on the couch. "I don't really know how to explain it, except to say I haven't wanted anyone. It wasn't worth it to just do it for the sake of it. My mother convinced me to see a therapist a couple of years ago. He seemed to think I was traumatized by what happened with Charisma, that I didn't trust anyone or maybe that I was afraid the same thing would happen again. Somewhere in the back of my mind that might have been the case, but I can tell you the desire for other women just hasn't been there."

"But you have the desire now?"

"That's two questions." His eyes lowered to my nipples that were standing to attention. "My turn. When was the last time you had sex with him?"

"Sometime before the night we went to Bev's. My turn. Do you have the desire back now?"

He just looked at me for the longest time then said, "Yes." His eyes traveled unapologetically down the length of my body, and his voice was lower. "My turn. Am I the reason you haven't slept with him since Bev's?"

I whispered, "Yes."

My foot accidentally bumped into his leg. After I moved it back on reflex, he grabbed it and began to lightly squeeze it, bringing in the other foot as well. Deep in thought, he stared down at his hands as they massaged my feet. I closed my eyes and enjoyed the sensation for several quiet minutes until he stopped suddenly.

"I think I should go." He got up and picked up his wet clothing off the floor.

"What? Why?" I followed him to the kitchen.

"Because I can't do this."

"It's okay. You don't have to leave. Things just got a little out of hand."

"I told myself I wasn't going to touch you until you asked me to."

"It was just a foot rub."

"It's not the foot rub. It's what I almost just did. It's what I still want to do. I want to know that you're not gonna turn me away because once I start, I'm not sure I could stop." He gripped the kitchen counter. "God, even the thought of being inside you makes me crazy. I get instantly hard. Just envisioning it is better than the real thing ever was with any one else." His arousal stretched through the fabric of the tight shorts. "You think sticking my dick inside another woman was ever going to help me get over you? It never has, and it never will. Does it help you, Skylar?"

"Sticking my dick inside another woman? I've never tried it, but at this point, maybe I should consider it as an option three."

He shook his head and startled me when he walked a step forward and put his hand on my cheek. "How do you do that, always make me laugh in a moment that's supposed to be fucking serious?" He moved his hand back. "What I meant was...does fucking him while you're thinking about me help? Based on the way you look at me, I would venture to say no."

"What way is that?"

"The same way I know I look at you, like someone who's wanted one thing practically his entire life and can never have it." His voice was strained. "I don't want to die not knowing what it feels like to be inside the only woman I've ever loved."

I closed my eyes.

What he'd said took me back to my cancer days when I'd spent many sleepless nights fearing that very same thing, that I would die before I had the chance to make love to him.

"I wish we had made love that night in Lake George when we had the chance."

"Me, too. I've never had more than meaningless sex. I don't even know what it feels like to make love to someone. You're the only woman I could experience that with. In ten years, I've had a lot of time to imagine what it would be like." He stared off and slowly shook his head with an indignant look. "It should have been me. I should have been your first...but I'd rather be your last."

"Mitch..."

His eyes darkened as he moved closer to me, just inches from my lips and said, "He's not giving you what you need. I can feel it." I was dying to kiss him, my breathing completely out of control. After a few seconds, he turned around and grabbed his keys off the counter. "I think it's time for me to go."

My underwear was completely soaked as I imagined him backing me against the counter and wrapping my legs around him as he pounded into me. I was throbbing between my legs. The look on his face was an expression of the same hunger I was feeling. I wanted him to touch me. I couldn't ask him to because I knew where it would lead, and I didn't want to cheat on Kevin, but I still needed to hear it like my life depended on it. "What would it be like?"

He stood still, staring at the ground with his keys in his hands. "I don't think I could be gentle."

My body was humming with an uncontrollable yearning. "What would you do to me?"

"Remember what I said earlier tonight?"

"Not to ask you a question if I don't want the honest answer."

"You still want to know what I would do to you?"

I was like someone who chooses to take drugs for the first time. You know full well the repercussions, but you say yes anyway. I nodded.

Mitch looked down at my shorts and asked a question he likely already knew the answer to. "Are you wet right now?"

My eyes were half-closed as I leaned my back against the counter. My voice was barely audible. "Yes."

"You want the honest answer? Baby, words can't do justice to what I would do to your body. I'm not going to tell you. I want to show you...when you ask me to." He exited the kitchen and opened the front door. He took a few steps toward his car, his feet crunching in the gravel before he turned around. "And Skylar? Restraint is the best foreplay."

TWENTY-SEVEN

MITCH

My morning wood was worse than usual. That didn't surprise me, considering I also woke up in the middle of the night with a wet dream. The years of celibacy were catching up to me all at once. When I got back to my hotel last night, I was like a rock star going off on a bender after five years of sobriety. I guess I was more like a *cock* star, since my drug of choice seemed to be jerking off repeatedly to thoughts of her.

My plan to weaken her resistance had worked. The problem was, I wasn't keeping up my end of the deal: no touching. Even when she had rubbed the sunscreen on my back earlier in the day, I kept my hands off of her.

It became exceedingly more difficult not to touch her once we started playing around at the beach. Still, I hadn't lost control until I started massaging her feet by the fire. I had gotten the sudden urge to kiss them and work my way up the rest of her body. I stopped it before my fantasy became a reality. Taking the next step was Skylar's decision to make, not mine. My job was to make her see that I was the *right* decision.

One good thing from last night: she finally admitted that she wasn't happy with him. Normally, that would have been grounds for a celebratory dance. But she followed it up with a major downer when she said it was more important to feel safe than happy. Screw that. If she continued to let her mind win over her heart, I stood to lose everything.

Her eyes confused me the most. They were basically commanding me to bend her over and fuck her hard. In all the years I'd known her, I'd never seen anything like it. It was proof he wasn't giving her what she needed. She practically begged me to tell her what I'd do to her like her next breath depended on it. *Dirty.* Needless to say, that nearly put me over the edge, which was why I had to get the hell out of there.

I emerged from the bathroom after my cold, morning shower. Instrumental music from the Weather Channel forecast played on the television. I dialed my mother before heading to the house for our last day of hard labor.

"Hey, Mom."

"Hi, honey. Is everything okay? You sound upset."

"It's going alright. Skylar's a confused mess. Nothing is going to get resolved on this trip."

"I hope you're prepared if things don't go your way."

"Look, I wasn't calling to discuss it. I just want to talk to Henry. Is he up?"

"Sure, I'll put him on."

I could hear the noises from his iPad, so I knew he was on the phone.

I lay back on the bed with a big smile. "Hey, buddy. It's Daddy. I miss you."

He hummed in reaction to my voice. Even though he couldn't respond to me in words, I truly believed he understood everything I was saying.

"I'll be home in a couple of days, okay? Be good for Grammy."

I could hear the computer-generated voice from the iPad. *"I want to go to McDonald's."*

I laughed. "Daddy will take you to McDonald's this weekend when I get back, okay? We'll go Sunday. I promise."

"I want Daddy."

"I know. I love you, buddy. I'll be home soon."

My mother came back to the phone. "He misses you. He keeps pulling up the picture of your face and pressing it."

"It fucking breaks my heart. I hate that he can't tell me whether he understands that I'm coming back."

"Don't worry about things here, okay? You deserve this break."

"Thank you, Mom. I'll talk to you later."

I missed my son, and I was feeling down on the drive into work. The phone call home had brought me back to reality. With only two days left, I was becoming more pessimistic that things would work out in my favor. Skylar was a good person. She wasn't going to do this guy dirty and dump him after a few days with me even if she loved me. She'd go home, probably still unsure then get sucked in again to the perfect, safe life he built for her. This trip would be a mere memory. She'd leave me and my baggage behind and take off to California for a new start.

When I walked into the house, Skylar was directing one of the guys as to where to hang a picture of a giant bass.

She stopped mid-sentence, and her eyes widened when she noticed me. "Hey."

I waved and silently walked right past her.

I was stewing while unloading my tools to finish off the electrical work in the upstairs bathroom. I could still smell her perfume while my head became lost in a sea of doubt. We belonged together. It just seemed so clear to me, but I couldn't force it. If she was intent on ending up with the *safer* choice, the one who never caused her any pain, there was nothing I could do. Fuck history. Fuck love. Fuck fate. Fuck happiness. Fuck mind-blowing sex. Fuck it all.

About ten minutes had passed when she appeared at the door then came in and shut it. "You forgot what I said."

The sound of her sweet voice alone immediately weakened my new supposed stance.

I put down my pliers and tried not to look at her. "What?"

"You're pretending I don't exist because you're scared. It's exactly what you used to do when we were teenagers. Remember how you would avoid me when you started to have feelings? You're doing that right now. Back then, I told you I didn't want to lose moments with you just because you were afraid. I made a promise, though, that I couldn't keep. I told you that if we screwed up, no matter what, you wouldn't lose me. I told you I would always be there, and I wasn't. When things got worse than either of us could have imagined, I ran. I lied to you, and I'm sorry." Her eyes started to glisten as she continued, "But we have two days left here. Again, I'm telling you I don't want to lose one moment with you. I realize I haven't given you any answers, but just know, I need every second of this time with you like my life depends on it."

Me, too. Fuck. I needed that too.

I had no resolve. I pulled her into a hug that lasted for at least a full minute. Her hair was practically in my mouth. I was breathing into her neck while my helpless dick swelled. I knew I had to stick this out. I'd be gambling with my heart because even a small chance of winning her love and trust was impossible to pass up.

That night, we watched old nineties movies back at the beach house and talked until all hours. There was no touching. I went back to my hotel, tossing and turning, knowing that the next night would be our last at the house on Sandbridge Beach. What really kept me up, though, was the fear that it would be our last night together period.

Friday had finally arrived, and all of the work at the house was completed. The unveiling was set for tomorrow morning.

Skylar spent the afternoon putting the finishing decorative touches on all of the rooms. She had picked a nautical theme with lots of blue and white, along with images of anchors, boats and the ocean. An actual oar hung on the wall. She laid throw pillows down, put out candles, silk flowers and seashells. Her skills were seriously impressive. She also managed to keep us 500-dollars under budget.

The last thing on my agenda was surveying the site along with the building inspector, making sure everything was up to code.

Skylar and I were able to make it back to the rental house in good time for our last night in Virginia Beach. The only other obligation we had was to show up for the big reveal tomorrow morning. Then, she would head to the airport in the early afternoon, and I would begin the long drive back to New Jersey alone.

Skylar said she wasn't hungry, so we had a small meal of appetizers at a local fried seafood shack. The mood was tense and somber like the cloudy weather outside tonight. Even though I felt like I knew where her heart was, I had no idea where her head was. Her expression had been stoic throughout dinner.

When we returned to the beach house, Skylar looked like she wanted to say something the second we walked in the door. She put her purse down and chewed her lip nervously. "I want you to spend the night here in the spare room. Will you?"

"I'm not sure that's a good idea."

There was no way I trusted myself.

"You paid for this house. I want you to enjoy it for at least one night. The second room overlooks the ocean, too. There's nothing like waking up to that view and smelling the salty air. I've felt guilty this whole time. We're both adults. There's no reason why you can't stay here for our last night."

"If that's what makes you happy, I'll stay." I had no idea what was going to really happen tonight. My heart started to beat rapidly. I smiled. She smiled back.

Her phone rang, interrupting our moment. She looked unsettled, and I immediately knew who it was. In the past, I walked away when she took his call. Tonight was different. I stayed looking at her the entire time she spoke to him, my heart mangled.

She picked it up. "Hey, what's up?"

"Yes, everything's still on target. We finished up today."

"Ugh...you know...just watching TV...relaxing."

Fucking around with my ex. Same thing.

"Yup."

"I'll call you when I land. I can just catch a cab."

"If you insist..."

"Me, too."

There was a long pause.

"You know I do."

Then, a longer pause. Her eyeballs were frantically moving back and forth.

"Kevin..."

Her breathing was rapid, and her face turned red as a beet. What was he saying to her?

Her gaze fell on mine. "I love you," she finally said to him.

She immediately closed her eyes in shame and hung up the phone.

She might as well have shot me at point blank range.

My eyes bugged out of my head. "What the fuck was that?"

"It wasn't what it seemed."

"You...just told him...you loved him and were looking straight at *me*. You just said 'I love you' to another man while looking into my eyes as if you were saying it to me." I yelled, "Do you know what a mind fuck that is?"

Skylar was shaking. "He made me say it. If I hadn't, he would have suspected something. I'm pretty sure he already knows something's up with me."

Wow.

I looked down at the floor, rubbing my chin and just knew. This was it. I'd reached the end of my rope.

I looked deeply into her eyes because she needed to understand what I was about to say. "From the moment you came into my life all those years ago, you made me feel like I had a purpose on this Earth. Over time, I discovered what it was. It was to love you. I don't know who I am without you. I'm Henry's dad. But Mitch...Mitch is lost. I feel stuck in a time warp, like I'm still that teenager waiting to make love to his girlfriend over Christmas break. Everything changed in a flash. Physically, I became a grown man, but inside, I'm still that lost boy waiting for you to come back. I think I finally just realized that's never going to happen."

Tears fell from her eyes. "Mitch..."

"Do you know how painful it is to love someone so fucking much that you'd die for them, yet they don't even feel safe with you? Go on and marry him. Have your perfect life on your perfect street with your perfect man...and see my face every night when he's fucking you. I'm DONE." I couldn't look at her as I headed straight for the door. "Goodbye, Skylar."

She didn't even bother to follow me out this time.

TWENTY-EIGHT

SKYLAR

My entire body was shaking as I fell to the ground. I stayed in the same spot, leaning against the wall with my head in my hands unable to handle the enormity of what had just happened. I had finally managed to push him away. The pain in my chest was overpowering.

He loved me, but he could only put up with so much. How could I have told Kevin I loved him while looking straight into Mitch's eyes?

Kevin suspected something. He was acting uncharacteristically insecure on the phone and kept hounding me to say those three words. I didn't know what to do because if I didn't say them, he'd demand an explanation. He would have kept me on the phone all night, and I didn't want to ruin my last hours alone with Mitch. But that was exactly what happened anyway. I thought I could sweep it under the rug after, but the hurt was beyond repair.

Letting him leave was cowardly. All of the things I wanted to say to him were at the tip of my tongue, but none would come out.

I should've been relieved, right? Wasn't that what I had been looking for...someone to make the decision for me? Mitch giving up the fight now meant I could walk off into the sunset with Kevin sans temptation.

So, why did I feel like my life was over?

My eyelids shut tight as the wind shook the windows on the French doors. It was starting to rain outside. I prayed to God to take this immeasurable pain away. The thought of taking a second chance on Mitch had always scared me, but nothing compared to how scared I was now that I'd pushed him away.

Love can't exist without fear.

The thought had come out of nowhere, almost as if a spirit guide had whispered it in my ear. Where had I heard that before?

I wracked my brain and remembered the conversation Jake and I had years ago at the engagement party right before the nightmare with Charisma happened.

"If the thought of losing someone doesn't scare the shit out of you, then it's not love."

Throughout all of this, not once had I been scared to lose Kevin. I was scared to hurt him but never scared to live without him. It finally became crystal clear to me. Kevin took care of me and made me feel safe. I cared about him, but there was no fear. *It wasn't love.* I couldn't marry someone I wasn't in love with.

On the other hand, the thought of living without Mitch made me physically ill. It terrified me. The agony in my chest worsened. Mitch left tonight thinking I didn't love him when that couldn't have been further from the truth.

He needed to come back. I reached for my phone and dialed his number, but it went to voicemail. I called the hotel. He should have been there by now. The front desk connected me to his room, but there was no answer.

My heart started racing. The roads were probably slick. What if he got into an accident because he was upset? What if something happened to him, and he never knew how much he meant to me?

I grabbed my keys in a panic. When I ran out the door, the wind blew sand in my eyes. As I was about to get into the car, I noticed a silhouette in the distance by the shoreline.

It was a strong, muscular, beautiful silhouette of a man with his hands in his pockets, staring out at the ocean with the wind blowing through his hair.

Mitch.

Drizzle hit my face as I ran through the damp sand, stopping a few feet away from him.

I was out of breath. "You came back."

He turned around. "I never left...not for a second."

I knew he meant that literally and figuratively. He'd always been waiting for me to come back to him.

I walked slowly toward him.

"Don't come near me," he said.

I ignored him and put my hands on his face. His eyes were dark, empty, devoid of all life.

I started to cry. "I'm sorry. I'm so sorry for putting you through that. It should have never happened. I don't love him, Mitch. I realize that now."

He took my hands off his face and held them in a firm grip. "Look into my eyes. What do you see when you look at me? Can you even fucking see me anymore? It's *still* me. Please tell me you still see who I am."

In that moment, I chose to set aside my fears and truly *saw* him for the first time since coming home.

My Mitch.

The boy. The teenager. The man. His eyes were the one constant and the window into the soul of all three. I'd loved them all equally.

I sniffled. "Yes. I see you. I *see* you, and I love you."

"Don't fuck with me, Skylar. I was mourning you out here, like it was the fucking burial of our relationship. Then, you come out of nowhere telling me you love me. What changed?"

"I chose to let go of the fear and saw the love that lies beneath. It was always there. It never left."

"You're serious?"

I didn't answer him. Instead, I lifted the dress off of my body and let it blow away in the wind. My breasts were bare as I stood before him in nothing but my lace underwear.

"Touch me." He didn't move, and I begged again. "Please."

"Don't do this if you don't mean it. Don't—"

I pressed my lips into his. He groaned down my throat the second our mouths touched as if an endless hunger had finally been satisfied. He put his hands around my face, holding it steady as he slipped his tongue inside my mouth and licked me ravenously. I had never been kissed that deeply. It was like he was fucking my mouth with his tongue, demonstrating what he wanted to do to my body.

I knew there was no going back now. Guilt was making an attempt to rise to the surface, but it wasn't strong enough. I couldn't stop if I tried. I moved back for a moment to catch my breath when he pulled me into him harder. Wetness trickled down my thigh. I was so incredibly turned on by the commanding force of his kiss.

When his mouth left mine, I panted and licked my lips, starving for more. The scruff on his face scraped my skin as he kissed my chin, and ended it with one slow, gentle bite. He pulled my hair back roughly and devoured the base of my neck, sucking so hard that it hurt. There would be marks tomorrow, but I didn't care. I was all in, wanting the pain, wanting everything he had to give.

He slowly licked a line back up to my mouth. This time, as he pressed his lips against mine, his hot erection also pressed against my stomach.

Misty rain continued to spray my nearly naked body as he kissed me with his palms placed firmly on my ass. The warm, humid air blew our hair around as he kept his forehead on mine. Neither of us moved as the waves crashed around us. He whispered against my mouth. "Tell me this is real."

I ran my fingers through his hair. "It's real. It's not a dream."

"I'm going to make love to you tonight in that big, white bed upstairs." I nodded against his forehead in agreement as he continued, "But first, I really need to fuck you...right here on this beach."

The muscles between my legs began to rapidly contract. "Please," I begged.

"Take off your underwear."

His chest was rising and falling as he watched me step out of the pink lace panties. Metal clanked as he unfastened his leather belt without delay and threw it onto the sand. When he unbuttoned his jeans and lowered the zipper, they fell to the ground. His swollen cock rested against his thigh through his tight boxers. I had forgotten how big he was, and my heart galloped. I couldn't wait another second to feel him.

He didn't have to direct me this time. I leapt into his arms. He kissed me harder than before and moaned into my mouth the moment he entered me. In one slightly painful thrust, he was inside of me. My muscles pulsed and squeezed around him in a way I had never experienced with anyone. My legs were wrapped around his waist as he fucked me with a force and depth I didn't even know was possible.

He let out a single, intense breath with each thrust. Each one seemed harder than the last, and I'd move my hips to keep up. It was never enough. His eyes were closed tight as if the pleasure were unbearable. I knew with every movement, he was taking me back, taking back everything we lost and at the same time, finally claiming me in every way.

He bit my bottom lip and growled, "Ten fucking years, I've been dying for this." In a rhythm that matched his thrusts, he repeated, "Ten...fucking...years. Promise me no other man will ever touch you again."

I could hardly think straight. "Yes."

"Say it. Promise me. When I come inside you, I need to know that I'm your last, that you belong to me now."

I bore down on him faster in an attempt to demonstrate my feelings. "I'm yours. Take it. Take it all." I remembered something I said years ago that made him crazy and repeated it. "I'm going to come all over your dick."

My words immediately set him off. "You little shit. You remembered." He laughed against my mouth, and his body shuddered. "Say my name then when you come all over my dick, baby. Say it."

"Mitch. Oh, God...Mitch. Yes!"

He screamed out in pleasure as he came, staring intensely into my eyes and pushing me down over his orgasm. I tightened around it as I climaxed, wanting every drop of his hot release in me.

My legs, now limp, were still wrapped around him as he stayed inside of me and kissed me softly this time.

I felt wetness on my face.

I looked at him and realized tears were pouring out of his eyes. "You'd better fucking mean what you said, Skylar. Because I can't go back now."

Neither could I.

The rain picked up, pelting us, but we didn't move immediately. He pulled out of me and put me down only to lift my naked body back up again and carry me into the house.

Once upstairs, he brought me to the bathroom and turned on the hot water in the tub, checking the temperature. He let it fill for a while before he grabbed my hand and led me in.

We said nothing as he poured liquid soap onto the sponge and ran it slowly down my body, washing in slow circles between my legs and down to my toes. He pumped some shampoo into his hands and massaged it into my hair. I closed my eyes in heaven as the bathroom filled with steam and the smell of mint. He was being so gentle, caring for me as if I were a delicate flower. It felt like he was trying to make up for what he couldn't give me in the past. It wasn't my first time, but it was *our* first time. This was what he would have done for me had we had that chance years ago.

I grabbed the sponge and began to wash his back. The water was still running, but it had nearly topped off, so I shut it. I massaged the sudsy bubbles over his cross tattoo.

"What does the cross stand for?"

"This one is more recent than the rest. It symbolizes the fact that everyone has a cross to bear. Henry has his autism, yours was the cancer and the domino effect that came along with it. Everyone has something."

"What's yours?"

"What do you think?"

"It was losing me?"

"Losing you and hurting the person who meant everything to me, having to live with that. You remember when we first met? How afraid of love I was because of my parents' divorce and what my father did to my mother?"

"Yes, of course I do."

"You made me believe in love. Then, when that shit happened with Charisma, I essentially became my father. I became the man who got some girl pregnant and devastated the woman who loved him. It was a sick twist of fate. The circumstances were different, but the outcome was the same. Everything I had ever feared had come true. I couldn't live with myself. I wanted to die. Up until now, Henry was the only thing that saved me. But what you gave me tonight...a second chance to love you...was a gift. I'll spend the rest of my life making sure you don't regret it."

I knew he would, but this night was bittersweet. I wouldn't be able to just return home and start a new life with Mitch. I had a major loose end to tie up, and his name was Kevin. It wasn't going to be pretty.

TWENTY-NINE

MITCH

Until Skylar was wearing my ring, nothing was set in stone. She was still technically engaged to another man, and there was always the chance that she would go home and get sucked into the safety zone again. I needed to do everything in my power to make sure she didn't forget one moment of this night. It was all I had.

Water bubbled down the drain as I lifted her out of the bathtub and wiped her down, delighting in the smell of her skin.

I threw the towel on the ground and pressed my cock against her, backing her into the wall, desperate to be inside of her again. "I need to have you again, but I just want to look at you first."

Her naked body was even more phenomenal than I remembered. A few extra pounds added dainty curves to her delicate frame. I cupped her cheek and ran my hand slowly down her neck to her tits. They were the perfect size, round and just big enough to fit in the palm of my hands. Her nipples were large and a delicate, blush color.

They hardened as I ran my hands down over them. Saliva gathered in my mouth as I dared myself not to lick them. I rubbed my index finger across the familiar cluster of freckles in between her breasts, smiling to myself as if they were old friends I never thought I'd see again.

My hand traveled down to her stomach. I couldn't help the stinging thought that crossed my mind: I would have given anything to see it swell with my baby inside. I loved her so much and wanted to be able to give her a child. I hated that I didn't have the power alone to make that happen, regardless of how desperately I wanted it.

Her pussy looked freshly shaved, and I wondered if she did it because she knew this was bound to happen. I slipped two of my fingers inside of her.

Shit.

"How could you be so wet when I've barely done anything?"

"I've been like that this whole trip. Even when you'd just look at me, it made me wet. No one makes me feel the way you do. What we did on that beach tonight...it's never been like that for me...ever."

"I can't even remember what being with a woman was like before tonight. That was the most incredible thing I've ever felt bar none." I pushed my hand deeper inside of her. "I've never come inside of anyone before...well, willingly at least. I've never done it without a condom."

"Neither have I."

I stopped moving my fingers in disbelief. "What?"

"Kevin always used condoms. He never wanted to take a chance...even though I likely can't...you know...anyway."

I cowered at the thought of anyone else inside of her but couldn't have been more pleased to know that.

"After five years, I wouldn't have guessed that, but I can't tell you how happy I am that no one's ever done that to you before and that I could be your first at something."

"You were my first kiss, too, remember?"

"Ah...the stolen kiss."

She whimpered as I suddenly kissed her greedily.

She licked my lips and said, "You're the first in all the things that have ever truly mattered. You were my first love, my only love."

I needed to continue to make sure I was the last. Feeling insanely possessive, I pulled my fingers out of her and led her to the bed in the adjacent room. Her damp hair fell across the pillow as I hovered over her. My own hair nearly covered my eyes.

My dick was painfully hard and a drop of precum dripped onto her stomach. I needed her now, but first I had to fix something that was bothering me. I grabbed her hand and slowly slipped off her engagement ring, placing it on the nightstand. It was a bold move, but I couldn't stand looking at it anymore. She didn't resist, and I was grateful, unsure how I would have reacted if she had protested.

The rain outside fell harder now against the window. I locked her in with my arms on each side. "Tell me what you want. You want me to be gentle this time? I was a little rough on you out there."

She bit her lip in apprehension. "Um..."

"What? Tell me."

"I don't...want you to go easy on me...at all."

I smiled mischievously. "You like it rough?"

"Yes...very much."

My already excited cock had now become engorged.

I bent down to nip her breast. "What else do you like?"

She was blushing and didn't say anything.

I lightly bit her earlobe, refusing to budge. "I'm not moving until you tell me what you want me to do to you."

"Actually, I like it when *you* tell me what to do, when you're demanding and when you talk dirty. That's what makes me the craziest."

Fuck yeah.

I slid my cock against her opening, "Don't ever be afraid to tell me what you want. I can't wait to try everything with you, things neither of us have ever done. I want to explore every last inch of you, push boundaries if you let me."

"I'll let you do whatever you want."

No, I definitely couldn't ever go back. I'd die.

I kneeled up off of her. "Turn around. I want to see that gorgeous ass."

When she did, I slid my cock between her cheeks and moved it along the top of her crease without entering her. "Remember when I did this to you in the tent years ago?"

"Mmm-hmm."

"I was dying to fuck you from behind so badly that night, but I stopped myself. Not this time." I entered her in one slow movement. "Fuck. Never again." I pulled out of her slowly and pushed myself back in even slower. "Never again," I repeated.

She gripped the pillow and started gyrating her hips into me.

I placed my hand firmly on her lower back. "No. Don't move. I want to take you slow until you can't stand it anymore and need to beg me to do it harder."

She breathed in quick, trembling breaths with each deep penetration and then again whenever I would slide myself out. My dick was drenched, and I couldn't tell if it was her essence or my own arousal. Moving slowly in and out of her like this was delicious torture. I wanted more of her. I licked my finger and slowly inserted it into her ass. Her breathing quickened in response, and she flinched.

"Does that hurt?" I asked.

"No."

"Stay still."

I pushed it in deeper. "Does it feel good?"

"Yes...really good."

I moved my finger at the exact pace that my cock pumped inside of her, slow and deep. I could have come at any second. This was the most erotic thing I had ever seen or done, and it was only the tip of the iceberg of what I wanted.

"Mitch..."

"Yes, baby?"

"I need more."

"You want it faster?"

"Yes."

"Harder?"

"Yes. Yes."

I pulled my finger out. "My turn to stay still. Ride my cock how you want to. Show me how badly you need it."

"Put your finger back there first. That felt good," she whispered.

I bent down and licked around her puckered hole before sticking my finger back inside. I rested my thumb in between her cheeks as she rode my shaft hard and fast.

My eyes drifted at one point to the ring taunting me on the end table. It set me off and a sudden need to own her body caused me to begin thrusting hard into her despite my vow not to move. My balls slapped against her, and she fucked me faster to keep up. I could feel her muscles contract and knew she was about to come. I let myself go at that exact moment and watched in amazement as she enveloped me, milking every last bit of my orgasm. My dick convulsed harder than I'd ever experienced.

Mind. Blowing.

Still pulsating, I continued to move in and out of her even when there was nothing left. Kissing the skin of her back softly, I said, "I love you so much."

She turned around and kissed me fiercely on the lips and wrapped her arms around my neck.

"Oh my God." She looked into my eyes. "You're crying again."

Fuck. What was wrong with me? When I'm with her, I cry like a baby every time I blow my load.

I sniffled and shook my head in embarrassment. "Apparently, there is a live wire connecting my dick to my tear ducts when I'm with you." I put my forehead on hers. "I'm going to be a fucking wreck tomorrow."

She smiled, wiping my eyes and kissing each one. "No one's ever made me feel like this. I've always loved you, but now...I'm absolutely addicted to you."

The morning sun shined into the bedroom, making the microscopic light blonde hairs on Skylar's body more prominent. I was still staring at her in disbelief over last night. After we made love a few more times, I spent the entire night just watching her sleep. It reminded me of the all-nighter I pulled years ago in her bed right before she moved to Brooklyn. The circumstances were different then, but the uncertainty I woke up to today felt eerily similar.

I didn't want to let her go back to him for even a second.

We were scheduled to be at the house at 11, an hour before the unveiling. We were running late, so I started to kiss her neck.

"Baby, wake up. We have to get going soon. There's something I want to do with you before we have to go."

She grunted in protest then stretched her arms into the air. I left the room and ran out to the car to get my swim shorts.

By the time I returned upstairs, she had dozed off again. I reached into her drawer and grabbed a black bikini bottom, slipping it up her legs.

She spoke through her yawn. "What are you doing?"

"I want to take one last dip with you in the ocean before we leave. We don't have much time."

I lifted her out of the bed and carried her in my arms down the stairs.

"What about my top?"

"I couldn't find it. You don't need one anyway. There's no one around."

I held her all the way to the shore before putting her down and reaching out my hand. We walked into the water until we were waist deep. The sun suddenly started to fade, and it looked like a morning rainstorm was looming. It was the perfect symbolism for my own feeling of joy, suddenly overshadowed by a dreary reality.

This was nothing like our last playful jaunt in the water. This time, we simply held hands, staring at the fading sun, knowing the next several days were going to put our love to the test.

"I'm just going to need some time when we get back, okay? I decided to be completely honest with Kevin about the trip. He deserves to know the truth."

A lump formed in my throat. "I understand."

A look of guilt washed over her face. It made me angry that she let it cast a shadow over our last moments together here.

I put my hands on her shoulders. "Don't ever be ashamed of what we've done. You're not a bad person. Last night was the purest thing I've ever experienced. Whatever happens tomorrow and beyond, I'll never forget it for as long as I live."

Skylar and I pulled into the driveway of the renovated house as scheduled in separate cars. A press release had gone out, so members of the media would be arriving in an hour along with local government officials, neighbors and relatives of the homeowners.

Skylar walked around opening windows and fluffing pillows. A few of my guys were hanging out having coffee and donuts in the kitchen downstairs. I pretended to be busy, but the entire time, I was really brooding over the fact that she had put her diamond ring back on. Maybe I was reading into things too much, but it pissed me off. After the reveal, she would have just enough time to drive back to the beach house, lock up and head straight to the airport. There would be no time to talk or say a proper goodbye.

I had actually been quite proud of how I handled things this morning, but seeing his ring back on her finger had sparked old jealousy again and a need for reassurance.

She stopped in the doorway of one of the bedrooms just as I had finished hammering a nail in a floorboard that had come loose.

"Can I do something to help you?" she asked.

The hammer banged against the wood when I dropped it. "Yes, you can. Close the door."

"What's going on?"

"Just close it. Lock it, actually."

The lock clicked. "What do you need?"

I stood up and walked toward her, rubbing my nose against her neck and inhaling the smell of her skin. "I need to taste you."

"There are people downstairs."

"Sit on the bed."

She looked worried about someone catching us, but it didn't stop her from doing as I said. I kneeled at the foot of the bed and pushed her hips toward my face in one swift movement, lifting her skirt and spreading her legs open wide. She was still wearing her underwear when I began to teasingly kiss her mound softly. Moisture seeped through the silky fabric. She pressed herself hard against my mouth and gripped my hair. Then, I used my teeth to slowly slide her panties off of her legs.

"Are you still worried about the people downstairs?" I whispered.

She shook her head and said something that was unintelligible.

"I didn't think so," I said before pressing my lips against her naked clit and sucking on it.

She wiggled under me as my tongue lapped hard against her while I twirled my fingers inside of her warm opening.

I loved the effect I had on Skylar. I could probably get her to do anything sexually. I definitely held the advantage in that corner. Still, her putting the ring back on had caused me to second guess everything that happened last night. I began to ruminate while I was eating her out. Was this a tryst after all, or did she mean it when she said she would leave him? Even though I knew it was cruel, I suddenly stopped.

She leaned up. “What happened?”

I was panting and stood up. “You’re wearing his ring again. If you’re really planning to end things, why did you put it back on?”

She sat up and looked down at the ring on her hand almost as if she were surprised to see it there. “I hadn’t even thought about it. It’s just a habit.”

“Well, it’s all I’ve been able to fucking think about.”

“I’m giving the ring back to him, Mitch.” She stood up and took my face in both of her hands. “I’m sorry my wearing it made you doubt my intentions. I should have made them clearer. I’m not thinking straight because I’m so nervous about having to tell him.”

My heart beat against her chest as I pulled her into me. “It’s just...I’m a little crazy when it comes to you if you haven’t already noticed. Last night obliterated any tolerance I used to have. I just can’t bear the thought of you with him anymore. I’m sorry I overreacted.”

“Don’t be sorry. It shows me how much you love me and helps me to know I’m making the right decision.” She kissed me softly on the lips. “I love you.”

Hearing it never got old. “I waited for five years hoping you’d come back to me but never imagined you actually would. Forgive me if I’m having a hard time believing it, because it seems unreal. I could spend the rest of my life trying to prove how thankful I am, how much I love you, and it still wouldn’t be enough.”

“You don’t need to prove anything. Just love me.”

“I should finish what I started before I freaked out, but I just really need to be deep inside you right now. Is that okay?”

"There's nothing I want more, but we have to be quick."

"Quick I can do." I unbuckled my belt. "How does five seconds sound?"

She giggled. "You don't need to be quite that fast."

I backed her onto the bed. My pants were only halfway way down my legs when I entered her and gasped at how incredible her hot pussy felt wrapped tight around my cock. It had only been hours since I'd last been inside of her, but it felt like forever ago. I could never get enough. I wanted this all day, every day.

While the other times we'd made love were frantic and desperate, this moment was different. I ended up relaxing into it, believing for the first time in my life that she was truly mine. I let myself experience every sensation and stayed in the present without clouding my mind with doubt and worry. That allowed me to truly feel with my body what she was telling me with hers. With every movement, she was giving me another piece of her: the way her muscles tightened around my cock, the way she grabbed onto me for dear life, the way she breathed as if every breath depended on our bodies being joined together. She was showing me that she'd made her choice.

Nirvana.

There were no words for the magnitude of my love for this woman. When we climaxed together, right on cue were those fucking tears again. My heart wanted to scream out, "Marry me, Skylar" as I came inside of her, but my brain intercepted. Proposing to her in the middle of my signature weeping orgasm wasn't exactly ideal. So, I nixed it.

There were voices coming from the bottom of the stairs. Car doors slammed outside. It was getting close to the start time for the unveiling, and people were arriving.

"We need to get out of here," she said, softly nibbling at my nose while wiping my eyes as she smiled. Still on top of her, I reluctantly pulled out.

Skylar went to the connecting bathroom to clean up while I fastened my pants and got my shit together. Walking downstairs in front of my guys looking like I'd been crying would not be a good thing.

We kissed passionately one last time before I left the room. She'd follow me out separately so that our sneaking around wasn't obvious.

Camera flashes and jumbled conversations greeted me on the first floor. Skylar emerged some time after, looking poised without a hair out of place. No one would have guessed that she had just been thoroughly fucked a few minutes earlier.

A local reporter interviewed Skylar in a corner. I watched from across the room, sipping my coffee as she eloquently explained the process of decorating the house on a budget in such a short period of time.

I got a call on my cell phone letting me know that the Johansen family was five minutes away.

When they arrived, everyone got emotional. Seeing their reactions as they went from room to room with looks of absolute joy and gratitude was priceless. They were especially touched by the wheelchair ramp we installed out front for their son. We had also made one of the bathrooms handicap accessible. All in all, the surprise was a huge success.

By the time the media left, we were free to go and let the family enjoy their new home. I followed Skylar back to Sandbridge Beach, so she could use the bathroom at the house and grab her things. She'd then drive her rental car to the airport before catching her flight. I'd close up the house and hit the road in the hopes of arriving in New Jersey late tonight.

I didn't want to let her go. I came up behind her as she fiddled with the handle to her suitcase. I kissed her neck and spoke into her ear. "Cancel your flight. Drive home with me. We'll stop for dinner in D.C."

She turned around and rubbed her thumb along the stubble on my chin. "I can't. I need to go home and get this over with."

"Are you gonna talk to him tonight?"

She looked down anxiously at the ground and let out a deep breath. "Depending on what time I get in, I'll either tell him tonight or tomorrow."

"Tell him tonight."

"Why?"

"I don't want him touching you. What are you gonna do if he tries something?"

"I guess I hadn't thought that far ahead."

"Tell him when you get home. Then, I want you to get your stuff and come to my house. My mother will let you in if I haven't gotten back yet."

"Mitch, I have to handle this a little more sensitively than that. He's going to have a lot of questions. I can't just tell him I'm leaving him after five years for the man he thinks traumatized me...then walk out the door. I care about him."

Fuck. I suppose she was right. Knowing all too well what it felt like to lose her, I should've been feeling really badly for the poor bastard, but I couldn't seem to get past my own excitement and jealousy. I just wanted her in my house and in my bed as soon as possible.

"Okay. I understand. I won't pressure you. Are you sure you won't change your mind about driving home with me, though?"

She shook her head no.

I kissed her, sucking on her bottom lip hard. "I love you, Skylar Marie Seymour."

"I love you, too."

"Have a safe flight. Please call me when you land. I'll be in the car."

"I will."

She rolled her suitcase out the door as I followed her. After I put the luggage in the trunk, we kissed one last time before she got in and drove off the gravel onto the road. I watched until her car was completely out of sight.

The house was eerily quiet. She was gone, but the smell of her flowery perfume that remained in the foyer teased me. I missed her already. I picked up one of her hair ties that had fallen and played it with it as I pondered our week together unable to contain my smile.

I walked to the French doors to admire the ocean one last time before I'd lock up. This place would always be special to me because of what happened here. I made a mental note to book it for next year. We could take Henry and my mother and turn it into a tradition. My son loved to play at the beach. The water calmed him down. I always said I'd love to move close to an ocean for that reason alone.

As I daydreamed about a future that seemed brighter than ever, there was a knock at the door.

She came back.

My heart filled with anticipation as I walked over and opened it. That was when I realized she wasn't heading home to him after all.

Because he and his fist were right here, heading straight for my face.

THIRTY

SKYLAR

When my plane landed, and I walked out into the passenger area at Newark, I just knew something was wrong. Kevin was never late for anything. A couple of days ago, he had insisted on picking me up, but now, he was nowhere to be found.

With all that happened with Mitch, I had stupidly forgotten to charge my phone the night before. I realized it was dead after I got on the plane and had left my charger in the suitcase. I had no way to reach anyone. I didn't even know Kevin's number by heart since it had been programmed into my phone for so long.

My luggage was the last piece rotating around the conveyer belt when I grabbed it and conceded that he wasn't coming. An ominous feeling came over me as I stood in the crowded baggage claim area unsure of where to go or what to do. Boarding calls played over the intercom, and people were bumping into me as I stood dazed and confused.

An airline representative ended up calling me a car service that drove me all the way home.

My heart was palpitating as I approached our front door on Bayberry Lane. My hand shook as I put the key into the slot. It wouldn't budge. I double-checked to make sure I hadn't grabbed the wrong one and soon realized that the locks had been changed.

I heard barking coming from the upstairs bedroom. It was Seamus. He hadn't done that in years. Something was wrong. I couldn't get to him and started to panic.

Kevin knew.

Birds chirped as I looked from side to side paranoid, expecting him to jump out of the bushes or something.

I got into my car to connect my phone to a charger and drove aimlessly around the neighborhood. Stopping for a group of boys playing hockey in the street, I started to sweat. Something bad was about to happen.

When my phone eventually turned on, I pulled over to the side of the road. There were ten missed calls and several missed texts. All were from Mitch, except one: from Kevin.

It was a photo of Mitch and me taken early this morning while we were in the water holding hands.

My heart sank, and I covered my mouth with my hand in shock. The message under it was simply: **How could you do this to us?**

There were no further texts or calls from him. If he had taken this photo, that meant he was in Virginia. I wondered what else he had seen. Before my mind could attempt to compute it all further, the phone rang.

It was Mitch.

"Mitch? Kevin...he—"

"He knows."

I was speed talking. "I just got in. My phone had died. He sent me a pic—"

"Try to calm down. Listen to me, Skylar. He came to the beach house."

"What?"

"Right after you left, there was a knock at the door. I opened it because I thought you had come back. It was him, and he punched me."

No.

"Are you okay?"

"I have a slight black eye, but I'm fine. He tried to hit me a second time, but I tackled him and locked his hands. I'm stronger than he is. I just hadn't seen that first punch coming."

"Where is he now? Where are you?"

"I'm guessing he's on a flight back to New Jersey. I'm driving home. I got a late start because he was interrogating me for a while. He's a mess, but I can't blame him."

"What did you say to him?"

"I told him the truth about how we reconnected and that we were in love. I don't remember every detail of what I said, but basically, he accused me of manipulating you. He reminded me of how messed up you were when he met you. He said if you were stupid enough to go back to me after all that, then we deserved each other."

"Did he say how long he had been in Virginia? How much he saw?"

"It sounded like he caught an early flight down there this morning. I don't think he was there last night. He said he checked your laptop and found the email I sent you before the trip. When he saw my name on it, he figured it out. I think he was waiting for you to leave for the airport, so he could fuck me up man to man without you having to witness it."

I banged my head against the back of the seat and closed my eyes. "He must have snooped around after I was hesitant to tell him I loved him on the phone last night."

"Either way, he knows everything now. I'm so sorry this happened, but I want you away from that house."

"He locked me out, but I need to wait here and face him tonight."

"I don't want you doing that alone."

"He won't hurt me."

"He fucking hit me without thinking twice. If he ever laid a hand on you, I'd never forgive myself."

"He wouldn't hit me. I'm pretty sure he's never punched anyone before you in his entire life. It's not in his nature."

"I won't be there for a few hours. If he gets there before me and you insist on this, you need to charge your phone and call the police if he so much as touches you. Do you understand?"

"Don't worry."

After I hung up with Mitch, I drove back to the house and parked out front. The sun set into darkness and after two hours, still no sign of Kevin. He hadn't answered his phone, so there was no choice but to continue waiting. I didn't have anything to eat or drink, but my appetite was nonexistent regardless.

Around 11:30, blinding headlights approached from behind my car. Kevin pulled into the garage and immediately closed the electric door. I knew he must have seen me parked out front.

My mouth was dry, and I felt like I was going to pee my pants as I approached the front door and knocked. He wouldn't answer. I started to bang on it until my knuckles hurt and finally yelled, "Kevin, let me in!" as a tear drop fell. I hated myself for hurting him.

He still wouldn't come to the door. I heard a window open on the second floor and then it started raining clothes. Kevin was throwing all of my belongings down onto the bushes and grass. As I moved toward the window, one of my skirts fell on my head.

I screamed, "Please talk to me."

"There's nothing to say. I want you and all of your shit gone."

"I didn't mean to hurt you. I was going to talk to you about it when I got back. Nothing happened before the trip."

Seamus was barking again.

"I should let the bird out the window, too." I heard him say.

"Don't!"

He finally stopped and stuck his head out. His nostrils flared in anger. "I wouldn't actually do that, Skylar. That's the difference between us. I'm not a cold, heartless person."

After he seemed to have finished throwing every last item I owned onto the grass, he disappeared. I looked around in shame at my clothing strewn about. When Seamus stopped barking suddenly, the silence was deafening.

My heart broke for Kevin. I was a terrible person.

Suddenly, the front door creaked open slowly, and I walked over to it. Kevin leaned against it, blocking me from entering. His eyes were red, and his shirt was untucked. It devastated me to see him looking so disheveled.

His voice was hoarse. "Did you ever love me?"

Listening to crickets, I looked down at his shoes and thought about how to respond sensitively to that question.

"I thought I did. I care about you so much. You've been my world for so long. I love you in many ways, just—"

"Not the way you love him."

I started to cry. "No, not in the same way."

He shook his head and rubbed his unshaven chin. "I should have trusted my gut. I knew something was wrong for a very long time. I just tried to ignore it and hoped it would get better."

I had the urge to say a million things to try to make him feel better but knew it wouldn't matter. Making excuses for bad behavior doesn't change it. I cheated on him with the man I love. Last night, I had somehow justified it in my own mind because I'd mentally ended things with Kevin, vowing to tell him as soon as I got back. Explaining it that way wouldn't help him, though. This was going to sting no matter what I said, so I chose not to insult him with my own sorry excuse.

"I don't want to look at your face anymore tonight," he said. "You can take your clothes home...wherever that is now. I'll pack up the rest of your things and drop them off at your mother's. Please leave."

"I understand. I'll go. Can I please just get Seamus?"

He sighed and let me in. I walked up the stairs and when I entered the room, Seamus tilted his head at me. He squawked when I grabbed his cage and breathable blanket before carrying him downstairs. He'd been shuffled around so much, he was probably thinking, "not again."

Kevin was in the same spot at the door looking at me coldly when I returned. I put Seamus down just long enough to take my diamond off, placing it carefully on the small table in the foyer.

I took one last look around at the house that never felt like a home and didn't look back.

Darjeeling tea warmed my throat as I sipped it by the window at my mother's house and pondered what my life had become.

It had been a month since the altercation with Kevin. We met one time for coffee after that, mainly because I begged him. I needed to know he didn't hate me. I wanted to reiterate how much I appreciated our years together even if he felt I threw it all away. He didn't say much as I rambled on nervously that day. He was clearly still bitter and had closed himself off to me. I understood. A part of me would never forgive myself for hurting him, but the meeting gave me a little closure. At least we were on speaking terms. That was more than I would have given him had the roles been reversed. I offered to help take care of the house while it was still on the market, but he declined. He moved to California the next day. His moving away hadn't phased me, and that validated the fact that I'd made the right choice.

If someone had told me a month ago that I'd be living at my mother's house again, I wouldn't have believed it. Mom was absolutely shocked when she found out what had happened. She knew nothing about Mitch being back in the picture and had really loved Kevin, probably more than I ever did. She didn't try to push guilt, but things were tense for the first few days back here.

Mitch had begged me to move in with him. I wanted nothing more, but we needed to let Henry get used to me being around before I invaded their space. There was no need to rush things. Living in their world would also mean someday possibly facing the one thing I hoped I would never have to: Charisma. What if she came to visit? Seeing her was what I dreaded the most. There were a lot of things that scared me but not enough to live my life apart from him anymore.

In fact, over the past few nights, I couldn't get enough of Mitch. I felt like a kid again. Waiting for his nightly text would make me giddy. After Henry would fall asleep, Mitch would message me to come over. He'd be waiting at the doorway, watching me cross the street. He'd take me into his arms before I even stepped foot inside. Candles would be flickering in the living room and a bottle of my favorite wine opened. We were forced to be quiet like a couple of teenagers sneaking around. We'd make out on the couch while watching something on Netflix, and that would inevitably turn into mind-numbing sex before the movie was finished. It was the first time in our lives we could just enjoy each other.

This particular afternoon, when I got up to put my mug in the kitchen, I noticed a piece of white paper had been slipped under the door.

Meet us at the basketball hoop at three.

It made me chuckle, realizing he was recreating the first note he ever left me when we were kids.

My watch showed the time as 2:50, so I went back to the window to wait. About 2:55, Mitch and Henry came outside. Mitch was carrying one of those plastic kids' basketball hoops. He placed it down in the middle of the concrete driveway as Henry ran around in circles. Mitch was struggling to get his attention, but Henry wouldn't stop. Finally, he grabbed his son, lifted him up in the air and placed him in front of the hoop. He demonstrated how to throw the ball in, but Henry continued to be more interested in looking down at the ground and running. Mitch lifted him up again and held Henry's hands around the ball, guiding them into the hoop. When the ball went in, Mitch clapped excitedly while Henry started jogging around him in circles again, completely disinterested in the game.

Looking defeated, Mitch stood there with the ball under his arm. It made my heart hurt to see him trying so hard. He was such a good father. There was something about that moment, watching him standing there, facing the challenge alone. I really wanted to be a part of it...not tomorrow, not next year...but today and forever. I loved him so much.

I grabbed my jacket and ran across the street.

"Hey, you."

Mitch's face brightened when he noticed me. "Hey, you. You're right on time."

I wrapped my arms around him, and he kissed me.

"I've been watching you guys for a while."

"Yeah...Henry is more interested in chasing his own shadow in the sun than playing basketball."

"That's okay. Everyone has their thing."

He leaned into me with a smoldering look. "What's your thing?"

"You're my thing," I said, grabbing his shirt.

He kissed me again, teasingly nudging at my bottom lip slowly with his teeth and grunted. "Yeah?"

"Yeah."

He lightly pushed me away. "Alright, get away from me. I'm getting hard."

I laughed as he moved the plastic hoop to the side. Henry continued to run around in the middle of a patch of sun closer to the garage door.

I walked over to him and stooped down to his height. "Hi, Henry." He wouldn't stop or look at me.

"He's in rare form today," Mitch said.

"If that's what he wants to do, then he should be able to."

Mitch passed the ball to me. "You wanna play?"

"Sure."

He wiggled his brows. "Do you remember the rules to our game?"

"I made the rules to our game, Nichols."

"True."

We took turns throwing the ball into the hoop, and I was the first to miss.

"Alright," he said, scratching his chin. "Name one thing you love about me."

"I can't do that."

"You have to."

"There are too many things to name one. I love what an incredible father you are. I love that you never fully gave up on us even when I had. I love how your face lights up whenever you see me. I love how you know your way around my body like no one else. I lo—"

He cut me off with a kiss and said, "I've never felt so lucky in my life."

I wasn't finished. "And I love how you cry like a baby when you come."

"Ah....you like that? I've dubbed it the weeping orgasm. I'm thinking of turning it into a cocktail. It can be the signature drink at our wedding. We'll make up the ingredients, and only we'll know the true meaning behind it."

"Our wedding, huh?"

"Yeah. You okay with that?"

I felt my eyes watering. "More than okay."

"Good. Because I'm never letting you go again."

I played with the zipper on his hoodie, contemplating what I was about to propose. "I think we should move in first. How about today?"

He planted his hands on my face and his eyes widened in excitement. "Are you serious?"

"Yeah. I've decided to take you up on your offer. I'm ready."

Mitch let go of me. "Go! Grab your shit and come back here, then. I want you in my bed tonight."

"I just have a question."

"What?"

"Do you take birds?"

"Only old perverted ones."

As I was laughing, my eyes wandered to where Henry was playing. He had stopped running around and had picked up the basketball that rolled over toward him. "Check this out, Mitch."

Mitch turned around to look.

Henry walked over to the kid's hoop and casually dumped the ball in. Mitch shook his head. "He's got a mind of his own, I guess."

"That's a good sign."

Seconds later, he was back to chasing his shadow.

Mitch tugged at my jacket. "Come inside. Let's make dinner together. Then, I want to have you later for our celebratory dessert. I'll help you move in your stuff tomorrow."

"Let me just go across the street and get Seamus and some pajamas."

When I returned to Mitch and Henry, I laughed at the absurdity of officially moving out of my mother's house with nothing but a caged parrot and a handful of clothes.

Seamus started flapping his wings like mad when he saw where we were.

"He seems excited. You think he remembers this place?" I asked.

"I think he's looking forward to crapping all over me later. That's what I think."

Henry came over to the cage and peeked in.

Mitch tousled the boy's hair. "You see the bird, Henry? That's a bird. His name is Seamus. Say, 'Hi, bird.'"

Suddenly, Henry started mimicking Seamus' flapping. It was quite a sight, the two of them flapping at each other. Henry started to laugh and even looked back at Mitch for a reaction.

Mitch was beaming. "I've never seen him this pumped about anything non-electronic."

Seamus seemed to be encouraging Henry by flapping his wings faster. When the parrot started bopping his head, Henry let out a belly laugh then started to copy that, too.

Mitch and I smiled at each other.

"Well, I think this bird finally found his calling," I said.

When Mitch lifted the cage to bring Seamus inside with us, Henry squealed in protest. "Buh..."

"What did he just say?"

Mitch's eyes were glowing. "I think he's trying to say bird." He put the cage back down. "Henry, you want to stay outside with the bird?"

"Bud," he said.

I gasped. "He is saying bird!"

"I think that's his first official word."

This was definitely a day to remember for multiple reasons.

"Holy Toledo!"

Mitch and I looked at Seamus in unison.

"Mitch, he hasn't said that in years. That is so weird."

"Son of a gun. It's like he knows things are back to the way they should be."

That's the thing about true love. It can rise from the ashes because at its source, it's indestructible. Layers can be stripped away and lost, but if you're lucky enough to find them again and put them back together, the end result is stronger than ever.

That was all I could think of as I stood there with Mitch in our basketball court. After all we'd been through, we found ourselves starting a better life in exactly the place where it all began.

EPILOGUE

SKYLAR

We couldn't have gotten better weather for a Saturday backyard party. It was warm but dry with low humidity. Mitch was busy cleaning off the outside tables and setting up a makeshift bar in preparation for our guests. Janis was babysitting, so we could get everything ready.

When the postal delivery truck drove off, I walked down to the mailbox in my flip-flops and sorted through the stack of bills and coupon flyers. An international envelope with the words airmail stamped on the front immediately caught my eye. It was addressed to Skylar Nichols. The return address was London. The waffles I had just eaten for breakfast felt like they were coming up on me.

Not today.

There was no way I was going to let this ruin our day.

I looked around as I entered the house and ran to the upstairs bathroom, shutting the door. She'd better not be trying to make trouble for us. Charisma hadn't been back to the states once in the years since Mitch and I reunited. I never had to face her like I feared.

The envelope sliced through my hand, causing a paper cut as I rushed to open the letter. It was hand-written on expensive-looking stationery.

Dear Skylar,

I suppose I'm the last person you want to receive mail from. I fully understand. This letter is more for my benefit than yours.

I'll get to the point. Certain life circumstances as of late have caused me to reevaluate my actions over the years. I'm facing a health crisis, and while I will spare you the details, let's just say we now have something else in common besides a history with Mitch.

I'm writing because I feel as though I need to apologize to you before it's too late. I'm sorry for the hurt I intentionally caused both of you. My actions were immature, selfish and cruel. I don't expect you to forget, because that is likely impossible. I am, however, asking for your forgiveness.

I also want to thank you for giving my child the type of mother he deserves. I realize that I have all but abandoned my son. It's partly because I was never well-suited to be a mother and mainly, because I'm fairly certain he's better off without me.

Congratulations on your marriage. I really do wish you the best. Although I suspect you won't believe that, it's the truth. You and Mitch undoubtedly belong together and are evidence that fate will always get the last laugh. So will karma. I'm living proof of that.

Regards,

Charisma Warner

My eyes remained glued to the letter in my hands. I didn't know what to make of it. A vague feeling of sadness caught me off guard. I did pity her. She would never know the kind of joy I experienced with Henry on a daily basis, helping him learn and celebrating every single stride he makes. Moreover, he loved me and showed it in his own special ways. I was the only mother he'd ever known.

I folded the paper, closed my eyes and said a prayer. If there were any true sign of forgiveness, it would be praying for the well-being of your worst enemy. After that, I experienced an inner-peace that couldn't have come at a better time.

Mitch wouldn't find out about this letter today. I didn't want to upset him because this day was too important to both of us. I took the envelope into the bedroom and tucked it inside my drawer, vowing to show it to him tomorrow.

We'd been married now for almost three years. About six months after I moved into his house, he asked me to sit down one night to a movie after dinner. When he pressed play, what really showed up was a montage of pictures of us that Angie had taken over the years. *All of Me* by John Legend played in the background of the slideshow.

I was dumbfounded. There were shots of just our hands holding together and from when we were teenagers of Mitch looking at me adoringly when he didn't know his picture was being taken. The love was written all over his face even back then. There were shots of him kissing my head when I was sick, prom night and the Lake George trip. The five-year gap was painfully obvious, though, before photos that he had taken of us together with Henry appeared. At the very end, the words *To Be Continued* popped up on the screen, followed by *Will You Marry Me?* I'll never forget that moment when I turned to him and looked into his eyes. He was fumbling and nervous as he took the ring out of his shirt. Like I would ever say no.

It was my most cherished memory, second only to the day I married the love of my life during a small gathering of family and friends four months later. We let Henry have his iPad to stay calm during the ceremony. It was supposed to be on mute, but he figured out how to turn the volume on in the middle of the priest's asking if anyone objected to our union. Henry asked to go to McDonald's.

Today would end up being another fond memory someday.

Mitch appeared at the door to our bedroom, startling me. "How's my beautiful wife?"

He wiped his head with his shirt. Staring at my husband's body never got old. Men always seemed to get better looking with age, and Mitch was no exception. He was looking especially yummy today, unshaven and sporting a summer tan. He took his shirt off altogether and threw it on the ground.

"What are you doing?"

He unzipped his jeans and slipped his muscular legs out of them. "I just called my mother and they're not coming back until noon. I asked her to stay at the playground a little longer. Guests don't arrive until one. Guess who's fucking you as loud as he wants while we have the house to ourselves for the first time in months?" He pressed his solid chest against my breasts and lifted my shirt over my head as he said, "My appetite for you is off the charts today. I've been jonesing this since the second I woke up this morning. I couldn't concentrate outside just now because it was all I could think about."

"You're insatiable, you know that?"

He sucked on my neck and spoke into my skin. "I was gonna shower first, but I can't wait. I hope you don't mind me dirty."

"Would it matter if I did?"

"Hell no."

"You know I like you dirty anyway."

He planted soft kisses on my breasts then bent down and kissed my stomach. He stood up, and his cock twitched when he rubbed it against me.

"Shit, Skylar. Feel this, how hard I am."

I reached into his boxers. His dick was hot and throbbing in my hand.

I could always tell what kind of a sexual mood he was in by the look in his eyes. Sometimes, he'd want me to direct, but this wasn't going to be one of those days. This time, he would take what he wanted.

I whispered in his ear and slowly stroked him. "What do you want, baby?"

"I want you to suck my cock."

Yup. I was right.

I kneeled and flicked my tongue over the thin line of hair on his stomach leading into his shorts. I took him into my mouth and stroked him at the base, sucking hard to the back of my throat. He massaged and pulled at my hair as he bent his head back, struggling to catch his breath. Normally, I'd keep going, but I was eager to have sex with him when he was in this kind of a mood.

After a couple of minutes, I stopped. "Where do you want me?"

"You know where I want you."

Mitch lay back on the bed. Veins protruded from his cock, which was as hard it got and sticking up straight up in the air. It moved at the sight of my mouth lowering down on it as I sucked the moisture off the tip slowly one last time.

After I positioned myself over him, he moaned as he sank into me. He grabbed my hips and slid my body rhythmically over him. "This is heaven. I'm so deep in there," he said. "You feel incredible at this angle."

"I love it like this, too," I said as my ass rubbed against his balls.

He placed his rough hands over my breasts, squeezing them together. "Fuck...this was just what I needed."

I moved down on him faster. Being on top allowed me to see every inch of his hard body. I licked my lips and continued to ride him, ogling the cut muscles of his tattooed chest bearing my name. He'd thrust upward, and his six-pack would become more prominent as he tightened his ab muscles with each movement into me. I got off on watching it. Drool literally dripped from my lower lip onto him.

His pupils dilated, and I knew he was very close. "I love the way you look at me when we fuck," he groaned. "I want to fill you with my cum. Now. I can't hold back anymore."

My orgasm vibrated through me instantly. He knew I loved a filthy mouth. Sometimes, it only took one sentence to set me off. "Oh, yes. Yes!"

Because the house was empty, he held nothing back and yelled out louder than he had been able to in months. I watched his chest move up and down as he came almost violently.

My hair covered both of our faces as I bent down to kiss him. My breasts were plastered against his sweaty chest. We had to get ready, but a part of me wished we could stay in bed all day like this.

"It's fucking painful," he said.

"What is?"

"How much I love you."

I rolled to the side and wiped his eyes. "Is that why you cry?"

"Don't know. I can't stop them because these tears aren't derived from my conscious brain. I have a theory, though."

"What is it?"

"This is all coming from someplace deeper, like when we make love my soul cries tears of joy because it comes together with its other half."

"That's beautiful." I kissed his shoulder. "Or it could just be really good sex."

Mitch started to tickle me, and we went for another round before heading into the bathroom.

MITCH

The charcoal from the grill filled the air out back. People would be arriving any minute. As I dumped bags of ice into the two coolers, a little voice came up from behind me.

"We're back, Daddy."

That sound always tugged at my heartstrings. I'd never get sick of being called that name.

My mother had just arrived at the house with the kids about ten minutes after Skylar and I took our shower. It was good timing.

I lifted Lara up in the air. "How's my little girl? Did you have a good time at the park?"

"Grammy bought us some Fun Dip."

I looked at my mother. "Grammy, that'll rot their teeth."

Henry had red powder all over his cheeks.

My mother shrugged her shoulders. "It's Lara's special day. I told her she could pick one thing at the drug store, and that was what she wanted. She got some for him, too."

I put my daughter down. "I suppose we can make an exception for today."

She giggled, exposing her missing front tooth and licked the white stick before dunking it into the blue powder again.

Today, we were celebrating the fact that our adoption of Lara was officially made final yesterday. She had really felt like ours for a while, though. Now five, she'd been living with us for over a year.

Skylar and I had visited an adoption agency about a year and a half ago, looking to adopt a newborn, but they told us there would be a long waiting list. We were willing to be patient, but then they mentioned a little girl who had been in foster care since she was one and needed a home. She was only three and a half at the time and wore her hair in two little braids. When I saw her, I just knew she was my daughter. I never thought I'd be lucky enough to fall in love with two girls in braids over the course of my life. It happened with Lara, and it was instant. She almost looked like little Skylar, too, with her reddish brown hair and a few freckles on her face.

Lara was such a good little sister to Henry and even explained his autism in her own cute way to people who would stare at us in public. She'd say, "He's not being bad. He's just my brother and has autism. You should look it up on the computer." It was a relief to know that Henry would have a big sister to look after him someday when I couldn't.

"Daddy, will you chase me?"

"Just let me throw these steaks on, and then we'll play one round of tag." She stayed hanging onto my leg until I finished placing the raw meat down. I looked at her little hands wrapped around my knee and smiled at her big eyes looking up at me.

As I chased her around the yard, our guests started to pour in through the fence. A few of Skylar's friends from her volunteer gig at the hospital showed up at the same time as Davey and Zena and their baby daughter, Dena. Then, some neighbors started trickling in holding food and drink items.

Skylar's mother was next to arrive, followed by Jake and Nina who had come all the way from Boston.

Skylar had made about six different side dishes and started putting all the food out on the buffet table. Henry walked up to her requesting something on his iPad. She didn't know I was watching her as she stopped everything to lift him up and kiss him on the nose. Henry hadn't changed or improved dramatically over the years. His speech still wasn't developing as we'd hoped, but he did have two words: bird and mama. My son, who at one time was indirectly the catalyst for tearing us apart, had become *our* son and part of the glue that put us back together. I was a prime example of how one small decision can shape an entire life. Sometimes, if you're lucky, the biggest hardship can lead to your greatest blessing. It just takes time to see that God works in mysterious ways.

Jake came up behind me. "Hey, Bitch."

We smacked hands "Thanks for making the trek, Jake."

"No problem, man. I brought my karaoke machine for later." He was holding two glasses. "Where do you keep the good liquor?"

"That's my makeshift bar over there. Everything's underneath."

"How do you make that fruity drink they were passing around at your wedding? Nina wants one. It was some weird ass name, wasn't it? What was it called again?"

"A weeping orgasm."

"You make that shit up?"

"Yeah. It's Blueberry vodka, Sprite and fresh raspberries. We should have all the ingredients."

"Got it. You want one?"

"Why not?"

I looked around at my yard full of people. Henry was jumping on the trampoline with his sister. My mother and Tish clinked their wine glasses in a toast to their granddaughter. Much to our relief, they'd rekindled their friendship after we'd gotten back together.

Nina came by, kissing me on the cheek and squeezed my shoulders in passing. "Great party. Congratulations."

I'd spotted everyone but *her*. Where was Skylar? I finally caught her grinning at me from a corner of the yard as if she'd been waiting for me to notice her. Her hair blew in the gentle breeze and, as always, she'd rendered me breathless. We looked at each other, and my heart filled with pure joy, eternally grateful at how my life had fallen into place.

She walked over to me and placed her hands around my neck. Everyone else seemed to fade into the background.

I rested my forehead on hers. "Thank you."

"For what?" she asked.

"For giving me something happy to think about every single day of my life."

Jake came by with two drinks. "I friggin' rock at this bartending shit. Taste these."

"Is that a weeping orgasm?" she asked.

He nodded. "Your husband told me how to make it."

Jake handed one to me and then to Skylar.

She waved it away. "Thanks, but I'm gonna stick to soda tonight."

"Okay." He looked over to where Nina was chatting with a neighbor. "More for my little lush over there then."

When he left, I placed my hand over Skylar's stomach, and she looked up at me and smiled. They say these things happen when you're not trying, when you least expect it. No one knew the secret we were keeping just between us. It was too early and risky to say anything. The doctors had always told us it would be difficult—a long shot even—but clearly, it wasn't impossible. Miracles do happen, and we would wait month by month with bated breath, hoping and praying for the chance to meet ours.

Jake tapped the mic. "Is this thing on? Hello?"

Skylar and I looked up.

"I'm gonna start the evening's entertainment off with a slow song. It's an oldie but goodie." He pointed the microphone at me and winked. "Bitch, this one's for you."

Nina covered her face then mouthed, "I'm sorry."

It took me a few minutes to realize that the song was an old Roy Orbison tune called *Crying*.

My head turned slowly toward a guilty-looking Skylar. "You told Nina..."

Her complexion transformed into a bright shade of pink. “I was drunk once…at my bachelorette party, I think. It slipped out. She must have told him.”

I gave Jake the finger, and he stumbled over the lyrics in laughter.

I grabbed her. “You little shit. You’re lucky I love you.” If you can’t beat ‘em, join ‘em. “Let’s dance.”

We slowly rocked back and forth to the surprisingly good sound of Jake’s crooning. I was overcome with emotion as I peered into her eyes and saw my entire world staring back at me: my past, my present and my future.

My Skylar.

OTHER BOOKS BY
PENELOPE WARD

Moody
The Assignment
The Aristocrat
The Crush
The Anti-Boyfriend
The Day He Came Back
Neighbor Dearest
Just One Year
When August Ends
Love Online
Gentleman Nine
Drunk Dial
Mack Daddy
Stepbrother Dearest
RoomHate
Sins of Sevin
Jake Undone (Jake #1)
My Skylar (Jake #2)
Jake Understood (Jake #3)
Gemini

OTHER BOOKS BY
PENELOPE WARD & VI KEELAND

Well Played
Park Avenue Player

Stuck-Up Suit
Cocky Bastard
Not Pretending Anymore
Happily Letter After
My Favorite Souvenir
Dirty Letters
Hate Notes
Rebel Heir
Rebel Heart
Mister Moneybags
British Bedmate
Playboy Pilot

Acknowledgements

First and foremost, thank you to my loving parents for continuing to support me every day in every way.

To my husband, who puts up with a lot of crap so I can live out this new dream ...thank you for your love and patience.

To Allison, who always believed in me back when all of this was simply about telling stories and to Harpo, my agent in heaven: love you both.

To my editor, Kim York, thank you for your undivided attention chapter by chapter and for your invaluable facebook chats.

To my besties: Angela, Tarah and Sonia...love you all so much!

To all the bloggers who help and support me: you are the reason for my success. I'm afraid to list everyone here because I will undoubtedly forget someone unintentionally. You know who you are and do not hesitate to contact me if I can return the favor.

To Penelope's Peeps, my facebook fan group: I adore you!

To Donna Soluri of Soluri Public Relations who organized my book blitz and who always dishes out sound advice: Thank you!

To Hetty Rasmussen: for your support and for being my awesome Book Bash assistant!

To my readers: nothing makes me happier than knowing I've provided you with an escape from the daily stresses of life. That same escape was why I started writing. There is no greater joy in this business than to hear from you directly and to know that something I wrote touched you in some way.

To the autism moms (and dads): you rock!

Last but not least, to my daughter and son: Mommy loves you. You are my motivation and inspiration!

ABOUT THE AUTHOR

PENELOPE WARD is a New York Times, USA Today, and #1 Wall Street Journal Bestselling author. With over two-million books sold, she's a 21-time New York Times bestseller. Her novels are published in over a dozen languages and can be found in bookstores around the world. Having grown up in Boston with five older brothers, she spent most of her twenties as a television news anchor, before switching to a more family-friendly career. She is the proud mother of a beautiful 16-year-old girl with autism and a 14-year-old boy. Penelope and her family reside in Rhode Island.

Facebook Private Fan Group
https://www.facebook.com/groups/PenelopesPeeps/_
Facebook: https://www.facebook.com/penelopewardauthor
TikTok: https://www.tiktok.com/@penelopewardofficial
Website: www.penelopewardauthor.com
Twitter: https://twitter.com/PenelopeAuthor
Instagram: https://instagram.com/PenelopeWardAuthor